CONRAD EDISON AND THE INFERNAL DESIGN

OVERWORLD ARCANUM BOOK 4

JOHN CORWIN

BOOKS BY JOHN CORWIN

THE OVERWORLD CHRONICLES

Sweet Blood of Mine

Dark Light of Mine

Fallen Angel of Mine

Dread Nemesis of Mine

Twisted Sister of Mine

Dearest Mother of Mine

Infernal Father of Mine

Sinister Seraphim of Mine

Wicked War of Mine

Dire Destiny of Ours

Aetherial Annihilation

Baleful Betrayal

Ominous Odyssey

Insidious Insurrection

Assignment Zero (An Elyssa Short Story)

OVERWORLD UNDERGROUND

Possessed By You

Demonicus

OVERWORLD ARCANUM

Conrad Edison and the Living Curse

Conrad Edison and the Anchored World

Conrad Edison and the Broken Relic

Conrad Edison and the Infernal Design

STAND ALONE NOVELS

Mars Rising

No Darker Fate

The Next Thing I Knew

Outsourced

For the latest on new releases, free ebooks, and more, join John Corwin's Newsletter at www.johncorwin.net!

DARK DESIGN

When Conrad learns his father has perfected a way to create demonic clones of living people, he realizes it's only a matter of time before the Overworld falls once again to Victus.

The Arcane Council is already in flux, and Max's father, Xander, is running for primus. If he wins, it will give Victus another solid rung to climb to the top. Several ministers already seem in favor, and with a little push, the entire council could belong to Victus.

The only way to stop Victus is to destroy the foundry. But to do that, Conrad will have to figure out who is friend, who is foe, and who might be a demon clone. If the infernal design is not broken, Victus will soon control everything.

CHAPTER 1

The stranger appeared inside the mansion without warning. Zarin called out to his bodyguards, but they ignored his summons, their eyes surveying the nearby hallway and parlor room as if nothing was even the slightest bit amiss despite the man in robes and a cowl no more than ten feet from them.

The stranger waved a wand toward Zarin as he rose from his chair. "Please sit. I have a matter to discuss with you."

"Wizard," Zarin hissed. "Do you know who I am?"

"I prefer the term Arcane," the stranger said. "I am here precisely because of who you are."

"Hmm. British," Zarin said. "Well educated and arrogant. There aren't many Arcanes who fit that bill these days. They're all gone—trapped in Seraphina."

"Likewise, there are not many of your kind left in Eden either." The stranger raised his hands and lowered the cowl. Shaved head, thin face. A deep scar traversed diagonally from above the left eyebrow, narrowly missing the eye and ending at the nose. He smiled, but it was not a kind smile. It was the sort of smile one might expect to see on the face of a boy maliciously tearing the wings off flies.

"I don't recognize you," Zarin said. "Yet you seem to know a great deal about me."

"In the absence of the great houses, you have made quite a name for yourself," the stranger said. "You have built a small empire on the backs of mortals and broken every rule of the Overworld Conclave."

"Bah." Zarin slashed the air with a hand. "The Overworld government is in disarray. Weak. After the death of the Overlord, Galfandor and those fools at Arcane University tried to piece it back together. But without Templars to enforce the laws, without structure in the factions, there is no glue to hold it together." He bared his teeth. "Who are you, Arcane, to come into my home and make such accusations?"

"Not accusations. Observations." The stranger shrugged. "You are a man without a house."

"I'm no man."

"Man enough," the stranger said. "Yes, there are others of your kind still in the far-flung reaches of the world. Japan, perhaps."

"The few left alive." Zarin shuddered. "I heard the stories. I know what that girl did."

"Ivy Slade is no longer a threat." The stranger's cruel smile turned pleasant for a moment. "There's little standing in the way of someone ambitious."

Zarin barked a laugh. "You want to rule the world?" He laughed again. "How cliché."

"And yet it has never been done." The stranger shrugged. "What if I told you we could achieve great power? What if I told you, the Overlord could rise again?"

Realization lit in Zarin's eyes, and his smile vanished. "You look very different with a shaved head, but it's you, isn't it?" He leaned forward. "You had us all fooled with your death."

"I was quite dead, Zarin." The man shrugged. "Were it not for the teachings of your sister, I might still be so."

"Yes, well—" without warning, Zarin exploded from his seat, pectoral muscles popping the buttons from his oxford, quads ripping through silk slacks. Horns spiraled from his forehead and a great forked tail sprang from his backside. His mass expanded to nearly three times his original size as he crossed the room in a blur. Thick black claws sparked against an invisible shield around the Arcane.

Zarin reared back his head and roared. Even now, his bodyguards remained oblivious thanks to whatever spell the Arcane cast on them. Zarin raked his nails across the invisible shield, failing to draw even a look of concern from the man beneath its protection. "Tell me, Victus," he growled in a guttural voice, "what made you think I'd let you live after what you did to my sister?"

Victus inspected a fingernail and buffed them on his robes as if he were not in imminent danger of a disemboweling. "*What* do you think I did to her?"

"She's gone. Dead for all I know." Zarin bared his demonic fangs and huffed against the shield, a panther fogging the window of the observation glass at a zoo. "You cannot maintain this shield forever, Overlord." He loaded the last word with scorn.

"Your concern for Aerianas is touching, Zarin." Victus stood, the air shimmering around him as the shield extended. "She is very much alive and has hopefully completed her mission in Seraphina by now."

"Mission?" Zarin's eyes glowed red. "Why should I believe you?"

Victus placed an arcphone on the tea table near his divan and flicked on the screen to reveal a password lock. "This is your sister's device. She encoded it with a word only you would know to prove it is hers."

"Why did you not bring it to me years ago?" Zarin remained in his demon form, pacing back and forth like a hungry lion. "You are nearly a decade late, wizard."

"One of her acolytes remained behind to assist me," Victus replied. "Only he was skilled enough to work the demonic magic I needed in her absence. Unfortunately, he was killed by the girl."

"The *girl*." Zarin spoke it like a curse. "You are one of the most skilled demonologists among Arcanes. What could a Daemos do for you that you could not do yourself?"

"The window in your soul provides a much stronger link to the netherworld than I could ever achieve." Victus touched his chest as if indicating the physical location. "Not only that, but I require a very lifelike quality to the summoned demons."

Zarin stared at the arcphone for a long moment. At last, he spoke the word he had spoken only to his sister. "*Jaitini.*"

The lock screen vanished and a holographic image of Aerianas sprang into the air. Thick black hair hung around her narrow face, cascaded down her petite shoulders. Her lithe form seemed ready to spring to life from the recording and grip him in a crushing embrace. Zarin forgot himself and his demonic form melted away to its thin, athletic origin.

"Jaitini, I hope this finds you well." Aerianas held out her hand as if wishing she could touch her brother across the years and virtual divide. "The Alabaster Arches have been restored and Victus sees an opportunity to harness the Seraphim to our will. I do not know when I will return and there is a chance things will go badly." She wiped a tear from her eye. "If I am successful in my mission, perhaps you could join me here, far from the rules of the houses. We could live as we once dreamed, masters of our own destinies."

"Yes, my love." Zarin dropped to a knee before her image. Hot tears stung his eyes.

"I leave this message in case Victus ever needs your help, brother. I know you like to keep to your own in matters of state, but I beseech you to consider joining him." Aerianas's right forefinger tapped her left thumb twice, a secret code she and Zarin had shared. *This is the truth.* The imaged puffed away.

The message was genuine and sincere. Zarin frowned. "When did she leave for Seraphina?"

"I freed her from the Templar prison holding her and together we went to Seraphina—more specifically, to the nation of Pjurna." Victus sat back on the divan. "I left her to study the local politics so we could enact our plan. The Second Seraphim War, unfortunately, did not cripple the Eden army nearly as much as I'd hoped. We enlisted the aid of a Seraphim named Cephus to further weaken Justin Slade and his army."

"The crystoid incident." Zarin narrowed his eyes. "It nearly destroyed all magic in our realm."

"It was a carefully staged ploy, nothing more." Victus flicked a bit of fuzz off his robe. "Aerianas saw the opportunity to trap them over there, so we did. With our carefully planned plot to take over the Darkling and Brightling governments from the inside, we would eventually control armies of Seraphim, destroy the remnants of the Templars, and shatter the alliance."

"That was over nine years ago," Zarin said. "Why have you not reopened the way to Seraphina? Surely Aerianas has failed or succeeded by now."

"And that is where we miscalculated." Victus deflated ever so slightly. "I used a Relic of Juranthemon to seal the arches so I could reopen them at my convenience. It appears that while I can repair the magical connections on this side, the same must also be done on the other side, unless Serena knows another way."

"The blond witch?" Zarin's eyes narrowed. "From what I know of her, she is the foremost expert on arches."

"Yes. And soon we can test her theories on the Grand Nexus."

"So your tinkering damaged the arches in Seraphina too?" Zarin dropped back into his chair and tugged at his torn shirt. "Expert or not, I don't see how Serena can repair both sides without access."

"Precisely." Victus shrugged. "We will figure it out. In the meantime, I have great need of your help."

"Great need indeed." Zarin leaned back. "You would not have risked death otherwise."

"I also know of a possible way to cross back into Seraphina without an arch, but it requires a dangerous journey into a land from which I have been banned." Victus unconsciously touched the scar above his eye. "It is time to restore my rule. It is time to reopen the way to a conquered Seraphina where your sister reigns."

"I truly hope that is the case." Zarin nodded. "I will work with you to that end, Victus."

"You swear on your sister's life that you hold no ill will toward me?"

"I hold ill will toward anyone who takes my lover from me," Zarin said, "but I understand why she went, and you are safe from death by my hand unless I discover subterfuge on your part." He stood. "Should I find that deceit led to the death of my beloved, there will be no safe place for you in any realm, wizard."

"Understood." Victus rose and held out his hand. "To an alliance."

Zarin reluctantly took the now unshielded limb and shook it, squeezing perhaps a bit harder than necessary. "We are allies. Everything you know, I know. Is that understood?"

Victus nodded. "So far as it pertains to our mission."

Zarin looked at his bodyguards. "Free them from your curse."

Victus tapped on his arcphone and the guards blinked, staggered. They saw Victus. Eyes widening with alarm, they drew weapons.

Zarin held up a hand. "All is well. Victus is my guest."

"But, sir, I swear he wasn't—"

Zarin nodded. "Yes, yes. I brought him here in secrecy. Resume your duties."

The bodyguards looked at each other, exchanging the looks of mortals who have only glimpsed bits of the supernatural and not quite believed it. They holstered weapons and tried to act as if nothing strange had happened.

"Now that is settled, I must know something," Zarin said.

Victus raised an eyebrow. "Yes?"

Zarin tapped his eyebrow. "Who did that to you?"

The Arcane's fists tightened. He blew out a long breath. "My son, Conrad Edison."

CHAPTER 2

"Conrad? Conrad Edison?"

I jerked from a daydream about Cora and saw my friend Max Tiberius pointing to a poster on the hallway wall. *Join us for the Founders Day Celebration in the Grotto!*

"Can you believe it?" Max said. "They haven't held one of these in nearly ten years! We definitely have to go."

"Certainly sounds exciting." My other best friend, Ambria Rax read the fine print. "After being cooped up on campus all summer, it would certainly be nice to get out."

I took the next left and ascended a narrow staircase. "Let's pass it by Galfandor first."

GALFANDOR LEANED against the sturdy oak desk in his study and shook his head after I told him what we wanted to do. "I would caution against leaving Queens Gate, Conrad. Campus and, to a lesser degree, the city below are warded against your father. I cannot make the same guarantees for the Grotto."

Ambria leapt up from the plush chair to my right. "But we've been trapped in Queens Gate all summer. Surely Victus hasn't spent all his time lurking in the shadows waiting to kill us."

"He's an evil mastermind," Max said. "I'll bet he's got plenty of other things to do."

"I've spent the entire summer dreading a knife to the back or a spell to the chest every time I walk around a corner." I gripped the armrests and tried to look braver than I felt. "I don't think I'm at the top of Victus's priorities right now."

A brilliant red spider the size of a large dog crawled from a square vent in the wall. "Can I go? I would make sure nothing happens to them." An enchanted gem hidden in her soft fur amplified her whispery voice.

The headmaster stroked his long white beard and cast a pensive look at the three of us. "With Shushiel watching, perhaps you'll be safe."

"I will use camouflage and remain on the rooftops." The ruby spider bobbed up and down with excitement. "No one will even know I'm there."

"Then it's settled." I rubbed the fur on Shushiel's leg. "We'll leave for the Grotto tomorrow."

Galfandor stepped around his desk and leaned on the edge. "A large group departs through the Obsidian Arch tomorrow after breakfast if you would like to avoid paying the standard toll."

"Splendid." Ambria wiped her hands together. "Will you go, sir?"

Galfandor nodded. "The Arcane Council decided to hold its annual meet and greet at the Grotto, and I must attend."

Max's face turned pale. "We're not required to go, are we?"

Galfandor's eyebrow perched atop a wrinkle. "You look rather concerned, young Tiberius."

My friend swallowed hard. "I would rather avoid it."

"Your parents will be there won't they?" Ambria crossed her arms and challenged him with a questioning glare.

Max nodded. "Reason enough to avoid it."

I'd never met his parents, though they sounded perfectly nasty if Max's every word was to be believed.

"I don't believe your parents have taken the trouble of coming to an annual meet and greet in years." Galfandor's wrinkles creased even more. "I would be surprised if they showed up to this one."

"I want to meet them, Max." Ambria clapped her hands together. "Your stories make them sound so despicable, I just have to see for myself."

I shook my head. "I think Rhys and Devon are proof enough."

Ambria refused to relent. "Come to think of it, Max, I've never met your sisters, either. Will they be there?"

Max scowled back. "If you want to meet the rest of my terrible family, you can do it alone."

"Family can be difficult," Shushiel said. "I prefer my friends."

Her optimistic tone melted the knot of sorrow and anger twisting in my guts—a knot caused by simply thinking about Victus.

"Truer words have never been spoken." Max flicked his gaze to Ambria. "Though some friends certainly test my limits."

Ambria stuck out her tongue.

Max, Ambria, and I left to attend our daily arcnology session with my odd cousin, Ansel Moore. Shushiel remained behind to continue her job of shuttling documents back and forth across campus for Galfandor. Few students attended summer semester, but with the fall semester right around the corner, more returned to campus every day.

I polished the arcwand Ansel had given me as we walked toward the broom closet to retrieve our brooms. The aether battery and magical processing unit inside allowed me to store complex spells and retrieve them on command. I tried not to rely on such a crutch, but kept it on my person just in case I encountered one of Victus's minions.

We boarded our brooms outside the main atrium and flew over the trees. The valley opened up below, the city of Queens Gate nestled in the middle. Cottony puffs dotted the green lands below, sheep and goats on the farms at the outskirts of town. As the towering spires of Arcane University fell behind us, the chromatic, organically curved buildings of Science Academy came into view.

Academy students on the moving walkways below looked up at us with suspicion or gawked with outright confusion. Rocket sticks and robots were the norm on this campus, not broomsticks and wands.

A shiny chrome flying saucer with a blacked-out glass dome paced us. The glass slid back to reveal a girl wearing a pair of bronze goggles and an old-school aviator helmet. She laughed. "Aren't you on the wrong campus, magicians?"

Ambria shot an angry glare back. "We're Arcanes, not magicians!"

The girl laughed again and jetted forward, her UFO leaving behind rings of vapor.

"I hate science students," Max said. "They think they're so much better than us."

"Well, we *are* better." Ambria guided her broom through a loop of dissipating vapor. "If it would do any good, I'd outrun her on my broom just to prove it."

We passed by the main lab buildings. Electricity arced between the towering Tesla coils of Tesla Labs. A bulbous building with a narrow base—a light bulb—represented Edison Labs and a twisting DNA ladder stood for Curie Labs. My mind drifted back to the first time Esma Emoora had brought me here.

Oh, how I'd admired her and looked up to her as a mother figure. It turned out she was actually my biological mother, Delectra Moore, in disguise. Twisted by abuse and demonic possession, my mother had been a tortured soul. Our brief time together had rescued her from the darkness my evil father had instilled in her. I only wished she could have lived longer instead of dying by his hand.

Why did you kill her, you bastard? My hands trembled, a vision of Delectra's final moments flickering through my mind's eye. Victus, running away like the coward he was. I hated living in fear of the man. I almost wished he would try something. I'd rather die fighting than by a spell in the back.

Ambria drifted closer to me and patted my hand. "Don't be sad, Conrad."

I swallowed hard. "I'm trying."

"Every time we come by here, you get that same look on your face." Her forehead pinched with concern. "Don't bottle up the anger. It just makes it worse."

"I'm not angry." The broom's saddle horn cut into my palms, my grip too tight. "I'm frustrated. I want justice."

"Ansel taught us some good defensive spells over the past month," Max said. "Maybe he can help us with some offensive ones too."

"I don't like Ansel even a little bit." Ambria took back her hand and shuddered. "He's rude and acts like a know-it-all."

"He certainly knows a lot more than us." Max steered down toward a mundane building of gray stone and rectangular dimensions. "I don't mind learning with the arcnology tutorials we found in Moore's vault, but having a live teacher is easier."

We'd found a number of helpful videos from famed Arcnologist, Adam Nosti, inside Ezzek Moore's secret vault, but the more advanced areas of arcnology stumped us and sent us back to Ansel for answers. He was all too happy to rub our ignorance in our faces and put us through a number of meaningless tests before agreeing to tutor us.

Ansel might be family, but I didn't think I could ever be close to the man. It seemed he barely tolerated me or anyone else except the stream of random women he carried on with. It seemed I was doomed to dislike my living relatives. I might have actually loved the woman my mother was before Victus corrupted her with demon magic.

The three of us landed and headed inside the building with the plain placard above the door that read, *Arcnology Labs*. I opened the door and promptly collided with a man just on the other side. I bounced back and landed on my rump. He looked down at me with cool, expressionless eyes. A shiver of ice ran up my spine.

"I-I'm sorry, sir." I pushed myself up. "I didn't see you."

The thin man wore dark slacks and an expensive shirt, a strange ensemble for this campus. He merely gave me an annoyed look and skirted past, nearly bowling over Ambria and Max just behind me.

"How rude!" Ambria grabbed Max for support. "Don't they teach manners over here?"

"Who was that?" I asked, not really expecting an answer. "I've never seen him here before."

Max rubbed the gooseflesh on his bare arm. "I don't know about you, but he gave me the creeps."

Ambria narrowed her eyes. "There is something strange about him."

I watched the man step onto a moving walkway and shook my head. "It's not like he tried to kill us. Maybe he's an administrator." I motioned the others inside. "Let's get to Ansel before we're late."

"Heaven forbid." Ambria picked up her broom off the ground and stomped inside. "That man can certainly throw a fit."

We walked down the hallway and entered the last door on the right. Ansel sat on a stool, his profile to us. A blank whiteboard seemed to have captured his attention.

"Ansel?" I said.

His lips moved, but whatever he said was too faint to hear.

I stepped closer. "Ansel, we're here for our lesson."

His mouth continued to move, face otherwise locked in a catatonic stare at the blank board.

Though my cousin was odd, this seemed strange even by his standards. My heart beat a little faster. I stepped directly in front of him. "Ansel?"

"Dark, so dark. So many undead. Why, why, why? What did you do to me, witch?" Ansel repeated his words over and over, barely taking time to breathe between sentences. Purple stained his lips and his breath smelled pungent.

"Who did what to you?" I stepped closer, daring to reach out a hand and shake his shoulder.

Ansel flinched and leapt up. The stool toppled, clattered on the floor. "That witch!" He grabbed my shoulders. "She put it in my head! I can't get it out!"

I tried to pull away, but his grip was maniacally strong. "Who?"

He bared stained purple teeth. "Your mother!" Ansel raced to the whiteboard and began frantically drawing on it. "Dark, so dark!" He drew a circle filled with crooked rectangles. "So many undead."

"I don't understand," Ambria said. "What are you drawing?"

Max picked up a nearly empty glass vial from Ansel's desk and swished the purple liquid inside. "I think your cousin is high, Conrad."

Ansel grabbed me again. "No, no, no. Mind clearing. Open the mind."

"Open your mind to what?" I said.

"The nightmares." His eyes lost focus, arms dropped to his sides. "It worked until—" His eyes widened. "Something tore me inside." Ansel gripped his chest. "Hurts so bad."

"We need to get him to a medical facility," Ambria said. "Your cousin is as high as a kite!"

Max sniffed the purple concoction and wrinkled his nose. "Smells like lavender."

I took Ansel by the arm, but he shook me off. "Dark, so dark!" He turned on me and blinked as if waking from a dream. "She left you a message too. You have to find them." Fear lit his eyes. "My soul is torn. I can feel the shards."

Even though I didn't personally like Ansel, my heart wrenched at his distress.

His mutterings grew incomprehensible and try as I might, I couldn't snap him out of it again.

Ambria stepped into the hallway to find someone to help. She returned moments later with a tall thin man in a red uniform. His gaunt cheeks and short brown hair gave him a familiar look, though I couldn't quite place where I'd seen him before.

"What's the problem?" He saw Ansel gibbering in the corner and grunted as if the question just answered itself.

"I think he drank this." Max held up the vial with the lavender contents.

The man took it, sniffed it, grunted. "It's a clarity potion. Students use them all the time to help study."

"Do they react like this?" Ambria said.

The man opened a pouch on his belt and took out a strip of yellow paper. He dipped it into the potion and held it up to the light. The purple liquid turned brown. He frowned and sniffed the liquid. "Something is off about this potion, but I don't have the equipment to analyze it."

Ambria gave him an incredulous look. "Aren't you a medic?"

"Yes, a science medic, not an Arcane healer." He found a cork and stoppered the vial. "My brother might be able to help you."

"Well, bring him here," Ambria said.

"He loathes coming here," the medic said. "Better we take the poor lad to him." He took Ansel by his bicep and guided him toward the door. "Come now, lad. I have a sky sled just outside."

"Dark," Ansel murmured. "Undead. Broken souls."

"I hope he didn't try mixing a potion with recreational drugs," the man said.

The medic helped Ansel onto a silver sled hovering outside, and strapped him down tight. He looked at the brooms in our hands. "What brings Arcane students to Science Academy?"

"Arcnology lessons," Max said.

The medic offered another grunt. "I thought they frowned on such things there."

"There's no law against it." Ambria tilted her head. "Is there?"

The man stepped onto the sky sled and gripped the handlebars. "None that I know of." The sled rose above the trees and turned toward the valley. The medic twisted a handle and the sled took off across campus. The three of us hopped on our brooms and paced him.

We passed a gleaming tower with a white cross on the front of it and continued toward the cliff.

"Wasn't that the medical center?" Max said.

"Useless, as I said earlier." The medic nodded toward the spires of Arcane University across the valley. "My brother can help."

I realized whom he resembled. "Is your brother Percival?"

"You know him?"

Max chuckled. "Too well."

I grimaced. "Let's just say we're regular patients."

"I'm Arthur." The medic raised an eyebrow. "And you are?"

I pointed to myself and my friends. "Conrad, Max and Ambria."

"Delighted," he said in a bland tone.

"Why did you become a medic instead of an Arcane Healer?" Ambria asked.

Arthur pursed his lips as if he'd encountered a bad taste. "My Arcane talents are limited compared to his and our father is a doctor in a nom clinic. I decided to pursue a scientific medical career instead of one involving magic." He looked back at his cargo. "Unfortunately, its applications are limited not by science, but by oath."

"Oath?" Max dodged around a stray bird. "You mean you're not allowed to treat magical medical issues?"

"Except in case of extreme emergencies." Arthur directed the sled down toward the main gates of Arcane University. "I need to get a ward pass from the gate guard."

"Dark!" Ansel screamed. "Broken souls!"

Ambria shrieked and nearly fell off her broom.

Foam flecked Ansels lips and a terrible scream erupted from his throat. In that moment, I felt certain my cousin was about to die.

CHAPTER 3

"**M**edical emergency," Arthur told the guard.

The guard backed far away from the stricken patient. "Is he contagious?"

"No, poisoned."

The guard scanned them with a spell and then marked them as safe so the wards would let them through. "Get on with it then."

"Thank you." Arthur directed his sled into the main building. We drifted alongside on our brooms, ever watchful of professors since they frowned on indoor broom flying.

Percival's eyes widened with joy when we entered the healing ward ahead of Arthur. "Is one of you injured already?" He got up and walked around to meet us. "Did anyone lose a limb, perchance? I fashioned a potion that shows great promise in reattachment."

Ambria grimaced and backed away. "No, we have another problem."

Arthur entered the door pushing Ansel on a smaller floating gurney. "Good day, Percival."

"Arthur!" the healer clapped his hands together. "It's been months since you brought me anyone."

"I do so try." Arthur pushed the gurney into the back and he and his brother slid Ansel onto a bed. "This one seems to be suffering from a spiked clarity potion."

"Oh." Percival's grin flattened. "Well, that's easy enough to treat."

Max rolled his eyes. "Not challenging enough?"

Percival rummaged around on his workbench, sorting through jars filled with dubious ingredients until he found a small one filled a quarter of the way up with what appeared to be dirt. "Without challenge, how are we to advance?" He unscrewed the lid and took a pinch. "Do you believe stagnation in magical research is acceptable?"

"I think avoiding serious injuries is better than being your guinea pig," Max shot back.

Percival motioned toward Ambria. "Hold open his mouth."

She backed away. "Why me?"

Arthur gently squeezed Ansel's jaw and pried open his mouth.

"Children these days." Percival huffed and dropped the pinch into his patient's mouth.

Arthur closed Ansel's mouth and rubbed his Adam's apple until the man swallowed. Ansel's eyes shot wide. A tortured scream ripped from his throat and his entire body convulsed.

"Hold him still!" Percival shouted and we each took hold of a flailing limb.

Ambria cried out as my cousin's hand smacked her in the face. Max held onto a bucking leg, face red with exertion.

"What in the world did you give him?" I asked.

"Powered newt's eye and ghost pepper extract, of course." Percival stared at us as if we were complete fools. "It purges most poisonous effects within minutes."

"Ghost pepper?" Max lost his grip and fell on his backside. "Are you mental?"

"Poor man," Ambria said. "His mouth must feel like an inferno!"

Ansel's convulsions calmed after a few minutes whereupon his head lolled to the side and foaming spittle dripped from the corner of his mouth.

"How awful." Ambria averted her eyes. "I think you killed him, Percival."

A dagger of ice slid into my heart. "Is he dead?"

"Oh, don't get melodramatic on me." The healer peeled back Ansel's eyelid and shined a light from the tip of his wand. The dilated pupils remained fixed. He frowned. "Are you certain a spiked clarity is the only thing ailing this man, Arthur?"

His brother shrugged. "Nothing showed up on my medical scanner, so I assumed it was all magical."

Percival pursed his lips and strolled to a nearby shelf. He leafed through several parchments until a grunt told us he'd found the right one. He unrolled it on a table and pinned down the corners with smoothed pebbles. He read the text and examined the diagram of a human body, looking back and forth between it and his patient several times before making a thoughtful sound and shaking his head. "This is not poisoning. This man took a clarity potion, but whatever happened to him has nothing to do with it."

"Well, what's wrong then?" Ambria said.

"Probably ghost pepper poisoning at this point," Max said with a pointed look at the healer. "That's going to burn like an inferno when it comes out the other end."

I shot Max a grimace. "Is that really at the top of your mind right now?"

"I just don't want Percival shoving ghost pepper down my throat the next time I end up in here."

"Momentary pain is a fair tradeoff for prolonged nausea and vomiting, young man." Percival pinched and prodded Ansel but failed to elicit much more than a groan. He muttered an incantation and ran his spell from Ansel's head to his toes. "I believe the diagnosis is more severe than poisoning."

Ambria peered over at the parchment. "Which is?"

The healer rested his chin on a hand. "I don't know yet. I need time." He rolled up the parchment and tucked it back on the shelf. "Where to start?"

"Wish I could be of help, but I need to get back to the academy," Arthur said.

"Yes, yes, of course." Percival gave his brother a curt nod. "I will notify you of my progress."

Arthur nodded at the rest of us and left.

"Did your scan spell reveal anything?" Ambria asked.

"Oh, yes." Percival's forehead pinched seriously. "This man is quite sick."

Max clapped slowly. "You're truly a genius, Percival."

Percival's gaze shot daggers at my friend. "My scan revealed no obvious underlying cause to his symptoms."

"Perhaps it's demonic possession," Ambria said.

"My scan would have revealed a demonic presence." Percival shook his head. "This is quite the mystery." A smile spread across his lips. "Perhaps you've brought me a worthy challenge after all."

"Not exactly what we aimed for," I said. "Ansel was tutoring us in arcnology and we'd like to have him back."

"And he's Conrad's only living cousin." Ambria looked at me uneasily. "That we know of."

Percival's smiled faded. "I will get to the bottom of this and return him to full working order." He made a shooing motion with his hands. "Now, if you'll kindly leave, I can get to work."

I hesitated. "Please don't fail him, Percival. I can't lose another relative."

The healer nodded somberly. "I will do my best, boy. Now go."

I hoped his best was good enough. *Ansel is mean, but tolerable. I'd prefer to have him around.*

We'd barely stepped into the hallway when Max's stomach grumbled loudly and announced our next destination.

Ambria raised an eyebrow. "Lunch time already, Max? It's not even noon."

"Close enough," he said, and set out toward the dining hall. "Nothing like a good mystery to make me hungry."

"You certainly don't need a mystery for that." Ambria whisked the bristles of her broom across the floor. "I wish we'd left these at the broom closet instead of lugging them around."

"I can take them if you want," I offered.

"That would be awfully sweet." Ambria pecked a kiss on my cheek and gave me her broom.

Max sniffed the air. "Mm, I smell roast."

"Your broom?" I said.

He blinked as if coming out of a trance and handed me his broom. "Oh, thanks!"

"No problem." I slung the three brooms over my shoulder and headed back down the hall toward the broom check near the main entrance and hung them on the hooks covering the walls of the round room. I chose

22

the three closest to the door and hung the brooms. Each hook zapped my finger with a charm that would allow me to release them when I came back.

The main door opened and a figure stepped inside, a shaft of sunlight glinting off her glossy black hair.

Remember.

Cold air raises the hair on my arms. Dim torchlight illuminates a wide room filled with coffins. It smells musty like a cave. The drip of water echoes. I take a step toward the nearest box. The top is transparent, like glass. I look inside and shout in fright but no sound comes from my throat.

A withered face stares back with glassy eyes, mouth locked in one last scream.

I gasped and staggered back a step.

Full red lips parted in a greeting smile morphed to surprise. "Conrad, are you okay?" Asha Fellini took my hand and squeezed it.

I dared meet the eyes of the woman who looked so much like Delectra even though it knotted my heart with sorrow. The afterimages of my vision faded, but I recalled everything with perfect clarity. *That voice. It sounded like Della.*

Della had been the soul fragment left inside me after the demon preserving my parents' souls had been released. When Delectra died, Della went with her. Her last words to me were, "I left you something. Goodbye." I wondered if this vision had anything to do with that.

"Conrad?" Della touched my cheek with her cool fingers.

I flinched back. "I—I'm fine, Professor."

She stepped back. "What is it about me that offends you, Conrad?"

"Nothing, Professor." I'd so rudely rejected her touch, it probably hurt her feelings. But what could I tell her? *Excuse me, but you look just like my dead mother.* No, that wouldn't do at all. "Your hand was cold."

Asha narrowed her eyes. "I won't let you off that easy. Ever since the first day we met you've always given me such strange looks." Her forehead pinched with concern. "I am quite certain until I moved here from Italy, we had never met, so I don't know what I could have done to wrong you."

I tried to smile, but my face trembled with the effort of painting a façade over the intense pain of looking at this near clone of my mother. "I really don't want to talk about it." I backed away, blinking back tears. "I hope you had a wonderful summer." With that lame statement, I turned and ran back toward the dining hall.

Before entering, I took a moment in the hall to collect myself. A few other students walking past spared curious glances my way but mercifully left me alone. I went inside and found Max and Ambria at our usual table in the far corner. The vast dining hall boasted dozens of large round tables, but with over a week to go until the start of school, few students were here to fill them.

Wooden serving golems marched about the room efficiently delivering trays of food to the smattering of students. Max was already halfway through a haunch of roast beast and mashed potatoes. Ambria smiled brightly at me as I walked over. She smoothed down her long brown hair as she often did and wiped her mouth with a napkin.

The small bushy-haired girl I'd rescued from slavery at the hands of Little Angel Orphanage had grown tall and fierce. Together, we'd faced so many dangers and rescued each other so many times, I wondered what I'd do without the first real friend I'd ever had. Max was my best friend as well, but Ambria and I had a shared past that formed an even deeper bond.

I took a seat and leaned my head on Ambria's shoulder.

"What's wrong, Conrad?"

I told her about Asha. "Should I tell her that she looks like Delectra?"

Ambria squeezed my hand. "Will it help the pain?"

"Which pain?" I sighed. "I don't know where one begins and another ends anymore."

Max paused his chewing. "I'd tell her. It can't hurt anything and maybe it'll make you feel better."

"Max isn't right very often," Ambria said in a serious tone, "but he might be right this once."

Max chomped into a biscuit and rolled his eyes. "Mff."

Ambria flashed a grin. "I'm glad you agree."

"I also had a vision."

Max narrowed his eyes but never stopped chewing. "What was the vision about?"

"I heard Della's voice. She told me to remember." I closed my eyes and recalled what I could. "It was cold and musty—like a cellar. There was a red coffin with a glass top." I swallowed the dread in my throat. "And a body inside."

"A body?" Ambria's exclamation echoed in the nearly empty dining hall.

A few eyes darted our way, but the attention didn't deter Max from eating as if it were his last day alive.

I told them about the last thing Della had told me before leaving me. "I think she left me that vision, but I don't know what it's supposed to tell me."

"Could be a warning," Max said. "Stay away from cellars and dead bodies."

Ambria flicked a bit of mashed potato at Max but missed. "That's just common sense."

Max grinned.

Ambria shook her head. "I don't like it, not one little bit." She squeezed my hand. "If Della left behind memories, why haven't you had any visions since then? Why now?"

"Maybe Asha's face triggered it," Max said. "She does look a lot like Delectra."

"I saw Asha plenty of times after Delectra died." I cut into my slice of roast. "Maybe the memory just got stuck, or maybe Della timed it."

"True." Max stabbed the last bit of his beef. "Must be something else then."

"If it's an omen, we need to be very careful." Ambria bit her lower lip. "I don't want us to end up in those coffins."

CHAPTER 4

After breakfast the next morning, we joined a group of students and university staff on the flying pirate ship that ferried people back and forth between the university and the Queens Gate waystation. The cabin was full of people going to the Founders Day celebration.

Shushiel had already climbed onboard, camouflaged and nearly invisible. Once we reached the Grotto, she'd remain as invisible as possible since many people reacted unfavorably to giant red spiders in their midst.

Asha sat in the lower galley, the plump history teacher Eleanor Beetle firmly sandwiched between her and Gideon Grace. Grace's lip curled into a sneer the moment he saw the three of us. Asha smiled kindly but didn't call out or wave.

A stocky, freckled ginger shoved past us. "Watch yourself, Edison."

Harris Ashmore followed his friend, Baxter Troy, using his shoulder to push past us despite ample room. "You're blocking the way, idiots."

A tall girl with curly brown hair smiled at us as she followed in the wake of her friends. "Hello, Max. Hi, Conrad."

Max's face flushed. "Oh, hey, Lily."

Lily Crown seemed taller than the last time I'd seen her. My eyes felt drawn to the curve of her waist, the dimples in her cheeks. "Is there something different about her?"

"Yeah." Max tugged at the collar of his shirt. "I wish she didn't have such rotten friends."

Ambria grabbed our shoulders and turned us around. "Stop staring like fools. You'll just work Harris into a lather."

According to a foreseeance, Harris was supposed to stop a great evil. Since I was the son of Victus Edison, the former evil Overlord, many people assumed I'd be his target. By now it was evident to me that if Harris was going to save us, it would probably be from my father and not me.

"Just because Lily's pretty doesn't mean she isn't rotten to the core." Ambria sniffed. "It's too crowded down here. Let's go to the top deck."

Max and I followed her up a winding staircase to the top deck as the ship began to drift away from the clifftop and toward the landing pad far below. The sun glinted off the distant chrome rocket that ferried students to and from Science Academy as it began its descent into the valley.

The cool wind blew back the hair from Ambria's face and turned her cheeks pink. She touched a cheek with the back of her hand and sighed. "I wish Harris and Baxter would leave us alone. We might have evil parents, but haven't we proven by now that we're not like them?"

"Harris is too consumed with his own greatness to worry about that." I leaned over the railing and spit.

Max hawked up a gob and spit it after mine.

"Ew!" Ambria shivered. "Why are boy so gross and what's so fun about watching your spit fall to the ground?"

"I don't know." Max scratched his head. "I just like watching rocks and stuff like that fall a long way."

I couldn't answer her question either. "One of my foster parents had a tall hill in their backyard. Almost every afternoon, her sons would roll tires down it for fun. I liked watching them do it. It was also the only time they didn't bully me."

"How boring." Ambria leaned her chin on the railing. "If you want real fun, you should go shopping with me sometime."

"Shopping?" Max snorted. "The only thing I like to shop for are gag spells."

"Yes, that sounds about your speed, Max." Ambria looked him up and down. "Your clothes look like something a four-year-old would pick off the rack."

The two of them managed to fill the rest of the time it took us to reach the bottom arguing about shopping and dropping things from great heights. I followed the rest of the crowd off the pirate ship and through the ornate double doors leading into the Queens Gate waystation. Transitioning from a wide green valley and into a massive cavern with a giant black arch in the middle of it was still something of a shock to me.

Queens Gate and the Grotto were both considered pocket dimensions by most of the Overworld community, but I'd discovered they were actually fragments of Eden trapped in a strange juxtaposition with the Glimmer, the world that anchored all the realms together.

The university group headed for the towering Obsidian Arch, the source of a low humming noise as it powered up. Bright light slashed the air and a giant portal opened between the arch columns. It was almost like looking into a mirror. People in a similar way station somewhere across the earth looked back at us from the other side. One group came through on camelback, though not a one of them looked dressed for travel through the desert.

Once they cleared the black-and-yellow-striped markers around the silver circle bordering the arch, the portal flickered away. The professors leading the group went to the ticket booth and spoke with a portly man behind the counter. He motioned us into the waiting area where two smaller groups waited their turn.

An Arcane in yellow robes with black stripes did a headcount and gave us instructions, buzzing about us like a worker bee. "Stay close to each other and move through the portal in an orderly fashion. Whatever you do, don't cast any spells during the portal opening or you risk a Gloom fracture."

"What's that?" a young girl asked.

"A tear in reality that'll suck you into the dream world where you could be trapped for all eternity," the man said curtly. "So don't do it, okay?"

Nervous laughter fluttered through the group, but no one challenged his instructions. When our turn came, the arch hummed to life and the portal flashed on.

"Go!" the arch operator ordered.

Everyone took off like a shot, many with fear in their eyes, as if a vortex might open up and swallow them whole at any moment. We reached the portal without incident. The world stretched like a rubber band followed by a moment of disorientation, and we emerged on the other side of the pond deep beneath the city of Atlanta in the United States.

The Grotto waystation looked virtually identical to Queens Gate, complete with double doors. The group veered left around a waiting line and skirted past a parking lot packed with cars.

Ambria pointed to a brilliant orange sports car with tiger stripes. "Someone's got more money than sense."

"I sort of like it." Max peered inside the window, but the dark tint obscured the interior. "I wonder who owns it."

"Someone important, I'm sure." I pushed them forward before the group left us behind.

We stepped through the double doors ahead and onto a cobblestone road lined with shops that might have hearkened from the Victorian Era. Templars stood on the sidewalks to either side, motioning people onward.

"Keep moving," they said. "No loitering near the exit."

Despite the size of the pocket dimension, I felt a little claustrophobic. With the record-sized crowds expected for the celebration, the small exit to the waystation formed a terrible bottleneck in case of an emergency. What if Victus planned to strike while everyone was in one place? It seemed the perfect opportunity for an act of violence.

We continued through the town and into a large green park overflowing with people. I saw Galfandor near a group of kiosks promoting the Arcane Council, deep in conversation with a tall, thin man. As we neared the tents, the man turned and looked out over the crowd.

He looked familiar, and I soon realized why. It was the same man I'd seen at the arcnology building the day before.

I wasn't the only one who noticed. "Haven't I seen him before?" Ambria said.

Max squinted. "Yeah, I remember him."

"I wonder if he works at in the arcnology building with Ansel," I said. "Maybe he knows what happened to him."

Sharp green eyes locked onto mine through the crowd. A woman in blue robes bowed out of a conversation with a group of Arcanes and weaved her way through a sea of Arcanes on a course toward me. Her bobbed blonde hair bounced as if it had a life of its own. I looked behind me, wondering if perhaps Gideon Grace or another professor stood nearby. When I looked back, the woman offered me a smile from only a few feet away.

"Good day, Conrad Edison." She held out a dainty hand. "I'm Esmerelda Quiff of the Arcane Council." Despite her cute button nose and rosy cheeks, she looked businesslike. Something hard glinted in the depths of her eyes, and I wondered what hid behind her smile.

I took her hand and shook it. "Um, hello?" I had never met this woman before and had no idea why a member of the Arcane Council would want to speak with me. "It's a pleasure," I hastily amended.

"Yes, quite." She released my hand and smiled brightly. "I've heard a great deal about you, young man. I believe it's time we set aside some time to discuss in depth your role in some rather disturbing incidents on campus."

Ambria's forehead pinched with suspicion. "What is your role on the council, Ms. Quiff?"

The woman smiled again. "Oh, Esmerelda, please." She stared at Ambria, the smile etched unmoving on her face.

Ambria cleared her throat. "Um, what's your role on the council, Esmerelda?"

"I am chief security advisor." Esmerelda clasped her hands and looked at us as if we should be delighted. "Arcane University has been a hotbed of problems during your educational tenure, Mr. Edison. I believe it's time the council took a closer look."

"Are you accusing Conrad of causing problem?" Max asked.

"That is a pertinent question, Mr. Tiberius."

"You can't blame him for what happened at school!" Ambria protested.

"Who said anything about blame, dear girl?" Esmerelda patted Ambria on the shoulder. "I believe it's important to keep a detailed record of such incidents for further study."

"Well, well, Esmerelda. I see you've met Mr. Edison." Galfandor nudged between Max and Ambria. "I believe I asked you to save this discussion until after the elections."

"An efficient investigator wastes little time on formalities," Esmerelda said. "It is still a week until we decide on the next Arcanus Primus. I see no reason to delay."

"Perhaps the next primus will have something to say about that," Galfandor replied, an undercurrent of challenge in his tone.

"Perhaps," she said. Esmerelda bobbed her head at me. "I will be in touch, Mr. Edison. Enjoy the festivities." She turned and bounced away through the crowd.

"You should watch yourself around that woman," Galfandor said.

"She doesn't seem dangerous," Ambria said. "Just strange."

Galfandor grunted. "She is a dagger in a fluffy sheath."

"I don't see the harm in her questioning me about the problems my father caused." I looked up at Galfandor and shrugged. "Wouldn't it be a good thing to get the truth out?"

"Many do not wish to hear the truth," he replied. "Many wish to believe the Overlord is gone for good, never to return."

A portly man in gold robes huffed and puffed his way up stairs to a stage near the Arcane kiosks. He tapped a wand to his throat and began to speak in an amplified voice to the crowd of Arcanes. "Welcome, one and all." He bowed this way and that, his face red from the effort. "Today marks an important occasion in Arcane history. Today we celebrate when Ezzek Moore, the first Arcane, brought together the factions of the Overworld and bound them with a treaty. The Arcanes are proud to lead the Overworld into a peaceful and united future."

While most of the crowd burst into cheers, a group of people in the back booed the announcement.

A thickly bearded man in a blue romper cupped his hands around his mouth and shouted, "Leaders my ass!" His fashionably dressed friends burst into laughter.

"Bloody vampires," Galfandor muttered. He nodded at us. "I have to go for now. Do keep your wits about you, yes?"

"Yes, Headmaster." I looked up at the nearby rooftops and wondered which one Shushiel perched on. Even though Max and I were fairly tall, our view was obscured by two tall men. A short wall bordering the plaza provided a perch for several other people, so we stepped up on it to see over the heads of everyone.

The crowd stretched from one corner of the plaza to the other. Ambria pointed out a sea of Arcane robes at the core, with a fringe of vampires in their stylish clothing and lycans in their outdoorsy gear.

The speaker ignored the jibes of the vampires and continued speaking. "For those who don't know me, I am Alfred Jefferies, the acting Arcanus Primus until the election is held four days from now. It is my honor to introduce the candidates and allow for a short question and answer session."

"What does it even matter?" Max grumbled. "We don't get a vote."

"Actually, you do have a voice," Ambria said. "All Arcanes may participate in a popular vote in their district. Their representative is encouraged to cast their vote accordingly."

"Yeah, but they don't have to." Max shrugged. "We're not old enough to vote anyway."

"The general vote will be held tomorrow in Queens Gate," Alfred continued. "All travel by Obsidian Arch will be free for the duration of voting."

"Even for vampires?" someone shouted.

Alfred's sigh echoed across the crowd thanks to his amplification spell. "Free for Arcanes only, I'm afraid."

A chorus of boos scattered across the crowd. A group of young Arcanes pulled out their wands and thrust them into the air. Neon signs burst into life above their heads.

Free travel for all!

Vampires are people too!

No discrimination by supernatural affiliation!

More popped up across the crowd, much to the amusement of the lycans if their howls were anything to go by. Arcanes in tight blue robes, gold medallions shining on their chests, moved into the crowd and began scuffling with the protestors.

Alfred spoke louder to cover the shouts. "Lest you forget, the Obsidian Arches are run at great expense by the Arcanes. We must offset the costs by charging for travel."

"That's a lie!" a protesting Arcane shouted. One of the security guards hit him with a stun spell and the protestor collapsed in a heap. Within minutes, the guards quelled the protest and dragged the perpetrators out of the crowd.

Despite their shouts and heckles, the vampires and lycans were not ejected by security. Apparently, the Arcane guards only had jurisdiction over their own faction.

"Now, back to business," Alfred said. "I will introduce a candidate many of you know and admire. He has long avoided the spotlight, but many of us are glad to see his name on the ballot. Galfandor, will you please join me on stage?"

Max and Ambria met my surprised gaze with raised eyebrows.

"I didn't know Galfandor was running for primus." Max stared with confusion as the headmaster joined Alfred on stage. "I wonder why he never mentioned it."

"Hush and maybe we'll find out," Ambria said.

"Thank you, Vice Chancellor." Galfandor's voice boomed out across the crowd. "It was not until quite recently that I decided to run for primus. Though I find my job as headmaster of Arcane University immensely fulfilling, I realized that there was more I could do to make a difference." His gaze swept the crowd, but his eyes seemed to linger on me for a moment. "The Overworld is in a delicate state. The factions distrust each other, and Arcane arrogance has only worsened the situation."

The vampires burst into cheers. While some Arcanes looked at each other uneasily, others nodded quietly as if hearing a truth they already knew.

"Travel via the arches is too expensive for other factions. Magic that could improve the lives of others is no longer shared. The felycans drift apart from the lycans, the vampires apart from the Daemas, and the Arcanes hold themselves above everyone else." Galfandor pounded the bottom of his staff against the stage, sending a boom across the now silent crowd. "We must break down the walls that separate us and unite. We must help one another as family. Division will weaken us and tear apart the fabric of the great society that is the Overworld."

The crowd exploded into applause.

Galfandor waited patiently for it to die away. "I promise you that as primus, I will seek out the path to a better future for us all. Thank you."

Even Alfred seemed impressed by the short speech, a delighted smile on his face. His smile faded slowly, settling into a grimace, as if awaking from a beautiful dream only to find himself in a pile of rotting garbage. "Thank you, Galfandor. I will let the next candidate speak, and then open the floor to a few questions." He swallowed hard and took a deep breath. "Please welcome—"

The next candidate had already walked onto the stage, and we could hardly believe who it was.

CHAPTER 5

Alfred scowled, but introduced the next candidate anyway. "Please welcome Xander Tiberius."

Max blanched and stumbled back. "My father?"

"Is he bloody joking?" someone nearby said.

A woman gasped. "Not a chance in hell I'd vote for that scum."

"This must be a mistake." Max's shoulders hunched as if he were trying to make himself as small as possible. "He couldn't possibly win."

Judging from the scattered shouts from the crowd, many agreed with him.

"Get him off the stage!"

"Arrest him!"

"Overlord collaborator!"

Alfred raised his hands and beat the air with them. "Quiet, please while the next candidate speaks."

Aside from a few scattered hecklers, the noise level dropped to a discontented murmur. Xander brushed back platinum blond hair from his face and flashed brilliant white teeth. He looked like an older version of his twin sons, Rhys and Devon, only taller and with a more pronounced jawline.

"My opponent uses flowery words and beautiful promises to lure you to his side. He avoids the truth and tries to win you over with platitudes." Xander shook his head sadly. "The Overworld is in shambles, my friends."

A chorus of boos countered his words, but the amplification spell over-powered them.

"Arcanes cannot walk the streets of Queens Gate without worry. Entire sections of the town are no-go zones because they are overrun with rogue vampires who lie in wait for passersby." Xander narrowed his eyes at a group of vampire hecklers near the back. "The Daemos remain aloof and do whatever they will, and the Templars are too few to police the factions."

"Go back home, Tiberius!" someone shouted.

"Overlord lover!"

Xander spoke over the insults. "We need a strong leader. We can police ourselves. We can fix the vampire problem by barring them from Queens Gate. We can control Arcane destiny!"

A small section of the crowd burst into cheers. Distrust blended with curiosity on the faces of several nearby. Though a disliked messenger, it appeared to me that Xander had a compelling message to some.

"To fix the Overworld, we must first fix our own ailing cities, and bring back jobs." Xander held up his hands as if the scattered applause was a standing ovation. "As primus, I promise to put Arcanes first." He looked around until the few people cheering him ran out of breath and then strode off the stage. A throng of Arcanes in black robes swirled about him in a protective barrier and escorted him through the crowd.

Alfred cleared his throat uneasily. "We will hold another more formal meeting for only Arcanes on Monday in Queens Gate. Until then, I hope everyone has a marvelous Founders Day."

Max glued his eyes to the ground as if wishing it would open up and swallow him whole. "Why in the world is he running for primus? There's no way he can win."

"Well, you told us your father loves power," Ambria said. "Maybe he thinks there's a chance."

"You heard the crowd." Max glanced around uneasily. "They hate him. Well, most of them, anyway."

I looked around for Galfandor, but he was preoccupied with Alfred and a group of grim-faced Arcanes. "I'm surprised no one else is running."

"No one else thinks they can beat Galfandor." Max groaned. "My father is going to lose so badly, it'll just be another embarrassment for the family."

Ambria patted his shoulder. "Max, you're not the brightest and your hunger is insatiable, but you are not your father. If he wants to embarrass himself, it's all on him."

"Agreed," I said. "Though I think you're smarter than Ambria gives you credit for."

Max cracked a smile. "I suppose you're right. Maybe I could dye my hair and change my last name."

Ambria clapped her hands together with delight. "What a splendid idea. I say you go with blue or dark green."

Max stuck out his tongue. "And give you something else to make fun of? No thanks."

I looked around the crowd. "Maybe now we can find that odd fellow from the arcnology lab."

Ambria stood on her tiptoes and looked out at the sea of people. "In this crowd?"

The rhythm of a chant cut through the roar of the crowd. "Equal access, no more charge! Equal access, no more charge!"

I turned and saw a large crowd of Arcanes mixed with vampires pushing at the fringe of the crowd. A thin line of Blue Cloaks tried to stop them, but they surged through, pushing into the crowd and toward the stage.

A ball of flame soared. Someone shouted. A scream. Sparks flew. Wands and staffs were drawn. In an instant, the peaceful gathering exploded into violence. Fire blasted one of the nearby buildings and a tree burst into flame.

The crowd turned into a stampeding mob. A force of Blue Cloaks flew in on carpets, firing spells into the crowd. Vampires clambered up buildings and launched themselves at the airborne defenders, fangs flashing. The mob jostled the three of us, knocking Ambria from the wall. I cried out and grabbed her hand, holding on for dear life as a sea of bodies tried to drag her under.

Max gripped my waist and kept me from toppling off after her. I groaned and strained with all my might. Her hand slipped.

"Conrad!" She shrieked and then the current of frightened people carried her away.

"No!" I ran along the low wall my heart thudding, trying to find her, Max on my heels. I saw a flash of red and eight legs skittering across the heads of people. The screams intensified as the giant red spider became visible.

Shushiel dove into the throng and emerged an instant later, a frazzled Ambria dangling by a thread as silk webs pulled the ruby spider out of harm's way.

"There he is," someone shouted.

I turned. Two Arcanes in black robes glared at me with ill intent. Before I could react, one of them thrust a wand toward me. A searing bolt of light sprang from the tip. My wand hung in a holster on my back. Even if I'd had it out, I didn't have the reaction time to stop this surprise attack. In the end, the mob saved me. A tall man slammed into the dark mage. The attack nicked my shoulder. Blistering pain ignited my flesh and I spun off the wall as if someone had kicked me.

"Conrad!" Max's voice sounded as if he were underwater.

The world blurred and tears stung my eyes. I tried to move my left arm, but it wouldn't respond. A foot slammed into my head. Someone in the fleeing mob kicked my rib and fell in a heap on top of me. More weight slammed down. Brilliant light flashed, cutting through the haze for an instant, and I saw a someone bending down toward me.

Dark almond-shaped eyes gazed calmly down at me despite the chaos all around. Hands gripped me and the world spun. My stomach hit a shoulder and my face rested against dark blue fabric. Light flickered and flashed, but I was too woozy and weak to see what happened.

"Drop my friend or die!" Max shouted.

"He is safe," a calm voice replied. "Come."

"Wait a minute—" Max gasped. "Hey are you—wait up!"

My face bobbed as the person carrying me jogged through an endless stream of panicked people. As if someone had shut off the faucet, we reached a quiet place, the cries far away. I felt cool stone through my robes and against my back. The almond eyes hovered in my view once again.

The man wore his black hair cropped so short it looked almost shaved. A pointed goatee hung from his chin. He didn't look like someone who'd just fought his way through a crowd to save me.

Max ran around the corner, huffing and puffing, sweat dripping from his forehead. "Holy—" He panted a moment. "That was scary!"

I tried to speak, but my lips felt heavy, my eyelids wouldn't stay open. The man didn't speak as he prodded my wounded shoulder, but he grunted as if confirming a suspicion. His eyes betrayed very little emotion, but they seemed concerned.

He looked back at Max and waited until my friend stopped panting. "A healer is not far. Can you keep up?"

Max gulped a breath. "Yes."

Shushiel dropped from above, mandibles spread in attack. The man rolled out of the way and stood facing the ruby spider with no more concern than he might spare a ladybug.

The spider shielded me. "Stay away from my friend!"

"He's helping!" Max shouted. "We have to get Conrad to a healer."

"Percival is somewhere around here!" Ambria said from the side. I couldn't seem to move my head to look. It felt as if frost was working through my shoulder and toward my heart.

"Where?" Max said.

"Well, I mean, I saw him earlier. I don't know where he is now."

"This way," the man said. He slung me over his shoulder again and began to jog. I expected pain, but my cold flesh turned numb. I felt oddly detached from the world, as if riding a train into a dark tunnel, farther and farther from the light of day.

A door. Muffled but urgent conversations. A table. Pressure on my skin. A sudden jolt of pain and fire spreading through my limbs. I shouted and tried to flail, but something held me down. I sagged and felt moisture trickling down my skin. Something cold pressed against my shoulder and for a moment, I thought it was the same sensation I'd felt earlier.

I blinked open heavy eyelids and turned my head left. White moss bound to my shoulder. Cold air drifted from the compress like smoke.

"The poison is purged," a familiar voice said. I blinked a few more times and looked into the lovely face of Asha Fellini.

"Poison?" I moaned weakly.

She smoothed back the hair from my forehead. "Yes, Conrad. Those battle mages hit you with a frost poison spell. If you'd gone much longer without treatment, it would have frozen your heart."

"Why are you here?"

Asha tilted her head. Frowned. "I was here for the event. After the riots broke out, I came to the nearest healer ward in case they needed help."

I tried to sit up, but my arms trembled with the effort. "My friends?"

"In the waiting area." She put a hand to my back and helped me sit. The room overflowed with bloodied and bruised people. Healers bustled about, checking on the injured and helping others through a door and inside. "When I saw it was you, I brought you in immediately."

"Battle mages." I groaned with weariness. "They were looking for me."

"I was on the far side away from the rioters," Asha said. "Do you have any idea what started it?"

I lay back down and looked up at the glow ball drifting near the ceiling. "I think it was deliberate. My father must have realized I was here and needed a diversion so the battle mages could kill me."

"How can any person be so awful?" Asha took my hand and squeezed it. "To kill your own child takes a special sort of evil." Tears pooled in her big eyes and in that moment, she reminded me so much of Delectra I nearly cried myself.

She is not my mother. Delectra is dead.

"This isn't the first time you've looked at me like this, Conrad." Asha leaned closer. "You shrink away from me and look at me as if I'm out to steal your soul. Why?"

I hadn't realized that was the impression I gave her. Guilt hung heavy on my heart and I knew I couldn't keep this from her. She'd saved my life. She deserved the truth. "You look very much like my mother—like Delectra."

Asha gasped. "Really? I saw a few pictures of her in the newspapers, but the images were blurry."

"You didn't see her when she and my father ruled the Overworld?"

"No, I grew up in a remote part of Italy." Her gaze grew distant. "I learned magic from—from someone very special to me." Asha smiled sadly. "I went to Arcane University a year after the defeat of the Overlord. Because he had killed so many Arcanes, there was a shortage of teachers. It was then I decided that would be my profession. I would help magic return to the world." She spoke hesitantly, as if unaccustomed to telling others about her past.

"Who are your parents?"

"Dead." Asha smoothed her robes, eyes distant. "In any case, I never saw the Overlord or Delectra in person."

I tried to sit up again, but gravity pinned down my weary muscles. "Who were your parents?"

Asha blinked and shook her head. "Perhaps another time, Conrad." She walked over to a table of potions and brought back one filled with blue liquid. "Drink this, please. It will restore your strength." She held it up to my mouth since my arms felt too heavy to move.

The potion was so bitter I gagged, but managed to keep it down. She helped me lie back down and left to help attend other patients. A dull ache worked into my muscles followed by a soothing warmth not unlike the menthol salve Cora used on my chest when I caught cold. I must have fallen asleep for a brief time. When I woke, I felt well enough to sit up. I saw Asha across the ward talking to the man who'd helped me.

She smiled at me, but the man's face remained as impassive as ever. I stood on wobbling feet and made my way through the crowded ward.

"Thank you for saving me," I told the man.

He nodded. "It was time."

"Time?" The man didn't answer, but I asked another question anyway. "Who are you?"

He bowed ever so slightly. "Conrad Edison, I am Kanaan."

CHAPTER 6

My eyes went wide and I stumbled back. Kanaan's hand flicked out and steadied me. "The magitsu master?"

He nodded. "The stage is set. The players have arrived. Emily told me it was time to act."

"Emily?" I looked at Asha for guidance, but she frowned and shrugged.

"Emily Glass." Kanaan nodded toward the exit. "We should go. Another assassin might look for you here."

"Story of my life," I said. "It's not the first time my father tried to have me killed." I had a million questions, but the moans of the injured and the smell of blood flooded my senses and scrambled my thoughts. I walked out of the ward and into the waiting area.

"Conrad!" Ambria jumped up off the floor and squeezed me, peppering my face with kisses. "They wouldn't let me go in."

I squeezed her with what little strength the potion had restored and rested my head on her shoulder. "I'm so glad Shushiel saved you. I thought for sure the crowd would trample you."

Max stood behind Ambria grinning ear to ear. He reached out to slap my shoulder, saw the moss compress and took his hand back. "I knew you were too tough for a bunch of stupid assassins."

I let go of Ambria and felt oddly cold as her heat receded from me. "No, I'm not too tough. They nearly got me this time, Max."

He looked over my shoulder. "Professor Fellini healed you."

"You may call me Asha outside of the class room, Max." Asha walked to my side and inspected the moss compress. "Leave this on until it turns black and falls off."

Max leaned over and whispered in my ear. "You'll never believe who that man with the goatee is."

"Kanaan." I chuckled at his disappointed look.

"You could have at least pretended not to know." I looked back at the magitsu master who now stood near the exit to the building a few feet away. "He said Emily Glass sent him."

"Whoa." Max's jaw dropped open. "I thought she was dead."

"She vanished years ago," Ambria said. "Or so I read in the history books."

"You should go with Kanaan," Asha said. "There are probably other assassins in the Grotto who will do whatever it takes to kill you."

"Why would my father put so much effort into killing me?" I pressed a hand to my forehead as if that would quiet all the conflicting thoughts. "It's not like I'm dangerous to him."

Kanaan tapped his temple. "You have something dangerous up here."

"My brain?"

"Memories from your parents," he said. "The demon who held their souls inside told Emily that parts of your parents remained."

"No, the soul shards are gone," I said. "I don't hear them anymore." I thought back to the vision about the room and the boxes. "Well, except for a memory that Della left me."

"Della?" Asha said.

I felt like a mental patient revealing their problems to an outsider even though I'd heard the voices of my parents not due to mental illness, but because parts of their souls had been left behind after their resurrection. "I called Delectra's soul shard Della, and Victus's Vic so I could tell them apart."

Asha winced. "You had them trapped in your head?"

"They're gone now."

"Tell me about the memory," Kanaan said.

I recounted the incident.

"A clue." He nodded once. "Victus suspects you have information that could harm his plans."

"That seems like an awfully big stretch." Max shook his head. "I mean, how would Victus know about the memory?"

"He probably doesn't know specifics," Ambria said, "but remember, Delectra spent a lot of time with Conrad as Esma Emoora. Victus probably thinks she told him something."

Sorrow pierced my heart, but I took a deep breath and tried not to show it.

Asha touched my good shoulder. "I'm so sorry, Conrad. I talked with Esma—with Delectra—many times and she spoke fondly of you."

"She did?" My heart rose. "I didn't know you spoke with her." *Of course teachers talk to each other, dummy.*

"We spoke quite often." Asha sighed. "I was surprised when the dreaded Professor Emoora wanted to have tea with me the first time. The other professors said she was not very sociable."

"Duh," Max said. "It's because she was Delectra, not Esma Emoora."

Ambria punched him on the shoulder. "None of us knew that, Max."

It seemed I had more reasons to talk with Asha. "I would very much like to hear about your conversations."

"We will make time for it Conrad, I promise." Asha turned to Kanaan. "Can you get them back to Queens Gate safely?"

"I will do my best," the magitsu master replied. He looked straight up at the ceiling. "Shushiel, will you scout the way?"

"How did you know I was here?" said a disembodied voice.

"Ancient Chinese secret," he said and opened the door to leave.

Max's mouth dropped open. "Did he just make a joke?"

"He was probably serious," Ambria said.

I saw a blur move through the door as the camouflaged Shushiel crawled outside after Kanaan. Asha touched my arm. "Make sure you get plenty of rest. Whatever you do, don't let Percival give you any of his experimental potions. That man is a menace."

I smiled. "I'll avoid him the best I can."

More injured people lined the street outside, though most looked far better than those inside. Among the healers tending to them, I saw Percival, a delighted smile on his face.

He handed a weary-looking man a vial. "I swear this will make you right as rain!"

The man looked warily at another person retching into the gutter and shook his head. "I'll take my chances without your snake oil."

"Snake oil?" Percival shouted. "This is a highly effective experimental potion!"

Our group slipped around the corner before Percival saw us and followed Kanaan down a narrow street. Shushiel left red-tinted arrows made of webbing on the buildings to let us know which ways were clear as we proceeded through the town. Before long, we passed through the plaza where the riot had broken out.

Yellow lines glowed around the crime scene, barricading it from public access. Templars and Blue Cloaks huddled around covered bodies. I counted a dozen still figures, two of which lay close to our route through the zone. The buildings on the perimeter bore scorch marks and the trees were blackened by fire. It looked like a warzone.

Xander Tiberius stood with a group of Blue Cloaks, his face clouded with anger. He glanced our way and his eyes widened as they settled on Max. Max turned his face away and shivered. "Is he still looking?"

His father scowled and turned back to the investigators.

"No," I said.

We entered an alley marked safe by Shushiel and stopped at the end while Kanaan looked for her next arrow. Instead, the ruby spider shimmered into view at the end of a thread.

"Bad men come," she said. "Run the other way."

"How many?" Kanaan asked.

"Three."

He pursed his lips. "Few enough." Kanaan motioned us against the wall. "Stay hidden."

"Wait, I have a spell for that," Ambria said, and flourished her wand.

Kanaan held up a hand to stop her. "The hook is baited. Do nothing." He touched a ruby on the silver bracelet on his right wrist and blurred into camouflage with the wall. Three men in black robes burst around the corner seconds later, staffs at the ready.

The skull of a ram stared blankly at us from the top of one man's staff. He stood over six feet tall, thickly proportioned and bald. Gray streaks laced his long, wooly beard and tattoos patterned his face. The man's black eyes sent chills down my spine. He stood back while the other two men advanced on me.

They were shorter and thinner than the man with the ram staff. One had similar tattoos on the left side of his face, but far fewer. The other one had no ink that I could see. They held their staffs out like professional battle mages.

"We can take him alive, Garkin," said one of the men.

Garkin held up a hand, narrowed gaze surveying the area. "No, they are not alone." He pounded his staff on the ground and a shockwave reverberated through the air. Shushiel flickered into view on the wall behind them and Kanaan appeared to our left.

"I heard you were back, Kanaan." Garkin pursed his lips and looked up at Shushiel. "New friends, I see."

"There is no need for bloodshed." Kanaan twirled a wand in each hand. "I am the guardian of the boy."

"I agree," Garkin replied calmly. "There is no need for anyone to die." He nodded at me. "Not even the boy. Give him over to me and I will ensure he survives whatever Victus plans for him."

"Not good enough." Kanaan's eyes darted back and forth among the three men.

My stomach twisted and churned at the thought of merely surviving what my father wanted to do to me. *Death would probably be better.* The name Garkin sounded familiar to me, but I felt certain I'd never met him before. I stared at the ram's skull. A purple jewel in its forehead glittered.

A dim cave. Dripping water. Victus stands next to a coffin, speaking with Garkin. I cannot hear what they say. Victus trusts me only so far. He has seen the cracks in his control over me. It will not be long before he recalls the demon to corrupt me once again. He will need me by his side now that the Overworld is his for the taking. Never again will he let me run away.

Garkin looks over at me. Nods grimly. He despises all that the Overworld stands for. He sees unity among the factions as weakness. It is his wish for Arcanes to rule supreme even if Victus is the leader and not him. If only I could save my son from this torment.

Victus meets my eyes. Anger flashes as he recognizes the weakness in my face. No, there is no escape this time.

I gasped and jerked back into reality. Ambria gripped my arm with one hand, wand out in the other. I didn't know how long I'd been gone—seconds? Minutes? The standoff hadn't changed. Garkin still spoke with Kanaan.

That man helped Victus imprison my mother. Anger swelled like a black churning mass in my gut. "What did Victus do to my mother? What is that room with all the coffins?"

Garkin raised an eyebrow and turned to me. His attention settled on my shoulders like lead weights. "Did Delectra tell you about that, or is it a memory from the soul shard?"

I realized I'd just confirmed Victus's suspicions about me. Then again, he'd already tried to kill me with no solid evidence, so it probably didn't matter. "Victus failed the last time he tried to rule the Overworld, and he'll fail again."

"The last time, he had Ivy Slade to contend with." Garkin held his heavy gaze on me. "All of his principle enemies are no more, boy. In a short time, even your knowledge will be no threat to him."

"He doesn't know anything!" Ambria shouted. "Leave him alone, you evil bastards."

"He doesn't know what he doesn't know," one of the other men with Garkin said. "He could remember at any time."

And therein lay the problem. So long as I had the potential to recall more about this coffin cave, Victus would do his best to take me out. From what Garkin said, it sounded like I had very little time to stop him from doing whatever he planned. What was the short time he needed? Days? Weeks? A month?

"Last chance, Kanaan." The purple jewel on the ram's skull began to glow. "Things did not go so well for you the last time we fought."

"My duty is clear." Kanaan brandished his wands.

"You're not serious, are you?" Max said. "No one can beat Kanaan!"

My grip tightened around my wand. "My father underestimated me in our last fight." I gritted my teeth and tried to look fierce, but my lanky teenage frame was nothing compared to this bear of a man facing me. "I'm not a helpless boy anymore."

"You're a helpless teenager," the mage to Garkin's left said. "Enough talk, Garkin. Let's do our job and have an ale."

"Really, Boris?" Garkin gave the other man a sideways glare. "You think it so easy to defeat Kanaan?"

"The man is all legend, no substance." The mage spat on the ground. "I fought in the war with him. He didn't impress me."

"Let's kill them all and be done with it," the other mage said.

Garkin sighed. "It appears we must fight." He slammed his staff on the cobblestones. Brilliant light flashed.

Kanaan slashed a wand through the air and a dark wave countered the light. Purple energy poured from Garkin's staff, a scorching ray of magic that tore through stone. Kanaan rolled beneath the death ray. His second wand shot a beam of webbed light at Boris, but the mage leapt over the spell.

The unnamed mage parried Kanaan's first wand with his staff. Kanaan gripped the staff and catapulted himself up into the air. The tips of his wands glowed orange and he drove them into the man's ears. The mage's head lit up inside like a jack-o-lantern. A brief scream ripped through his throat before brain matter exploded from his nostrils and his eyes popped from their sockets.

Kanaan wasted no time, spinning to block a beam of magic from Garkin. Wands and staff whirled into blurs as each man parried the other.

Boris ignored the fight and came for us, a sphere of red energy pulsating atop his staff.

Ambria flicked her wand and a shield spell flickered in front of me. Max took out a black glass marble and blew on it three times then threw it toward the feet of the mage. A bolt of red intercepted the marble. Black liquid spattered the ground and spread.

Boris's lip curled into a sneer. "What was that, a smoke bomb, little boy?" His smile vanished the instant his feet touched the dark liquid and lost all traction. Arms windmilling, the mage went down hard and slid help-lessly across the slick.

"That's what you get for being a smart ass!" Max shouted.

Esma had taught us a simple spell for shocking each other during magical sparring matches. She'd also taught me its more powerful sibling. I flicked the wand through the pattern. I no longer needed words to help focus my spells, but I was too angry to remain silent. "*Amparus!*" Electricity buzzed from my wand and hit the helpless mage in the face.

Skin sizzled, hair burned, and a horrific odor filled the air along with Boris's scream of pain. His head cracked into the stone wall and his body went limp. Shushiel bounded from the wall and wrapped the mage in silken threads.

Kanaan flipped backward and fired shots from both wands. Garkin spun his staff and the shots ricocheted, knocking the wand from Kanaan's right hand. The mage advanced, casting small shield spells to intercept every shot his opponent fired. Kanaan ducked beneath Garkin's slashing staff and jammed a wand into the other man's knee.

Green light splashed across Garkin's robes. The mage flipped backward, his foot catching Kanaan in the chin and throwing him against the wall.

"Get him!" I said to the others.

Max threw another slick ball. I fired electricity, and Ambria launched a volley of blinding spheres. Garkin caught the sphere of potion with a web of light and threw it against a building. He dispersed Ambria's flash spell with a gout of dark light, and shielded himself from my attacks.

Shushiel dropped a web from above. The mage rolled away before it could land on him. Kanaan recovered his wands, and climbed to his feet. Blood trickled from a cut on his chin and burn marks marred his form-fitting robes.

Garkin looked down at his fallen companions and shook his head, turned his gaze up to Kanaan. "We'll have to reschedule, apprentice." He backed down the alley and vanished around the corner.

CHAPTER 7

Kanaan dropped to a knee, wands clattering to the ground. "That was close."

"Are you okay?" Ambria rushed to his side and checked his wounds.

"The student has not surpassed the teacher." Kanaan took a vial from a pouch and drank the green contents. He corked it and put it back.

"Wait a minute," Max said, "Garkin was your teacher?"

Whatever the magitsu master drank seemed to give him strength and healing. The cut on his chin zipped shut right before our eyes. He patted Ambria's hand. "I am fine, thank you." Kanaan rose to his feet and flicked his wands into their holsters.

Max balled up his trembling hands. "Is that a yes?"

Kanaan knelt next to the unnamed mage and examined him. "The first masters devised three paths of mastery, the rock, the tree, the monkey. Those aligned with the rock stand firm and unyielding. They align with strength." He stood and walked over to Boris and felt for a pulse. "Those who follow the way of the tree bend in the face of adversity. They dodge and weave, observing their enemy for weakness, but will only strike if necessary. They align with intelligence."

Max frowned. "So they avoid fights?"

"The monkey slips beneath his opponent's defenses, punishing him with speed and trickery."

"Agility?" Ambria said.

Kanaan nodded. "Precisely."

Max groaned. "Is this the really long way to answer my original question?"

"Garkin taught me the path of the rock," Kanaan replied. "I had already mastered agility, but in my youthful hubris, thought I could master all three paths."

"Is it impossible?" Max asked.

"No." Kanaan rolled Boris onto his back, careful not to touch the sticky threads binding him, and peeled back the man's eyelids. The dilated pupil shrank in response to the light. He took out another vial of green liquid and dripped it into the stricken man's mouth. "Each path is a different way of thought. One must hone their reflexes and physique to suit the chosen way."

I nodded. "In other words, switching from a rock to a monkey is difficult."

Kanaan continued administering the potion to Boris. "A mind does not easily switch modes of thought. If I gave you a broom where left was right and up was down, could you adjust?"

"Sure, it's easy," Max said.

I gave it some thought and imagined how my reflexes might betray me if I tried to fly a broom like that through an obstacle course. "It would take time, but I could do it."

"Yes. I learned the path of the rock, but I cannot switch between it and the monkey without preparation." Kanaan felt Boris's neck again and nodded. "He will survive."

"Why save him?" Max said. "He'll only come after us again."

"He's a murderer." Ambria's hand curled into a fist.

Kanaan brushed off the knees of his pants. "I agree with the way of the tree in some regards. Life is precious. If it must be taken, then take it. If it can be spared, spare it." He looked at the downed man. "He is a battle mage, not a follower of magitsu. I will end his life if he makes it necessary, but for now, he lives."

I felt mixed emotions about letting Boris live. The man had shown us no mercy and I doubted sparing his life would change his feelings, provided he had any. I had killed in defense, but to set out with the intention of murdering someone twisted my insides with horror. If he were my father, I would show no mercy, if only to spare the world a madman. Boris was just a minion. We'd injured him so badly, he might not be back on his feet for a while, anyway.

I looked at his more unfortunate companion whose brains still dribbled from his nostrils, and shuddered. Kanaan had executed him in an instant. How much stronger, then, was his teacher, Garkin?

I thought back to the first time I'd heard of Kanaan and wanted to be a magitsu master so I could fight my parents. Two years later, I now realized how long such an endeavor would take. "How long did it take you to master agility, Kanaan?"

"Mastery is never-ending." He turned to Shushiel. "Will you scout ahead, friend?"

"Of course, Master Kanaan," Shushiel said in an awed whisper. "Watching you fight was like art in motion."

Kanaan bowed slightly. "You are a master of threads. Thank you for binding the other attacker."

Shushiel bobbed up and down like she did when happy or laughing then climbed the wall and shimmered into camouflage.

"He is quite good," Ambria said to me. She took my hand and leaned against my shoulder. "But we made a pretty good team against Boris, didn't we?"

I let the heat of her body chase away the chill of fear still lingering from the encounter. "Yes, we did, but we can't stand against someone like Garkin."

Kanaan went to the corner and peered around it. He turned and looked me up and down. "One year."

I didn't know what he meant by that and jumped on the wrong conclusion. "It took you only a year to master agility?"

"That is what it will take to teach you the basics." Kanaan motioned us on and we followed a series of webbed arrows through empty alleys and streets. We came to another stop and waited on another signal from Shushiel, so I took the opportunity to ask another question.

"When do I begin?"

"Tomorrow."

"Um, can I learn too?" Max asked.

"Me too," Ambria said.

"I will teach anyone willing to learn." The magitsu master spotted another arrow and we continued on.

When we at last reached the doors leading into the waystation, we encountered our next obstacle—a human dam of bodies blocked the way out. People shouted and demanded to be let through, but only so many could fit through the narrow exit.

Kanaan didn't seem discouraged and continued across the main road and down a narrow street until we stood at the very end of the Grotto where it ended in a dense bank of fog.

Max tried to put his hand in the fog, but encountered an invisible barrier. "What now?"

Kanaan rested his gaze on me. "Tell me what you see."

I looked around. "A tree, some houses, a wall of fog behind an invisible barrier."

"Tell me what you sense."

I wasn't sure what he meant, so I sniffed. "Smells like wet rocks and grass."

He nodded. "Continue."

"I think he means to use all your senses, Conrad." Ambria sniffed and ran her hand along the invisible barrier. She stopped and backed up, running her fingers along a certain spot. "This barrier has lumps."

Max joined her and ran his hand up and down. "It's smooth like glass, but bumpy."

I walked closer and noticed the scent of damp rock grew stronger. It reminded me of freshly dug earth. I felt the barrier and noticed the same thing. Magical shields were usually uniform in shape, though from what I'd learned in history, the barrier in the Grotto was something of a mystery.

Queens Gate was a walled-in valley with a clear view of the sky. The Grotto was similar except an invisible barrier and thick fog surrounded it. I'd been through a crack in the world of Queens Gate and as I stood close to the fog, I realized how much it smelled like that rocky tunnel.

"Is this an illusion?" I asked.

Kanaan watched me but said nothing.

I closed my eyes and touched the barrier, sniffing like a dog hunting a fox. Despite the smooth feel of the barrier, it smelled like rock and earth. I kept walking, feeling the imperfections until I found the corner.

Here the barrier took a right turn to block off the front section of the city. It was there that I felt a small hole just large enough to slip a finger into. Hoping it wasn't a trap, I inserted my index finger and found a lever. I depressed it. Something clicked and a four-by-four opening silently appeared.

Kanaan offered a curt nod. "This is an emergency exit built by Underborn. Proceed."

I crawled through the opening and emerged in a huge hall filled with arches from one end to the other. I recognized the black and white stripes of an Alabaster Arch rising above dozens of smaller black arches. A niche to the left held even more. It looked just like the pictures from the history book.

"Whoa!" Max brushed off his knees and looked around. "So this is a control room."

An Arcane in worker bee robes stood at the far end of the great hall, connecting cities on the large map by manipulating a rotating sphere on a pedestal.

"It's a madhouse, I tell you, a madhouse!" another Arcane said as he stormed into the control room.

We took cover behind a nearby arch while Kanaan closed the secret door and walked over to the niche of small black arches.

"What happened?" the controller asked.

"A riot. That weasel Xander Tiberius announced he's running for primus and all hell broke loose." He shook his head. "There's no way that collaborator is getting any votes."

"Wow, I never expected him to run for election." The controller activated the arch and a deep hum resounded through the room. "You know, not all of his policies were bad. It was nice having Arcanes put first for a change instead of the vampires running the show."

"You can't be serious." The humming arch in the cavern beyond the room drowned out the rest of the words.

Kanaan motioned us over to the niche and walked among the small black arches. A silver circle surrounded each one, many marked with red Xs. He stopped in front of one with a green slash and knelt to press his thumb against the circle. Static brushed against the hairs on my arm as a magical circuit closed.

"Where do these arches go?" Max said. "What's with the green slash?"

"Anywhere but here is good," Ambria said.

I didn't have much experience with arches and only knew the bits and pieces taught in the history books. I suspected they kept the information intentionally vague since arch operations required a technical university degree.

Kanaan stepped inside the circle and concentrated on the arch. A silver line split the air vertically from top to bottom and peeled open into a portal the same shape and size as the arch. Familiar gray stone floors lay on the other side. "Enter," he said.

I stepped through. The world warped like a fishbowl and snapped back in place. I stood in the main hall of Arcane University. The portal hovered just above the floor behind me without a corresponding arch to support it. I gaped in disbelief until Ambria leapt through and knocked me on my backside.

"Oh, Conrad!" She giggled and took my hand to help me up.

Max, Kanaan, and Shushiel came through one at a time, then the portal winked into a white dot that faded like an afterimage burned into my retina.

"How was that possible?" I asked. "There's no arch here."

"An omniarch," Kanaan said in his usual brief manner.

Max scratched his head. "Never heard of one. You're saying it can open portals anywhere?"

Kanaan let us figure that one out ourselves and set off down the hall. We hurried to catch up.

"Where are we going?" Ambria asked.

"The mansion." He said it like it was a proper noun.

The mansion used by Arcanus Primuses of the past lay in ruins. The mansions of former Greek Row had been leveled by war. The only one I knew of was Galfandor's house. "Why are we going there?"

"It is a safe place." We continued down the main hall, through the many twists and turns that made the school a maze where many a student had become lost. We went down several flights of stairs until we reached a small room hewn from rock. Kanaan flicked his wand and one of the walls shimmered away to reveal a door.

"This is the Burrows, isn't it?" Max said. "We're not supposed to go in here."

Kanaan twisted his wand in the lock and the door creaked open into a black space. The tip of his wand glowed. He tossed it inside and the wand hovered in a tunnel. "Enter."

"I have always wanted to explore the Burrows." Shushiel bounced on all eight legs. "May I run ahead?"

"Of course," Kanaan said.

The ruby spider vanished into the dark.

Max stepped over the threshold. "Won't she get lost?"

Kanaan touched a slender silk thread on the tunnel wall. "She can find her way back."

"Where is this mansion you mentioned?" Ambria rubbed her arms in the cool air. "I don't like this place at all."

With Kanaan's floating wand leading the way, we followed him. "These were once dungeons. Later, a secret place for the Arcane Council to meet. Not so long ago, many called the Burrows home."

As we went deeper, we found old prison cells converted into living quarters, the dust-covered cross of the Templar order on a rocky ledge, moldy clothes, and even silverware. As we crossed the dark dungeon, I saw a dim yellow glow emanating around a curve ahead.

Max jumped at every noise, holding his glowing wand defensively. "I don't like this place at all. How much further?"

We turned the corner and entered a wide hall lit by magic sconces on the walls. Kanaan flicked his wand and another light source brightened until the huge space glowed bright as day. Standing grandly before us stood a huge mansion even larger than Galfandor's.

"An underground mansion?" Max rubbed his eyes as if they might be deceiving him. "Where are we?"

Kanaan pointed up. "The original once stood above. Destroyed by Daelissa, now a pale imitation."

"It's a replica of the original mansion!" Ambria clapped her hands together. "How beautiful."

Shushiel appeared at the top of the roof and crawled down to join us. "Why did people live below ground?"

"Daelissa planted an arch in the goliath arena and invaded Queens Gate." Ambria tapped her bottom lip with a finger. "This was probably a safe place to hide."

I blinked a few times and tried to process what this meant. "Are you saying we need to live down here?"

Kanaan shook his head. "This is where we train." He walked past the mansion and into a small door at the end of the tunnel. Inside stood a black arch about ten feet tall and just as wide. "I will reside in the mansion. You must find your way down here each day we train. In case of emergency, I will use this omniarch to assist."

"Why can't we just come through the arch?" Max shivered. "I don't want to go back through those dark tunnels."

"You may choose not to come." Kanaan's face betrayed no emotion as he regarded us. "But without proper conditioning, I believe you will die."

CHAPTER 8

Kanaan's stark appraisal was enough to bring us bright and early to the Burrows once again the next morning. The secret entrance he'd opened the day before was gone.

"How does he expect us to get down there?" Max ran his hands up and down the wall where the entrance had appeared before.

Ambria looked up the center of the stairwell. "We did come down the right stairs, didn't we?"

"I'm positive." I'd made a note of the particular statues and paintings we'd passed.

Shushiel dangled from a web attached to the ceiling. "Did you wave your wand like he did?"

Ambria looked at me. I looked at her. Max threw his hands up and groaned.

"I don't remember the pattern," I admitted. *Stupid! I should have been more observant.*

Shushiel raised a foreleg and flicked through a quick pattern. "Does that help?"

Ambria took the spider's foreleg and pressed it to her cheek. "What would we ever do without you?"

Shushiel's mandibles twitched with laughter.

I took out my wand and waved it through the pattern, but the pattern without context was useless. Though spells didn't require words to work, they needed will and focus to shape them. Words helped novices like us shape the spell into the required form. Or maybe they just helped us focus the purpose of the spell. Despite everything we'd learned, it was still confusing.

Max seemed to have reached the same conclusion. "I don't suppose he said any words, did he?"

"No, but he looked at the wall in a determined way." Shushiel dropped to the floor between us, her padded legs making no sound. "Perhaps that will help."

"It's simple," Ambria said. She flicked her wand in the pattern. The solid wall illusion shimmered away, revealing the entrance. She grinned when she saw the confusion on our faces.

Max's jaw dropped open. "How did you get it to work?"

"Spells work with patterns and willpower to focus them." She reached over and gently pressed up on his chin to close his mouth. "All I had to do was will the entrance to reveal itself."

"Because it was a solid illusion," I said.

She quirked her lips. "Well, I asked it to reveal and open just in case."

Shushiel bobbed up and down. "That was very smart of you."

Ambria rubbed the spider's soft red fur. "That's because girls are smarter than boys."

"I think you are right!" Shushiel tilted to the side. "Though I am not a human girl."

"You're a girl spider, so that counts."

Max waved his hands. "Shushiel, don't encourage her."

Ambria laughed. "Don't be frightened of my superiority, Max."

I checked the time on my arcphone. "We're running late. We need to hurry."

Max bounded through the opening. Bright lights flashed and he shouted with alarm. Shushiel skittered through after him and the rest of us followed. I turned off the illumination spell hovering over us since bright glowballs lit the once-dark tunnel.

A tall wooden wall with ropes blocked our way. Shushiel climbed up and over. She bobbed with agitation and returned to us. "I think it will take some time to reach the mansion."

Max's forehead pinched. "What's on the other side of the wall?"

"Many traps that we must get past." Shushiel's multiple eyes blinked at once. "It looks dangerous."

"That's a tall wall," Ambria said. "Maybe we should go get our brooms."

"I don't think Kanaan would be happy if we cheated," Max said. He blew out a sigh and went to the wall. It stood about ten feet tall with three knotted ropes hanging from the top. He gripped the knots and shimmied up, his body bouncing off the wall with each wriggle upward. After a lot of grunting, he dragged himself atop the wall and lay down. "Oh, man. This is going to take all day!"

Ambria grabbed the rope, braced her feet on the wall, and walked up in half the time it took Max.

"How in the world did you get up here so fast?" Max asked.

"I joined the summer athletic courses." Ambria pulled up her sleeve and flexed an arm to reveal a nicely formed bicep. "After our adventures in the Glimmer, I decided to get in better shape. I asked you and Conrad to join the courses too, but you were too busy."

I vaguely remembered her asking us. It involved hiking, sports, and gym activities, but I was too intent on improving my magical abilities and spent a great deal of time exploring Ezzek Moore's hidden vault that we'd found last year. Between that and learning arcnology from Ansel, I didn't have the time for athletics, although right now I wished I had found the time.

Shushiel crawled onto the ceiling and moved ahead while I followed Ambria's example and walked up the wall instead of shimmying up the rope. I didn't quite match her pace, but I wasn't nearly as tired as Max.

A pendulum with a padded burlap sack on the end swung back and forth across the tunnel a few feet from the wall. Beyond that, I saw a series of ropes hanging over a trench filled with water. Whatever surprises came next were hidden around the bend.

We made our way down the ropes on the other side of the wall. Timed our way past the pendulum. Swung our way across the water trench, though not without mishap. Max and I both fell in once. Since the trench was deeper at the far end, we had to go back to the start to get out and reach the ropes.

When we caught up with Ambria around the corner, she already faced the next challenge. The floor, walls, and ceiling shined like polished glass up a slight incline for about forty yards. Shushiel slipped across the surface, her legs struggling helplessly, unable to find purchase and came sliding back down toward us.

"Easy," Ambria said without prompting. "We run at it, slide up, and reach the other side."

Max knelt and examined the slope. "You'll never get enough momentum."

"I haven't sat on my backside all summer, Max." Ambria backed up a good ways and dashed toward the slick surface. She leapt at the last minute and landed on her feet, hunched over like a snow skier. The surface proved too slick, even for her improved body conditioning.

Her feet flew from underneath her and she landed on her backside, sliding at a mad pace halfway up the incline, slowing, and then gliding back down toward us. Max and I caught Ambria before she hit the rough floor, despite our gales of laughter.

"Oh, man that was funny!" Max howled with laughter. "You sure ended up on your backside that time."

I wiped tears from my eyes. "That was very athletic, Ambria."

Even Shushiel bobbed up and down in hysterics. "It was a good try and very funny."

Ambria was not amused. "That hurt."

Max held his stomach and managed some words between giggles. "Your ego, or your bottom?"

"Both." Ambria huffed and stood up. "Well, laughing isn't going to get us to the other side."

I took a few deep breaths to ward off another giggle fit and looked at the floor. *Max is right. We can't get enough speed to slide up the hill.* I imagined flinging someone across the floor, but even if I had the strength to spin someone around and toss them, it still wouldn't be enough. I knelt and touched the glassy surface with my bare hand. The surface felt cool and nearly as slick as Max's potion.

"Can you shoot a web across it?" Max asked Shushiel.

"My web does not shoot," the spider said. "It extrudes and I attach it."

Max frowned. "We should make a web shooting charm. It'd be bonkers if you could shoot your webs."

As they continued to talk about making slingshots from her web and propelling us across, I wondered if maybe we were thinking about this all wrong. The first few obstacles required physical exertion, but this one defied our abilities. Kanaan hadn't told us about his gauntlet, or explicitly stated any rules.

Why not use magic? I took out my wand and focused a fire spell on the slippery surface. It bubbled and melted away like ice, leaving behind bare rock. I swept the spell up the incline, clearing a path. After a few seconds, the rock glazed back over.

"Are you kidding me?" Ambria followed close behind. "It's so simple."

"I didn't even think of using magic." Max blasted a section with his wand. "For some reason, I thought we couldn't."

I cleared a trail and led the way up the path, hurrying since it returned to its slippery state after a brief time.

"Obviously we're supposed to use magic on this one." Ambria huffed and put her hands on her hips when we reached the top of the incline where the slick coating ended. From here, the tunnel floor dipped at a shallow angle. About fifty yards ahead, a humongous bull grazed in a small patch of dark green grass. Its head jerked upright when it saw us, hoof stomping in warning.

"How in the world did Kanaan have time to set up this crazy obstacle course?" Max said. "Where did he find a bull?"

"Probably with the omniarch," I said.

"There's no room for you to get past the bull." Shushiel crawled to the ceiling. "I can go over his head."

"Simple." Max flourished his wand. "Let's use magic."

"A blinding spell ought to do the trick." Ambria stepped toward the bull until it stood twenty yards away while the rest of us readied our wands in case it charged. She traced a pattern and a flash of light speared toward the bull's eyes. The spell splashed off the bull to no effect.

The creature bellowed angrily and stomped its front hoof. Then it lowered its head and charged.

"Run away!" Max shouted before taking his own advice.

Ambria sprinted past both of us, her summer of training proving its worth. Shushiel crawled overhead and dropped from the ceiling just ahead of us, a thin thread of silk stretching behind her.

"Hurry!" She said. "Press yourselves against the wall."

We ran past her and stopped at the edge of the slippery slope where we followed her advice.

The bull charged over the rise, pounding straight for us when its front legs struck a nearly invisible tripwire. With a bellow of surprise and wide bovine eyes, the bull faltered. It hit the slippery slope obstacle and slid all the way down, coasting to a stop at the bottom. It gained its feet and tried to charge us, but the slick surface confounded it as much as it had us.

Max brushed off his hands. "Well, that was easy enough."

Ambria hugged Shushiel. "Girl power."

"Yes." The spider bobbed up and down. "Girl power."

Max groaned.

A rhythmic pounding echoed from somewhere ahead. We walked over the bull's patch of grass and followed the curve to the source. Wooden beams jutted from the ceiling, walls, and floors, their surfaces studded with rods of varying lengths. The beams and rods rotated, extended, and retracted, opening and closing gaps along several yards of the passage. The floor was divided into hexagonal shapes that also shifted up and down just enough to trip someone trying to run across it.

"Reminds me of the gauntlet for kabash," Max said. "But those openings look a lot smaller."

I walked to the edge of the area and watched the first row of beams, counting the seconds between openings. A gap between the first and second series would allow us to gauge the next pattern. "Let me get to the other side."

"Maybe I should go first," Ambria said.

Max grunted. "How about giving boy power a chance first?"

Ambria rolled her eyes. "Fine, but don't hurt yourselves too badly."

I timed the pattern and ran, but the moment my foot touched the first hexagonal tile, the rhythm of the gauntlet shifted and changed to a new beat. The openings I'd timed before vanished, replaced by new ones.

Max slapped his forehead. "This is mental!"

I stepped back onto the normal floor and watched the new pattern. The openings in the first row were in opposite places now. If I'd tried to run straight through like originally envisioned, I would've been swatted like a fly. I watched the new pattern for a moment before realizing that it might change again when I stepped on the floor.

I put some weight on the same hexagonal tile. A loud click echoed and the pattern shifted to something even more chaotic. The floor tiles rose and dropped like ocean waves, the wooden beams shot up and down faster and faster. I pressed the tile again. Another click. Another pattern change. I pressed it again, giving myself a moment to analyze the pattern. The fifth time I pressed it, the pattern became familiar again and I realized it was the first pattern.

"There are five patterns," I told the others. "So far the first one seems the easiest."

"No, there is another problem," Shushiel said. "On the third pattern, there were no openings in the first row. I climbed higher and was able to see between the gaps. On some patterns, there are no openings in the other rows."

"How many rows are there?" Ambria asked.

"Six." Shushiel's eyes blinked. "I will have to crawl along the floor with the rest of you."

I blew out a breath. "Great, so we have to change the pattern to open gaps in different sections. That means someone over here will have to change the pattern for me while I make my way through. Once I hit the other side, I can tell you the pattern order."

Ambria pressed her hands to her temples. "This is awfully confusing."

"We'll be lucky to reach Kanaan today," Max said. "If there wasn't a bull between us and the exit, I'd leave right now." He rubbed his belly. "Also, I'd really like some donuts."

Ambria poked his stomach with a finger. "You don't need more donuts, Maxwell Tiberius. You need a diet."

Max pushed her finger away. "Hey, I'm not fat."

"Save the arguing for later, please." I pushed them apart. "We need to get through this challenge."

"Stupid challenge!" Max pressed on the first hexagonal tile, switching the patterns rapid fire. Something groaned. Cracked. Splinters exploded from beneath the floor tiles and the floor dropped a foot, leaving a gap between the ceiling and floor beams as the apparatus ground to a halt. Max's mouth dropped open. "Whoops."

"You broke it!" Ambria's lips spread into a wide grin. "Max, this is wonderful."

"Boy power," I muttered. "Guess it's good for something."

Shushiel bobbed up and down in amusement.

We squeezed through the gaps in the broken rods and with the aid of Shushiel, climbed over the places where no openings presented themselves. We continued down the tunnel, relieved to find no more obstacles. We emerged in a gauntlet room twenty minutes later. Just outside the room was the corridor leading to the mansion and the omniarch.

Max looked back at the tunnel exit. "Was that a different route from yesterday?"

"Looks like it." I wondered if we'd have to go back through it on the way home, or if Kanaan would let us use the omniarch.

Kanaan sat on a stone column in the center of the gauntlet room. Behind him were rows of progressively larger stones, monkey bars, and other equipment. He nodded curtly as we approached. "You made it. Now for the hard part."

CHAPTER 9

"The hard part?" Max looked flabbergasted. "If we hadn't broken the last gauntlet, we'd still be stuck out there."

"You broke it?" Kanaan raised an eyebrow.

Max gulped. "Um, it was an accident."

"What did you learn?" Kanaan asked.

Ambria sniffed. "That flying brooms through all of it would've been easier."

He nodded. "Why did you not?"

I frowned. "Wouldn't that be cheating?"

"In a game of no rules, there is no cheating." Kanaan pushed off the stone column. "Use what you can to reach your goal."

"Does that include breaking a challenge?" Ambria asked sweetly.

Kanaan nodded. "Sometimes you must break things to survive." He led us to three identical rows of stones. "Line up each stone in its place across the room." He pointed to three chalk lines on the opposite side.

"I will watch," Shushiel said, and climbed up a tall stone pillar.

The three of us started with our smaller stones, moving them in order. Ambria struggled with the fifth, a smooth round stone the size of her head. Despite our lack of exercise, Max and I were able to carry ours across without too much trouble. Ambria waddled across the room, huffing and puffing, and dropped it into place.

The sixth caused Max and I to struggle mightily. Ambria had to roll hers. Though it took her several minutes to get it into place, she didn't fall behind me and Max since our seventh stones had flat bottoms making them impossible to roll or lift. Even if we moved them, we still had the final stone to move, and it was the size of a small boulder.

I was the first to take out my wand and use a spell to levitate the stone into position. Kanaan watched and remained silent. Apparently, there were no rules to this challenge either. Max and Ambria followed my lead and within a few minutes, we'd relocated our final stones.

Kanaan clapped his hands together once. "Cross the rungs of the climbing frame. Repeat until you can hold on no longer." He pointed to the monkey bars.

The frame was about fifty feet long and ten feet wide, giving us room to cross beside each other. Max made it halfway across before his hands gave out and he dropped to the sand pit beneath it. Kanaan motioned him over to his side while Ambria and I continued. I fell short of the end by ten feet. Ambria made it three rungs more but couldn't hold on long enough to reach the end.

Kanaan clapped his hands. "Gather."

We walked over next to Max.

He led us to a track in another section of the gauntlet room. Progressively higher hurdles stood in our way. Beyond that, the track twisted and turned through stone walls. "Run the course as many times as possible."

I leapt over the first four hurdles, but the fifth was as high as my waist and I plowed into it. Thankfully, it bent over like rubber, allowing me to continue without tripping and falling on my face. I ran the course four times before I was too tired to continue. Ambria jogged past twice more before stopping.

Kanaan traced his wand over each of us and nodded.

"What in the world does this have to do with magitsu?" Max said. "I'm sick of your rat mazes."

The magitsu master turned to him. "Perform a flip."

"A flip?" Max grimaced. "I'd kill myself."

"Precisely." Kanaan led us to another section of the room where the floor emitted a sullen glow. "Do your flips here."

Ambria stepped tentatively onto the floor. It sank slightly beneath her weight. She jumped. The floor rebounded and propelled her several feet into the air. "It's just like a trampoline!" She did a perfect backward flip. "Oh, it's so much fun."

Max blew out a sigh, but went a safe distance from Ambria and tried to flip. He landed on his face, his back, and even his head. On his fifth attempt, he managed to land on his feet.

"What's this all about?" I asked Kanaan. "Why the gauntlet? Why flips?"

"Is it not clear?" He watched Ambria bounce up and down. "The monkey requires agility. You must condition your bodies as well as your minds. Magic alone is not enough."

Max scratched his head. "Do we have to do less exercise if we take the path of the rock?"

Kanaan offered a glimpse of a smile. "Then I would have you lift heavy weights to improve your strength. For the path of the tree, you would do yoga."

"In other words, there's no way to avoid exercise."

He shook his head. "To become a master, one must achieve balance in many aspects."

I went out onto the floor and practiced my flips.

We were exhausted by the end of our physical exercises, but Kanaan had more in store for us. "Light as many candles as possible with magic." He revealed a section filled with row upon row of candles.

Lighting candles should have been easy, but I was so tired, I could barely stand, much less concentrate on making a flame. I gritted my teeth and forced my tired mind to focus. Twenty candles later, I had to stop and close my eyes. Max and Ambria lit just over ten candles each before they could go no further.

Kanaan brought us tea and a plate of fruit and nuts. "Eat."

Shushiel perched on a nearby stone pillar. "You did well. I wish I could do magic so I could train with you."

"You could use eight wands," Max said with a grin.

Shushiel blinked. "It would be hard to walk."

Max dug into the fruit with abandon. I ate some blueberries, an apple, and a handful of almonds. The tea tasted slightly bitter, but it must have had extra ingredients, because by the time Kanaan returned for us, I felt refreshed.

Max noticed it too. "Did you give us an energy potion?"

"A drop of refresher potion in the tea." Kanaan set down his cup. "It will accelerate your physical conditioning, but you will require more sleep. After training, I suggest you eat an early supper."

"Is the potion harmful?" Ambria asked.

"In large doses and over long periods of time, yes." Kanaan held a small vial between thumb and forefinger. "Only one drop a day." He picked up a wicker basket at the foot of the pillar and put it on the stone block next to the fruit. He opened the lid and removed three jars. "Drink the red one in the morning, the green one after lunch, and the white before supper."

Ambria looked inside the basket. "What do they do?"

"They will enhance muscle growth and ligament strength." Kanaan tucked the jars back in the basket. "It is vital." He set the basket back by the pillar. "Come. Time for more exercises."

Max grimaced. I held back a groan. Though I felt refreshed from the tea potion, I didn't look forward to more trials.

Ambria clapped her hands together and jumped up. "I'm ready!"

Our teacher led us through more exercises. By the end, I lit fourteen candles while the others stopped at nearly half that. Apparently, the refresher potion had its limits. Even so, my muscles swelled more than usual, as if all the blood rushed inside and filled them like balloons.

After training, Kanaan opened an omniarch portal to the hallway outside the dining hall in the university.

"You read my mind!" Max rushed through despite having complained of being too tired to move just moments before.

"Tomorrow, same time," Kanaan said.

Ambria hesitated in front of the portal. "How did you get all those obstacles in place so fast?"

"The Burrows hold many secrets left by the builders. There are tunnels, other challenges." Kanaan folded his arms low over his waist. "Tomorrow you will face new gauntlets."

"What about the bull?" Ambria's forehead pinched. "Surely it hasn't been down here all this time."

"I borrowed it." Kanaan motioned us through the portal. "I will see you soon."

We stepped through and the portal winked away, leaving me and

Ambria alone in the hallway since Max had already vanished into the dining hall.

"Do you sometimes feel as if we're training for too much all at the same time?" Ambria said. "We're still learning basic spells, arcnology, and now magitsu."

"Everything feels like too much." I sat down on a wooden bench and sighed with relief. "I don't have my parents' soul shards to rely on for advanced magic anymore. I have to be better if I want to survive."

Ambria sat down next to me. "Even though we've been at the same place since escaping the orphanage, it feels like we're always running, doesn't it?"

I hadn't thought of it that way, but Ambria was right. We'd never stopped running from the specter of my parents. "Maybe I didn't run far enough."

"Do you think we should go somewhere else?" She touched my hand. "Leave Queens Gate?"

I met her big brown eyes and realized with a start just how different she looked from the little orphan girl I'd saved all that time ago. Ambria had lost her round cheeks and gained dimples. Her hair was glossy and groomed instead of fuzzy and unkempt. She was growing into a woman, and I still felt like a little boy. No matter how hard I trained, I still felt helpless in the face of my father's power.

She deserved a wonderful future, but if I ran, I knew she would come with me out of a sense of obligation. I might have saved her from the orphanage, but that didn't mean she owed me her future. "No, Victus has to be stopped. I know he still wants power, so he'll be back."

Ambria squeezed my hand. "You've grown so much, Conrad. I know that together we can stop him."

My heart turned to ice at the thought of what might lie in store for us.

My friends and I had been through a lot, but we'd always had help surviving.

Shushiel shimmered out of camouflage next to Ambria. "Am I interrupting?"

I flinched, having forgotten she was there. "No, of course not."

"I will help you defeat your father, Conrad." Shushiel touched my arm with her foreleg. "He created the ruby spiders, but he is a bad man."

"Hey!" Max poked his head out of the dining hall. "Are you all coming to eat, or what?"

Ambria laughed and wiped a tear from her eye. "We should eat before we get too tired."

"Agreed." I let go of her hand even though a part of me wanted to keep holding it, and we joined Max for supper.

True to Kanaan's warning, by the time we ate and got to our brooms in the check-in closet, we were shuffling like zombies. Flying our brooms while tired proved hazardous. After Max nearly collided with a tree, we slowed down. Instead of flying up to our rooms and risking a fall, we went through the main entrance and dragged ourselves up the stairs.

Thankfully, very few students had returned from summer holiday yet, so there was no one to make fun of the way we walked.

Max's jaw cracked with another yawn. "I don't know if I can make it up the rest of the stairs." He gazed longingly at the sofas in the coed sitting room. "Maybe no one will bother me if I sleep here."

"You'll probably wake up with lipstick and a new haircut," Ambria said. "But go to sleep there if you want."

Max seemed too tired to groan and trudged toward the stairs leading to the male dorms.

Ambria stood on tiptoe and kissed my cheek. "Sleep well, Conrad."

"That won't be a problem." I hesitated, then leaned down and kissed her cheek. It felt so soft and warm to my lips that I let them linger for several seconds before realizing what I'd done. "Oh, I'm sorry."

She giggled. "Falling asleep on your feet?"

"Maybe." The couch began to tempt me as it had Max, so I managed a weary smile. "Good night."

I stumbled up the stairs after Max, into the male dorm sitting room, and toward the tower stairs. Max had already vanished around the bend and I found it increasingly hard to move my feet.

A white house. Rolling green hills. The sun shines through the red leaves of an oak. Desperation chokes me. This is my only chance. He doesn't know what I've done. He cannot find out or we will both die. Will she survive or did I use the spell too early? I look down at blood-stained hands. My knees are weak, my stomach roils with nausea. He is my last hope.

I blinked. My head ached, each heartbeat pulsing in my skull. *Where am I?* I sat up, slowly, every fiber in my muscles aching nearly as much as my head. I touched my left temple and found drying blood on my fingers. I was still in the stairwell. "I must have fallen asleep and hit my head."

Every time I blinked, the afterimage of the white house appeared in stark relief to the darkness behind my lids. The red leaves whispered in a cool wind, and the green grass of the nearby hills waved. "That wasn't a dream." I'd had another vision, but it was so different from the previous ones.

I checked the time on my phone. *Two in the morning.* At least I still had time for more restful slumber.

I pushed to my feet and recovered my broom. Steeling myself against the pain and exhaustion, I pushed onward and upward until I reached the room I shared with Max. He lay fully clothed on the bed. The basket of health potions from Kanaan sat at the foot of my bed. The magitsu master must have put it there with the aid of the omniarch.

I changed into my pajamas and crawled under the sheets, replaying the vision over and over again in my mind.

Where is that house? Who lives there?

"Della, what did you do to me?"

If only she were there to tell me.

CHAPTER 10

Dawn arrived too soon, but I got up anyway and drank one of Kanaan's morning potions. My muscles felt sore, but stronger. My head still hurt from hitting it on the stairs. I shook Max awake.

"Go away." He tried to pull the covers over his head, but he'd slept on top of them all night.

"Get up, Max." I shook him again. "Drink the morning potion. It'll make you feel better."

"I'm done training." He kicked off his shoes and wrestled the covers over him. "Go without me."

My stomach rumbled ravenously, dissuading me from arguing with my friend. I took a quick shower and headed into the common sitting room. Ambria jumped off the sofa when she saw me, an empty potion jar in her hand. "Oh, thank goodness! I'm so hungry I could hardly wait! Kanaan left a basket of his training potions, so I drank this one, hoping it would make me feel full."

"We should get you an arcphone so you can tell me when you're ready," I told her.

"It would make meeting for breakfast easier." She climbed on her broom and whisked through the open window, apparently eager to be on the way.

I followed after her and checked our brooms into the broom closet in the main hall. Aside from a smattering of students, the dining hall was empty. The wooden serving golems had just laid out a breakfast of eggs, bacon, and toast, when Max charged inside.

"Food! Now!" He dropped into the chair next to me and stared at my toast. "Food, please, please, please. I'm dying."

I gave him my toast, but was too hungry to share my eggs. Ambria and I polished off two servings of breakfast, and Max three. As we sat there sipping our orange juice and moaning contentedly, Shushiel appeared next to Ambria, bouncing in amusement.

"You must be very hungry," she said. "I have never seen Ambria eat so much."

Ambria smiled. "It's the training."

I turned to Max. "Are you coming or not?"

He sighed and rubbed his belly. "Well, now that I'm not tired anymore, I guess so."

We returned to the keep and changed into more athletic wear and took the pre-lunch potions with us to meet Ambria outside her window. Once again, we returned to the Burrows. The secret entrance led into an earthen tunnel this time where we faced another a long mud pit beneath rope swings with metal rings on the ends.

"I'm using my broom to fly across," Max said, and took off. He made it ten feet over the mud pit when his broom nosedived into the mud. Max squawked like a wounded bird and struggled to drag himself from the thick muck while Ambria and I laughed.

"That must be Kanaan's way of saying no brooms," Ambria said.

Max growled and slung mud at us. "Why didn't he just tell us not to!"

Since it was still early, we reversed course and flew back to the dorms so Max could clean off. We checked our brooms into the broom closet before returning to face the gauntlets. After the mud pit, we climbed a rock face. At the top, we found a tunnel entrance so low, we had to crawl inside. The inside was a claustrophobic maze with a central chamber large enough for us to sit in.

I'd programmed a pathfinding spell into my arcwand that helped us navigate through, but the only way out required us to crawl on our bellies through a swarm of roaches. Ambria handled it with only a few squeals, but Max screamed the entire way. The last part of the gauntlet required us to piece together a wooden puzzle to find the secret word to open a lock. Naturally, the word was 'cockroach'.

Ambria growled. "Kanaan has an evil sense of humor."

When we finally reached Kanaan, he allowed us a short break, then led us through a similar routine as the one the day before. The rest of the week followed the same pattern, leaving us exhausted beyond belief each day, but making us feel stronger and more sure of ourselves after a good night of rest. While the potions accelerated the effects of our efforts, each day felt harder than the previous.

Soon the end of the week arrived and with it, familiar faces. Rory Culpepper and his sister, Marisol, showed up early Friday to ensure Professor Gideon Grace renewed their tenures as resident keepers since they enjoyed bossing around their peers. The rest of the student body appeared en masse over the next two days, filling the keeps and school grounds with the sounds of children.

"I wonder what our magitsu schedule will be like during school," Max mused as we ate breakfast Sunday. Though students filled the dining hall, few of the senior staff or professors were yet present.

"This is the year for determining advanced placement." Ambria chomped on her toast and hardly bothered to chew before swallowing. "We can't afford to miss classes."

"We can't afford to miss training either." I pointed a finger in the general direction of *somewhere out there*, and said, "Victus is plotting and planning to kill his enemies and rule the Overworld. School is important, but we can't ignore reality. We have to be ready for anything."

"I'm tired as a salty slug, but I agree with Conrad." Max finished his potatoes and ordered another round. "I have a bad feeling that Victus is on the verge of something awful, especially with that Garkin fellow."

"Absolutely." Ambria looked up at the head table. "Usually, all the professors are present for the Sunday before classes, but I haven't seen Galfandor all week."

"Probably still tied up with investigations about the Founders Day riot," Max said. His face paled and he looked away. "Professor Fellini is up there."

Asha smiled at me when I glanced at the head table. I'd meant to speak with her more about her talks with Esma, but just hadn't had the time with our magitsu training. I smiled back and waved. Gideon Grace, sitting to her right, scowled at me as if I'd waved to him.

After filling ourselves, we set off for practice, weaving through the crowd of students milling in the halls. Seeing the new students reminded me how much I'd changed over the past two years and how far I still had to go. Despite my time here, I still didn't feel like I quite fit in.

A group of new students stared at me, mouths opened in horror. They shrank away as my friends and I passed.

"That's Evil Edison!" I heard one of the girls hiss to the others.

Judging from the whispered rumors I heard in passing, it seemed someone had been busy spreading this new nickname. I saw Harris Ashmore and his best friend, Baxter Troy talking to a group of new students. Baxter's ginger eyebrows pinched into a malicious V when he saw us. He smirked and elbowed Harris who turned and glared at me with pure hatred.

Ambria hooked her arm in mine. "What's wrong, Conrad?"

I looked away from the stares and shrugged. "Nothing that hasn't been wrong from the start. I think Harris and Baxter are spreading lies about us. I heard one girl refer to us as Evil Edison, Maniac Max, and Abrasive Ambria."

"Abrasive?" Ambria glared back at Harris and Baxter. "Is that really the best they could come up with?"

"Harris is trying his best to make us miserable. Everyone believes him because he's the son of prophecy." Max made air quotes around the title. "I'd like to make him the son of a punch to the face."

Ambria raised a clenched hand. "I'll abrade him with my fist."

We ducked out of the press of students and took the path down to the Burrows.

Shushiel uncloaked herself when we reached the secret entrance, bobbing up and down with excitement. "I wonder what challenges we will face today."

Max scowled. "You like watching us struggle, don't you?"

"It is quite entertaining," the spider agreed.

We stepped through the door and into a vast rocky cavern. A large glowball hung over a rocky island in the middle of a black lake. Glowing forms writhed beneath the surface of the water, ghastly faces staring up at us, eyes full of longing.

Ambria gasped and stepped back from the water's edge. "What are those things?"

I gazed out at the island and saw a golden key dangling in the air. A stout wooden door with a golden lock sat on the other side of the lake. "There's the way out."

"I will climb across the cave and retrieve the key." Shushiel's forelegs touched the rocky wall but slid off. She tried to climb a different place but her feet wouldn't stick. She rotated back to us and moved her mandibles in a shrug. "My feet do not cling to the wall."

"What about your web?" I asked.

She extruded a thread and pressed it to the wall, but it also refused to adhere. "It seems we must find another way to the island."

Max wandered down the narrow shore around the lake, looking behind rocks. "I don't see any boats or way to float."

The crescent shore ended forty yards to either side of us and there seemed to be no ledges or other way to walk around the lake.

"Maybe we should go get our brooms," Max said.

"I'm sure they'll fail just like with the mud pit." Ambria pursed her lips. "No, there must be a way across."

I looked down into the waters. Ghostly forms stared back. Scores of men, women, and children, rotting flesh trailing from skulls, held their hands toward us as if beckoning us to join them. I shuddered. Even Shushiel quailed.

"We cannot swim across." She backed away. "Those ghosts do not look friendly."

"Are they really ghosts?" Max picked up a rock and threw it. A hand shot out of the water and caught the rock, threw it back. Max shrieked and jumped behind Shushiel.

"Definitely not ghosts," Ambria said.

Max remained crouched behind Shushiel. "They're water zombies."

"Does that mean they'll eat our brains?" I stared at the water, unwilling to get closer. "Even if we had a boat, they'd probably capsize it."

"Maybe Kanaan doesn't want to see us today," Shushiel said hopefully.

"I wish." Max kicked a rock, but made sure to aim it anywhere but the lake. "Let's get our brooms and at least try to fly across." He turned for the wall where the door had been and flicked his wand. Nothing happened.

Ambria tried. I tried. Shushiel touched the wall and shook her body back and forth.

"The door will not reopen." She rotated toward the water. "We are trapped."

"No!" Max howled, pounding the wall. "Let us out of here, Kanaan!"

If the magitsu master could hear us, he didn't reply.

I searched up and down the shore for anything that could possibly aid us. There wasn't so much as a twig of wood for flotation and no sign of a rope or anything else. It appeared the only things that could get us to the island and the other side were our bodies. *Surely we can't swim with those zombies in the water!*

Did Kanaan mean for us to fight the creatures? I counted nearly a dozen eagerly waiting just ten feet off the shore, their bodies glowing a slight radioactive green. I took out my wand and tried to think of a spell that might help.

Ambria gasped. "I think I have it."

"What?" I prayed she had some brilliant insight.

"We use a freeze spell to make a bridge." She flourished her wand and cast a deep blue beam of aether toward the water. The water crackled and hardened.

"Brilliant!" Max followed her lead and I did the same. Before long, we'd formed a ten-foot length of ice nearly five feet wide and a foot thick.

"Maybe we can use it like a boat," Shushiel said. "I can fashion an oar from silk."

"Yes, do it!" Ambria said. "See, we can get past anything with ingenuity."

We froze the water until our ice platform formed a nice large square we could all fit on.

"I'll test it." I stepped onto it. My feet slipped, but I spread my arms and managed to stay upright. The platform wobbled slightly, but seemed stable enough. "Yeah, I think it's ready—"

Crack!

Zombie bodies crashed into the bottom of the ice float. Arms windmilling, I fell toward the water. Shushiel darted out and caught me before I fell into the waiting arms of a rotting child and dragged me back to shore just as the ice boat shattered into pieces.

"No!" Ambria shouted. "We worked so hard on that, you mean zombies!"

Anger boiled up in me. I wanted to sear the zombies with flames, or blast them apart with spells. But the water protected them from my wrath just as it prevented us from going anywhere. I sat down and glared at the ghastly creatures.

We couldn't fly, couldn't float, couldn't use ropes to swing across this barrier. Once again, our only option was to enter the water and fight the monsters in their domain. But if they could destroy our ice boat so easily, what chance did I have against them? They would drown me before I could do a thing.

There must be a way! I wondered if, like fish, these water ghosts could survive on land. Maybe the only way to beat them was to coax them out of the water somehow. Unfortunately, we had no bait except ourselves.

I pushed up and turned to Shushiel. "Wrap silk around my waist and be ready to pull me out."

"What?" Ambria grabbed my arm. "Are you going in the water?"

"It looks very dangerous," Shushiel said, even as she extruded silk and wrapped it around me waist with her forelegs.

"I'm going to fish them out," I said.

"Are you mental?" Max jabbed a finger at the water. "They'll drag you to the bottom before you have a chance to do anything."

"Shushiel is strong enough to pull me out," I said. "Maybe they can't survive out of the water. It'll be just like fishing."

"Yeah, except you're the bait." Max gritted his teeth. "I don't think this is the solution."

"On that we agree," Ambria said. "Conrad, you're not thinking straight."

"What else is there to try?" I tugged on the thread. "Besides, Shushiel is incredibly strong. Even if five of them grab me, she can pull me out, right?"

Shushiel bobbed up and down. "My feet may not stick to the walls, but they stick very well to the floor. The monsters are in water, and I am anchored to land."

Ambria shivered. "Well, let's hope this challenge isn't as deadly as it looks. Maybe Kanaan doesn't mean to drown us all."

"That is one huge maybe." Max shivered. "Are you sure, Conrad?"

"No." I took off my shoes, my shirt, and stared at the water.

Ambria raised an eyebrow. "Keeping on your trousers?"

My face suddenly felt quite warm. "I don't want you seeing me in my underwear."

Max barked a laugh. "You're about to jump in a lake filled with murderous ghosts, and you're worried about prancing around in your underwear?"

Ambria giggled and touched my bare shoulder. Her smile quickly vanished and she kissed me on the cheek. "Please be careful." She turned to Shushiel. "You're quite certain you can fish him back out?"

"My thread is strong as steel," the spider said. "And I will be stronger still to rescue my friend."

"Remember when you saved me at the edge of the Glimmer?" I rubbed her fur. "I know I'm safe with you."

Shushiel bobbed up and down. "Yes, cousin, I will not let them have you."

Max grimaced. "Let's just hope they don't skin you to the bone like piranha."

I tried not to think how that would feel and put a foot into the water. Before I could even blink, a soft hand gripped my ankle and jerked me. I plunged into the lake, water rushing past me, the light growing dimmer. Glowing figures swirled around me.

A woman, her face vibrant and lovely instead of decaying and grue-some, stopped in front of me. "Why do you disturb our lake, boy?"

I heard her voice clear as day despite the pressure of liquid all around me. I hadn't taken a good breath before submerging, and already my lungs burned. I felt the silk tightening as Shushiel reeled me in. Hands grasped me, but the power of the ruby spider dragged them all up with me.

But I was too deep. The burning grew so intense I couldn't take it.

I gasped for air.

CHAPTER 11

I expected a lungful of water. Instead, I drew in air despite still being below the waters. I flew up out of the water. Furry red legs caught me and put me safely on shore. I sucked in another breath, no different than the one I'd just taken underwater.

"What in the world?" I staggered toward the water and saw the decaying face of an old woman looking back. "We need to cross your lake, please!"

She gave no indication that she heard or understood me.

"What happened?" Ambria dragged me back from the edge. "I thought we'd lost you!"

"It happened so fast, I was not ready to pull you up," Shushiel said. "I'm sorry, Conrad."

"It's okay." I waved them away. "Be ready to pull me up again, okay?"

"Are you insane?" Max gripped my arm. "I thought we'd lost you!"

Though the cool air raised bumps on my skin, the lake hadn't seemed cold at all. How had I breathed underwater? "This lake is a puzzle, and the only way to solve it is going back under." Before they could stop me, I jumped back in.

The glowing figures grabbed me once again. This time, I spoke. "Wait!" My voice rang out clear as a bell.

The woman appeared once again. "Why do you disturb our lake?"

I dared take a breath and discovered it was no different than breathing on shore. The water felt warm, comfortable. "We need the key on the island."

"And why should I let you have it?" An inhumanly wide smile stretched across her face, revealing sharp teeth. "Why should I not eat you now?"

My inside froze in horror. *What if this challenge is lethal?* I gripped the thread, ready to tug it so Shushiel could rescue me. "I don't taste very good?"

She burst into laughter. "You're probably right." Before I could say anything else, she gripped me and we jetted toward the island, stopping just at the shore. "Retrieve your key, and I will take you to the other side of the lake."

My mouth dropped open. "That simple?"

"Was it really so simple?" Her lips quirked into an amused expression. "It took you quite some time to build up the courage to step foot into the water."

"Because you look like decaying water ghosts!" I protested.

"Oh, that Kanaan." She tutted. "He is a sneaky devil."

"Do you really live in the lake?" I asked.

"No," she replied. "We are water spirits. Kanaan asked us to help with this challenge."

"Water spirits?" I'd never heard of such a thing. "How do you know Kanaan?"

"He saved our waters from mortals." She grimaced. "If not for him, we would have lost our home." She pointed up. "Retrieve your key. My people and I are eager to leave this dark place."

"I will, thanks." I pulled myself out of the water and took the key.

Max cupped his hands and shouted, "What happened?"

I did the same and yelled back. "They're friendly water spirits. Get in the water and they'll take you to the other side."

"Are you sure?" Ambria said.

"Well, they haven't eaten me yet!" I shouted.

I got into the water. The woman took my hand and jetted me to the side of the lake with the door. "We will bring your friends to join you."

"If you're a spirit, how can you touch me?" I asked.

"The water makes us solid." She shifted into the shape of an otter and swam in circles around me, then morphed into great white shark, and back into human form. "When we are close to water, we can remain solid, even in the air for a brief time, but when water is far, we become pure energy, slowly dissipating and dying."

"Do you live in a lake or the ocean?" I asked.

"We prefer fresh waters," she said. "Others enjoy the salt and sea, but those waters have become too polluted for our tastes."

"Thank you." I squeezed her hand.

"You are welcome." She pushed me up. I shot up into the air, a jet of water holding me up until I stepped onto the solid rock. The water receded from my body and clothes until I was completely dry.

A moment later, my friends jetted out of the water, Ambria crying out with delight, Max shouting in alarm. Shushiel pounced lightly to shore, turned and waved her mandibles at the ghostly creatures.

"Thank you," she said.

"That was fun!" Ambria clapped her hands together. "Oh, can we do it again sometime?"

Max touched his clothes. "Hey, I'm dry!"

Shushiel removed my clothing from a silk pouch on her abdomen. "I thought you might want these again."

"Thank you." I dressed quickly.

Max took the key from me and twisted it in the lock, but hesitated before opening the door. "I hope there's not another bleeding challenge on the other side."

Ambria twisted the handle and tugged it open. The hallway near the mansion waited on the other side. We breathed a sigh of relief and stepped through.

Kanaan was reading a book in the gauntlet room when we stepped inside. He closed the book and directed us toward our first exercises.

I held up a hand. "What was the point of the lake challenge? Once I got in the lake, the water spirits helped us get the key and reach the door. There was nothing to it."

"Were you frightened?" Kanaan asked.

"Heck yeah!" Max shivered. "I thought they were going to kill us!"

"Me too," Ambria said.

Shushiel hung from a stone column overhead. "They did not look friendly."

Kanaan nodded. "Why did you go into the water?"

"I thought I could fish them out," I admitted. The idea seemed foolish in retrospect.

"You risked death to cross."

"Well, I suppose. They weren't really deadly," I said. "In fact, they were polite and helpful."

"You did not know that." Kanaan cast his gaze at each of us. "Fear of the unknown will paralyze even the greatest warriors. You must be willing to accept the unknown and face it so it will become known."

Max scratched his head, mouth gaping open. "Huh?"

Ambria sniffed. "I think the short version is face your fears."

Kanaan didn't answer and led us through our exercises. As we lunched, he poured himself a cup of tea and perched on a stone pillar.

"You have done well." He took a sip and looked up at Shushiel who swung in lazy circles overhead, snacking on a rat or two. "Since you start school tomorrow, you will meet me here after classes. There will be no more challenges. I will open a portal instead." He gave me a pendant shaped like a blue shield. "Tap this and will it to contact me after classes. Then I will arrange for the portal."

Max breathed a sigh of relief.

"Have we really improved?" Ambria asked. "I feel just as exhausted every day."

Kanaan nodded. "Even with the potions, progress takes time." He stood. "Practice is over for the day. You should prepare for school tomorrow."

Max pumped a fist but kept his celebration silent.

"Did they ever get to the bottom of the Founders Day riots?" I asked Kanaan.

"I requested information from the investigators," he replied. "So far, they have ignored me."

"Ignored you?" Ambria's voice rose in disbelief. "Aren't you a Blue Cloak?"

"A Blue Cloak no longer," he replied. "Until our lost people return from Seraphina, I will remain independent."

"That's something else I want to talk to you about." I brushed the crumbs off my pants and stood up. "I think Victus used a Relic of Juranthemon to disable the Alabaster Arches."

"The Hand of Jura." Kanaan nodded. "The hand unbound magical properties from the Alabaster Arches, but even with it, repairing them would be almost impossible."

"Impossible?" Ambria plucked a grape and rolled it in her fingers. "I thought the hand was the only thing that could fix it."

Kanaan motioned us to follow him and led us out of the gauntlet room, down the corridor, and into the omniarch room. He removed a glass lens from inside his robes and held it up in front of Ambria's face. "What do you see?"

Ambria's eyes widened. "All sorts of glowing lines and symbols."

I leaned over and peered through the glass. Thousands of tiny glowing lines no thicker than spider silk stretched in all directions, each one emanating from tiny symbols etched in the obsidian columns and connecting them to others. Max pushed us both aside and took in the sight.

"Are those the enchantments that power the arch?" Ambria asked.

"Precisely." Kanaan flicked his fingers and the lens vanished. "Any enchanted object appears just so when viewed through a crafting lens."

"We read about those in enchantments," I said. "They're used to help enchanters verify their work."

"The Hand of Jura allows one to unbind enchantments." Kanaan held out his right hand. "Imagine tearing through many of the threads and having no idea which ends to rebind."

"You've looked at the Alabaster Arches?" I asked.

Kanaan knelt and sealed the silver circle around the omniarch. A window to another place flicked open. Beyond stood a massive black arch with white stripes. He stepped through and we followed.

The cavern beyond spread out for what seemed like miles in every direction. We looked up in awe at the Alabaster Arch before us. It easily dwarfed the one we'd seen in the control room at the Grotto.

Ambria spoke first. "It's the Grand Nexus."

Kanaan held up the crafting lens and we took turns peering through it. Like the omniarch, thousands of threads connected symbols in the stone columns, especially from a socket where a small orb might fit. It was there that I noticed the damage.

It appeared as if someone snipped the strings on a harp, leaving the loose ends to curl up on their binds. Except in this case, there were thousands of broken strings. Reconnecting them to their correct counterpart seemed impossible.

Max frowned. "Can't we match the symbol at the base of a thread to the identical symbol at the other end?"

"No," Kanaan said. "Threads are not necessarily bound to identical symbols. The magic behind the arches has long eluded even the most brilliant enchanters."

I walked across the dozens of yards separating me from the orb-shaped pocket and examined the bindings up close with the lens. The symbols seemed to hover just off the surface and grew blurry when viewed from certain angles. I recognized Cyrinthian characters, but most were something else—another language alien to me.

Each of the torn threads curled near a darkened symbol. When Victus had damaged the magical bindings, he'd simply torn through them. Either he'd assumed he could easily repair them, or had been in a hurry.

I returned to the others. "Even with the hand, we can't possibly repair this without more knowledge."

"So much for reopening the portal to Seraphina." Max crossed his arms and glared at the arch as if it was at fault. "I guess we'll never see Justin Slade or the others again."

"That's a glum outlook, Max!" Ambria tutted. "I just know there's someone in Eden who can fix this thing." She turned to me. "That means we still have to find the Hand of Jura."

"Perhaps not." Kanaan took the crafting lens from me and headed back toward the portal leading to the omniarch. "The arch is an apparatus that can open the curtain between realms. I believe there are other methods."

I stepped through the portal. The world bent like a fishbowl and snapped back into place. I waited for the others to come through and said, "Do you know of any specific ways to cross realms?"

"No." The portal winked away behind Kanaan. "But I have heard tales of broken arches carrying people into other realms."

"Using a broken arch to travel?" Max waved his hands in front of his chest. "No, thanks. I watched a documentary on the people who tested broken arches during the war and some of them vanished forever."

"There might be another way." I touched my chest where the green gem Cora gave me had once hung. Now she had it. "The realms are anchored in the Glimmer. Maybe they can be reached from there."

"We can't get into the Glimmer right now." Ambria puffed out her cheeks and released the air. "Cora closed it off until she gets her kingdom in order."

"School, magitsu, Victus, and repairing the Grand Nexus." Max blew out a sigh. "As if being a kid wasn't hard enough."

Ambria sniffed. "We're hardly kids anymore, Max. We're teenagers."

Max threw up his hands. "Even worse!"

The corner of Kanaan's lip quirked up as if amused. "The path of the young is treacherous." He closed the circle around the omniarch and summoned a portal back to the wide grassy field behind the university. "I will see you tomorrow."

We departed through the portal and gazed at the university grounds. Students bustled back and forth on last-minute chores before school started. We had already procured our textbooks to avoid the rush.

Shushiel turned to face the Dark Forest only a few yards behind us. Spider bats fluttered fitfully in the boughs of a massive oak just within the shield wall. Strange calls and shrieks echoed through the dense woods. A group of students some distance from us threw sticks and stones at the shield, shouting for the tragon to make an appearance.

"I will visit my family," Shushiel said. "I have not seen them for a week."

"How do you get through the shield?" Max asked.

She tapped the amplification gem. "Galfandor charmed it to allow me through."

I peered into the darkness, and it seemed to look back at me. "Do you ever see frogres or other monsters my father created?"

"All the time." Shushiel's mandibles twitched. "Some roam in packs, killing and eating one another. The frogres are solitary. Most live in caves. My kind prefer to live in the trees where we can catch plenty of spider bats and stay out of reach of monsters."

Ambria rubbed Shushiel's soft fur. "I would love to see where you live sometime."

"That would be wonderful." The spider bounced with excitement. "I think you would like it very much."

"Yeah, but what about the monsters?" Max shivered. "I'm not going in there without monster repellent."

Ambria laughed. "Just bring a pair of your dirty underwear, Max. That should keep the monsters away."

"Ew." I wrinkled my nose. "I don't want Max swinging his dirty underwear around me."

"I suggest you bring your brooms," Shushiel said. "Very few of the carnivorous monsters can fly."

Max snorted. "As long as they can't fly fast."

We said our goodbyes to Shushiel and headed to the university where we swung by the healing ward to check up on Ansel's condition. Percival looked up from patching a first-year's knee, his eyes scanning us for injuries.

"Are you hurt?" he asked.

I shook my head and pointed to the back room. "How is Ansel?"

"Ah." Percival patted the child on the head and promptly shooed him out of the door. "No running in the halls next time, boy," he called after him then turned to us. "I diagnosed Ansel's problem, and the prognosis isn't good."

"What does that mean?" Max said.

Percival frowned. "It means, he may never recover. He could very well die."

CHAPTER 12

"Die?" I rushed into the back and found my cousin staring blankly up at the ceiling. I looked around and saw he wasn't the only one in the ward. Six other people of all ages seemed to be in the same exact condition. "What's wrong with them?"

"Rather large chunks of their souls have been torn out." Percival held up a parchment with the ghostly outline of a human body that looked as if someone had taken a bite from the left side. "All the others fell sick the same way just in the past week."

Ambria took the parchment and examined it, nose wrinkled in concern. "How did it happen?"

"There are few creatures who can cause this sort of damage, and those that can, are not of this world." Percival took a leather-bound tome from a shelf in the back of the room and flipped it open to a bookmark. "At first, I thought it might be a rogue Daemos, but they simply don't devour souls in such a manner. Even with them, it takes time, and it's more like a smooth wearing away of the spirit, not a brutal bite."

I looked at the shiny black creature on the page. It resembled a spider, but with far more than eight legs. A humanoid head pressed against the carapace from the inside, a scream frozen on its agonized face. The thought that something like this had taken a chunk of my cousin's soul made me sick to my stomach.

Percival moved his hand to uncover the name—*demon crawler*. "It appears we have a monster on the loose."

"No, that can't be right." Max shook his head. "Crawlers don't just take a bite of a soul and let the victim live."

Percival huffed. "How would you know what crawlers do and don't do?"

"War documentaries." Max jabbed a finger at a paragraph further down the page. "Plus, it says so right there—crawlers devour the soul through a straw-like mouth, often leaving bodies intact."

The healer frowned and glared at Max. "Well, it's the best theory I have at the moment. If you children are so smart, perhaps you can come up with something better."

Ambria patted Percival's hand in a soothing manner. "I think you're on the right track. These attacks must be demon related."

"Well, of course they are." Percival flipped through pages of a seemingly endless variety of hell spawn. "It must be some form of lower demon, but I simply don't have the information in this book."

"I will handle this investigation from this point on."

We spun to face the source of the voice. Percival stiffened at the sight of a thin woman, her face lined with age. "Minister Grint? Whatever are you doing here?"

"As I said, taking control of this poorly handled investigation." She looked down at the affected people, some students, others professors I recognized only because I'd seen them from time to time in the hallways or dining hall.

"Minister, I have things well in hand." Percival's chin jutted up and out in defiance. "I will accept assistance, but not interference."

"I am the health minister, *boy*." Grint's withered lips curled up into a sneer. "You have no say in the matter."

"This is outrageous!" Percival threw up his hands. "I am the chief healer for Arcane University. You have no right to interfere in my duties unless I have displayed gross negligence."

"He might be guilty of that," Max whispered to Ambria and me.

"Maybe we should come back later," Ambria said.

"Agreed." I slid past Percival and toward the door, but Minister Grint barred the way with her arm.

"You don't look injured, children." She bored through us with her eyes. "Why are you here?"

"Visiting friends," I said, feeling defensive and squeamish in her glare. "I hope that's all right."

"Conrad Edison." She looked at each of us in turn. "Ambria Rax. Maxwell Tiberius." A scowl turned her unfriendly face downright frightful. "I should have known you'd be involved."

Ambria's mouth dropped open. "We weren't involved in this. Our friend was injured and we came to visit him."

"Friend, hmm?" She looked around the room. "Which one?"

"Him." I pointed to Ansel.

"Ansel Moore, the *Arcnologist*." Grint spat the last word as if it were a curse. "You will stay out of this healing ward unless you're dying. You will have nothing to do with this investigation, or I will have you expelled." She leaned into my face. "Understand?"

Onion breath hit my face and nearly made my eyes water. I flinched back from the twofold horror of her face and odor and nodded. "Yes, Minister."

Grint moved her arm. "Very well. You may go."

We wasted no time fleeing the healing ward and kept running until we reached the broom closet.

"Wow." Max shivered. "I met Minister Grint two years ago and she seemed awfully nice." He plucked his broom from a rack. "Kind of grandmotherly and not such a b—"

"Maxwell!" Ambria said. "Don't you dare."

"I was going to say bossy woman." He stuck out his tongue.

"People change." I grabbed my broom and went back into the hallway. "Then again, Percival might have just upset her. He's not very pleasant either."

"True." Ambria bit her lower lip and looked down the hall. "Speaking of the investigation, I think I know where to find a complete book of lower demon spawn."

I could think of only one place. "In Moore's vault."

"Yes, the demonomicon of Emily Glass."

I fished my phone from a pocket and scrolled through the apps. "Actually, Ansel loaded that onto my phone when I first met him."

"I looked at that one," Ambria said. "It's abridged. I saw a full copy in the vault not long ago."

"I thought we weren't supposed to investigate," Max said.

I grunted. "Ansel might not be the most likeable, person, but if we can help him recover in any way, I'm for it."

Ambria patted his shoulder. "What Minister Grint doesn't know won't hurt her."

Max groaned.

We flew our brooms to Moore Keep and went in through the main entrance. A few twists and turns later, we entered a gallery of paintings documenting important historical events in Arcane history. Serpus

Mandracorn had used magical brushes to paint everything in incredible detail, including a door that looked as if it actually worked. A large painting of Daelissa delivering the deathblow to Jeremiah Conroy hung near the fake door. I pulled it loose to reveal another painting hiding behind it.

Three circles intersected and inside that juxtaposition stood a tree. The image seemed to hang off the wall right in front of my eyes. I plucked it and a copy of it manifested in my hand, no larger than a pendant. Max hung the decoy painting and we went to the fake door. I pressed the symbol into a blank circle, and the painted door jumped off the canvas into something real.

I clicked the handle and the door opened into darkness. As we stepped inside, glowballs flickered on overhead, lines and lines of them stretching down aisles so long it would take hours to traverse just one by foot. I closed the door behind us, and we climbed on our brooms.

"Which way?" I asked.

Ambria set off for the G section of shelves and took a hard left. A couple hundred yards down, she stopped in front of an odd collection of statues, busts, jewelry, and other trinkets, most encased in crystalline material we'd discovered was more for our protection than the preservation of the objects within.

Max flinched and nearly fell off his broom. I drifted past the statue of a howling man and gasped. Someone had peeled the face off a monkey and animated it. Its mouth stretched open over and over again in silent screams.

"Must be the cursed section." Max guided his broom far from the monkey face.

Indeed, the section was filled with objects from Custodian investigations led by Emily Glass, the famed demon hunter. I could only imagine the terrifying stories behind many of these objects. Ambria glided a few feet down and hovered up to a higher shelf.

"Here it is." She grabbed a thick black tome inscribed with a golden eye on the front. "If there's anything to find, it'll be in here."

Max looked warily at our foreboding surroundings. "Are you sure that book isn't cursed?"

Ambria rolled her eyes. "Why would Emily curse her own book, Max?"

"I don't know." He shuddered. "Maybe something rubbed off from one of the other cursed objects here."

Ambria pshawed. "Curses aren't contagious."

"They are if they're designed to be," I reminded her. "Let's find a table not in this section."

"Amen to that." Max wasted no time speeding toward the end of the aisle and a seating area there.

Ambria set down the book and opened it to the table of contents. The first section described various demon types and attributes. The second contained names and patterns for hundreds of demons. Patterns for powerful demons were so intricate, I could barely make out the separate lines.

Ambria tilted her head and looked sideways at the writing on the page. "Is the ink moving or is it just me?"

"I thought I was just seeing things." It seemed the longer I stared at a page, the more the ink seemed to squirm and flow.

"Ooh, magical ink." Max went back to the table of contents and tapped a finger on the section titled, *Lesser Demon Spawn*. The pages flipped themselves to the section.

"Wow!" Ambria traced her finger on the page. "Why doesn't it flip pages when I touch it?"

"Just like a spell, you need intent," Max said

"Does it allow editing?" I asked.

Max held up the pages and looked on the inside of the cover where a red star symbol glowed. "It does, but this security charm only allows certain individuals to do that." Max turned back to the demon spawn section. "Emily probably added to it with every adventure."

Ambria tapped on a heading and the book flipped to a page detailing aspects of lesser and higher demon spawn.

In general, lesser spawn lack sentience and operate solely on instinct. Higher spawn such as hellhounds possess varying degrees of intelligence some Daemos argue equals sentience. Spawn only refers to non-humanoid demon forms which is why Daemos take such offense at being labeled demon spawn.

Lesser forms come in all varieties, from the soul-devouring crawlers, to the flesh eating scorps, to the parasitic wyrms. The higher forms tend to be more physical in nature, with the ability to telepathically communicate with their masters. They typically do not demonstrate the same hunger for consuming souls as their lower brethren.

We read the introduction then skimmed through pages and pages of different spawn. It seemed the ecosystem of such creatures was nearly as extensive as that of the animal kingdom.

I groaned and leaned back in my chair. "This will take ages."

"Maybe we could search the book," Max said.

Ambria's forehead pinched. "Isn't that what we're doing?"

"No, this is called reading." He smirked. "Books this fancy usually come with search functions."

I ran a hand across my tired eyes. "Well why didn't you mention that before?"

"It's so interesting." Max shrugged. "I got caught up in it."

"How do we search, Max?" Ambria jabbed a finger on the page. "Show me before I tweak your nose."

Max gave her a hurt look. "No need for threats. Geez." He reached toward the top margin of the page and paused. "Um, what search terms?"

Ambria tapped her chin. "Soul damage?"

I modified her terms. "Torn souls."

"Sounds good." Max tapped the top margin and the ink swirled on the page. "Search for torn souls."

The ink reassembled into several separate sentences with the search terms highlighted.

...torn souls would be the least of our worries...

"Torn souls?" The demon laughed at me...

...souls torn from their bodies...

Max touched the first one and the pages flipped to an anecdote about an encounter with a demon. The second and third headings referred to the same stories. We tried Ambria's search term as well and came back with too many results to search.

I wracked my brain for a better search term and came up with a slightly better solution. "Can you cross reference? Try spawn with soul damage."

"I think so." Max submitted the request and the book returned with thirty results.

We hunted through them one-by-one until arriving at a subsection of parasitic demon wyrms called sickle wyrms. Emily nicknamed them rippers and for good reason. Most spawn parasites occupied the host body siphoning bits of soul and causing physical ailments, but this one was different.

Rippers burrow into the host through an open orifice—an ear, a nostril, the mouth—and phase into the spiritual plane to carve out a hunk of soul which it stores in a pouch. The ripper exits the body and crawls into a dark space where it will slowly consume the soul fragment. It prefers the souls of murderers and the truly wicked, but will settle for ordinary folks if pressed. Rippers must feed within twenty-four hours of summoning or their physical body will wither and die.

The next page displayed the sickening image of a ripper wyrm. It resembled a fat slimy slug. A mouth with a wide serrated lower jaw allowed it to rip through souls when it phased into ethereal form. The next page displayed diagrams and magical scans of affected hosts. Apparently, someone had unleashed a plague of the creatures during the early days of the Seraphim War and leading up to the Demon War.

"Why haven't we heard more about this Demon War?" Ambria asked.

"I've heard of it, but it happened around the same time as the Seraphim War, so most people probably never knew it happened." Max shuddered. "God, I hope we don't have another epidemic of rippers on our hands."

"The people in the healing ward weren't murderers or criminals," Ambria said. "If they're truly the victims of ripper wyrms, it's only because the little monsters couldn't find wicked souls nearby."

Max turned to the spawn introduction and ran his finger down a few paragraphs. "It says right here that lesser spawn can't manifest physically without help."

My insides twisted and churned at the thought of demonic parasites unleashed in Queens Gate and elsewhere. I might lack information, but this plague bore my father's fingerprints all over it.

Ambria touched my hand. "What's wrong, Conrad?"

"I think"—my mouth went dry with horror—"Victus plans to start another demon war."

CHAPTER 13

"Another demon war?" Max nearly toppled over backward in his chair. "That's insane!"

"Maybe you're jumping to conclusions," Ambria said. "Demons usually want power, right?"

I shrugged. "I don't know what demons want."

"What I mean is that I don't think Victus could get demons to help him without giving up power." She leaned her elbows on the table. "The whole point of taking over the Overworld is power, right?"

"That's all Victus cares about," Max said. "He wants to be the top dog, not some demon overlord."

"He might try to summon an army of lesser spawn," Ambria said.

"Doubt it." Max turned the page and pointed to a subsection of the demon spawn general information section. "Says here that most lesser spawn take way too much power for an Arcane to control more than one at a time. Only Daemos can do it, and even then, they can't manage more than a small force. If an Arcane loses control of a spawn, they're free in the mortal world until their body dies."

"So an Arcane could summon wyrms and just let them loose?" I said.

Max winced. "Yea, but once they're free from the binding, they're just as likely to attack the summoner as anyone else."

Ambria read another supporting sentence. "Lesser spawn are notoriously difficult to control, as one must overcome their blind instinct to consume. Each summoned spawn adds additional weight to the mind of the controller."

I held up my hands in surrender. "Fine. Maybe Victus isn't planning an infernal uprising." I sat back and tried to piece together the puzzle. "Do we agree that a ripper wyrm put those people in the healing ward?"

"There's one sure way to find out." Ambria leafed through the pages until she reached the end of the spawn introduction. "Aha!" She pressed a finger on a subsection entitled, *Diagnosis.* "We can use this ritual to determine if a spawn is the cause."

Max's forehead pinched into a worried V. "It says here we'd have to ink a diagram on their stomach and light it on fire!"

Ambria grimaced. "Well, if we want to know for sure, this is the way to do it."

"Essence of dill, toasted snails, fruit fly feces?" I continued listing the ingredients needed to make the ink. "We'll have to break into the storeroom to get all this stuff."

"And set a patient on fire!" Max reminded me.

Ambria pshawed. "The diagram, not the patient."

"On their stomach around their belly button." Max closed the demonomicon. "Minister Grint already told us not to interfere. If she catches us lighting fire to someone's belly button, we'll be suspended for sure."

"Then let's not get caught." I turned back to the page with the ritual and took a picture with my arcphone. "I think I know how to get the ingredients."

"Can you pick magical locks?" Max said.

I shook my head. "No, but I'll bet Kanaan can." I tapped the pendant he'd given me and willed it to contact him.

"Yes?" Kanaan's voice crackled with static.

"Kanaan, we need your help." I explained what I wanted and why.

"This is not for me to do," he replied. "Use what I have taught you, for one day you must fly free on your own."

"But we really need your help!" I waited for a response, but Kanaan cut the connection.

"Now what?" Max said.

Thankfully, I had a backup plan. "Let's visit Galfandor."

I took pictures of a few more pages from the demonomicon and we left the vault. We checked the headmaster's office first, but he wasn't there so we left campus and flew our brooms to his residence, the manor above the underground mansion.

Galfandor answered on the first knock, broom in hand. "Conrad, Maxwell, Ambria." He stepped outside and closed the door. "I suppose you're here to discuss the riots. My apologies for being absent, but I have been inundated with meetings."

"Where are you off to?" Ambria asked.

"A public debate with Xander Tiberius." He glanced down at Max. "Did you know your father planned to run for primus?"

"Absolutely not." Max bared his teeth. "I hope you kick his teeth in, Galfandor."

"I certainly don't think his policies will win him many friends on the council." Galfandor stroked his long beard. "Though the debate is public to all Arcanes, the only vote that matters is that of the council this week."

"I actually have a favor to ask," I said.

The headmaster raised an eyebrow. "Yes, what is it, Conrad?"

"My cousin, Ansel, is in the healing ward because part of his soul was ripped out."

"Percival sent me a detailed letter on the stricken souls in his ward." Galfandor frowned. "He also told me Minister Grint has taken over the investigation and forbidden him from looking into it."

"We were there when it happened." Ambria scowled. "She told us to keep our noses out of it too."

"I'm certain she has good reason," Galfandor said. "I've never known Agatha to be anything but professional and thorough."

Ambria scoffed. "I'd hardly call her patronizing tone professional. She treated Percival like an idiot."

Galfandor's bushy eyebrows rose. "Percival must have argued with her. She doesn't abide insubordination."

"Percival did protest," I admitted, "but I don't see how she can tell us what to do when it involves my cousin."

"Do you want me to talk to her?" Galfandor asked.

"Actually, we think we know the cause of the illnesses."

The headmaster removed a pocket watch from inside his robes, checked it and nodded. "I have a few minutes to listen."

"We could go to the debate and talk on the way," I said.

Galfandor shook his head. "I'm afraid it's for adults only."

Ambria planted her fists on her hips. "We're nearly adults."

I waved her off before she got started. "Sir, we think a parasitic demon spawn called a sickle wyrm or a ripper wyrm is responsible for my cousin's condition, but we need to confirm it."

"A demon spawn?" Galfandor pursed his lips. "Agatha told me it was a physical ailment and that Percival was on the wrong track entirely."

"Percival might be unorthodox, but he's a good healer," Ambria said.

"If you don't care about ghost peppers," Max grumbled.

"We can prove it with a few ingredients from potion storage." I didn't go into further detail, hoping he might approve.

Galfandor returned to stroking his beard. He nodded. "I will speak with the minister and gain her approval, then I will—"

"She won't agree," I said. "If she doesn't believe Percival, why would she believe me?"

"You mean to sneak into the ward and conduct a demonic divination ritual?" The headmaster chuckled. "She has posted guards outside the ward, Conrad. You can't simply wander inside without approval."

"That won't be a problem," I said, ignoring the flummoxed looks from Ambria and Max. "I can't get the ingredients without your help."

Galfandor sighed. "I believe you, Conrad, and I want to help, but I must go through proper channels." He climbed on his broom. "Go inside the manor, take a left, and the first door on the right is my study. Fill out the request form you will find in the third drawer down on the left side of the desk. Set a completed form on my desk and I will look at it."

"A request form?" I couldn't believe my ears. "If you believe me, why can't you just help?"

Galfandor narrowed his eyes and put a hand on my shoulder. "Do as I say, lad." He hopped on his broom and tipped his tall pointed hat at us before zipping away into the sky.

"A request form?" Max squinted up at the headmaster's dwindling form. "What nonsense is that?"

Ambria frowned. "I think we need to find out." She marched inside and we followed her into the study. A thick oak desk squatted between book-laden shelves and ornate chairs. She opened the drawer in question to reveal a variety of glass and stone paperweights, but no forms.

Max pulled out a couple and stared at them in disbelief. "What's this, Galfandor's idea of a joke?"

"Apparently so." I pulled out the paperweights and tapped the bottom of the drawer to see if a hidden compartment held the punchline.

"Hang on." Max picked up an upside-down paperweight. "This one has a wand inscribed on the bottom."

"This one has a broom, and this one has a bottle," Ambria said.

I sorted through the others and found one with a stoppered vial engraved on the bottom. "Is that a potion?"

"Looks like it to me." Max held the green glass up to the light. "What does it mean?"

"I don't see a key inside." Ambria rubbed the paperweight.

I smirked. "Trying to summon a genie?"

"These are paperweights, Conrad, not keys." Ambria dumped it on the desk. "I'm sick of solving puzzles. Why can't we ever get a straightforward answer from people?"

Max sucked in a breath. "Maybe it's more straightforward than we think." He grabbed the green paperweight. "Let's go find out."

Ambria sniffed. "Do you plan to hit the door with a paperweight until it breaks down?"

Max didn't look back at her. "If that's what it takes."

We left the manor and flew back to campus. We took two flights of stairs down, a spiral staircase up a tower and then walked upside down on the other side of the stairs, slid down a long brass pole, and navigated a small maze of corridors before reaching the ingredients storage room. Students weren't authorized, under any circumstances, to enter or even go near it, but Shushiel had shown us the path to this place and other hidden gems around the castle.

Max inspected the door and grimaced when he found the ordinary lock. "Well, maybe I was wrong."

Ambria snatched the paperweight and pressed it to the lock. The latch clicked and the door creaked open. "You give up so easily, Max."

"You're just rude." Max shoved past her and into the room.

The storage room stretched on for nearly a hundred yards in all directions. We referenced the picture I'd taken from the book and tracked down the ingredients without much trouble since they were in perfect order.

We were down to the last few items when Max froze. "Do you hear footsteps?"

We stopped what we were doing and listened. Hard soles clomped on stone in the distance.

"There's no way out but the way we came in." Ambria ran in a circle like a frightened squirrel. "We've got to hide!"

I ran to the door and eased it shut while Max and Ambria searched for a place to hide, but the warehouse was so impeccably neat, that there was nowhere to go. The ceiling was only twenty feet high and the entire room brightly illuminated so we couldn't hover out of sight on our brooms. Max pointed frantically toward burlap sacks on the bottom shelf near the back wall. We tugged out one and Ambria climbed behind it, then Max. The door clicked open and I clambered behind another sack, wedging myself between it and the back of the shelf.

The door clicked open and hard soles stomped inside. "My supply is on aisle three, case four, shelf two, section one." Gideon Grace's sneering voice echoed down the aisles. "I am still unclear as to why you need it."

"Must I give a reason?" Agatha Grint replied.

"It would certainly be polite."

"I am here to do a job, not waste my time with explanations." Grint huffed. "However, we have decided to move the victims to a dedicated facility in the Grotto first thing in the morning."

"There's nothing in the Grotto better than our healing ward." Grace scoffed. "What Percival lacks in bedside manner he more than makes up for in skill."

"Bring me the lavender sap, Professor." Steel laced Grint's tone.

"The patients are already asleep," Grace said. "Are you certain you know what you're doing?"

"Professor. The sap, now."

"Minister or not, I will not brook that tone," Grace hissed. "I have personally gathered every ingredient in this warehouse and reserve all rights to them."

"The council can commandeer whatever it needs." Grint sniffed and smaller shoes tapped down the aisle. The silence endured another moment and the feet tapped further away.

"That sap is ultra-pure and concentrated," Grace said. "Use it properly or your patients will become corpses." The door clicked open and shut and the voices faded down the hallway.

We must have remained cowering behind the sacks for another five minutes before we dared make a peep. Ambria crawled out while Max and I poked out our heads like frightened prairie dogs.

"Put the sacks back exactly as you found them," Ambria whispered. "I'm certain Professor Grace will notice our theft soon enough as it is."

Max and I replaced the burlap sacks as we'd found them and rejoined Ambria who'd collected the rest of the ingredients in the meantime.

"Agatha Grint is completely unreasonable." Max pulled our brooms from behind a sack and handed them out. "Why would they move the patients to another facility?"

"I don't like it one little bit." Ambria zippered the pouch of ingredients and put it in the saddlebag on her broom. "I hope they don't move them before we have a chance to use the ritual."

"Something feels horribly wrong about all this." I closed the door to the warehouse and climbed on my broom. "We need to do this tonight."

"Agreed." Max rubbed his belly. "Let's eat first."

We made our way back into the main halls, treading carefully in case Grace or Grint happened to be in our path. Explaining why we'd taken the upside-down staircase would be difficult since it led to an area off limits to students. We encountered no trace of the unpleasant pair and ate dinner in the crowded dining hall.

All the professors were absent, presumably attending the debate and the noise level seemed louder than usual without the watchful eye of authority present. A heated conversation at a nearby table abruptly escalated into full volume.

"You're full of it," a burly fifth year named Josh Cole shouted at an equally proportioned Paul Thomas. "We own the arches. The other factions need to pay their fair share."

"It's bleeding magic, you imbecile!" Paul slapped a hand on the table. "It doesn't cost a thing to run the arch."

"Time and labor," the other shot back.

"Is this really worth arguing about?" Nancy Mayhew held up a hand between the boys as they leaned across the table, faces red.

"Josh is a bloody traitor if he supports Galfandor's open Overworld platform." Paul leaned back, fists flexing atop the table. "It's about time we stopped getting pushed around by the vampires and lycans and commanded some respect."

"Arcanes First is a bunch of factionist imbeciles," Josh growled. "The Overworld is a steaming turd pile and guess what? We live in it. Making the other factions hate us even more won't help."

Paul made it clear he'd had enough by lunging across the table. Dinnerware and plates scattered and clattered. Fists pounded faces and the pair wrestled in a mound of mashed potatoes spilled during the melee.

"Stop it!" Nancy screamed. "I thought you were friends!"

School security rushed in and separated the boys, dragging them away even as the pair still shouted at each other. A crying Nancy and two other boys trailed in their wake.

Shouting echoed from the opposite side of the lunchroom and another fight erupted.

"What in the world has gotten into everyone?" Max shielded himself from a gob of hurled potatoes with his empty dinner plate.

"It's insanity!" Ambria ducked as the food fight in the middle of the hall exploded out of control.

I grabbed her hand and made a run for the door, ducking flying food on the way out. Max squawked and slipped in a puddle of gravy. "Man down!" he shouted.

I burst into laughter and dragged Ambria out into the hallway.

"Conrad!" She shook her hand loose and wiped pudding off her cheek. "You pulled me right into the line of fire."

I couldn't stop laughing at the absurdity of it all while a part of me wanted to go inside and throw food with the rest of them. "Here, you missed a spot." I wiped a glob from her cheek and wiped my hand on my pants.

It suddenly occurred to me how close we stood, our faces only inches apart, her other hand touching mine, and a lovely smile spreading across her lips. Heat flushed my face and my knees didn't want to support my weight.

"My knight in shining armor." Ambria pressed a hand to my cheek. "It looks like someone hit you too."

Mouth dry, I tried to respond. *What's wrong with me?* I'd never felt so awkward around Ambria before. Never been so entranced with how her eyes shone when she smiled, or how her smooth cheeks begged my hands to touch them.

"It's a warzone!" Max crashed into the middle of us, his pants and shirt coated with food. "I took down three bogies with potato bombs, and winged another with a cupcake."

I finally found my voice. "You wasted a perfectly good cupcake?"

He looked down, eyebrows pinched with regret. "It was the only way I could survive."

Ambria's eyelids fluttered as if waking from a trance. "Max, you're such a warrior."

I looked down at my clothes, splotched and stained from the food war. "Well, we can't break into the healing ward like this. Let's get cleaned up first.

Ambria swallowed. Nodded. "I need to prepare the ritual ink."

Max flashed a toothy grin. "And then it's go time."

CHAPTER 14

W e met on our brooms outside Ambria's window, several stories above the ground beneath a starry sky. A crescent moon offered little light, leaving the trees in shadow, highlighting the Dark Forest like a cutout against the sky. An owl's hoots echoed from the trees below. In the distance, a flock of spider bats screeched.

Ambria produced a sealed inkpot. "This is it."

Max arched an eyebrow. "You're sure you made it right?"

"Shall we put some on you and set it ablaze to test?" Ambria said sweetly.

Max stuck out his tongue. "You'd like to set me on fire, wouldn't you?"

Ambria held her thumb and forefinger apart by an inch. "Only a little."

"Let's save the ink for the ritual," I said. "You can use the rest to set each other on fire all you want afterward."

Max snorted.

We flew down to the university castle and sneaked through the halls until we reached the corridor with the healing ward. As Galfandor predicted, two guards in the blue livery of the Arcane Council security forces stood outside the main entrance. We bypassed the hallway and took a different turn down to the Burrows.

Since Kanaan had removed the challenges, the route took us through the old dungeons until we reached the corridor with the gauntlet room on one side, the mansion on the opposite, and the omniarch at the end. We sneaked past the large opening leading to the mansion and entered the omniarch room.

I stepped inside the silver circle around the arch and took a breath. "I hope I can do this."

"You can." Ambria patted my arm.

I touched a thumb to the circle and willed it closed. The static rush of aether tingled against the hair on my arms. I looked at the image of mine and Max's room on my arcphone, fixed it in my mind and willed a small portal to open there.

The air between the columns split and a window to our room appeared.

Max pumped his fist in the air. "Great job!"

I stepped through. The world warped for an instant and snapped back. I stood in the room, an oval portal a few feet tall and wide hovering just above the floor. I walked to the side of the portal. It was paper thin, and invisible from the back, allowing a clear view of the wall behind it.

When I reached my hand around to the other side, however, I couldn't see it. "That's odd." I knew as long as we didn't cross through the portal, no one could see us, but I'd expected to become visible once we stepped through. I picked up a sock from the floor and tossed it on the other side. The portal blocked it from view as well.

I stepped to the front of the portal and motioned to the others. "Come take a look at something."

They stepped through and I showed them what I'd discovered.

"I wonder if what we're seeing is an afterimage of the wall," Max said. "When the portal appears, the image of whatever it's facing is captured like a picture until the portal is off."

"I suppose that makes sense," Ambria said. "At least it's something to hide behind."

"Well, let's get to it then." I led the others back through and deactivated the portal.

Max took out his arcphone and thumbed through the pictures. "Here's a picture from the summer."

It was a picture of me and Ambria standing in the back corner of the healing ward. We'd taken Max there after he knocked himself unconscious in a broom racing accident. In the picture, I faced the camera. Ambria looked at me, a smile on her face.

"I look awful in this," she said.

"What's that stupid grin for?" Max said.

Her face turned pink. "I was probably happy you'd injured yourself."

"Figures."

I ignored their banter and concentrated on the wall in the picture. *Does Ambria like me in a different way than just friends? We're best friends. I shouldn't feel like this around her. I like the way she smiles.*

"Problems?" Max nodded toward the inactive arch. "You've been staring at the picture for a full minute now."

I cleared my throat. "Sorry. I guess I can't see the wall behind us well enough." I refocused my efforts, clearing the stray thoughts from my mind and stared only at the image of the wall instead of the smile Ambria wore in the picture. The portal flickered on, the very same wall only a few feet away.

Finally. I stepped through and peeked around the portal. A nearby empty bed had been shoved a few feet to the side by the edge of the portal. I hadn't even considered the dangers of opening a portal in a space occupied by a person and gave silent thanks it didn't slice right through matter.

Ansel lay in the bed nearest the door leading out into the lobby. I saw no guards inside this room, but took a moment to thoroughly survey it before motioning the others to join me. Ambria stepped through. Her body seemed to warp and stretch ever so slightly before snapping back into shape on this side of the arch. Max joined us an instant later.

"The room is clear," I whispered.

"Tonight?" a deep male voice said. "I thought it was tomorrow."

"I want it done tonight." Grint's voice emanated from the next room. "Clear out the ward and transport them all to the new facility."

"Yes, Minister," the man replied.

"We'd better hurry." I stepped out from behind the portal and padded across the room.

"Let's get it over with, Clancy," another man said. "I've already got the gurney carpets here."

Clancy, the male with the deep voice groaned. "Man, I was hoping to pass this on to the next shift."

Boots clomped our way. I spun around and fell over Max and Ambria in my haste to get back behind the cover of the portal. We scrambled to our feet in silent panic and cowered behind the portal as the men came into the room.

"Let's start at the back, Harold," Clancy said. "Put 'em on a carpet and take them into the hallway."

"You got it."

I peered around the portal and watched two orderlies in white robes head our way, their target, a comatose boy lying on a bed only feet from us. One orderly unrolled a carpet and left it hovering next to the bed then lifted the boy beneath his arms while the other gripped the patient's feet. They carefully slid him onto the carpet and then guided it out of the door and presumably into the hallway beyond the lobby.

"We need to abort," Max whispered. "We don't have enough time to do the ritual."

"Not in here," I said. I counted the seconds until the orderlies returned for a middle-aged woman in the bed next to the boy's.

Ambria's brow pinched in concern. "What's that supposed to mean?"

I mimicked grabbing something. "We're taking Ansel with us."

"You're mental," Max hissed.

Ambria put a finger to her lips and glared.

"Did you say something, Clancy?" the other orderly said.

"No, why?"

"Thought I heard something."

"Wasn't me." Clancy paused. "Got her?"

"Yep. One, two, three." A pair of grunts sounded.

I peeked and watched them push out the carpet with the woman. The instant they stepped through the door, I motioned to the others and raced across the room to Ansel. His face was pale, lips slightly blue, but his breathing sounded regular. He wasn't the most pleasant person in the world, but I hoped he wasn't dying.

I grabbed one of the carpets from the pile the orderlies brought in and unfurled it to hover next to the bed. Max unceremoniously rolled Ansel onto the carpet where he ended up facedown. Footsteps sounded in the hallway. I grabbed the carpet and dragged it through the air after me, pulling it behind the portal just as I saw the orderlies enter the room.

"Hey did you see that?" Clancy said.

"Huh?" Harold said. "See what?"

I pushed the carpet through the portal.

"Thought I saw a boy in the back of the ward."

"A patient?" Harold asked.

Max and Ambria dashed through the portal.

Hard soles raced across the floor. "I don't know."

I jumped through the portal and willed it to shut just as the footsteps were nearly upon me. It winked out. I panted as if I'd just run a mile. Max leaned against the wall, holding a hand to his heart, eyes wide.

"That was too close." Ambria hugged herself and rubbed her arms. "I can't imagine what Grint would to do us if those orderlies caught us in there."

I rolled Ansel over onto his back and put a hand on his forehead. His skin felt clammy and cool. "I can't tell if he's getting better or not."

"Doesn't look like it," Max said.

Ambria removed the ink from her pouch. "Shall we?"

I took out my phone and projected a holograph of the image I'd taken of the ritual page. Ambria pulled up Ansel's striped pajama shirt to reveal pasty white skin while Max lowered the flying carpet to hover waist-high to her.

"No hair, thankfully." Ambria grimaced. "I'd have let you boys shave his belly if necessary."

"Yuck." Max tugged the shirt up to Ansel's neck. "Where does the symbol go?"

"Right here." Ambria traced a circle around Ansel's belly button. She took out the inkpot, dipped the tip of her wand in it, and scribed a neat circle. Aether crackled in the ink, the wand infusing it with magic. She drew a nine-sided star inside the circle, and wiped off her wand while inspecting her handiwork.

"Wish I could draw perfect circles," Max said.

Ambria smirked. "I cheated and used a guiding spell."

"I didn't know there was such a thing."

"I discovered it in an Arcane architectural textbook in the vault." She shrugged. "I knew it would come in handy someday."

I read the rest of the instructions. "All that's left is sparking the ink." I began recording with my arcphone so we'd have something to show Galfandor.

"Got it." Ambria flicked her wand and a stream of blue fire struck the diagram in the center. The ink blazed into black flame and a thick cloud of black smoke drifted up.

Max pinched his nose. "Gah, it stinks."

After a moment, it seemed apparent that smoke and flame were all we'd get from this ritual spell. I continued recording while I re-read the instructions. Unfortunately, my picture of the page cut off the bottom section detailing the results.

"Maybe the stench identifies the cause," Ambria said.

Max sighed. "Or maybe we were completely wrong about the cause."

The fire died and the smoke cloud dissipated as it drifted to the floor. A high-pitched shriek assaulted my ears and a slimy black slug erupted from the cloud straight at my face. I screamed and fell over backward in my haste to get away. The ripper wyrm landed on the floor between my legs, a low-pitched gurgling emanating from its orifice. A dozen eyestalks extended from its head and glared my way.

I vaguely heard Max and Ambria screaming and shouting in the background. Felt my hand tug my wand free of its holster, a spell forming in my mind. The wyrm sprang for my face. I flicked my wand and a shield solidified. The creature hit the shield and drifted apart like smoke.

"What?" I could hardly hear my own words over the sound of my pounding heart. "Where did it go?"

"Was it just smoke?" Ambria said. "Was it not real?"

Max whimpered. "I thought my heart exploded from fright."

"Interesting."

We three shouted and jumped in alarm, but it was just Kanaan, a flicker of amusement hiding behind his eyes.

"I knew you could accomplish what you needed." The magitsu master walked around the flying carpet holding Ansel's still form. "I suspect the hand of a powerful Daemos behind this."

Ambria recovered first. "That would make sense, but how would Victus recruit such help?"

"With leverage." Kanaan brushed the ashes of the ink off Ansel's stomach. "In the meantime, this man requires medical attention."

"Do you know a good healer?" Ambria said.

"I suggest Percival," Kanaan said.

"But Agatha Grint took him off duty." Ambria raised an eyebrow. "Do you know Percival?"

"Not personally." Kanaan pulled the flying carpet after him and left the arch room. "There is a small healing ward in the mansion. I will keep Ansel there."

"We can bring Percival in by the arch," Max said.

"We have to find him first." Ambria sighed. "I have no idea where he went after Grint relieved him of duty."

"She didn't relieve him of duty," Max said. "She told him to butt out of the torn soul investigation."

"Yes, but knowing his ego, I'm sure he took it hard." Ambria tutted. "I don't care for his methods, but he does get the job done."

An idea sparked in my head. "We can ask his brother at Science Academy."

Ambria frowned. "Do we plan to open portals all over the academy campus looking for him? You realize we'll have to leave the portal open if we plan to return through it."

"We can open the portal in Ansel's office," I said. "We'll leave the portal open and use our brooms to fly to the medical center."

"What if someone walks into his office while the portal is open?" Max asked.

"I'll open it to face a wall in the back." I knew the details of the office far better than I wanted, thanks to Ansel's harsh arcnology lessons.

We followed Kanaan into the mansion. An ornate foyer led to wide dual staircases that curved around an open space beneath a giant crystal chandelier. Wooden golems no more detailed than stick figures in servant livery dusted the neglected furniture and swept the floors. Kanaan paid them no mind and took a right down the hallway.

"The ward is in the east wing." He swung open double doors at the far end of the hallway and showed us into a room that looked very similar to the healing ward in Arcane University, albeit on a slightly smaller scale. Kanaan rang a bell and a servant golem clomped in. "Fresh linens."

"Please," Ambria said and darted a daring look at the magitsu master. "It's always good to be polite."

Max snorted. "I can think of plenty of times you're not."

"Quiet, Max." Ambria bared her teeth. "Please."

Kanaan stripped dusty sheets off a nearby bed. "Politeness is a commodity afforded only the civil."

I couldn't resist needling him. "Did you read that off a fortune cookie?"

He flicked his wand at the mattress. A funnel of wind drew out the dust and delivered it into a rubbish bin. The golem returned moments later and fitted the sheets on the bed.

"He looks worse," Ambria said after we slid Ansel into place. "His face is starting to look withered."

I looked down at the sunken cheeks, the loose skin on his neck, and flashed back to the dark room filled with coffins. I must have gasped because the others gave me concerned looks.

Ambria gripped my hand. "What is it, Conrad?"

"This reminds me of the memories Della left me." I described the faces in the coffins. "I think whatever afflicts Ansel is wrong with those people too." I felt sick.

"But this just started happening," Max said. "Did she give you a fore-seeance, or does that mean this has happened before?"

"It's not the future." I recounted the vision with Victus and Garkin. "That was my mother's past. It confirms that Victus is behind this new epidemic."

"He's using ripper wyrms to spread spiritual diseases." Ambria's eyes widened. "That's horrific."

"The demonomicon said ripper wyrm attacks aren't fatal." Max shook his head. "The victim should recover."

"Maybe Victus did something so the wyrm poisons the person," I suggested.

Kanaan looked down at my stricken cousin. "Masters of healing, we are not. I suggest you find Percival."

Ansel wasn't my favorite person in the world, but he'd taken time to teach us arcnology. He was the only blood relative I knew of besides Victus. I didn't want him to die. If anything, I wanted to use a ripper wyrm on Victus and watch him die a slow painful death.

CHAPTER 15

We had little time to waste, but it was late, and Arthur surely would be at home asleep at this hour. We portaled back to Moore Keep, opening a gateway to Ambria's room first, and then one in mine and Max's quarters, leaving it open and facing the wall so we could use it in the morning.

The next morning, we reversed the process, stepping through the portal and back into the arch room, closing it and opening one to Ambria's room. She came through, already dressed and ready to go.

"This is brilliant," Max said. "I wish I could use this omniarch to go everywhere."

"Unfortunately, someone has to be here to control it," Ambria said. "Perhaps we could come up with a remote way of activating it."

I pictured the corner of Ansel's office in my head and willed the arch to open a portal there. A silver line sliced through the air and gaped open to reveal a window to the desired location. I stepped through and looked around to make sure no one was there, then motioned the others through.

Max stopped near the spot we'd found Ansel and paused. "Hmm, I wonder."

"What's for breakfast?" Ambria inserted.

"No. I wonder if that man we saw coming from Ansel's office had anything to do with his injuries." Max turned to me. "Or maybe he found Ansel and ran because he was frightened."

"Why be frightened?" I said. "Ansel was acting drunk or high. The man should've been running for help."

"We thought he might've given Ansel drugs like Arthur said." Max shook his head. "But we know that's not the case now."

I pictured the man and felt the same chills I'd felt the first time I saw him. "I think you're right."

Ambria looked shocked at what she said next. "Me too."

"Put it on the back burner," I said. "For now, we focus on finding Percival."

We boarded our brooms and flew to the medical center, but were saved from having to go inside. Percival and Arthur sat outside on a bench, gesturing as if engaged in a spirited conversation.

"It's ridiculous!" Percival shouted.

"I bloody know it is, but you've got no standing." Arthur blinked twice when he saw us land behind his brother. "What are you doing here?"

Percival spun and saw us. "Oh, it's you, children. Tell my brother what that old hag said about me."

I waved him off. "Look, that's not important right now. What is important is that we need you to save a life."

"Duty calls, Percy." Arthur patted Percival on the shoulder while giving us a thumbs up and a grateful look behind his back.

Percival waved us away. "No, what's important is that I be allowed to cure those soul-torn patients!"

"We have patient zero," I said. "My cousin Ansel."

Percival's eyes brightened. "Well, why didn't you say so?" He pointed toward Arcane University. "Let's go."

"Uh, we need to go the other way," Max said.

Percival frowned. "But the university is that way."

"Just trust us." I waved goodbye to Arthur as he hurried off toward the medical center, and then led Percival toward the arcnology lab.

"I don't see how we're supposed to return to campus by walking away from it," the healer complained. "Where are we going?"

"Through a portal," I said.

His forehead wrinkled. "A portal in the middle of this campus?"

"It's from an omniarch," Ambria explained. "You can portal anywhere."

Percival gasped. "What sorcery is this?"

"It's been around forever." Max shook his head. "Just trust us, okay?"

"Well, I've already walked this far. A little further won't hurt." Percival brushed something off his robes and straightened his shoulders. "Patient zero, you say?"

"We know what caused his condition and diagnosed it with a ritual." Ambria flashed a grin at his confusion. "It's a demonic ripper wyrm."

"You did what?" Percival wagged a finger at us. "None of you are qualified to practice medicine."

"It's not medicine." Max pshawed. "We can't heal him. That's why we need you."

"His condition is worsening." I walked through the entrance to the arcnology lab and led Percival to the portal in the office. "Ansel isn't the most pleasant fellow, but he's all the family I have."

Ambria grimaced. "Victus *not* included."

"Goodness." Percival stepped through the portal and looked back in wonder. "I've never heard of these omniarches."

We followed him through and I closed the portal. "Can we trust you not to tell anyone about this portal or what I'm about to show you?"

"Where are we?" Percival touched the walls. "Is this a basement?"

"Can we?" I insisted.

He pursed his lips. "Children with secrets are usually up to no good."

Ambria set her fists on her hips. "We don't want Agatha Grint or her cronies finding out."

"Ah." A smile spread across the healer's face. "In that case, absolutely. I will keep your secret to the grave."

He seemed serious despite the smile, so I motioned him to follow us out of the arch room and into the corridor. We stepped in front of the arching entrance leading to the cavern with the mansion and Percival stopped in his tracks, a dumfounded look on his face.

"Are we underground?" He looked around at us. "Is that a mansion in a cave?"

"It's from the old resistance." Max grinned, pleased at the reaction. "Justin Slade and his people built it after Daelissa destroyed the one aboveground."

"You children really do have the most interesting secrets." Percival walked to the mansion and opened the door where he paused again to take in the magnificent interior. "Simply amazing."

Ambria took a turn playing gracious host. "The healing ward is this way." She led him to Ansel's bed.

Percival's wide-eyed wonder turned to a frown as he took in Ansel's pale face. "Oh, he doesn't look good at all."

"Is that your professional opinion?" Ambria said.

"Shush, child." Percival took out his wand and ran it up and down the patient's body. "Are there any supplies here, or must I procure my own?"

"The supply room is down the hallway," Ambria said. "Have a look inside and if you need anything else, we can get it with the portal, provided we have a detailed image of the destination."

"I keep ample supplies at my residence," Percival said. "Must I use the portal, or is there a way to walk from here?"

"I suggest you use the portal," I said. "It's much faster." I explained the simple mechanics of it. "Do you have an arcphone?"

"Yes, but don't tell anyone." Percival retrieved a small thin tablet from within his robe. "You know how the university frowns on such devices."

I bumped mine against his. "I exchanged our contact information. That way if we need you to activate the portal remotely for us, you can, and vice versa."

"Indeed." Percival bent over Ansel and continued to scan him. "I need more information about ripper wyrms. In the meantime, I'll prepare a preservation tincture to stabilize his body functions until I discover the cause."

"Isn't the cause part of his soul being ripped out?" Ambria said.

"He should still have enough soul essence to regrow it," Percival replied. "These physical symptoms might be something else—a poison left by the wyrm, possibly."

"Wyrms aren't poisonous," Max said. "Then again, we think Victus is the one using them, so maybe he modified it somehow."

Percival jerked upright. "Victus Edison? The Overlord?"

"My father." I scowled.

"I thought he was dead."

"It's a long story, but he's back and he's up to no good." I touched Ansel's hand and recoiled at how clammy it felt. "Look, we've got to get to class. Let us know how it goes."

Percival nodded solemnly. "I will heal your cousin, Conrad."

I returned a brief smile. "Thanks."

We used the portal to take us to the field behind the university. I closed it and we rushed to the dining hall to eat with only fifteen minutes before the first class. The corridors were uncommonly empty when they should have teemed with students rushing from breakfast to class.

"Strange," Max mused. "Where is everyone?"

We rounded the bend near the dining hall. The double doors were closed, but a magically amplified voice echoed off the stone walls from the other side. Max eased open the door and peeked through the crack.

"...required of every student and professor." I recognized the voice of Esmerelda Quiff. "Security is of paramount importance, as I'm sure you all understand."

"Must be about the riots," Max whispered.

The door shoved open, sending Max stumbling backward. Two Blue Cloaks with stern faces grabbed us by the arms and pulled us inside. The dining hall was full to bursting, each table full, and every chair at the head table occupied.

Minister Quiff smiled brightly at us from the podium. "Conrad Edison." She spoke my name as if deliriously happy to see me. "How nice of you to come."

Two tables away, Harris Ashmore bared his teeth at me while his best friend, Baxter Troy, snickered with glee at our predicament. Lily Crown offered a smile and a covert wave our way. Laughter rose from other tables, but Quiff snuffed the amusement before it spread further.

"There is nothing funny about this, children." She paced to her right, blond hair bouncing. She stopped. Faced us. "Do you want to know why security is such a problem?"

Galfandor gave her an uneasy look from his position in the middle of the table and then met my eyes for an instant.

As the silence hung, the Blue Cloaks pointed us to stand against the back wall where the overflow of students and faculty gathered.

Minister Quiff smiled sweetly. "Poor student quality." She looked at a short man with a disproportionately large head and nodded. "Education Minister Jonas and I have spoken about this extensively and we are on the same page."

Jonas nodded sternly at her, his large head tipping so precariously, I thought it might pull him off balance.

"We will conduct an educational audit." Quiff waved a hand across the crowd. "We will find the low-performers and determine if it is the fault of our teachers"—she turned and ran her eyes over the professors, then turned back to us—"or the students."

Galfandor stood. "I'm sorry, Minister, but weren't we discussing security?"

Quiff laced her fingers together. "It is all intertwined, Headmaster." She folded her hands together. "I and the other ministers will be auditing classes today. We expect to have results within a week."

Galfandor frowned. "I think that is more than enough for now." He held up his hands. "Students, you are free to go to class."

The room erupted into chaos, children racing from the dining hall as if fleeing wildfire. The school faculty did likewise while the ministers circled like vultures around Galfandor. Among them stood Max's father, Xander.

"What's he doing here?" Max's face paled. "My brothers are here, too!"

Ambria looked around in confusion. "But they graduated."

"I don't think they're here as students." He stared at the identical twin boys standing at a table near the front, amused expressions on their faces.

Devon and Rhys were unpleasant and downright cruel. They'd threatened me to keep me from playing kabash the previous year so they could go out with a championship, and done far worse to their little brother, Max. It now appeared they were in Xander's entourage.

"I wish I could hear what they're saying to Galfandor," Ambria said.

The headmaster's bushy eyebrows pinched into an angry V, but he remained still and calm even as Minister Quiff and her compatriots took turns talking.

"The first day of classes and you're already up to no good." Gideon Grace had approached us unseen from the side.

Max stiffened. "We weren't doing anything wrong, Professor."

"This gathering was mandatory." Grace stepped in front of me. "Where were you earlier?"

"We didn't even know about it," I said, doing my best not to be cowed by his angry sneer. Grace despised our parents and us by relation.

"If I discover you're the ones behind these illnesses around campus, I will lock you away myself," he hissed. His arm rose and a finger pointed to the door. "Now get to class."

I wanted to shout back at him that I had nothing to do with it. *It's not me, it's my father!* But I didn't feel innocent. I felt guilty by association.

We didn't escape Grace's sneer for long since he taught our first period class, Advanced Spellcasting. Harris and his friends sat on the opposite side of the room near the front, so we took desks in the far back corner.

Professor Grace marched in, gray robes swishing, and gave us a sideways glare in passing. "Advanced Spellcasting." He dropped a huge leather-bound tome on his desk and spun to face us. "The spells you've learned were mere rungs on a ladder so you could reach out your tiny hands and grasp the true core of spellcasting." He flicked his wand through a complex pattern and a small dark cloud gathered before him. "Some spells requires you to layer the magic. One mistake, and your casting falls apart, or"—a bolt of lightning shot from the small cloud. Thunder boomed and everyone cried out in surprise—"it blows up in your face."

A tiny smile tugged at the corner of the professor's lips. Rain sprinkled on the floor beneath the tiny cloud even as more lightning and thunder rolled in miniature sound. The storm drifted toward Baxter's desk. Eyes wide, the ginger scooted back to avoid the tiny bolts of lightning. Grace slashed his wand through the cloud and it dissipated to a fine mist.

"Now it's your turn." Grace diagrammed the wand pattern on the chalkboard with a series of dotted lines, pause marks, and circles for the cast points. "Complete it successfully by the end of class, or receive a failing grade for the day."

"That spell looks familiar," Ambria said.

I stared at it for a moment and realized it was actually three different patterns, three cast points, layered into one spell. I opened the textbook to the spell and circled where each pattern segued into the next. "The first part condenses mist, the second adds electrical current, and the third ties the spells into a repeating loop."

"We've done those spells before." Max practiced waving his wand through each pattern. "I think I've got it." He concentrated on the air in front of him and began the patterns. Gray mist condensed, growing thicker and thicker until it was nearly black. Streaks of brilliant yellow lanced through the cloud, and thunder boomed.

It was a beautifully rendered spell, a point not lost on the professor.

Grace's eyes shot wide as he realized Max was the first student to complete the spell.

Ambria clapped her hands. "Excellent, Max!"

He grinned. "Easy, peasy."

The cloud drifted down the aisle, leaving a puddle behind it. Max jumped up and slashed his wand through it to cut the spell binding before it created a huge mess.

Grace narrowed his eyes. "Passing grade, Tiberius."

Max's grin stretched ear-to-ear before he hid it. "Thank you, sir."

Ambria and I replicated Max's success and received our passing grades as well. Lily Crown, ever the perfectionist, earned her mark fourth.

Halfway through the class, Grace allowed those who had passed to leave early, so we wasted no time departing and headed down the hallway for the next class.

"Wait for me," Lily called out behind us.

Max cringed. Ambria groaned. I stopped and directed a suspicious gaze at her.

"Aren't you going to wait for your besties?" Max said.

Lily quirked her lips. "I don't want to wait another thirty minutes in there." She shifted her book bag on her shoulder. "How did you all do the spell so quickly?"

Max shrugged. "Easy. It was just a combination of other spells."

"And we've practiced all summer," Ambria said.

"Harris is convinced he'll have to fight and kill you all," Lily said in a matter-of-fact tone. "When he saw how fast you did the spells, I think it scared him."

"Harris is demented." Ambria threw up her hands. "Why does he think we're the evil in his stupid foreseeance?"

"I told him I don't think you're bad just because your parents were." She twirled a lock of brown hair on her finger as she walked alongside Max. "Unfortunately, I don't think he cares." She looked sadly at me. "Harris hates you because your parents murdered his."

"I know that already." Lily sounded so reasonable, I wondered why she hung out with Harris and Baxter in the first place. "I guess we won't be friends anytime soon."

"Just be careful, Conrad." Lily looked over her shoulder. "I think Harris wants to force a fight very soon."

CHAPTER 16

L ily's words chilled me to the bone. I had enough to worry about without Harris's vendetta.

Ambria huffed. "Can't you talk sense to the boy? Does he really mean to murder Conrad?"

"You should report him to the headmaster," Max said. "I didn't realize he was so unhinged."

"I have spoken to him," Lily said. "He tells Baxter how evil you all are, and Baxter echoes everything right back. They feed off each other's anger and won't listen to reason. I just thought you should know." She veered off toward the bathrooms. "See you in class."

We sat on benches in the hallway outside the classroom to wait for the class to end and the room to empty. Lessons in basic magical defense emanated from the open doorway. It seemed so odd to hear them in Asha Fellini's voice instead of Esma's. My chest tightened and salt stung my eyes. *I'll never see Esma again.*

Esma, my mentor, and the woman who'd never existed. Sometimes I had trouble seeing Esma and Delectra as the same person. Other times it seemed I could hardly separate the two.

Ambria's hand closed around mine. "I know this will be a tough class." Her voice broke. "Esma was my favorite professor."

Max chuckled. "She was mean, but effective."

"She wasn't real." I twisted my hand free and wiped my eyes. "It is what it is, and I'm fine." *Never see her again. Ever.* That infinite expanse of emptiness opened like a hole in my heart. I'd avoided thinking about this for so long, but reality refused to let me duck it any longer.

The bell rang and children flooded out of the classroom. Even after it was long empty, I remained seated while Ambria and Max watched in concern. I steeled myself and stood. *Esma—my mother—is gone. Accept it and move on.*

Asha looked up from a book on her desk. I already knew how much she resembled Delectra, but memories of a ghost haunted me.

Professor Fellini smiled. "You three are here early."

Ambria returned the smile. "We got out of our last class before it ended."

I tried to smile, but my heart felt like lead. I chose a desk in the row nearest the door and opened the textbook, pretending to read it so I wouldn't have to look at Asha's face. I caught a glance of concern from her, but she turned back to her own book and waited for class to begin.

Harris delivered a black glare at me when he walked in, Baxter close behind and mirroring the expression. They took desks across the room next to Lily who'd slipped in when I wasn't looking. I stared at my textbook, eyes blind to the words as thoughts and regrets consumed me. In the distance, I heard the bell ring. Heard a low electrical hum building in the air.

My hand reflexively grasped my wand, flicked through a pattern etched in my mind. A three-layered shield sprang into place before me and intercepted a bolt of harmless electricity before it zapped my nose.

Satisfaction flashed across Asha's face before she turned and tried to zap another student. Nearly everyone passed her impromptu test, but only because Esma had launched surprise attacks nearly every day on her unwitting students until they adapted and learned that danger could come at any moment.

A part of me felt happy that Asha decided to continue with the tradition.

"Shields are wonderful for blocking attacks," Asha said, "but what happens when you're injured?"

Lily thrust a hand into the air. "You escape."

Asha pursed her lips and nodded. "That's one option. But sometimes, you can't escape, or your injuries keep you from leaving. Sometimes, you have to patch yourself up before you can go."

"Isn't that healing?" Lily frowned.

"Yes, it is." Asha stood in front of the desk and leaned back on it. "While healing is considered a branch all its own, what you will learn today is more about field healing so you can get on your feet in a hurry." She held her wand over the palm of her other hand. Azure energy flashed out and crackled.

Asha winced. The odor of cooked flesh filled the room. Gasps rose as we realized she'd just burnt her own hand. The professor turned her hand to us, displaying blackened skin. "The first thing you want to do when injured is deaden the pain."

"You burned your own hand!" Lily cried.

Asha's eyes hardened. "Listen to me, children." She clenched her injured hand. "I have seen combat. I've seen people die because they weren't capable of staunching blood, or patching a broken limb." Her gaze raked across the room and seemed to lock onto me. In that instant, I saw an echo of Delectra in her more clearly than ever before and it shocked me to the core.

Could she be Delectra's sister? A relative I don't know about?

"Please, please, please, heal yourself," Lily moaned. She wiped tears from her cheeks.

Asha flicked her wand through a pattern and relief flooded her face, though her hand looked just as gravely wounded as before. "That was a numbing spell." She slapped the palm of the injured hand on the desk.

Students gasped and looked away.

"I can still function. I can still escape and heal later." Asha traced her wand in slow irregular circles over the flesh. Moments later, the blackened flesh sloughed off, revealing raw new skin beneath. "Today, students, you will learn how to numb small injuries."

"I think I'm gonna be sick," Max groaned.

Ambria rubbed her eyes as if she couldn't believe what she was seeing. "And I thought Esma was hardcore." She grimaced and looked at me. "Sorry, Conrad."

I nodded absentmindedly, still shocked by Asha's demonstration. This was a side I hadn't seen of her, but it was a side I liked.

By the end of class, we'd learned how to numb small wounds and make magical splints for broken limbs.

Baxter sneered at me as he and Harris left the room. "Hope you learned something today, Edison. You're gonna need it."

Lily offered an apologetic smile and followed after them.

"I really don't like them," Max growled as we headed to our next class.

Eleanor Beetle bored us to tears in Overworld Social Studies by reading straight from the textbook for a solid hour. I wondered if she actually knew anything about her subjects, or if she learned by reading the textbooks along with us.

The dining hall was abuzz with activity. Unfamiliar faces crowded the head table along with a few I recognized—Esmerelda Quiff, Agatha Grint, and Galfandor. Due to the lack of seats, most professors sat at tables normally used by students. Gideon Grace looked particularly peeved, casting venomous stares at children when they threatened to sit nearby. One look from him sent most scurrying away.

A wide, black curtain emblazoned with the glowing blue orb of the Arcane Council hung from the wall behind the table.

"Who are all those people?" Ambria said.

Max took out his arcphone and scrolled to a news page with the headline: *Arcane Council Holds Election at Arcane University.* "That's odd."

"Where do they usually hold the election?" Ambria asked.

"The council chambers in Queens Gate." Max scanned the article. "They decided to hold an early vote instead of waiting for this evening."

I looked up at Galfandor to see if he looked upset or worried, but the headmaster carried on a conversation with Agatha Grint as if nothing was the matter. Not more than three chairs away sat Xander Tiberius, his nose angled up at a noble bearing, a smirk on his face as he appeared to humor a pale waif of a man next to him.

The serving golems set food in front of us, but for once, Max didn't seem to notice. His gaze darted from his father to the other people near him. "I can't believe the council would let him sit with them."

"Well, he *is* running for primus," Ambria noted.

Max pointed to the thin man next to Xander. "That's Marcus Welby, minister of Arcane law. He promised to send my father to prison if it was the last thing he ever did. Not two months ago, he gave a speech about rounding up Overlord collaborators and used my father as an example."

I observed the smile on Welby's face as he talked to Xander. "He doesn't look angry with him now."

"I don't know anyone on the council who's ever had a favorable thing to say about my father." Max ran a hand down his face. "I know he didn't bribe them to like him. He tried that once, and Minister Welby tried to prosecute him for it."

"In other words, Galfandor has this election in the bag." Ambria gave him a questioning look. "Right?"

Devon and Rhys hovered behind their father, eager smirks on their faces. Devon whispered something in his father's ear, and Xander's gaze locked onto Max. The three of them shared a laugh.

Max shrank in his seat. "I hate my family."

Xander waved a hand and the twins walked down off the stage and sat at a table on the right side.

"Where's your mother?" Ambria asked.

Max looked down at the floor and shrugged. "I'm sure she's here somewhere."

Minister Quiff banged a gavel on the main table and the dining hall went quiet. "For too long the council has gone without a primus. Today it is time to inject all Arcanes with a renewed sense of purpose and give them a government they can trust." She beamed a too-sweet smile across the room.

"Hear, hear," Welby called out.

The others on the council clapped. Gideon Grace exchanged a perplexed look with other professors at his table even as he joined the scattered clapping. Nearby students looked around, half-heartedly applauding if they saw their peers doing the same.

"I hereby call the voting into session," Quiff said. "Do I have a second?"

Agatha Grint banged a fist on the table. "Seconded!"

"Thirded!" Welby said with a wild grin on his too-thin face.

Galfandor frowned, but said nothing while Xander bared his teeth in a confident smile.

A stout councilwoman shoved back her chair and stood. "This is highly irregular! I hereby call to dismiss this vote and hold it at the scheduled time in the council chambers."

"I second Minister Bell," said a burly fellow next to her. He tweaked the end of his magnificently groomed mustache and stood. "There is no need to rush the process."

"Is that so, Minister Moon?" Quiff raised an imperious eyebrow. "Let us vote on the matter. All in favor of voting now?"

Six members raised their hands.

"All opposed?"

Six more raised their hands.

All eyes turned to a trembling woman seated between Ministers Welby and Bell. She hugged herself and looked down at her food.

Quiff raised another eyebrow to join the first. "What is your vote, Minister Lutz?"

Welby nudged her ribs from one side. Bell elbowed her none-too-gently from the other side.

Xander leaned around Welby and said something that made Lutz stiffen. She looked up sharply, eyes wide. Her voice cracked as she said, "I vote in favor."

The table burst into an uproar, both sides shouting over the others.

Minister Moon jumped to his feet, towering over the others. "What the bloody hell is wrong with you, Quiff? Not a week ago you shouted down Grint for suggesting an early vote, and now you're the one leading the charge?"

Quiff banged her gavel until the handle broke and at last the shouting subsided. "The matter has been settled." Another smile. "Now, let us vote."

Moon bared his teeth and sat back down. "Fine, let's get it over with, shall we? I don't suppose we'll be voting by secret ballot as per council rules either?"

Grint turned to him. "We will keep voting transparent for all to see."

Quiff wasted no time. "All in favor of Galfandor, let it be known."

Six hands rose. Minister Bell elbowed Lutz until she hesitantly raised her hand, making it seven out of thirteen for Galfandor.

Max gasped in relief along with the rest of us at the table. "I can't believe six people are voting for my father."

Quiff glared at Lutz. "All for Xander Tiberius."

The same six hands that called for an early vote rose, but they had lost by one vote. Cheers rose from the end of the table with the victors. Galfandor watched on, eyes wary, and stood.

Xander stared at Lutz. She averted her eyes, but still trembled as if she could feel the malevolence. Welby whispered something into her ear and the woman wilted. She stood and raised her hand.

Quiff smiled. "Yes, Minister Lutz?"

"I wish to change my vote, Minister." Lutz hugged herself ever more tightly. "I change my vote to Xander Tiberius."

CHAPTER 17

T he hall burst into an uproar. Galfandor narrowed his eyes in suspicion, but said nothing. Max went white as a sheet. Ambria shook her head in disbelief. "Impossible!"

I watched Galfandor for any clue this might be a trick. A shadow seemed to move against the black curtain on the wall. I glimpsed it beneath the head table, a silhouette so small, I might have missed it if not for my fixation on the headmaster. I blinked, thinking my eyes were playing tricks on me, but when I opened them, the object moved into the light.

Shiny, black and slug-like. *A ripper wyrm!* "Galfandor!" I shouted, but the roar of the crowd drowned my terrified voice.

Galfandor walked over and spoke with Agatha Grint, one of the very council members who'd voted against him, unaware of the monster creeping up on him. I leapt from my chair and ran toward the head table, heart thrashing in my chest. Students looked up at me in surprise as I raced past shouting for the headmaster.

My foot caught on something. The floor rushed to meet me. Either adrenalin or Kanaan's training kept me from falling. I stumbled, caught myself. Something slammed me in the back and I went down hard.

"Watch where you're going Edison!" Baxter shouted.

I leapt to my feet and looked forward. The wyrm slithered beneath Galfandor's robes. The headmaster stiffened, face turning ghostly white. Grint kept talking as if unaware of what was happening right under her nose.

"Galfandor!" I cried.

The wyrm dropped to the floor out and snaked back toward the dark curtain. Galfandor collapsed in a heap.

Baxter laughed and jeered at me. "Watch your feet, Edison!"

I roared and spun to face the red-headed menace. I grabbed two fistfuls of his hair and slammed his face into the potato soup on his tray. Jerked his head up and slammed it down again.

"Agh!" Baxter cried, hands flailing at me. I let him go and raced for the fallen headmaster.

Minister Grint looked down at Galfandor. She looked oddly calm, almost satisfied even, before backing away and shouting, "The headmaster has fainted!"

I clambered up on the platform and rushed to Galfandor's side. "He's been attacked by a ripper wyrm!"

Grint's eyes narrowed. "What was that?"

"Clear the way!" Percival pushed past the health minister and ran his wand over the stricken headmaster.

"He fainted, Percival." Grint tugged on his robes. "Give him space to breath, and get that boy out of here!"

Council security leapt onto the stage and pulled Percival away. Large hands gripped me and tore me from Galfandor's side.

"Let me go!" I struggled to free myself, but their grips were like iron.

"I will tend to the headmaster myself," Grint said to the other council members swarming around Galfandor's prone form. "I'm certain he's simply overworked himself."

Horace Moon looked at her with narrowed eyes and his gaze wandered over to meet mine.

"He didn't faint!" I shouted. "It was demon spawn!"

A tall silhouette against the black curtain caught my eyes. A hood fell back from a familiar face—that of the man we'd seen coming from Ansel's office. His cruel eyes chilled me to the core. I felt something tingling, pressing against me, but it wasn't physical. It was as if something tried to worm its way into my soul.

Fear gripped me. Who or what was that man? The tingling intensified. I felt it now—like someone tapping on a window, trying to get in. It reminded me of the sensation I'd felt when Cumberbatch exorcised the demon from me that had preserved my parents' souls, but the feeling was somehow different. I hardened my will, refused to let it take hold of me.

The man's forehead pinched with confusion.

He wasn't using any Arcane magic I knew. It felt demonic. I realized he might not even be an Arcane. Puzzle pieces clicked together even as council security pulled me off the stage and let me go.

That man is Daemos. He controlled the ripper wyrm that attacked Galfandor!

Even if true, security now surrounded the head table. Two men in healer robes put Galfandor on a flying carpet while students and professors watched in shock. Ambria and Max joined me.

In the distance, I heard Baxter shouting, "He's over there, Professor!"

"We've got to get out of here," Max said. "Baxter went to Professor Grace after you dunked his head in soup."

"What good would it do to run?" I muttered. "Grace will just find me back at the keep."

Ambria got in front of me. "What happened to Galfandor?"

"A ripper wyrm." I trembled with anger. "I saw it coming for him. Baxter tripped me."

Someone shoved me hard in the back. I stumbled into Ambria and we tumbled to the ground.

"You're mine, Edison!"

I didn't have to see Harris to recognize his voice. I grabbed Ambria and rolled her on top of me and out of the way just as a jolt of magical energy struck the floor where we'd been.

Max reared back his arm and blind-sided Harris in the jaw. "Leave us alone!"

Ambria climbed lithely to her feet and pulled me up just as Baxter let out a battle cry and ran straight for Max. Max dodged to the side and Baxter missed, crashing into a group of students, bits of potato flying from his hair.

"Enough!" Gideon Grace roared.

Harris wobbled on his feet, tears of pain in his eyes as he favored his jaw. "He punched me, Professor!"

Max clenched his fists. "He shoved my friends and tried to kill Conrad with a spell!"

"You." Graced jabbed a finger at me. "What was the meaning of attacking Baxter?"

"He tripped me and hit me in the back." I fought to keep my voice calm. "I defended myself."

Baxter disentangled himself from the students he'd run into. "He just attacked me for no reason."

"Liar!" Ambria poked him in the chest. "I saw you trip him."

"I've had enough." Grace's voice went cold. "Edison, you are to report to detention directly after supper tonight."

"But Conrad didn't do anything!" Max said. "It was Baxter and Harris!"

"One more word, Tiberius, and you'll join him." Grace looked at Baxter and shook his head. "Clean yourself up, boy." He spun on his heel and left.

"I know you did something to Galfandor," Harris hissed. "Try anything else, Edison, and I won't go easy on you."

Baxter smirked. "Aw, does the poor baby have detention?"

A feline growl sounded to my left. Ambria lunged forward and punched Baxter square on the nose. He yelped and went down like a sack of potatoes. Ambria stared at her fist as if she couldn't believe what she'd just done, then looked guiltily at me. "He deserved it."

Harris backed away from her. "You're all insane."

"You're the insane one," Max shot back. "If you want to fight evil, you're on the wrong side."

Harris gripped Baxter under the armpits and dragged him to his feet, all the while glaring at Ambria. "Let's see if Professor Grace has room in detention for you."

Baxter held his nose to staunch the bleeding and shook his head desperately. "No, let's just go."

Lily smirked and gave a thumbs-up to Ambria. "Don't want to tell the professor a girl put you down, Baxter?"

"Shut up!" He ran away, tears streaming down his face. Harris scowled at us one more time before rushing off.

I squeezed through the crowd and reached the head table, but the ministers crowded around Galfandor. I ignored a look from a nearby Blue

Cloak and ran over to the stricken headmaster. Minister Grint noticed me trying to get through and nudged Minister Quiff. The pair blocked my path.

"What peculiar claims you made a moment ago," Quiff said.

Grint raised an eyebrow. "Yes, what's a ripper wyrm, Edison? What makes you think it's responsible for Galfandor's fainting episode?"

Their tones set me on the defensive and I instantly regretted shouting about the wyrm. I scrambled to come up with an explanation, but Horace Moon jumped in. "Ripper wyrms are rare demon spawn." He patted me on the shoulder. "Did you see something, lad?"

I wanted to tell them that I'd read a great deal on demon spawn recently, but couldn't think of a good explanation as to why. They would probably assume I was up to no good and intent on summoning spawn for nefarious purposes. Then again, Moon seemed much friendlier than Grint and Quiff and might support my assertions.

"Demon spawn?" Quiff sniffed. "Why would a boy know about a rare form of demon spawn unless..." She trailed off and narrowed her eyes. "Victus Edison was a known demon collaborator."

"Boy, do you intend to follow in your father's footsteps?" Grint took a step closer. "Did you summon a demon spawn?"

"Impossible," Moon shot back. "A boy his age and skill level couldn't possibly summon spawn. Demonologists study for years before attempting their first summoning."

I tried to speak again, but the ministers seemed intent on arguing among themselves. I slipped past them and knelt next to Galfandor even as healers prepared to move the carpet bearing him. "Galfandor?"

His eyelids fluttered, but the headmaster didn't respond.

I touched his hand. It felt warm and sweaty. I had no doubt he'd soon exhibit the same symptoms as Ansel. I looked up and locked gazes with

Percival who stood behind a wall of security, a helpless expression on his face.

"Step away, lad." One of the healers gently pushed me back. "Don't you worry. We'll take good care of him."

I stood and backed away, swallowing hard in a vain attempt to quell the rising desperation and hopelessness draining the warmth from my insides. I couldn't believe this was happening. I closed my eyes and tried to wish it away. Instead, I saw my mother dying in my arms. I heard Della's voice whisper in my mind, *Remember.*

I blink bleary eyes. I cannot move my arms or legs or lift my head to look around. A sheet of glass slides away and a face leers down at me. I gasp and strength returns. I'm in a box—a coffin. Victus steps back, ice glinting in his eyes as he takes me in.

"Who is your master?" he asks.

Something dark and malevolent rises inside me and consumes my self-control. "You are my master." I hear my voice, but it isn't me speaking. I feel as if my consciousness drowns in a pool of inky pitch.

"I will suffer no more insubordination, wife." He grips my hand so tightly, knuckles crack. "You are mine. Any fruit you bear is mine to do with as I please."

"I understand," my body replies, though my soul rages against it. "All I am is yours, master." All I wish is to please him. I will lie for him, fight for him, kill for him. I will even give him our children to do with as he pleases. A voice cries out in opposition, but it fades, darkness drowning the light.

"You will never find her," the voice whispers before fading away.

Victus leads me through the chamber, wending his way through more coffins. "The new foundry works even better than the first. I have prepared a surprise for you."

"Yes, what is it?" My voice seethes with dark excitement.

He grins. "Something I made to keep up appearances while you were in holding."

Fingernails bite into the palms of my hands. I clench my fists hard enough to draw blood. The pain invigorates me. I wish to see blood spilled. I am ready to be let loose upon the world.

Victus steps into a hallway and stops at the first door on the right. He lifts a black iron bar and pulls the door open.

"Master?" A familiar voice calls from within.

"Yes, love." He smiles and shivers with delight. "I want you to meet Delectra."

"She is here?" A figure emerges from the shadows.

I clap with glee when I see her lovely face. "Oh, she's perfect!" I inspect her closely. There are small differences—a dimple here, a freckle there—but in every other regard, she looks just like me. "Have you made others?"

"No." He takes the woman's hand. "To craft a perfect replica takes weeks of effort. I can make others who look similar, but this one is virtually identical to you."

"My very own demon golem." I can hardly believe it. "Does my soul fragment keep the demon flesh intact for longer than a few hours?"

"She is nearly a month old, love." Victus chuckles. "She is like the real you in every way."

"Are there others?" I ask.

He shakes his head. "She is the first of the infernus, but soon there will be many more."

My infernus looks at me and beams a brilliant smile. Joy sweeps through me, for this is the beginning of the end for all who oppose our master.

I staggered back, knees weak, and stifled a shout of terror. *Infernus? Victus used a demon to clone my mother?* I saw Grint and Quiff turn away from Horace Moon. Their eyes locked onto me and I knew they meant to interrogate me more about my wyrm claim. A great weight settled on my chest until I could barely breathe.

I turned and bumped into—*Mom?* No, it was Asha. I knocked her back a step and elicited a surprised gasp. Seeing her familiar face only doubled the horror blossoming inside me. There was no question in my mind now why she looked so much like Delectra. She wasn't the perfect clone from my vision, but she was close enough.

Asha Fellini was not a real person. She was an infernus.

CHAPTER 18

"What's wrong, Conrad?" Asha gripped my hand. "You're white as a sheet."

"No!" I jerked my hand free. "Not real!" I bolted down the stairs from the platform and sped out of the dining room, tears burning in my eyes.

"Conrad!" Ambria shouted from behind. "Wait!"

I didn't want to stop. Didn't want to face the creature Victus created in his infernal labs. I looked back and saw Asha talking with Max and Ambria. Fear and loathing jerked me to a halt. *I can't let her near my friends.* A lucid thought penetrated the haze of terror fogging my brain. *I can't let Asha know that I know she's an infernus. This is why Victus wanted me dead. This is why Garkin tried to kill me. Victus plans to use these demon golems to conquer the Overworld.*

I had to get my friends away from that creature without her knowing why. I took deep calming breaths and tried to maintain a grip on rational thoughts. Asha might be an infernus, but in all the time I'd known her, she hadn't tried to harm me. Victus must have known how deeply it would affect me having a teacher who so closely resembled my mother.

Asha had certainly thrown me off balance and caused me emotional turmoil all because she looked like Delectra. With the truth revealed, I could finally see past the illusion and know this creature for what she really was—an impostor.

I gathered my wits and walked back to the others.

Wide with concern, Asha's eyes looked so real—so human—I could hardly believe she was a copy of my dead mother.

"Conrad, are you okay?" She reached out to touch me, but seemed to remember my earlier response and lowered her hand.

"Where were you running?" Max said.

"I was upset." My thoughts scrambled for a solid excuse. "A wyrm—" I stopped talking, suddenly realizing that if I told Asha about our knowledge of the wyrm, she would tell Victus.

"Did you actually see one?" Ambria said.

I changed the subject. "Grint and Quiff kept interrogating me. I wanted to get out of there."

Asha's nose wrinkled. "I do not like that pair one bit. Minister Quiff asked me all sorts of personal questions about my history and threatened to hold a formal review if I didn't answer her thoroughly."

"What sorts of questions?" Ambria asked.

"Where I was from, my parents' names, and so forth." She shrugged. "It was unexpected and bizarre, especially since all of that should be on file in the human resources office."

Except you don't have a real history. Victus must have created her shortly after his resurrection. Of course, if that was the case, why hadn't she killed me? Asha had the opportunity any number of times. Then again, so had Delectra while disguised as Esma.

I wondered if perhaps Asha as a clone of Delectra had the same emotional conflicts as my mother. Perhaps she was here to kill me, but maternal instinct had transferred from the soul fragment used by my mother.

Another loose puzzle piece clicked with the larger picture. *Soul fragments—the ripper wyrm.* The man with the ripper wyrm was collecting soul fragments for Victus. He planned to create copies of important people and use them to control the Overworld!

I nearly blurted out my thoughts, but bit my tongue. *Asha is a spy.*

"Where are you from?" Ambria asked.

"I was born and raised in Italy," Asha replied. "My mother was Italian, and my father British." A sad smile lifted the corners of her lips. "They died when I was too young to remember, so I lived in the countryside with my adoptive grandfather."

Lies. I wondered how deep her false history went. "What is his name?"

"Stan." Her face flushed. "He's one of my favorite people in the world."

"Stan doesn't sound Italian," Max noted.

"Oh, he's British," Asha said.

"Still alive?" I asked.

"Yes." Her head tilted. "You sound upset, Conrad. Are you certain you're okay?"

"I think Minister Quiff is full of hot air." Ambria huffed. "Then again, most adults are." Her eyes flashed wide. "No offense, Professor."

Asha laughed. "None taken, because I happen to agree with you."

"Thank goodness." Max breathed a sigh of relief. "For a moment, I thought Ambria made us fail your course."

"No, you'll have to pass or fail on your own merits, Mr. Tiberius." A smile lingered on Asha's lips. "Oh, how I miss Granddad Stan. I really should visit him soon."

I wondered if Victus implanted her with memories, or if Asha had simply rehearsed her lines over and over again. I wanted so badly to challenge her but didn't want to arouse her suspicions either, so I held my tongue and let the others talk.

"You certainly should," Ambria said. "I have no family, well"—she flashed a grin—"except for these two bumblers."

"You're one to talk." Max snorted. "My family is awful, and I prefer to avoid them whenever possible." He sighed. "My grandparents were just as bad as my parents."

Asha's smile faded. "None of you were blessed with good family, and for that, I am truly sorry." Her gaze lingered on me. "But sometimes, the family we make in life is every bit as good."

How can she sound so nice? I wanted to hate this demon clone, but a part of me wished more than anything that she was a real person—someone genuine instead of evil hiding behind an illusion. *If Delectra changed, why can't Asha?* Another realization hit me. *She might be a demon clone, but she's made from a fragment of my mother.* I allowed hope to penetrate the wall of anger. Maybe I could turn this infernus into my ally and preserve a small portion of the woman Victus had so callously murdered.

Determination swelled the hope, and my anger crumbled. I would turn Victus's own creation against him. Asha would become my ally. But I had to take it slow. The memories Della implanted in my mind had revealed a great deal about Victus's plans. I couldn't reveal to Asha what I knew until I felt certain she was on my side.

For now, everything had to remain between true friends.

"We should really get going," I said. "Class starts soon."

Ambria's forehead wrinkled, but she picked up on my hint and sighed. "Yes, I suppose we must."

Max, however, didn't get a clue. "Ugh, really? Galfandor is in a coma, I'm in emotional shock, and you want to go to class?"

"Yes, Max, we have to." Ambria elbowed him in the ribs.

Max grunted and blinked as he caught our mood. "Okay, then."

Asha smiled gently at us. "I'm certain the headmaster will recover from his episode. I'll see you tomorrow."

"Goodbye, Asha." I touched the top of her hand. "Thank you for your concern."

Emotion filled her eyes. "Any time, Conrad." She turned and walked back toward the dining hall where security now clustered around the doorway.

We headed toward our next class, Advanced Potions.

Ambria raised an eyebrow. "What's going on Conrad? Why were you so eager to leave Professor Fellini?"

I waited until we rounded the corner and made sure the hallway was clear before detailing the horrific revelations from my vision and summing it up with the terrible conclusion. "Asha is a demon golem and I think Victus plans to clone Galfandor so he can control the entire school!"

Ambria leaned against the wall, face ashen. "Asha is an infernus?"

"It makes sense now." Max slapped a hand against the stone wall. "No wonder she looks so similar to your mother."

"What do we do?" Ambria's question emerged like a frightened whimper. "Who else has Victus cloned? Who can we trust?"

I had no easy answer for her. I spun my finger in a circle between us. "Us three and Shushiel."

Max grunted. "In other words, the usual suspects."

"Exactly." I gave him a grim smile. "It's no different from any other time." That wasn't completely true. Galfandor and even Delectra had helped us and proven they could be trusted. But now the people we thought we knew could be impostors.

"The healers took Galfandor for treatment," Ambria said. "If his copy simply shows up one day, won't everyone know it's a fake?"

"Not if the healers are infernus working for Victus," Max said. He grimaced. "My god, there's no telling how deep this runs."

"What do you suppose those coffins are used for?" Ambria asked. "You said Delectra woke up in one?"

"Probably enchanted with preservation spells," Max said. "I'll bet Victus kidnaps people and puts them in the coffins so he can take soul fragments whenever he wants."

"Then why didn't he kidnap Galfandor?" I asked. "Why put him in a coma with a ripper wyrm?"

Ambria pursed her lips and tapped the bottom of her chin. "Maybe we're looking at this wrong." She stopped tapping. "Ansel and Galfandor were our supports. I think Victus wanted to remove them from our lives, not clone them."

Max sucked in a breath. "Wyrms don't take enough soul essence to harm unless the controller knows how to make them do it."

"Exactly." Ambria shook her head slowly. "And if you want to clone people so you can covertly take over the government, don't copy the most recognizable people. Copy the ones who support them."

"Like healers and clerks." Though I'd encountered plenty of them over the years, I couldn't remember a single face. "They're invisible to most people, unlike the politicians."

"Victus could have an entire network already." Ambria shrugged. "It just depends on how long it takes to make an infernus."

"Did you see where the foundry is?" Max asked. "If we could find it, we could look inside the coffins and know exactly who's affected."

"No." In the few visions I'd had, I hadn't walked outside of the building. The memory of the white house on the hill flickered like an afterimage in my mind. I tried to link the visions of the foundry with that place, but it didn't feel right. Delectra had been desperate in that memory, as if she were on the run.

"We need you to remember," Ambria said.

"I wish I could, but the memories come back at random." I leaned back against the wall and gently banged my head against it. "I need to know more."

"They're triggered somehow." Ambria stepped in front of me. "Haven't you been in unpleasant situations each time?"

I tried to remember specifics. "I think so."

"Maybe we need to replicate them." She shrugged. "It's worth a try."

"Too complicated," Max said. "What we need is a hypnosis spell."

"Or a memory extraction spell," Ambria replied. "Can't you just tap a wand on someone's head and pull them out?"

Max shook his head. "Never heard of such a thing. If I could do that, I'd pull out tons of memories and flush them down a toilet."

I laughed. "That's awful."

"Awful, but true." Max sighed. "My brothers once used a hypnosis spell on me. They told me I was a frog and made me hop around until my hands were bloody, and my knees were bruised and raw."

Ambria grimaced and put a hand over her mouth. "That's horrible, Max."

I put a hand on his back. "Do you remember being hypnotized?"

"Oh, yes," he said. "They ordered me to remember everything." His fists clenched and his face reddened. "That's a memory I'd love to flush away."

"Well, if Devon and Rhys managed a hypnosis spell, then we can." I looked inside the classroom to make sure it was still empty. "I'll bet there's one on file in the vault."

"How is hypnosis supposed to help?" Ambria said. "Can we order you to remember?"

"Absolutely," Max said. "It'd certainly be more convenient than waiting for another episode."

"Let's go there after class." I took a lab table near the back. Ambria nabbed the seat next to me.

"Hey, I wanted to be Conrad's lab partner," Max said.

Ambria shook her head. "It was punishment enough having to be your potions partner last year, Max! I want a better grade this time."

Max sighed and slumped into the seat at the table next to us. "I'm almost afraid to see who I get."

Lily was the first person to enter the classroom. She smiled brightly at us and considered Max for a moment. "I'm curious to see what disasters you brew up this year, Max!"

He groaned and looked down. "No one wants to be my lab partner."

"Well, you caused six of the ten potions accidents last year," Lily said. "I think it's safe to say you'll continue that trend." She took the table on the far side of the room. "I'll observe from a safe distance."

The other students filed in, all of them assiduously avoiding Max's table. Harris and Baxter entered, the latter holding a cold pack to his nose. Ambria giggled. Harris sat next to Lily, and Baxter took a seat next to the short and talkative Kimmy Kaspersky. Before long, everyone had seats and partners except for Max.

Professor Rhona McTrask entered, worry etched into the lines on her face. She began roll call only to be interrupted by a late Geoffrey Simmons. He saw the empty seat next to Max and groaned.

"It would seem you have the honors, Mr. Simmons," McTrask said in a sharp voice.

Max grinned at his new partner only to receive a glare from the short boy in return.

"It's the first day of class," McTrask announced. "A long road and a difficult year lies ahead as you start your advanced classes. Today we will learn a helpful potion that will strengthen your memory without any ill side effects."

"A forget-me-not potion?" Lily said brightly.

"Do not interrupt, child." McTrask gave her a stern look. "No, this is the Fortify Memory Longevity potion, or as we call it, the FML potion."

Lily didn't seem the least bit deterred and rubbed her hands with excitement.

McTrask wrote the ingredients and instructions on the board. "This potion helps your short-term memory convert into long-term storage in short ten-minute spurts. I recommend that you not use it more than once a day, as too much can cause diarrhea."

Snorts and murmurs of laughter echoed around the room, quickly quashed by a stern look from McTrask. "Start now."

The potion was fairly complex, requiring freshly squeezed fish oil, shaved carrots, and the crushed petals of forget-me-not flowers, among a host of other items. Ambria and I finished in thirty minutes, boiling the dark mixture and then rapidly cooling it with a freeze spell to turn it crystal clear.

Max and his unwilling potions partner bickered constantly until the two of them stopped working together and began mixing their own separate potions.

McTrask tested our concoction, declared it acceptable, then did the same for Lily and Harris's. Nearly half the class had finished when Max reached the final stage of boiling. He aimed his wand at the potion and zapped it with a stronger freeze spell than the one prescribed by McTrask.

The mixture froze in an instant. The beaker cracked and broke apart, leaving a black cylinder of ice behind.

Geoffrey finished his potion, managing a cloudy solution that barely earned a passing grade from McTrask.

"No, no, no." Max threw up his hands. "What happened?"

Harris and Baxter burst into laughter.

"Making popsicles, Tiberius?" Baxter said. "What flavor is it? Dirt?"

Max snapped off a chunk of jagged ice from the top of his ruined potion and threw it at Baxter. "Why don't you taste it!" The ice shattered on Baxter's lab table and vaporized into black gas.

Kimmy threw up her hands and shouted in surprise, as the vapors flashed past her and Baxter before dissipating. The pair of them blinked and stared at their completed potion with almost comical confusion.

"What?" Baxter rotated the beaker. "How is it done? We were only halfway there!"

"It just changed right in front of my eyes!" Kimmy said. "How did you do that?"

"What do you mean?" McTrask said. "What stage were you working on?"

"Heating up the solution," Kimmy said. "We have to heat it for eight minutes, then cool it for two."

"You don't remember doing any of that?" McTrask asked.

Baxter and Kimmy looked at each other, foreheads furrowed, then shook their heads. "No."

"Don't remember making fun of Mr. Tiberius's botched potion?" she asked.

Baxter looked at the black ice on Max's desk and burst into laughter. "What happened, Tiberius? Making popsicles?"

Max ignored the jibe and grinned at the frozen concoction on his lab table. "It made them forget the last ten minutes!"

Rhona McTrask face-palmed and shook her head. "Only you could turn a memory fortification potion into a memory loss potion, Mr. Tiberius."

Max clapped his hands and grinned. "Awesome!"

"You have thirty minutes to clean up that mess and create the proper potion before I give you a failing grade for the day."

Max bit his lower lip and nodded. "Got it." He grabbed a mason jar and put the ice inside, closing the lid tightly. "Maybe I can use this stuff to make me forget my father is the new Arcanus Primus."

Ambria giggled. "Max, you're a mess."

Max managed to earn a satisfactory grade before the end of class, and we hurried to Advanced Enchantments with a new professor, Devon Mallory.

It was hard not to compare the tall, flamboyantly dressed professor to the bald and often absent Professor Sideon he replaced. Sideon, of course, had been Victus in disguise. In retrospect, is lessons about enchanted objects now seemed more about what relics he wanted to enhance his own power.

Mallory started with basic enchantments, quizzing us on what we should have learned in previous years to make sure our false professor hadn't led us too far astray. He stroked his silky pink tie as he listened to our answers, nodding and applauding as appropriate.

"Wonderful, children." He clapped, moving his hands in a circle as he did so. "Give yourselves a round of applause for remembering the basics!"

Ambria and Lily mimicked him, delighted smiles on their faces, though other students looked perplexed at the marked difference in this man's attitude compared to other professors. Praise was rarely, if ever, handed out by the likes of Gideon Grace and Rhona McTrask.

"Advanced enchantments are just basic enchantments layered together," Mallory said piling his hands one over the other repeatedly. "Just like advanced spells, you need to know how to merge them together so you don't get any unexpected explosions."

Ambria and I gave Max a wary look to which he shrugged and said, "I'll do my best."

By the end of class, I couldn't help but feel empowered by Professor Mallory's encouraging attitude. He was certainly a far cry from the false Professor Sideon.

After class, we hurried to the broom closet so we could get to the vault and test a hypnosis spell on me. Max carefully tucked his anti-memory potion in the saddlebags on his broom so it wouldn't break in transit.

"I wonder if I invented another new potion," he said as we boarded our brooms.

"What good is a potion that makes you forget the last ten minutes?" Ambria said.

Max grinned. "I'd love to use it repeatedly on my brothers. Maybe I can make them braindead."

"Just don't go testing it on me," Ambria said.

My arcphone buzzed with a call from Percival. "Yes?"

The healer spoke without preamble. "Did your cousin suffer from any allergies? Did he take any prescribed medications?"

I'd seen Ansel take all sorts of medications and recreational drugs during our training sessions. "Yes, why?"

"I need a list," Percival said. "Do you know where he lives?"

"Down in Queens Gate." I'd been there once to get a new spell program from him. "Do you think he keeps a list there?"

"A list?" Percival sniffed. "No, of course not. I need you to check his medicine cabinet and send me a list of potions he's taking."

The hypnosis spell would have to wait. "Okay, we'll do it." I ended the call and told my friends what Percival wanted.

Ambria hopped on her broom. "Well, let's do it, then we'll find the hypnosis spell."

"Should we fly or use a portal?" Max said.

"I don't remember what Ansel's house looks well enough like to open a portal there," I said. "Let's just fly."

We headed out over the cliff on our brooms and dove into the valley below, heading toward the dingy gray and decrepit northeastern side of Queens Gate. Hulking mansions packed the cobblestone streets, but they'd seen better days. Shuttered windows and peeling paint told a story of neglect and abuse.

Most of the houses were abandoned, making the neighborhood a lonely place, and probably the reason Ansel decided to squat in this part of town. We set down in front of a dark gray house with barred windows and stout steel doors. The house stood two stories high with hardwood porches wrapping around the front and sides. It could have once been a quaint bed and breakfast, but now it looked like a stylish prison.

Max opened his mouth to say something, but Ambria clamped a hand on his face and pointed at the doors. One of them hung slightly ajar. I guided my broom closer so I didn't have to walk across the wooden porch, and peeked inside. I couldn't see anything so I landed the broom and got off.

Footsteps clomped on the porch from the left, but I couldn't tell if they were upstairs or on our level. I motioned for Ambria and Max to go. They zipped across the street on their brooms and hid inside an alley between houses. Ambria spun around and gave me a horrified look when she saw me still on the porch. I grabbed my broom and slipped inside the house.

The smart move would have been to run, but I had to know what was going on. The scene inside made it clear—broken furniture, strewn books and paper, shattered glass. Someone was looking for something. I slipped into the kitchen and ducked behind a broken cupboard as the front door opened.

"Nevil, the place is trashed," a woman called. "There's nothing good left!"

Hard-soled shoes clomped down the stairs. "Those men were looking for something valuable, and I don't think they found it."

"They looked for three days, Nevil!" The woman sighed. "What makes you think we can find something they didn't?"

"I'll bet it's in the walls," Nevil said. "Let's go get a sledgehammer."

"Are you kidding me? I'm out of here!" The front door slammed.

"Hey, baby, wait!" The door opened and shut again. I peered through the window and saw a short, bald man chasing a skinny woman down the front sidewalk. He grabbed her arm and the pair got into a heated shouting match.

The woman jerked free and walked away. The man threw up his hands and looked back at the mansion, back to her, to the mansion again, and finally took off running after her. Max and Ambria ran across the street and into the house once the couple of looters walked around the corner.

"Conrad?" Ambria whispered.

I came out of the kitchen. "I'm here."

She shook a fist at me. "Don't you ever do that again."

"I thought it would be easier if just one of us had to sneak inside." I gestured at the wreckage. "Maybe there's no connection, but what are the odds that Ansel was hit by a wyrm and then his house was tossed?"

"Oh, it's gotta be connected," Max said. "Maybe Ansel had something Victus wants."

"What do you think it could be?" Ambria said.

I shook my head, unable to come up with anything. "Victus probably knew Ansel is Delectra's nephew. Maybe he thought she gave him something."

"Maybe." Ambria stepped carefully through the wreckage and peered into the neighboring rooms. "There's so much furniture and this house is huge. I'll bet there are lots of hiding spots."

"Yeah. From what those two said, whoever did this didn't find what they were looking for." I wondered what it was, but in the short term, I had another mission. I went upstairs and looked through the bedrooms. Broken wood and glass strewn everywhere, the mattresses ripped open, stuffing hanging out. Only one bathroom had toiletries, and they were smashed open, toothpaste and even soap squeezed out into the sink. The potions cabinet hung open, the glass vials empty or broken on the countertop.

I dug through the broken glass for the labels. Careful not to cut my fingers, I picked up the four I found and took pictures of them. *Clarity, Probiotic, Dandle, Kefarin.* I knew what clarity and probiotic were, but hadn't heard of the other two. I sent the image to Percival along with a query.

Ah, yes, he texted back. *Dandle and Kefarin are used to combat hyper-allergenic response.*

"Should we look around?" Ambria said.

Max looked around warily. "What if that couple comes back?"

"I don't know how we could find what they were looking for," I said. "Let's take care of the hypnosis thing first, then we can come back here."

Ambria nodded. "Agreed."

I grabbed my broom. We went back out, made sure no one was in sight, retrieved Max and Ambria's brooms, then flew back up to the university. We headed back to the keep, to the vault's hidden door and inside. Instead of searching the aisles, I flew to the table where we'd left Adam Nosti's spell coding tutorials and looked through the library of pre-programmed spells—or spellgrams, as he called them.

Max vanished into the aisles and returned with a box of empty glass spheres. He opened the jar with his still frozen potion.

"How in the world hasn't it thawed?" Ambria peered closely at the black ice. "It's been nearly two hours now."

Max carefully sliced a chunk of ice and tossed it several feet. It shattered and vaporized into black gas. "I don't know, but it sure is neat!" He carved the ice with an enchanted heat knife and traced a symbol on a glass sphere. The side split open wide enough for him to drop the ice inside and then closed up again. He continued the process until he had at least a dozen potion bombs.

I continued searching the spell index until Max jabbed a finger at the screen. "Right there."

The category read, *Neuro Magics*. I touched it and found a list of individual spells in alphabetical order. Hypnosis spells were right where they should be. Some of them were for hypno-therapy, and at least five of them were designed to play jokes on specific individuals. Max downloaded those to his arcphone.

Ambria narrowed her eyes. "I hope you don't mean to use one of those on me, Max."

Max grunted. "Don't worry. I'll only use these on my brothers."

I opened the spell titled *Hypnosis Memory Therapy*. The code looked complex, but Adam Nosti had simplified the execution of the spellgram to a simple button touch. I handed the device to Max. "Don't scramble my brain, okay?"

Max chuckled. "I'll try not to mess you up too badly."

"I'll make certain he behaves," Ambria said.

I handed her my arcphone. "Can you record everything?"

"Yes." Her hand lingered on mine. She blinked rapidly and pulled it away. "Recording." She held the phone camera toward me.

"It says in the instructions that you have to be relaxed," Max told me. "Take deep breaths and clear your mind."

I leaned back in the chair and did as instructed. "I'm ready—I hope."

Max pursed his lips and fiddled with the arcphone. Forehead furrowed in concentration, he flicked the screen and frowned. "I think this is it."

"It's just a button, right?" I blinked and the world changed in a heartbeat.

I stood in a grassy clearing, tall trees all around me. Sunlight shone on my face. Birds chirped and something rustled in the bushes at the fringe of the meadow. I gasped and backed up a step. My heel caught on something soft. I fell and landed in a puddle.

Crimson splashed around me. Dead eyes stared from a pale face—the face of a young woman.

CHAPTER 19

Burn marks covered the woman's flesh. Blood dripped from a gash in her throat. Horror squeezed my heart. I tried to shout, but my throat closed with terror.

Is this a dream? Am I still under hypnosis? I held up my hands. A wand clenched in my right, the left, open and empty but for mud and blood. My shoulder ached and I quickly discovered why. My shirt was charred, the skin beneath blistered and raw.

"This isn't a dream," I rasped. I stood up and instantly regretted it. Daggers of pain stabbed into my head. I staggered, recovered. My shoulder hurt so much, I could barely think straight. I saw another huddled form in the grass not far away.

Dread swelled in my chest, but I stepped closer. A middle-aged man splayed on his back, a gaping hole in his midriff. A third body lay not far from his. I didn't understand what I was seeing. Had I been in a fight? Had these people attacked me?

Did I kill them?

The breeze blew a rotten stench in my face. I gagged and put my shirt over my nose to block the assault. A long mound of dirt near the edge of the meadow caught my eye. I walked toward it. The stench in the air and the dread in my chest grew stronger with every step. I walked up the mound and fell to my knees.

So many! I heaved and emptied my stomach, unable to hold it in any longer. Flies buzzed around a pile of bodies, horrified faces frozen in death, bodies lying haphazardly where they'd been thrown.

Voices echoed from the forest.

"This way," a deep male voice shouted.

I bolted like a panicked cat and tripped over my own feet. The world spun. I rolled down the mound and into the corpses at the bottom of the trench. The empty eye sockets of a rotting old man gazed back at me. I stifled a scream. My stomach heaved, but I had nothing to throw up this time. The voices grew closer.

Scrambling out of the trench, I rolled into the bushes at the fringe of the meadow and lay on my belly in a blanket of pine needles. Two men in black robes emerged from the opposite side. I recognized them from the riot in the Grotto. They wore thick beards and held gnarled staffs, pale imitations of their master, Garkin.

The first stopped at the dead woman and nudged her with a foot. "She's definitely dead, so it wasn't her I saw."

"Two measly days, Chachi," the second said. "The last pair took us a week of camping and hunting to track down."

"These idiots tried to circle around," the first, Chachi, said. "They must think we're stupid." He looked expectantly at his companion. "So, Jonas, if it wasn't one of these you saw running through the woods a moment ago, then who the hell was it?"

Jonas shrugged. "I saw something running through the bushes at me so I hit it with a spell. When I went over to find the body, nothing was there."

"Something or someone?"

"Um, I didn't really get a good look."

"They wouldn't release another candidate from the white boxes without telling us. Probably just an animal." Chachi scowled at the bodies. "Let's get these in the trench then head back and tell Garkin."

Garkin, a familiar female voice growled in my head. *Jonas and Chachi must die.*

I almost gasped. *Della?*

Hatred. Fear. Seething rage.

Emotions that were not my own roiled inside me. My fist clenched around my wand. I crawled from cover, slithered onto the grass and along the mound of dirt on the backside of the trench.

No! Stop! I couldn't control myself. Couldn't fight off the inferno of hate burning in my heart.

Jonas and Chachi each carried a body slung over their shoulders. I sneaked around behind them as they joked about easy kills, about the hunts to come and the fun they would have tracking down helpless unarmed prey.

I stood, feeling taller, more powerful, and seething with the uncontrollable urge for revenge. "Looking for me?" My voice hissed with a feminine quality.

The men dropped the bodies and spun, hands reaching for wands. Two quick blasts from my wand severed their hands at the wrists. They screamed, hands clutching cauterized flesh, mirroring each other in a dance of pain.

"Who are you?" Chachi shouted. "Who the hell are you?"

I walked closer, wand out, a cruel smile stretching my lips. "Remember when your master made me your prey? Remember what you did when you caught me? How he allowed you to torture me?"

Jonas's eyes widened with surprise even as he nursed his stump. "That's Conrad Edison!"

Recognition flared in Chachi's eyes. "But we never caught him."

"Conrad?" My voice hissed with derision. "I am Delectra, you fools."

Their mouths dropped open, eyes blank with incomprehension.

"But—but you're dead," Jonas whispered.

"You hunted me," I hissed. "You caught me."

"That was years ago," Chachi said. "Victus told us to punish you!"

"And you did." My voice cackled madly even as I struggled to overcome whatever possessed my body. My arm thrust out the wand. "Now it is my turn."

"Impossible!" Jonas said. "He's just a boy. Delectra is dead!"

"How would this kid know anything about—" Chachi's sentence ended in a scream of pain. Sizzling light from the tip of my wand sliced through his arm just below the shoulder. Rage burned through my veins, matched only by the energy surging through my body. The spell flicked off an instant, just long enough to switch to the other side of Chachi's body and slice off his other arm.

Jonas bolted to his feet and tried to run. Another laser blast lopped off a leg below the knee and he went down in a heap. My possessed body butchered Chachi, cutting off his legs above the knees, leaving cauterized stumps behind. His torso wriggled in the grass, his screams abruptly ending as he lost consciousness.

Jonas rolled on his back, whimpering and looking up at me. He was a burly man, but he looked helpless as a little boy in that instant. "Perhaps I should dismember the offending bits first," the angry spirit within me said. "Perhaps emasculation is enough."

"God, no! Victus told us to punish you!" Jonas held up his arms defensively. Two angry swipes with the wand sliced them off at the elbows. He screamed in agony.

The wand slashed back and forth, burning orange rays carving Jonas from a man to a squealing pig. Flesh sizzled, instantly cauterized. Not even a drop of blood was spilled as the ghost of Della delivered what she believed was justice.

STOP! I screamed over and over again, struggling to take back control. These men were terrible, inhuman creatures, but butchering them like this was just as bad as their crimes. My knees went weak and my vision flickered. I stumbled forward, fell.

When I opened my eyes, the screaming had stopped. The sun hung lower on the horizon. Bushes rustled, leaves crackled. I heard murmurs near the tree line and staggered to my feet. Two figures burst through the bushes. I threw up my wand hand, but it was empty. I looked down in confusion and saw it poking out of the mud.

"Conrad!" The shadows hid the face, but I knew Ambria's voice instantly. She sprang forward, embraced me. "You're injured! What happened?"

Max lurched from the bushes. His eyes locked onto something behind me and went wide as dinner plates. He made retching noises and dropped to his knees.

Ambria looked in the direction and shrieked. "What happened?" Wild emotions flickered in her eyes. "My god, what's that smell?"

"Where am I?" I rasped. "How did I get here?"

Max tried to speak, but bent over and heaved again.

Ambria took my hand and led me into the forest. Tears brimmed in her eyes. "Conrad, something went horribly wrong with the hypnosis. Max and I asked you questions about the foundry, but you kept saying you didn't know. Then Max asked if Della was still inside your soul."

"She's not." At least her soul fragment wasn't. "But she left something behind. Memories, I think."

"Well, whatever she left you with, it took over." Ambria winced. "At first, she answered our questions, but then Max asked her to show us where the foundry was. He meant for her to show us on a map. Instead, you ran out of the vault and vanished. We looked everywhere, but couldn't find you."

I looked around at the trees. "This isn't the Dark Forest."

Ambria shook her head slowly. "No, it's not. We realized that you might be travelling to the foundry, and the quickest way would be through the omniarch."

"I took a portal here?"

She nodded. "Yes." Ambria held up my arcphone, a map on the screen. She tapped a finger on the blue dot indicating our location then pinched to zoom out. We weren't in England or even Europe anymore, but all the way across the pond in the United States—Montana to be precise.

"We're in the middle of nowhere." I flinched as Max gasped for air.

"What in god's name happened to that man?" he asked.

I blinked as Jonas and Chachi's earlier discussion echoed in my mind. "We're near the foundry now." I turned toward the trench. "All those dead people are somehow connected."

"Did you say people, as in plural?" Max shuddered. "I'm feeling sick again."

"Two men hunted down unarmed people and killed them." Gory images of their mutilated flesh flashed before my eyes. "I was hiding from them, but something up here"—I tapped my temple—"snapped. Della took control of me and attacked them."

"Attacked is a mild term for what you did to that man," Max said. "He's got no arms or legs!"

Ambria shivered. "Della killed them?"

I looked back over my shoulder, but the bushes obscured a view of Jonas. "They weren't dead earlier. Her spell cauterized the wounds."

"You said something about dead people," Max said.

"There's a trench where Jonas and Chachi dumped them." A faint rotten odor ticked my nose, or was it just my imagination?

"Chachi and Jonas?" Ambria raised an eyebrow. "I didn't realize you were on a first-name basis with them."

"I overheard their names." I choked down my rising gorge. "Apparently, Victus let them punish Delectra after she disobeyed him some time ago. They did something so terrible to her that Della took revenge." I took a deep breath to ward off the nausea. "I don't want to think about it anymore."

"Neither do I." Max squeezed his eyelids shut and opened them.

"I take it the foundry is nearby?" Ambria said.

I nodded. "Yes, but I don't know where."

Max peered into my eyes. "Is Della still lurking in there?"

I took a moment to evaluate my mental state. My shoulder hurt. My knees ached. I felt sore all over. But the presence I'd felt earlier was gone. "I think I'm more or less back to normal."

"You look awful," Max said. "Percival needs a look at you."

"Can he help me unsee what Della made me do?" I looked down at my filthy hands. Even now, they seemed like foreign appendages.

Ambria put a hand on the side of her face and stared out at the meadow. "We should get Conrad patched up, then come back and find the foundry."

"No." I shook my head. "Let's find it now."

"You sure?" Max put a hand on my good shoulder and peered into my eyes. "I don't want Della taking over again."

"She won't." I wished I felt as certain of that as I sounded.

I led the others around the edge of the meadow, determined to avoid the trench of bodies and the unfortunate Chachi and Jonas. I heard moaning and tried to ignore it. Apparently, one of the men was still alive.

"It would be a mercy to kill them," Ambria murmured. She gasped. "Is that an evil thought, Conrad?"

I shook my head. "You don't have an evil bone in your body." My body trembled as I suffered another flashback to the butchery.

"You don't either," she said quickly. "It wasn't you who did that, Conrad."

"I wonder what they did to Delectra," Max wondered aloud. "Must have been awful."

"Maybe she was justified." Ambria looked back and forth at us as if seeking agreement.

Max shrugged. "All I know is that I'd have to be insanely mad to cut off someone's arms and legs for revenge."

I let the conversation die, since talking about it served as a constant reminder. Thankfully, a well-trodden footpath caught our attention and drew us back into the forest, this time on the opposite side of the meadow. We remained quiet and alert, keeping a steady pace through the woods. The path widened and the trees thinned until we stood at the edge of a field of towering mud buttes, their steep sides riddled with holes.

Most rose the equivalent of three stories. I ran a finger along the rough surface as we followed the path inside a tunnel. Grit sprinkled down the side. We emerged from the other side and wended our way through a sandstone canyon. Small caves and dead-ends provided the only hiding places, should anyone come.

We listened for voices, heard none, and continued down the path until it ended at a sprawling butte with a gaping cave mouth. I hesitated outside and cocked an ear toward the opening. The ache in my shoulder grew with every passing minute, but I didn't want to leave without seeing the foundry. Della had imprinted the memories, burned them into my mind, for a reason.

Faint noises emanated from within, but I couldn't tell if they were voices, or simply the susurrus of wind blowing through an empty space.

Ambria gave me a worried look, quickly joined by Max. I steeled my nerves and pushed onward. The air cooled noticeably the moment I crossed the threshold. Small glowballs provided dim, yellow light. The tunnel curved and ended less than fifty feet later in a large, empty room. It looked circular at first, but I picked out edges and corners. Nine walls in all. The dim light glinted off faintly glowing lines in the floor.

I edged toward the center and my perspective changed, revealing an intricate pattern carved into the bedrock. My vision swam when I tried to follow even one line, like looking at a three-dimensional painting designed to trick the eyes.

Ambria knelt and looked sideways. "It hovers off the floor," she whispered.

Max dropped next to her and gasped. "I've never seen anything like it."

"It's a demon summoning pattern." In all the demon patterns we'd seen in Emily Glass's demonomicon, none of them looked quite like this. It seemed to be several patterns all drawn into one intricate diagram by a master. *Victus did this.* "Demon flesh, soul fragments." I darted my eyes toward the others. "This must be the foundry."

"This is where Victus makes the infernus?" Max hugged himself and shivered. "What kind of demon does this pattern summon?"

Ambria backed away from it. "Something powerful."

An open doorway on the opposite side of the room drew my attention. I started to walk over the pattern, changed my mind, and skirted around it. I had a feeling that even touching the pattern might alert the demon it summoned. I wasn't sure if my caution came from my own thoughts, or one Della had left behind.

Max and Ambria caught up with me. Neither looked eager to keep going, and both had their wands out at the ready. I reached down to draw mine, and realized it was already in my hand. I reached the doorway and peered through. A narrow passage stretched for only ten feet before ending in an exit.

I crept through, ears and eyes alert, poked my head around the edge of the exit. Another large space stretched out before me, but this one wasn't empty. Coffins ranging in appearance from plain to ornate occupied most of the floor space. *They're not coffins.* Della had described them as preservation chambers. I still couldn't help but feel like I was in a morgue or a funeral home. I'd been to a lot of funerals, seen a lot of people die due to the living curse Victus had put on me. This place felt no different.

Dozens of plain white coffins were piled in a corner, some stacked atop one another in lopsided fashion. Shiny black coffins occupied much of the middle of the room, most bearing white stickers with names on them. Isolated from the others in the far corner sat ruby-red preservation chambers shaped like flat-topped ovals and covered in intricate runes.

"I get the feeling that the red ones are more important than the white ones," Max whispered.

"Yeah." I tried to take another step, but apprehension filled me. *We should leave this instant.* Victus could walk into this room at any minute. But I couldn't leave, not now. I had to see what was inside the red coffins.

Ambria beat me to it, jogging through the aisles between the black coffins to the back of the room. Max and I caught up to her and stopped in front of the first red chamber. It had more runes than most, but was slightly smaller than the others, a diamond-shaped glass lid on top.

Unlike the black coffins, there were no name tags to tell us the identities of the occupants. But it only took a quick glance to recognize the girl who slumbered inside, a peaceful look on her face. I'd seen pictures of her and heard the stories.

"My god," Max whispered. "That's Ivy Slade!"

CHAPTER 20

I t was no wonder Ivy Slade had vanished all those years ago. The mystery instead was, "How in the world did my father capture her? I thought she helped defeat him."

"Maybe Cumberbatch did it," Ambria said.

"If that's Ivy, was does she look so young?" I peered through the glass. "Shouldn't she be eighteen or nineteen by now?"

"Maybe these preservation chambers keep people from aging." Ambria touched the glass near Ivy's face. "I can't believe it's really her."

"How does this thing open?" Max ran his fingers along the edges. "We've got to get her out."

I searched my memories, but found no solution to the puzzle. While Max worked on it, I darted to the other boxes. One held a lovely woman with dark hair, the next two nothing, and the fourth preserved a withered husk that might once have been a man. I rushed past the other coffins, but none of the faces looked familiar.

"Can't get it," Max growled. He grabbed my shirt. "Conrad, don't you see? If we rescue Ivy, she can defeat Victus again. We'll be unstoppable!"

Ambria gripped his wrist. "You sound mad, Max. Calm yourself."

Despite the pain his grappling caused my shoulder, I agreed with Max. Voices echoed behind us. I looked toward the back wall not far away and saw another doorway partially concealed by the stack of white coffins. Footsteps and loud voices filled the corridor beyond.

We were out of time.

I thought of hiding so we could stay and figure out this puzzle, but I didn't dare hide inside one of the preservation chambers. The white coffins were too tightly packed to hide behind. Besides, I was injured and tired. We needed to return home to heal and think. Worried looks from Max and Ambria told me they were thinking the same thing.

We raced across the room, through the connecting corridor, and into the foundry. Once again, we skirted the huge pattern and made for the exit.

A tall, thin figure appeared from the exit. Black suit, a crimson tie patterned with pentagrams, shiny leather shoes. Shaved temples bordered thick black hair on the crown. His cold gaze and flickering blue eyes sent shivers down my spine. It was the same man we'd seen outside Ansel's office. The same one who'd unleashed a wyrm on Galfandor.

He didn't smile, didn't alter his expression when he saw us. Instead he stopped as if to block our retreat. The ground to either side of him turned oily black. A head, still covered in the dark slime, pushed through the puddle to his left. A long muzzle formed, glowing red eyes flickered on. A body stood on wobbling legs and the shape became all-too familiar.

"He's summoning hellhounds!" Ambria shouted.

Max fired a shot of electrical energy from his wand. The man—the Daemos—blurred to the side. Much as I loathed what Della had done to those men, I took myself back to those terrible moments and remembered how she'd cast her deadly spell. It was a multi-pattern spell, one that would have taken me months if not years to master by myself. It required enormous power, explaining my fatigued state.

I didn't even try to land a hit on the man. I flicked the wand through the patterns, layering several destructions spells atop the other, weaving them into something far more malevolent, into something Della called *Fireblade*. The patterns melded and took form. All they needed now was focus and will.

The first shot flew wide, carving a gash into the stone wall. I slashed the wand downward and bisected the first hellhound as it struggled to break free of the primordial goo. The creature yelped, and the magic binding its form fell apart, the pieces melting into the oily substance. I dragged Fireblade straight across to the other hellhound. The Daemos blurred out of the path and slid to a stop. His teeth bared in anger as I sliced up his second demonic pet.

"Run!" I shouted, keeping the spell ready at the tip of my wand, but not firing it.

"Who are you, boy?" the Daemos said as we ran past.

I kept my wand leveled at him as I ran, aware he could probably blur over and snatch it from my hand in an instant if I let down my guard. "Who are *you*?"

He shot toward us. Max shouted in alarm. Glass shattered and a cloud of black gas billowed twenty feet from us. The Daemos whooshed through it and skidded to a stop, face screwed up with confusion. We rounded the corner and dashed through the exit.

"Was that your anti-memory potion?" Ambria panted, never looking back as she outpaced me and Max.

Max gulped air. "Yep—Memory Fog." He sucked in another breath. "I meant to grab Banana Peel!"

"What in the world is Banana Peel?" I asked.

"The slippery potion I invented last year." He stumbled over a root, but kept his balance as we left the trail and raced across the meadow. "I even made the last batch yellow to match the name."

During our potions class the previous year, Max had used peppered snails instead of toasted slugs for a cleansing potion and created an oily substance so slippery that it was nearly frictionless. He'd even been granted a certificate verifying that he'd created a brand new potion, albeit by accident.

I met the lifeless eyes of Jonas where I'd left him in the field. Not surprisingly, his wounds proved too severe to survive. I spotted Chachi face down in the dirt only a few feet away. He'd apparently tried to wriggle his way across to Jonas and died for his effort.

"Wait!" I stopped and steeled myself for what we had to do.

Ambria gave me a confused look but stopped. "Conrad, we can't just stop. That man could catch us in a heartbeat!"

"That's just it." I looked back but saw no signs of pursuit. "Max hit him with memory fog. He'll forget everything for the last ten minutes."

Max's eyebrows rose. "Hey, you're right. We don't need to run anymore."

"It's not just that." I swallowed the sickening knot forming in my throat. "It means he's forgotten that we know where this place is. It means we can come back and rescue Ivy without them expecting it."

Ambria's lips peeled back into a horrified grimace. "It means we have to hide these bodies, doesn't it?"

I nodded. "They can't find any trace of us here." I gagged just thinking about the trench beyond the piles of dirt on the other side of the meadow. "We have to dump the body parts into the trench and cover them with other corpses."

Max heaved and made retching noises. "I—I can't!"

Ambria shivered and hugged herself. "You can and you will, Max." She swallowed hard and looked at Chachi and Jonas's dismembered limbs. "Now, go grab those arms and throw them in the pit."

Max put a hand over his mouth and turned green. "I'm going to use memory fog on myself after this is over."

Ambria nodded fervently. "Oh, yes. Maybe on me too."

I knelt next to Chachi's torso. "Ambria, can you help me, please?"

She blanched, but knelt and grabbed handfuls of Chachi's shirt. "This is ghastly."

The effort of holding down my rising gorge prevented me from answering. We half-dragged, half-carried the torso to the trench and rolled it in. Then we retrieved Jonas's parts. Max located the limbs and threw them next to their previous owners before rushing into the woods and throwing up. When he came back, it took three of us to move some of the fresher bodies on top of Chachi and Jonas until they were fully concealed.

"That took much longer than ten minutes," Ambria said. "The memory fog won't help now, will it?"

Max shook his head sadly. "Now we can never unsee it."

I hadn't planned on using it anyway. "I don't think we should ever forget this." I realized that I could barely smell the stench of the dead anymore. "Victus is a monster. All of this is his doing."

Ambria nodded somberly. "Well, if we can't forget it, can we at least go home and bathe?"

"For once, I'm not even hungry," Max said in a small voice. "I just want to go home."

I couldn't agree more. We took one last look around to make sure we hadn't left any obvious traces and then headed into the forest, back toward the portal I'd left open while hypnotized. An old log cabin appeared between the trees, its roof sunken, weeds and flowers growing from the mud joints, but otherwise seemed in good shape for a building abandoned to the forest.

The gateway hung open in what had once been a small garden, evident by the chicken wire and log border around a patch of land. Something oddly familiar about this place tugged me toward the crooked door, a lone hinge holding it in place. I couldn't stop myself from walking inside.

I run giggling past the tall furniture. A simple leather couch sits in the middle of the room. Rustic wooden chairs surround a thick table, and a fire crackles in the brick hearth. This is where we come when Mommy needs to sneak away.

"Got you!" Gentle hands tickle my ribs and pull me in for a firm hug on the leather couch.

I burst into delighted laughter and look into the lovely young face of my mother. Delectra kisses my forehead and sighs. A lone tear trickles down her cheek. "I wish I could spare you, Conrad." More tears join the first. "I wish it more than anything."

"Spare?" I mispronounce the "r" like a "w", my tiny voice that of a toddler.

She doesn't seem to hear me, lost in her own world. "I can't risk it. Not again." Delectra wipes her tears and kisses my forehead. "I'm so sorry, my dear." Her face twists with pain. "No, go away."

"Is it the bad you again?" I ask.

She shivers. "Yes, Conrad. The bad me."

I flinched. The rotted leather couch sat in the middle of the room, its insides torn out. The remains of the table and chairs were scattered across the dusty floor. Cobwebs hung from the rafters, and the charred remains of old wood resided in the fireplace.

"I remember this place." The corner of a book protruded from beneath the couch. I knelt down and slid it out. Someone had scored the title with a knife, but I knew what it was without even thinking. *The Family Picnic.*

"I remember this book." Ambria took it and leafed to the first page. "It was in the library at the orphanage."

"I didn't read much at the orphanage." I looked at the illustrations on the first few pages, a perfect family preparing for a picnic. Mom, Dad, little Jimmy and Susy, and their pet dog, Patches.

"I hated it," Ambria said in a rough voice. "It was a reminder of something I could never have. Sometimes, I think the Goodleighs put it in the library as a cruel joke."

"I don't think we should stick around much longer," Max said. "I mean, what if that Daemos didn't lose his memory and is coming after us?"

"He would have caught us already," Ambria said.

I walked around the cabin, dazed at how familiar it felt. A bed, a small stove, and a kitchen counter occupied the two rooms. I vaguely remembered coming here on several occasions.

Delectra reads The Family Picnic *to me. The door bursts open. She screams. Two men rush inside and tear the book from her grasp. Jonas stabs it with a long knife, a cruel grin stretching his lips.*

"Well, isn't this a lovely refuge?" Chachi slashes the couch with his knife.

Delectra reaches for her wand on the nearby table, but Jonas kicks it away.

He waggles a finger at her. "Victus knows you plan to run again, Delectra."

"Yeah." Chachi tuts. "He asked us to talk to you."

Jonas laughs. "Yeah, exactly."

They rush her. I'm swept aside by their huge bodies and tumble into a heap in the corner where I cower in fear.

I shouted and flailed with my arms. The book flew from my grasp and tumbled onto the floor. My heart pounded and sweat beaded on my forehead. Thankfully, the memories from that night were too faded for me to recall much more. I had some inkling as to why Della's revenge had been so severe.

Some people need to die. Some deserve to die in agony.

I wondered what Chachi and Jonas's parents were like to have raised such wicked sons. Or had Victus taken ordinary people and turned them into monsters? If he did it to his own wife, I didn't see what would stop him from doing it to strangers.

"Do I even want to know?" Max asked.

"No, but I'll tell you anyway." I shuddered and told my friends what I'd seen when first entering the cabin, and the last vision.

Ambria wept and hugged me. "I'm so sorry, Conrad."

"I'm sorry too, but there's nothing we can do about the past." I stumbled back outside, eager to leave this place behind. I stopped before the portal. The small room on the other side beckoned to me, a safe space with no memory triggers. "At least now I know why Della's memories made me open the portal here." I stepped through. The world stretched and twisted, and I stood in the omniarch room near the underground mansion.

I closed the gateway the moment Ambria and Max crossed the threshold. Even though I hadn't looked long at the front of the cabin, its image was seared into my mind. I would have no problem opening another portal there.

A shadowy figure stepped from concealment near the wall.

We jumped in unison, gasping and shouting, but it was just Kanaan.

"You did well," he said. "You did what must be done to survive."

"You followed us?" Ambria's voice rose an octave. "Why didn't you help?"

"I would have if necessary." The magitsu master folded his arms and regarded me. "You have deep inner strength and conviction, but you will be very sick after casting such powerful magic."

Nausea had slowly squirmed its way up my guts ever since running from the foundry, but I'd thought it was from the dead bodies. Kanaan's words made me realize it was actually magic poisoning—common in novice Arcanes after channeling more aether than they were used to.

He tossed me a wax wrapper with purple gum inside—one of Percival's potion treatments for my symptoms. I gratefully tore it open and chewed it, hoping it would alleviate the sickness.

"You could have helped us rescue Ivy," Max said to Kanaan. "How could you just watch us and do nothing?"

"The case requires a magic word," he said. "When you ran, I remained behind in case Zarin chased you."

Ambria raised an eyebrow. "Zarin?"

"The Daemos you battled." Kanaan nodded at Max. "The potion you used made him forget the incident. When he recovered from his confusion, he went into the next chamber and met with Victus, Garkin, and Rufus Cumberbatch."

"Cumberbatch was there?" The mention of the demonologist sent a chill down my back. "What were they doing?"

Kanaan turned his gaze to me. "They removed a man from one of the white coffins and ripped a piece of his soul to create an infernus. It was at that moment I learned the magic words you can use to save Ivy."

CHAPTER 21

"Y ou saw them make an infernus?" Max said. "How did they do it?"

"Zarin used the wyrm as a receptacle." Kanaan cupped his hands to make a circle. "Garkin produced a crystal sphere used to contain the spark of a golem. With the help of Zarin, Cumberbatch threaded the soul fragment into the spark."

"How is it possible to do that?" Ambria said.

"Only a skilled Daemos and Arcane could meld the two." Kanaan paused as if to reflect on that and continued. "I sneaked through the room of nine sides before they entered and waited on the other side. Zarin summoned a humanoid demon and began molding its flesh into a likeness of the man whose soul they put in the sphere."

"Molded it?" Max shook his head. "When you summon a demon, don't they appear in their own form?"

"Powerful summoners can force them into shapes of their own choosing. Zarin held the demon in a fluid state, allowing it to morph." Kanaan pressed his lips together. "It was an impressive feat."

"He created a demon clone of the man?" Ambria asked.

Kanaan shook his head. "He had not finished when I left. It seemed a very slow, tiring process. I left and observed you in the cabin, then entered the portal shortly before you did."

"What are the magic words?" I asked, trying not to think of the poor man whose soul Zarin might even now be bonding to a demon.

"*Ehx voden na mihx.*" Kanaan tilted his head slightly. "It is demon language that means, "Your soul is mine.""

I tried to pronounce it the same way Kanaan did, but the guttural sounds didn't come easily to my throat. "Will you teach me how to say it, and more importantly, will you help us rescue Ivy and the other prisoners?"

"We have to do it soon," Max added. "We hid those bodies, but it won't take long before they get suspicious about their men disappearing."

"Sound reasoning," Kanaan said, "but I cannot defeat Garkin alone. With Victus and Zarin, they would make quick work of us."

The magic poisoning seemed to bloat my stomach and twist my insides. I chewed the gum faster, hoping the potion it contained would hurry up and work.

Ambria's forehead pinched with concern. "You're afraid of Garkin, aren't you?

"Afraid, no," Kanaan replied. "I am aware of his capabilities."

"I heard it in your voice," Ambria said. "You're convinced the way of the monkey can't beat the way of the rock. If you keep thinking like that, you'll never beat Garkin."

Kanaan grew still and quiet for so long, I thought he'd frozen in place. "You are right. I do fear I cannot beat him. My perception of Garkin is skewed and grants him power over me."

Max gulped. "Does that mean you won't help?"

Kanaan shook his head solemnly. "We are not rocks. We do not face down adversity with pure strength." He turned to Max. "We are not trees. We do not bend and sway to avoid adversity."

"We're monkeys," Ambria said. "We trick people."

Kanaan's lips hinted at a smile. "Correct. We do not have the strength to defeat our enemies in direct confrontation. We must devise a plan."

"How long before they notice Chachi and Jonas are gone?" Max said.

"Maybe longer than we think." I recalled the conversation the men had when I was in hiding. "They hunted and killed two people Victus didn't need anymore. I think they were probably people from the white coffins."

"That's barbaric!" Ambria squeezed shut her eyes for a moment. "I'm glad Chachi and Jonas are dead."

I didn't respond directly to her and continued my reasoning. "They'd been hunting and camping the forest for two days. Jonas said the last hunt took them a week. That means we have a few days before Garkin expects them back at the foundry."

"Time to plan," Kanaan said. He walked toward the door leading from the omniarch room. "Go home and rest. I will return to the foundry tonight and observe."

Ambria caught up to him and touched his arm. "Alone?"

Kanaan stopped walking. "Garkin is powerful, but he cannot fight what he does not know is there." He nodded at the omniarch. "I will use the portal after you leave, and reopen it to Conrad's room when I am done."

"Be careful, Kanaan." Ambria's forehead pinched with worry. "We need you."

He nodded, then opened a portal in the omniarch to the field behind Moore Keep. We walked through the portal and waved goodbye to Kanaan as the gateway flickered and vanished.

My knees felt weak. A cold sweat broke out on my forehead. The magic sickness was getting worse, but there wasn't much I could do except weather it.

"You look positively green, Conrad." Ambria took my arm. "Max, get him to bed straightaway."

"Of course." Max kept walking toward the keep, eyes lost in thought.

I leaned gratefully on Ambria, though I could still walk fine on my own. There was plenty to talk about, but really nothing to say that we hadn't already discussed, so I kept quiet and stumbled along into the keep, up the winding stairs, and into the common room between the male and female towers.

"Goodnight, Conrad." Ambria kissed my forehead. "Rest well."

Despite the chills plaguing me, the spot where her lips touched me felt feverishly warm. "Good night, Ambria." I reluctantly released her hand and watched her go.

Max seemed to snap out of his trance. "Well, let's get up to the room."

"What's on your mind?" I asked as we walked up the stairs to the male dorm's common room.

"Can't stop thinking about Ivy." A dreamy look came over his face. "If we rescue her, she'll help us with all our problems."

"Don't get too excited," I said. "She might not have all the answers."

Max had already retreated into his thoughts again and merely grunted.

When I reached my bed, I hardly remembered my head hitting the pillow. A solid night of sleep, however, didn't help me avoid a splitting headache and stomach cramps the next morning. Violent images of my encounter with Chachi and Jonas jerked me awake with a shout.

"Ah!" Max leapt out of bed, wand at the ready until he realized I'd just been dreaming.

"Sorry." I groaned and slid out of bed, another worry festering in my mind. I breathed a sigh of relief when I found a portal facing the corner, just as Kanaan had promised. It meant he'd survived spying on Garkin.

I felt sick as a dog, but missing classes wasn't an option. "Layering spells together is only one part of spellcasting," Gideon Grace announced as he entered the classroom that day. He raked his gaze across the classroom. "Just as important is predicting the spells cast by another person." Grace weaved his wand through a series of patterns.

I recognized bits and pieces, but was hard-pressed to identify the spells in their entirety.

Lily's hand shot up. "That was a shield spell combined with electricity."

The professor nodded. "Precisely." He repeated the process, this time tying off the spell. A sheet of shimmering electricity formed in the air before him. "If you were dueling another Arcane and recognized the patterns quickly enough, you could counter the shield with the proper spell."

"Dueling?" Harris glanced back at me, a devilish gleam in his eyes. "I didn't realize we got to duel anyone."

"Eventually, Mr. Ashmore." Grace also spared me a look, obviously wishing Harris could duel me now. "A good offense requires one to anticipate their opponent's spells so they can quickly counter them." He weaved another pattern.

His wand moved so fast I could hardly follow it, but I picked out two parts of the layers—a water spell combined with freezing. I didn't know the last pattern, but surmised it wasn't a projectile spell, but rather one you might use to trip up an opponent.

"How would you counter that spell?" Grace's eyes darted to me. "Edison?"

I hoped my gut instinct was right. "With a heat spell."

He paused for a moment and begrudgingly nodded. "Yes."

As class continued, I couldn't stop thinking about Kanaan and hoping he'd discovered a way to rescue Ivy without Garkin killing us. By comparison, all the homework Grace assigned us hardly seemed important. Though I hated to admit it, the professor had taught me something valuable today. If forced into a duel with my father, I would have a hard time anticipating and countering his spells.

I might have learned a powerful offensive spell, but Victus probably had a way to counter it. Until I increased my arsenal, I had to avoid a direct conflict.

The bell rang and students filtered out of the class. I dragged behind everyone else, the leaden sensation of magic poisoning pressing on my shoulders. Max and Ambria apparently hadn't realized I wasn't right behind them and were nowhere in sight. I shuffled one foot after the other, in no hurry to get to Asha's class.

It still seemed unbelievable that she was a demon clone of my mother. She seemed so real. So personable. I'd allowed myself to like her, only to find she wasn't even a real person. Depression snaked around my chest and squeezed. I looked up. The hall was nearly empty and I still had a way to go.

I picked up my pace, rounding twists and turns. Quick movement caught the corner of my eye, but my sluggish reflexes weren't enough to get me out of the way. A meaty fist caught me square in the temple.

My legs crumpled and I went down in a heap. Someone grabbed me under the armpits and dragged me a few feet before dumping me on the floor. I blinked the fog out of my eyes and saw Harris and Baxter smirking down at me.

"You're always avoiding me, Edison." Harris held his wand up. "Afraid to face me and get this over with?"

"I'm not your enemy." I pushed up to one knee. "The foreseeance isn't about me."

Baxter shoved me back down. "Don't deny it, you evil filth. You're gonna be just like your father."

"No." I dug deep inside, trying to find the strength to rise, but the blow to my head had nearly knocked me out. "I'm trying to stop my father."

"Stop him?" Harris barked a laugh. "He's dead, you idiot."

"He's alive again." I slid on my backside until my back met the wall. "Demon magic kept him alive."

"Just end it, Harris." Baxter brandished his own wand, but didn't raise it. "You have to be the one to do it."

"Kill me in cold blood?" I rasped, my throat suddenly dry. "What evil have I done to deserve that?" I swallowed hard. "What did I do besides being born, Harris?" Fear pumped through my veins, awakening a rush of adrenalin.

"Your parents murdered mine." Hatred inflamed his voice. "You don't deserve to live."

From the moment he'd discovered my true identity, Harris despised me for what my parents had done. This wasn't about me perpetrating evil, or even being the enemy he was supposed to face in the foreseeance. Killing me was pure revenge. Wiping out the bloodline of the Overlord, his twisted idea of justice.

"Do it before he gets back his senses, Harris!" Baxter came toward me, fist cocked to deliver another blow.

I wasn't anywhere close to a hundred percent, and the mere thought of casting a spell made me ill. Thankfully, I had a choice. I left my wand in its holster and let Baxter come. He must have thought our encounter in the dining hall was a fluke, because he left himself completely open. He swung his fist toward my face.

Moving to the side, I gripped his wrist and used his momentum to slam his head into the wall behind me. Harris flicked his wand. I rolled to the side, the heat from a fire spell jetting just overhead. Far from graceful, I hit my head and my elbow on the hard stone floor, but it was enough to get me close to Harris.

My legs flailed, caught his, and tripped him. His wand clattered to the floor. Face red with rage, he dove toward me. I lashed out with my foot, caught him in the stomach.

"Ungh!" Harris's eyes bugged.

I kicked him again, and he stumbled back. Before he could recover, I staggered to my feet and pressed my wand to his throat. I couldn't let this go on. Couldn't let Harris keep dogging me while the threat of Victus loomed.

My hand twitched and a bead of sweat trickled into my right eye. *Don't give him another chance to kill you!* I could end this right now.

I could kill Harris.

CHAPTER 22

Harris's face blanched and his eyes went wide. "Please, no."

Despite my rage and sense of self-preservation, I didn't want to kill the boy. I just wanted him to leave me alone. I leaned down, wishing I could look fierce, but felt too drained to think straight. Thankfully, Harris didn't know that. "Do you think I could kill you right now?"

Harris's breathing quickened. He nodded slightly, as if a mere twitch might cause me to slash his throat.

"Victus is still alive. He summoned a demon to possess my body. It preserved his soul and my mother's soul, binding them to mine, so they could pretend to be dead all these years." Anger and fear twisted my insides. "Victus never saw me as anything but a lab rat. Something to use and throw away." I tried to control the quaver in my voice but couldn't. "He wants to kill me. He wants to control the Overworld again. If you really want revenge, kill Victus, not me."

Baxter groaned and stirred on the floor behind me. I holstered my wand and shook my head at Harris. "Killing me will only make the man who murdered your parents happy."

"I don't believe you." With my wand off his throat, Harris regained confidence. "Victus is dead."

I took out my arcphone and projected a holographic recording I'd made while spying on Victus as he entered the crack leading to the Glimmer more than a year ago. He walked with Delectra and Serena, discussing their plans to conquer mortality with a part of the Anchor Stone.

"This is fake." Harris's face paled. "Or it's old footage."

I pointed to the timestamp. "Phone, has this video been altered?"

"No," the phone replied.

"Is the timestamp correct?"

"Yes," the phone responded.

I looked at Harris. "I took this video myself at the destroyed mansion near the Fairy Gardens."

Harris drew in a long, ragged breath. "No, it can't be!" He shook his head. "Your parents can't be alive!"

"My mother is dead." My voice cracked with emotion. "Victus murdered Delectra last year. He controlled her with demons just like he tried to do with me." I flicked off the recording. "The person you hate isn't your enemy. The real enemy is alive and out there." I wiped tears from my eyes and left the room. As I stepped outside, I heard Harris sobbing.

It was yet another depressing layer to add onto everything else. Remembering how Delectra died in my arms. How Victus controlled her. How he'd made her disguise herself as Esma and become my beloved mentor.

I kept walking.

Asha raised an eyebrow when I stepped inside, frowned, and motioned with her finger for me to come closer. "Conrad, what happened?" She took my chin and turned my head sideways. "The side of your head is bleeding!"

Ambria met my gaze with wide eyes and looked toward the empty desks usually occupied by Harris and Baxter.

"I slipped on a puddle of water in the bathroom," I lied. "Hit my head."

"You should go see Percival." Asha blinked. "Or whoever is in charge in the healing ward now."

"I'm fine, really." I touched the tender spot on my head and felt crusted blood. Baxter had hit me harder than I'd thought. I shuffled to my seat before she could object.

Ambria gripped my shoulder from the desk behind me. "Conrad, did Harris do this to you?"

I just groaned, too weary to explain.

Harris and Baxter walk in moments later, sheepish looks on their faces. Asha's face darkened into a scowl. "Why are you so late?" Her gaze flicked to meet mine, and understanding dawned. She grabbed Baxter's arm and held up his bruised fist. "What happened?"

"I tripped into a wall," Baxter replied lamely.

"Tripped into a wall?" Her voice rose in disbelief. She turned to Harris. "Did you trip into something too?"

Harris looked down at the floor.

Asha turned to me. I gave a slight shake of my head. *Please don't make a big deal of this.*

She pressed her lips together and jabbed a finger at their desks. "In your seats, now."

They wasted no time complying.

Lily whispered to Baxter when he sat down and looked aghast at his response.

I tried to be attentive, but the lesson droned in the background while thoughts and memories occupied my mind. When class ended, Asha put a hand on my arm. "A moment, Conrad."

Ambria and Max gave me worried looks, but left the classroom. Harris strode past, head down, and Baxter gave me an uneasy glance as he followed.

"Tell me what happened," Asha said when the other students left. "The truth."

"I'd rather not." I slumped into a front desk and tried not to meet her eyes. I felt so angry with her for not being real. For being yet another construct of my father's. I wanted to jump up and scream in her face, as if I could make her understand how much this betrayal hurt.

Is it even her fault?

No, it wasn't. Asha couldn't help that she was created from demon flesh and a fragment of my mother's soul. She couldn't help how she was born any more than I could. But that didn't mean I could trust her. Victus held her leash, no matter how loosely.

"Have you even heard what I said?" Asha took my chin in her hand and pulled my gaze up to her. "Conrad, what's wrong?"

My eyes stung, but I let the tears flow. I wanted to blurt the truth and be free of it, but I couldn't. "I practiced my spells too much and gave myself magic poisoning." That much was true. "I'm ill."

Her gaze softened. Asha took a handkerchief from the desk and gently wiped my eyes. She smoothed back my hair and smiled. "You need to rest, Conrad. You always look as if the weight of the world rests on your shoulders."

Her touch made me feel at ease, as if I could finally let down my guard and just rest. *She's not real.* For a moment, I didn't care. For just a moment, it was okay if I pretended she was more than an infernus. It was fine to play make believe as long as I could face the truth later.

I looked into that face that so resembled Delectra and shivered. Maybe I could kill Victus and free Asha. She might not be a real human, but she was real enough for me. "Could you tell me more about your childhood?"

A gentle smile. "Well, it was uneventful. My adoptive grandfather was a powerful Arcane, but he left the Overworld behind to raise me." Asha wiped the corner of my eye with her thumb and I tried not to shiver. "We lived near a small Tuscan village in Italy. For most of my life, it was all I knew. Though I attended normal school with the other children, my grandfather trained me in the Arcane arts." She sighed and smiled. "Everyone there loves him, and I hated to leave."

"Why doesn't he come to visit?" I knew it was because he didn't exist, but Asha's voice sounded so genuine when she told the falsehood, I found myself wanting to hear more of her fantasy.

"He came here once, to try to convince me to leave."

I frowned. "To leave? Why?"

"My parents were murdered, Conrad." Asha bit her lower lip. "Granddad Stan told me that he raised me in the country to keep me safe in case those people came looking."

I tried not to let myself be drawn in, but like reading a good book, I couldn't resist. "Why were they murdered?"

"He said my parents were mixed up with the wrong people." Asha seemed to swallow a lump in her throat. "Several years ago, he said he'd heard that those people were dead and gone, and that I was free to enjoy my life."

"Then why did he want you to leave the university?" I asked.

"Because he heard rumors that tales of their demise weren't true." Her forehead creased with worry. "That they might still be alive."

This is quite some tale. "Who are these people, Asha?" I sounded more demanding than I meant to be. The bell rang, signaling the start of the next period, but I ignored it.

Asha flinched. "My next class is waiting down the hall. I have to go."

I gripped her arm. "Who murdered your parents?"

Her face darkened. "I can't tell you."

"Please!"

"I won't." She shook her arm free. "Now go to your class, Conrad." She touched my cheek gently. "And do be careful in the bathrooms." With that, Asha whisked away like a kite on the wind.

I didn't like how she dismissed my questions, no matter the fact that her history was a cover story. I needed to dig deeper into her background. Find the cracks and weaknesses. Perhaps she didn't know that she was a demon golem, a tool used by her creator to spy on me. If I revealed her true nature, would it make her angry enough to betray Victus? Could she even betray him, or did he control her will?

I went into the bathroom and looked at the purple bruise spreading across my temple. A thin line of crusted blood formed a scab right across the center. I was surprised Baxter hadn't inadvertently killed me with the blow.

Eleanor Beetle barely looked up from reading the Overworld Social Studies textbook when I walked into the classroom, and didn't seem to care that the clock read ten minutes past the hour. Lily's forehead pinched with concern when she saw me. She bared her teeth and slapped Baxter on the back of his head.

"Ow!" he cried.

The professor didn't even look up from reading.

Harris stared at me with dead eyes, either still digesting that Victus was still alive, or deciding he wanted another crack at me after all. I planned to avoid him and Baxter. After all, we would soon be launching a rescue mission for Ivy that might result in our deaths. It would be better dying like that than allowing Harris his petty revenge.

"...it was a dire moment in Overworld social dynamics," Professor Beetle read from the textbook. "Though the Overlord had not risen to power, he had accrued enough support to make neighbor turn against neighbor. He killed dozens of people in his search for the one mentioned in Foreseeance Five Thousand. The one person he thought would bring him down."

Heads and eyes shifted toward Harris, but the boy didn't seem to notice that the lesson had suddenly become about him.

"Was that when the Overlord killed Harris's parents?" Kimmy Kaspersky asked.

Professor Beetle blinked and looked up from the book as if suddenly realizing she had a classroom full of students. "Unfortunately, yes."

"Why me?" Harris spoke in a bleak voice. "What made him think it was about me?"

I recognized the sad undertones of someone who wished the foreseeance had been about anyone but himself. I couldn't help but feel sorry for him, because I knew exactly how he felt. I wished more than anything that Victus wasn't my father.

Professor Beetle pursed her lips and closed the textbook. "Those with the gift often foresee many happenings in the future. The more momentous an event, the more likely many seers will prophesy about it, as was the case with Foreseeance Forty-Three Eleven."

"The one involving Justin Slade?" Max asked.

"Yes." Beetle smiled, as if enjoying her little jaunt outside the confines of a textbook. "There were exactly nine documented visions attributed to Foreseeance Five Thousand. It was the ninth that named young Harris."

"It specifically named him?" Lily frowned. "I've only ever heard the one version—*Once again shall the evil rise. The son of the fallen is the only hope for victory.*"

"That is the official abridged version." Professor Beetle pursed her lips.

"The first eight visions did not name anyone. After the Overlord's death, a ninth vision came to light. It was this foreseeance that specifically linked Mr. Ashmore to Foreseeance Five Thousand." She tapped a finger on her chin. "It's really quite odd when a foreseeance is so accurate."

Ambria's hand shot up. "In other words, the Overlord killed Harris's parents without realizing they were part of the prophecy?"

Harris's face grew tight, but he didn't seem overly upset about the discussion. As a child of prophecy, he'd probably heard people talk about his dead parents like this many times. As often as his parents were revered, I heard mine vilified.

"It would seem so." Professor Beetle's brow pinched into a confused W. "What is quite odd is that witnesses to the wave of murders during that time say that the Overlord was looking for something or someone in particular."

Baxter grunted. "Wasn't he looking for Harris?"

"Why would the Overlord search for Harris?" the professor replied. "Before the ninth vision, Foreseeance Five Thousand could have been about anyone who'd lost a parent. And why would the Overlord kill his parents and create a self-fulfilling prophecy?"

"What was the Overlord looking for?" Kimmy asked.

"Many scholars believe he was purging political opponents," Beetle said. "However, the majority of those he killed during his reign of terror had nothing to do with politics."

Lily raised her hand again. "Where can we read all the visions?"

"The Foreseeance section of the library, of course," Beetle replied.

"What's there to read that we don't already know?" Harris sighed and met my eyes. He looked like he wanted to say something else, but turned away.

"It's interesting," Lily said in a persistent voice. "I didn't realize there were nine visions. I thought there was just the one."

"It doesn't matter!" Harris burst out of his seat and stormed from the room.

Baxter got up halfway from his desk, mouth hanging open, forehead scrunched with confusion.

Professor Beetle frowned, then shrugged. "I suppose that is a rather delicate subject for Mr. Harris."

Lily put hands to her cheeks and managed to look ashamed. "I didn't mean to hurt him."

"I must say I've rather enjoyed this spontaneity," Beetle said. "Perhaps I'll allow more random questions in the future."

"It would certainly be better than reading the text book," Kimmy said, perhaps a bit louder than she'd meant to.

Eleanor Beetle didn't seem to mind. She opened the textbook and resumed reading. Boredom ensued.

Max turned around, ignoring the lecture. "I say we corner Harris and Baxter and beat them up. We can't let them get away with ambushing you like that."

Ambria touched my shoulder. "Why haven't you told us what happened, Conrad?"

"Later," I hissed, and put my head down on my desk.

I stare at the white house. It has been so long. I shouldn't be here. I don't want to be punished again. I don't want anyone to die because I couldn't stay away. Victus has me followed when he suspects the real me has emerged. I've grown accustomed to losing them, but what if I missed someone?

Fear grips me. I hop on my broom and speed away, desperate to put as much distance between it and me as I can. I can never come back. "My family is dead and gone," I say. "I have no one but Victus and Conrad."

My heart chokes with pain. If Victus knew I thought of our son as family, he would put me away for good. To him, our children have never been family, but guinea pigs in his quest for eternal life. How many has he used in his demonic experiments? Why must he use our children? During Conrad's birth, I emerged from the demon haze. Unlike so many before him, I saw my little boy come from my womb and open his eyes for the first time.

While I still had my wits, I made certain I could never bear another child. Conrad will be the last.

I look over my shoulder at the dwindling view. Hills, trees, and the one house in this world I can never visit again. I cannot lose the only family left to me.

"I think he's in a coma," Max said. "We need a healer!"

"No, he's awake," Professor Beetle said.

I blinked my weary eyes and looked with confusion at the concerned face of Max, Ambria, and Professor Beetle. "I'm sorry, I must have dozed off."

"We couldn't wake you," Ambria said. "You've been like that for nearly fifteen minutes."

"I thought that blow to your head must've given you a concussion." Max sighed with relief. "Thank god you finally woke up."

Professor Beetle pursed her lips. "You haven't been using drugs or narcotic potions, have you?"

"No." I got up from my desk. "I practiced magic too hard and got aether poisoning."

"Ah, that explains it." Beetle smiled and nodded as if everything was all better. "Perhaps you should go to bed early tonight."

"I'll do that." I gathered my books and made for the doorway.

Max and Ambria hurried after me. I took a right and headed downstairs.

"Where are you going?" Max jogged to pull even with me. "It's lunchtime and I'm starving."

Ambria came to my other side. "Did the blow to your head make you forget the dining hall is the other way?"

I focused on the image burned into my mind and shook my head. "No. Go to lunch if you have to. I have something else to do."

"What could be more important than eating?" Max said.

"Answers." I was afraid the memory would fade, but it remained vivid and focused, down to the smallest detail.

"Speaking of which, you still haven't told us what happened with Harris." Ambria gripped my arm and tried to slow me down. "Why won't you talk?"

"I'll tell you everything. Promise." We descended a ramp and entered a corridor not far from the entrance to the Burrows. The unused classroom with the portal was just down the way.

"We're taking the portal somewhere?" Max asked.

I nodded and hoped they didn't think I was crazy. "We're going to the place I just dreamed about." Concern flashed in their eyes, but I pressed onward. "We're going to the white house."

CHAPTER 23

I plunged through the portal and into the omniarch room on the other side before they could say anything. Ambria leapt through and grabbed my arm. "You saw the white house again?"

"Yes."

Max scratched his head. "This is one of those memories Della left?"

"Looks like it." I turned toward the omniarch and closed the portal hovering between its columns. I closed my eyes and saw the white house, the oak tree with red leaves, the hills behind it. *Open.* The omniarch hummed. I opened my eyes and a gateway blinked open.

The house was there, just as I'd dreamed it, a hundred yards across a grassy field. I stepped through the portal. Wind swept my hair. A blue sky and bright sun welcomed me to wherever in the world I now stood.

I started walking toward the house. The front door burst open and a massive white cat bounded outside and toward us.

Max stopped in his tracks. "Is that a lion?"

"It's spotted, Max," Ambria said in a disbelieving tone. "Since when do lions have spots?"

"A leopard." I looked back at the portal, now twenty yards distant. We could outrun the big cat if need be, but curiosity rooted me to the spot. "It was in that house and I don't see blood on its muzzle, so it must be tame."

"Just because it's someone's pet doesn't mean it won't eat us." Ambria gripped my arm. "We should run."

"Agreed." Max backed up a step.

"I dreamed about this house for a reason." I stood my ground. "I won't leave now."

Ambria sighed. "I really hope it doesn't eat us."

Max took out his wand, but I gripped his wrist and shook my head. "Don't threaten it."

I held up my hands and walked toward the leopard, shouting toward the house. "We come in peace!"

The leopard bounded up to us and circled around, a low growl in its throat. I froze with fear, but managed to repress the instinct to run. The feline turned toward the house and yowled in such a way it sounded almost like human speech.

A stout man with a Caesar's crown of gray hair stepped through the door, a staff at the ready. He made his way across the field, eyes never leaving us until he stood only a few yards away. He wore old-fashioned glasses with thick, wide rims, the side of which looked as if it had been taped together. I guessed his age to be in the seventies, or maybe older.

"Who are you?" His eyes drifted toward the portal. "Where are you from?"

I wasn't sure it was wise to tell this stranger.

"Max," Max said at once.

Ambria elbowed him and turned to me. "Well?"

If this man was an enemy, he had us completely at his mercy. I felt stupid for impulsively coming here without any planning whatsoever. "We're students from Arcane University."

The man frowned. "What are you doing here?"

I didn't know what else to say, so I took a leap of faith and hoped for the best. "Did you know Delectra?"

His bushy eyebrows shot up and his hand tensed around his staff. "Who's asking?"

Please don't let this be a mistake. "I'm Conrad, her son."

His mouth dropped open. "Sh—she had a son?"

I blinked, caught off guard by his question. "Yes, why?"

He shook his head slowly. "It's been so long since I saw her. So long since she died." He looked toward the portal. "Where does that lead?"

"Back to the university," I said.

"Who are you?" Ambria asked.

"I'm no one until I confirm who you are." He smiled as if to soften the hard words. "I'm sorry, but an old man can't be too careful." He motioned toward the portal. "Let's go."

The leopard yowled.

He nodded. "Yeah, you'd better come."

The big cat looked up at Max with intense green eyes and sniffed. Max jumped back a foot. The cat's mouth opened in what could only be described as a grin.

"That's a well-trained leopard," Ambria noted.

The man chuckled. "I wish. She pees all over the house."

The leopard growled and slung dirt at the old man with her paw. He chuckled.

We led him and his leopard back through the portal and into the arch room. He looked around intently. "Where is this?"

"It's underneath the headmaster's house at Arcane University," I said.

His eyebrows rose. "Wait, this is *the* omniarch used in the Seraphim War?" He headed for the exit. "Is it near the mansion?"

I hurried to catch up. "Yes. How did you hear about it?"

"Who hasn't heard about this place?" He snorted. "This was the resistance headquarters during the war." He stopped where the corridor opened into the cavern housing the mansion and blew out a long breath. "Amazing. How in the world do you kids have access to this place?"

I didn't know what to tell him about that. "I think everyone forgot it was down here. We just found it by accident."

"How sad. A lot's changed since the war ended." He shook his head. "And not for the better." He turned back toward the omniarch room. "Can you get us topside with that?"

"Of course, but why?" If he recognized the mansion, then he knew we were below Arcane University.

"There's someone I need to see." I couldn't imagine who that might be, but was too curious to stop now. "We don't want anyone knowing about the omniarch, so I'll open it in an abandoned wing of the university."

"Very well." The man watched patiently as I opened a new portal. His leopard prowled through the corridor outside and loped back in when we were ready to leave.

We stepped through the portal and into the empty room, then headed upstairs, through twisting corridors, and back into the main hallways. Lunch period wasn't over just yet, so the hallways were mostly empty.

The few students we passed gave startled looks at the leopard, some spinning on their heels and hurrying the opposite way.

"Well, if people only suspected we were evil before," Max said, "they're probably convinced now that we have a super-villain pet following us around."

The leopard growled and swiped at Max's leg.

"Whoa!" Max jumped to the side.

"She's not a pet," the man said.

Ambria's eyes narrowed. "Wait a minute—is she actually a leopard?"

"Yes." The man shrugged. "For now."

"She's a shifter, isn't she?" Ambria put her hands on her hips and frowned. "A felycan, and a very rude one at that!"

The leopard glared at her, but didn't swipe this time.

The air blurred ahead of us. Webs wrapped around the leopard and Shushiel scurried ahead of us, bouncing up and down on her legs, mandibles wide. "Did this man threaten you, Conrad?"

Max scrambled to the side, slipping and falling in his haste to escape the unexpected calamity. Ambria looked relieved.

The leopard yowled and tried to break free, but the tough webbing held her fast. The man's mouth dropped open in astonishment. "Is that a ruby spider?"

I held up a hand. "Shushiel, we're fine."

"I didn't realize they had such lovely red fur!" The old man leaned toward her, peering through his glasses.

Shushiel skirted sideways around us, her eyes blinking in rapid succession as she evaluated the situation. She stopped next to the leopard and snipped through the web bindings with her mandibles. The big cat scrambled upright and ran to hide behind the man.

"I am sorry to have been gone so long," Shushiel said, "but family matters and problems in the forest have kept me very busy."

"It's fine, really." Ambria rushed over and hugged our friend. "I'm glad to know you're watching over us again."

Shushiel stroked Ambria's hair with a foreleg. "I cannot stay long, but I heard of Galfandor's collapse and came back to see if he is okay."

"We don't know how he is," I admitted. "It all happened so fast, and then they whisked him away."

Max recovered his wits and sidled up next to me. "Things are bad."

"Well, Conrad, you certainly know how to make an impression." The man chuckled and looked down at the leopard. She stared with big green eyes at Shushiel, keeping the man between her and the spider.

Ambria stuck out her tongue. "Scaredy cat."

The leopard growled.

"Will you tell me who you are now?" I asked.

The man checked a pocket watch. "It's still lunchtime, yes?"

I nodded.

"Then take me to the dining hall, please."

"Best idea I've heard so far," Max said, and set out at a rapid pace down the hallway. By the time we caught up with him, he was already seated, looking imploringly toward the doors used by the serving golems.

Students at the closest tables went silent when they saw our strange group. Shushiel, at least, had camouflaged herself, but the leopard drew all manner of stares. Wolves were a more common sight around campus due to lycans attending shifter studies, but felycans were rare to the point of nonexistence at the university.

The man looked around as if searching for something or someone.

"May I ask what is going on here?" Asha Fellini seemed to appear from behind us.

The man faced her with a neutral expression. "Conrad is giving me a tour."

"You don't have a visitor badge." Asha raised an eyebrow and looked back and forth between me and our strange companions. "I require an explanation."

Max, meanwhile, received his food and dug in without giving the unfolding events another thought.

"Let's step into the hallway." Asha led the way without looking back. She took a right down an empty hallway and stopped. "Explain. Now."

"I wasn't expecting any visitors, but this boy appeared on my front lawn and demanded answers I'm not certain I should give," the man said. "I was merely ascertaining his identity."

Asha's lips flattened into a line, her eyes narrowing with apprehension. "Conrad, how did you find this man?"

I didn't want to tell her. Victus couldn't know that I had an—

"He used an omniarch," the man said. "Opened a portal nearly to my doorstep."

"Great." Ambria exchanged a worried look with me. "Well, I guess that little secret is out."

I couldn't believe I'd been so foolish to bring this man back with me. Now Asha had dangerous knowledge. As an agent of Victus, she could bring him or Garkin through a portal any time she wanted. I touched my wand, ready to use it. I hoped Shushiel could get into position and bind Asha.

"Conrad, answer my question." The steel in Asha's voice left me little room.

"I dreamed about it, okay?" I glared at the old man. "Why did Delectra go to your house? Who were you to her?"

Asha's face went white. Her legs wobbled and she stumbled back against the wall.

"Are you okay?" the man's face filled with sudden concern. He reached out a hand and touched her shoulder.

"Delectra went to your house?" Asha blinked rapidly. "When? I don't understand!"

The sudden emotion in her voice made me think I'd missed something. "Why are you so upset?" I asked.

Asha hardly seemed to hear me, focused as she was on the man. "It doesn't make any sense."

"I—I can explain." He stumbled over his words, tried to smile. "Really, I can."

Asha turned to me, tears in her eyes. "Conrad, when you asked me who killed my parents, I didn't want to tell you. More than anything, I just couldn't bring myself to hurt you."

"Hurt me?" I stepped backward, so confused at the twists and turns in the conversation. *She doesn't have parents. She's a construct of demon flesh and soul fragments!* "What are you talking about?"

"Asha," the man said softly. "We should talk about this elsewhere. Not here." The familiarity in the man's voice was unmistakable.

"Do you know each other?" Ambria said.

Asha didn't let him answer. "Victus and Delectra killed my parents." Her voice frosted over like a winter day. She turned to the man. "And now you tell me Delectra was at your house?"

"Not here!" The man turned to me. "Get us somewhere private, please."

"Who are you?" I said. "Tell me right this instant!"

"Please, not another word here," the man said. "I will tell you everything, but not here."

Asha blinked, as if coming awake from a trance. "I'm so sorry I told you that Conrad. I didn't want to burden you with more guilt."

I wanted to take her hand and tell her it was okay, but it was all a lie. Tears burned my eyes, but I couldn't bring myself to say anything. *Victus, you evil twisted bastard!*

"What in the world is going on here?" Ambria demanded.

I decided it was best to continue this in absolute privacy. There were better places to take the impostor, Asha, prisoner. I motioned everyone to follow me. We went back down the hallway toward the stairs leading to the underground classrooms.

"Delectra?" Asha muttered again.

The old man looked down, but said nothing.

A huffing Max caught up with us, a hand gripping his side. "Ow, I think I got a side cramp."

"Only you would consider food this important," Ambria said in a disapproving tone. "You didn't even think to bring us biscuits?"

Max looked down. "Sorry, but I couldn't think of anything except my stomach."

We reached the portal and stepped through it back to the omniarch room. I closed the gateway and hoped Kanaan was nearby in case I needed help.

Asha looked around in wonder. "Conrad, where are we? What is this place?"

"Oh, this is nothing, Ashes. You should see what's out there." The man motioned toward the corridor outside.

Ashes? The man spoke with such familiarity. Was he involved somehow?

Asha turned on him. "You will tell me this instant why Delectra was there."

"Tell me now," I demanded. "Why did you call her Ashes? How do you know each other?"

The man held up his hands defensively. "Please just give me a moment."

I turned to Asha. "How do you know him?"

Her angry glare softened as she turned to me. "This is my Granddad Stan."

I blinked. "He's real?"

The old man felt his chest. "Last time I checked, I was."

Asha looked confused. "Why wouldn't you think he's real, Conrad? Do you not believe me?"

"Believe you?" My voice was rough with emotion. "Is all of this a trick?" I spun on Stan. "Who are you, really? How did you know my mother?"

"Yes, why was Delectra there?" Asha's eyes tightened. "Did she want to kill me?"

Stan cleared his throat and looked down at the floor. "I'm so sorry, Ashes. I lied to you all those years ago." He met her eyes. "I had to. It seemed the best way to make you appreciate the danger. To keep you close to home."

"Lied about what?" Asha's voice cracked with emotion.

"Victus and Delectra didn't kill your parents." He looked back and forth from me to Asha. "They *were* your parents."

CHAPTER 24

I staggered backward. Ambria gasped and put a hand to her mouth. Max burped and grimaced apologetically.

Shushiel flickered out of camouflage, all eight eyes blinking rapidly. "This was unexpected."

The leopard melted into the form of a young girl with bright green eyes and shouted, "Are you bloody kidding me?"

Asha seemed the most shocked of all, suddenly discovering her parent's killers were actually family. Her face blazed bright red and she slapped Stan hard enough to make him stagger backward. "No!" Rage and sorrow roughened her voice. "That can't be true!"

"You're not a demon golem?" I said with wonder. "Y-you're my sister?"

Asha put a hand to her heart. "Demon golem?" She shook her head as if clearing a haze. "Sister?"

"I don't understand." I turned to Stan. "How can this be? I thought Victus made Delectra use their children for demonic experiments."

"I was best friends with Damien—Asha's grandfather. We served together in the Blue Cloak special forces. They asked me to be her godfather and I became like a second grandfather to her."

"He adopted me after my parents died." Asha scowled at him. "I can't believe you lied to me about my parents all these years."

Stan rubbed his cheek where she'd struck him. "Damien never liked Victus. He knew that man was no good from the moment he met him. God knows he tried to bring Delectra back from the darkness. But his little girl was so in love with Victus that she wouldn't listen." He bared his teeth. "That man and his demon magic corrupted her from the inside out."

"Does that mean you're my godfather too?" I asked, still too stunned to make sense of it all.

Asha interrupted. "What did you mean earlier about a demon golem?"

"Can we sit down and talk about this?" Max said. "My side is cramping bad right now."

"Yes, I think we should sit down," Ambria said. "Let's go into the mansion."

Everyone walked as if in a daze, Asha looked back and forth between me and Stan. I stared at them, while Stan cast worried looks at Asha. The leopard girl, now back in feline shape growled every time I looked her way.

I wanted to feel happy, but a part of me didn't trust this development even though it aligned with the visions from Delectra's memories.

I wasn't surprised when Kanaan opened the door and greeted us. "Come in."

Asha shook her head and backed up a step. "You're here, Kanaan?"

"Indeed." He motioned us inside. "There is tea in the sitting room."

Ambria led us into the large room on the right. The house golems had dusted and straightened the furniture. A steaming teapot sat on a silver tray, so we each poured ourselves a cup of tea and took a seat.

Asha and I looked at each other at the same time, neither of us averting our eyes.

"Now I know why Esma talked with you so much," I said. "She must have known who you were."

"Of course." Asha touched her cheek. "I never had the chance to tell you about those conversations, Conrad. She spoke highly of you, and seemed quite proud of your accomplishments, especially when you led your team to victory in kabash."

"How did she behave with you?" I asked.

"She tested me at every opportunity, despite my protestations." Asha frowned. "I am a professor, after all, not a student." She shrugged. "But Esma assured me it was absolutely necessary."

"How did you do?" I asked.

"Well, Stan taught me all I know, so I had little problem countering Esma's tricks most of the time." A smile flickered across her lips. "I even overpowered her a couple of times. I expected her to be upset, but she seemed delighted."

"Here's what I don't get." Max leaned forward in his chair. "How did Victus never suspect you were his child? I mean, you look just like Delectra!"

"That is curious." Ambria pursed her lips. "It seems highly unlikely he wouldn't have seen you or spoken to you when he was disguised as Professor Sideon."

"Oh, he spoke to me on occasion, but most of the time, he ignored me completely." Asha tapped a finger on her chin. "Perhaps Delectra persuaded him that I simply looked similar."

Stan shook his head. "Do you think I'd let you out into the world without protection, child?" He pointed to her neck. "The locket I gave you for your tenth birthday is enchanted."

Asha's eyes flared. She tugged on a silver chain and produced a heart-shaped locket from beneath her shirt. She opened it and a tiny holographic image of Stan hovered just above it. "You knew I would never take it off, didn't you?"

He nodded. "I warded it to shield your image from Victus. Should he ever look upon you, he would see a very plain young woman. The enchantment would also subtly encourage him to ignore you."

"Why didn't you ward it against Delectra?" I asked.

"I should have, but I didn't think Delectra would harm Asha." He pressed his lips tight. "Then again, when she was under demonic influence, she was capable of anything."

Asha directed her gaze on me. "Conrad, what is a demon golem?"

"Oh boy." Max leaned back and grimaced.

"Victus can create duplicates of people using their soul fragments," Ambria said. She looked from Asha to Stan. "I want to believe all of this, but Conrad, how can we be certain this isn't a trick?"

"Demon golems?" Stan blew out a breath. "The man's a bloody monster!"

The leopard morphed back into a scantily clad girl wearing what looked like black straps across her chest and lower body. The outfit was far too revealing to be proper.

"Conrad! Max!" Ambria snapped her fingers and the pair of us looked away.

"Natalia, you really shouldn't do that in front of these boys." Stan shrugged. "Teenagers."

"How does she fit into all this?" Ambria asked.

"Stan is part of a network that rescues children from bad situations," Asha said. "Natalia is one of several who still live with him."

"I grew up with her," Natalia said. "Asha and Granddad Stan are family."

"Does everyone call him Granddad Stan?" Max asked.

Natalia looked at the old man fondly. "He is a good man, even if he likes to squirt us with water spells by surprise."

Asha laughed. "He still does that?"

Stan chuckled. "Every chance I get."

Kanaan removed a small gray sphere from within his robes and walked to Asha. "I must ask that you hold this in your palm."

"What is it?" Asha asked.

"It detects demonic flesh," he replied. "You must hold it for thirty seconds."

Asha took it and held it in the flat of her palm. Half a minute ticked past, every second a hammer stroke in my chest. *What if she's a demon golem? What if this is a trick?* I could hardly stand it.

The gray in the sphere faded to white. Kanaan took it and nodded. "You are human."

I couldn't take it any longer. I jumped up and ran over to Asha, tears brimming in my eyes. "That means you're really my sister."

Her eyes wet with emotion, Asha stood and embraced me. "Yes, I am, little brother."

Stan choked up and wiped his eyes. "I can't believe Delectra saved you, lad." He got up and wrapped his arms around both of us. "I'd be honored to be your grandfather too."

I have a bigger family than I thought. It was one of the happiest moments of my life.

Natalia looked me up and down. "I suppose I can adopt you too."

Ambria clapped her hands and laughed. "Oh, Conrad, how wonderful!"

Max cleared his throat. "Does this mean we get an A in your class, Asha?"

Asha laughed and pulled away from the hug. "Not on your life, Max."

"A happy occasion, but dire times." Kanaan's words sobered the atmosphere. "Victus travels with his associates to Chernobyl this afternoon. They seek to repair the Grand Nexus to bring Aerianas back from Seraphina."

"What?" His announcement threw cold water on my spirits. "If they repair the Nexus, doesn't that mean Justin Slade can return?"

Kanaan hesitated before answering. "It means, if all went according to Victus's plans, Aerianas built an army of infernus and defeated Justin and his army. It means Victus now controls Seraphina."

"W-what?" Max sputtered. "Impossible. Justin Slade defeated the biggest supernatural army ever. If Daelissa couldn't beat him, there's no way Aerianas could build an army of infernus big enough."

"Unless they used subterfuge." Ambria bit her lower lip. "The key to winning with these infernus isn't by mass producing them. It's by replacing important people and taking over from within."

"Precisely." Kanaan poured himself another cup of black tea. "Zarin and Victus briefly spoke of her mission. She was to infiltrate the Darkling society, take control of their armies by duplicating their leaders, and repeat the same with the Brightlings. Once done, she was to unite the nations and prepare for Victus's eventual return."

"Destroying Justin Slade and the Eden army along the way." Max's face paled. "That's insidious."

"It's awful." Ambria wrung her hands. "Do they know if she succeeded?"

Kanaan shook his head. "They have had no contact with the other side for nearly a decade, and Victus doubts he can repair the damage he did to the Nexus. He and his partners will meet Serena and rely on her expertise for aid."

"It could mean another Seraphim invasion." Stan's hand tightened on the armrest. "Unless, of course, the Slade boy won. Then it could mean the end of Victus."

Max pounded the flat of his fist into the other hand. "We need Ivy. With her, we can stop Victus."

"Yes, you've made that point before," Ambria noted dryly.

Max raised an eyebrow. "And?"

"And, I agree with you, Max." She reached over and touched my hand. "Conrad?"

"Hmm?" I couldn't stop thinking about what might wait on the other side of the Grand Nexus. An invading army, or platoons of homesick soldiers ready to come home? "With Garkin around, we can't hope to beat Victus. I think we should do what we can to rescue the prisoners at the foundry and destroy the place if possible."

"I'm in," Asha said. "I can't let my little brother do something dangerous without me."

"Me too." Natalia bared her teeth. "I can sniff out any bad guys."

"As can I," Shushiel said.

Max flashed a grin at me. "You know I'm in."

Ambria snorted. "I would hope so, since this was your idea."

Max's eyes widened. "My idea?"

"I want to help, too," Stan said.

"Absolutely not." Asha took his hand. "You've got a bad leg, chronic heartburn, and…"

Stan laughed. "You can make that list a mile long, Ashes, but I'm coming." He looked at Kanaan. "I'm old, but I have a few tricks left."

"You taught Asha everything she knows," I said, "but are you strong enough to fight Victus?"

"I'm not letting my goddaughter go into battle without me." Stan flicked a compact staff from his side holster and expanded it. He slammed the butt on the ground. "I can hold my own."

"Perhaps you could squirt them with water," Natalia suggested.

"Hah!" Stan folded his staff back to a four-inch rod and put it in the holster. "If I get 'em in the eyes, you can bet they won't be able to see well enough to hit me."

Asha's forehead pinched with worry, but she nodded. "Be careful. There are many more people than me who rely on you."

"It appears we have much to plan." Kanaan set down his tea. "Destroying the foundry will present a serious challenge."

"I think you'd better explain more about the foundry," Asha said.

"It's the place where Victus makes the infernus." I tried to give her a brief description, but by the time I got into the preservation coffins and the demon pattern, I ended up spending half an hour on the story.

"The man is a monster," Stan said.

"I can't believe he's my father." Asha turned to me. "And I can't imagine how you've dealt with these awful feelings all this time, Conrad. It's as if his sins are suddenly mine."

I reached across and gripped her hand. "His sins are his alone, no matter what anyone says." I let go and leaned back. "All we can do is try to stop him from causing more harm."

"Amen," Max said.

Kanaan took out an arcphone and displayed a holographic image of a map. He drew an X with his finger where the abandoned cottage sat. "We use the portal to arrive here."

"Why not inside the foundry?" Max asked.

"I could not get a portal to open there or within a four-hundred-yard radius." Kanaan drew a circle around the foundry. "It is likely they have a portal-blocking statue inside."

"Like the ones they used during the war," Max said.

"Yes." The magitsu master traced a line from the cottage, through the woods, and around the field with the mass grave. "There are twenty-one of Garkin's battle mages living in the compound beyond the foundry." He zoomed in on a cluster of buildings to the north of the sandstone buttes. "I have not observed them patrolling. It appears they believe there is nothing to guard against since no one knows the compound exists."

Ambria sighed. "Thank goodness for your brain fog potion, Max. Otherwise Zarin would have alerted the others."

"Brain fog?" Asha looked confused.

"I'm really good at inventing potions," Max said. "This one makes you forget the last ten minutes."

Ambria tutted. "If by inventing you mean making terrible mistakes."

"If by mistakes you mean genius!" Max shot back.

I waved my hands to stop the argument before it consumed the entire meeting. "Provided we don't run into any resistance, what's the best way to free people from the preservation chambers?"

"I do not know if releasing them immediately is wise." Kanaan displayed the image of a red coffin. "It is possible the prisoners will be in a weakened state. They may not be able to walk on their own."

"Or they might need medical attention," Ambria added. "But we can't possibly move so many coffins ourselves."

"We will have to physically load them onto flying carpets," Kanaan said. "I tested a levitation spell, but the material resisted my efforts."

Asha inspected the holographic image of the red coffin. "Probably warded to prevent anyone without the proper passcode from breaking them open with magic."

"That was my conclusion as well." Kanaan rotated the image to show the pedestal holding up the box. "There is nothing holding down the coffin, but it weighs two hundred pounds."

Max whistled. "I don't know how much I can lift, but I know it's not that much."

"It will take all of us to move one coffin onto a flying carpet." Kanaan looked at Natalia. "Your felycan strength will help."

"Do not forget me," Shushiel said. "I can lower webs from the ceiling and swing the coffins onto the carpets."

"I have a better idea." I flicked to an earlier image of the chamber and rotated the view to the ceiling. Though the image wasn't perfectly clear, the surface looked smooth. "Maybe we could rig a pulley up there using Shushiel's webs."

Kanaan tapped his chin. "I had not considered a non-magical approach."

"You didn't grow up in an orphanage where they treated us like slaves," Ambria said. "Conrad used to help Brickle slaughter animals. He'd come inside covered with blood after hoisting them up with pulleys."

I shuddered at the memory of those days and tried not to think about how a demon had eaten Brickle alive. "Who's going to ferry the flying carpets? How many coffins can we fit on one?"

Kanaan swiped to the image of a double-wide carpet. "This will carry three coffins and still fit through the door to the foundry." He looked at Stan. "Can you guide the carpets to the portal?"

The old man nodded. "I'll take some extra painkillers in case my leg acts up."

"That's no short hike from the foundry to the portal," Asha said. "I'd feel much better if you only had to go halfway."

"Through woods and rough terrain?" Natalia pshawed. "I don't even think he should go halfway."

Ambria switched to a wide shot of the chamber holding the coffins and stared at the pile of white boxes. "Even if Garkin's men don't wander in and interfere, how in the world can we move so many coffins?"

I tried to count, but the jumbled pile of boxes defied my efforts. *Two hundred pounds each?* Our task didn't just seem monumental—it seemed impossible.

CHAPTER 25

"We will move what we can," Kanaan said. "I suggest we leave the white coffins for last."

"Because they're ordinary people?" Ambria shook her head. "It's not fair and it's not right."

"No, it's not," Asha said. "But if the people in those red coffins are as powerful as Ivy Slade, then we need them badly."

"I know that, but—" Ambria bit her lip. "All those poor people, copied and murdered once Victus is done with them."

The tortured faces of the dead in the trench flashed before my eyes. I shivered and choked back sickness.

Max gagged and ran from the room. His retches echoed down the hallway.

Asha's troubled eyes met mine. "We should save as many as we can, but there simply aren't enough of us."

"I spoke with Percival," Kanaan said in his quiet, undisturbed voice. "He will be here to monitor the health of those we free."

I barely registered his words, so focused was I on trying not to think of the dead. I'd seen so many horrors in my short life. I'd accidentally killed a man with a shovel. Watched a demon devour Brickle. Seen the Goodleighs die after their flying car crashed. Witnessed my parents rise from the dead. It should have prepared me for all the horrors one could imagine. But it hadn't, and maybe that was a good thing.

Much as I wanted Victus dead, I didn't relish killing him. I didn't want anyone else to die, but as long as such evil existed, I had no choice. There had to be some way we could rescue the people in those white coffins. They might be unimportant to Victus—just low-level people to copy so he could throw them away afterward—but they were *people*! Fathers, mothers, brothers, sisters—humans, all of them worthy of rescue.

We needed more people to help us, but who could we trust? There was no telling who Victus had replaced by now. If only the Glimmer was open, then Evadora could help. Galfandor was out of the picture, and I didn't know who else to ask.

I wondered if our vampire housemates might help. "Do you think Sonia and Desmond would come if I asked?"

Max shook his head. "Desmond might, but Sonia would just yell at you for asking."

"She's so mean, I wouldn't want her coming even if she did agree," Ambria said.

I pushed my seat back from the table and stood. "We need more hands for this job. I don't want to leave anyone behind."

"It may not be possible to save everyone." Kanaan took his arcphone from the table and deactivated the holographic image. "Sometimes there is no perfect solution to a problem."

I slammed my hand on the table. "The more people we leave behind, the more souls we give to Victus!" I pounded the table again. "I'll find a way to make it happen." I left the room, grabbed my broom, and stormed out of the house, furious that magic couldn't provide an easy answer for me.

I heard footsteps running down the gravel driveway after me. I didn't have to turn around to know who it was. "Yes, Ambria?"

She got in front of me, a smirk on her lips. "How'd you know it was me?"

"Because Max can't run that fast." I looked back at the house. "I'm surprised he didn't come."

"He was too busy stuffing his face with biscuits."

I grunted. "Food over friends. It figures."

Ambria took my hands. "We can figure this out."

I shrugged. "How? We don't have much time to find people we can trust."

"What about people we don't like but can probably trust?" she asked.

I frowned. "Who would that be?"

Ambria pressed her lips together as if considering her next words, then spoke. "What about Blue?"

"Blue?" I hissed a breath between my teeth. "She's the one who told Harris my real name. She's the reason he hates me."

"But she's a lycan. We could use her strength."

"I hardly see her around campus anymore since she's taking all shifter courses." I shook my head. "I wouldn't trust her to keep her mouth shut." I climbed on my broom and flew toward campus, Ambria pacing me on hers. "Besides aren't you the one who just said you didn't want to ask Sonia?"

"Yes, but that's because I know she wouldn't help." Ambria shrugged. "We could fly to the house and ask anyway."

I nodded. "Let's go." We flew across campus and dove off the cliff.

Queens Gate spread out below in the center of the valley far below. Sheep dotted the green fields like puffs of cotton and crops swayed in the breeze, a rippling sea of brown and red.

We reached the house at the corner of Dowling and Bucket and landed. A shout interrupted my march to the door. Harris, Baxter, and Lily emerged from the back yard, brooms in hand.

"Conrad." Harris spoke my name in a strained tone as his group advanced.

I took out my wand. "What are you doing here?"

"I couldn't find you on campus." He shrugged. "Figured you'd come back into the city."

Ambria stepped up beside me, wand held offensively. "What do you want?"

Lily held up a hand. "We don't want a fight."

"I know you don't," Ambria said. "You're the only decent one of the bunch."

"Hey, now," Baxter protested. "Just because we don't like evil—" Harris nudged him in the ribs and the bigger boy hushed.

"I want to…apologize." Harris's shoulders slumped as if someone had just removed a load of bricks from his back. "I'm sorry, Conrad."

His words so surprised me, that I nearly fell over backward. "What?"

"I said I'm sorry." Lily nudged him and he continued. "I don't think you're the evil I'm supposed to destroy."

"That's a relief," Ambria said. "I rather like Conrad."

"As do I," Lily added.

Baxter scowled. "I don't like him."

Harris put a hand on his friend's shoulder and shook his head. "I think

it's time we put the past behind us and concentrate on what's important." His shoulders straightened and he looked me in the eye. "Stopping
your father."

I holstered my wand. "No matter what?"

He nodded. "No matter what."

Even if I couldn't trust Harris, I could certainly trust his desire to fulfill
the prophecy. "If you're willing to risk your lives and do some heavy lifting, then you can start helping us today."

Harris's eyes brightened. "How?"

I looked around. "Let's go inside. I don't want to explain things twice." I
walked straight toward Baxter who stood in my way. Apparently
remembering his last two encounters with me, he jumped aside like he'd
just stepped on a snake.

The front door was locked but a tap from my wand and the secret word
opened it. At least the vampires hadn't changed the code just yet. I
stopped in front of a thick metal door halfway down the hall and next to
the stairs. It was still far too early for Desmond and Sonia to be awake. I
held up a fist, hesitated.

Ambria pounded on the door, ringing it like a bell. She grinned. "I'll be
sure to tell Sonia you're the one who knocked."

I pounded again until an unholy screech rose from below. Harris and
Baxter nearly fell over themselves backing up while Lily and Ambria
cackled with laughter. I swallowed the apprehension coiling around my
throat and hoped Desmond kept Sonia from ripping off my head.

"The house had better be on fire or I'm going to tear your arms off, you
little wankers!" Sonia screamed.

I jumped backward as locks clicked. The door swung inward and
slammed into the stone wall at the top of the basement stairs. Fingernails bared like claws, fangs flashing, Sonia leapt through the doorway
still wearing silky pajamas riddled with images of cats.

"I need your help!" I shouted before she ripped into me.

Sonia backed me up against the wall, pressing her body to mine, face an inch away. "What is the meaning of this?" she asked in a dangerously quiet hiss. "Who are these strangers in my house?"

"Hello, Conrad." Desmond appeared over Sonia's shoulder and put a restraining hand on his sister's arm. "I'm sure he has a good reason."

"Yes," I squeaked. Out of the corner of my eye I saw that Lily and Ambria were no longer smiling.

"Good reason or not, he woke me up." Sonia flicked a fingernail across my cheek hard enough to make me wince. She considered a drop of my blood and licked it. "The house is not on fire. I am not in imminent danger of dying. Therefore, he owes me more than this little drop of crimson."

Ambria took out her wand. Before she could aim it, Sonia blurred down the hallway and ripped it from her grasp. "And so do you, little girl." She poked Ambria in the chest. "You will give me a pint."

Anger boiled in my chest. Before I could stop myself, I drew my wand. Sonia spun, but a spell erupted, crashing into her chest and slamming her against the wall. I concentrated on her cheek and flicked my wand. A red streak formed on her pale skin.

Sonia gasped and touched her cheek. She pulled back her hand and looked at the blood. A slow smile spread across her lips. "So, the little dog has teeth after all."

"Enough!" Desmond shouted loudly enough to send everyone jumping back. He turned to me. "Conrad, what's the meaning of waking us up in the middle of the afternoon?"

"I'm very sorry to disturb you, but lives are on the line and I need all the help I can get." I looked over at Sonia. "Even yours."

She reared back her head and laughed. "Why should I help you?"

I holstered my wand. "Sonia, you're one of the most unpleasant people I know and we'd probably get more done without you, but we could really use both of you."

Sonia smirked. "Well, since you asked politely, I'll consider it. Now, tell me what this is about."

"You're just curious, aren't you?" Ambria said.

"Of course." Sonia sauntered down the hall, pausing long enough to run a finger under Baxter's chin. The big boy blanched, remaining still as a mouse in a cat's paw. "Aren't these the children who used to play next door?"

"I used to live next door," Harris said, unable to keep the tremor from his voice. "These are my friends."

Sonia pursed her lips, shrugged, and released Baxter's chin. "I'm having blood tea. Anyone else like some?"

Lily grimaced. "I'll take my tea black, please."

Sonia laughed.

After everyone settled around the small table, tea in hand, I told them about the infernus, the foundry, and our plans to rescue the prisoners. At the first mention of Victus, Sonia's eyes glowed red.

"Your bleeding father doesn't give up, does he?" Her fangs extended from beneath her plump lips. "If we kill him, will you bugger off and leave us alone?"

"I'll help," Desmond said. "Things are bad enough right now without the Overlord coming back into power."

Harris smacked the table with the flat of his hand. "I'm in."

"Me too," Baxter said.

"I'll help." Lily smiled. "Though, I certainly won't be much help lifting those heavy coffins."

"My aunt and uncle have a pair of worker golems that can lift heavy loads," Harris said. "I can bring them along."

"Every little bit helps." I looked at Sonia. "Well?"

"Hmm." She stood and stretched, her pajamas tightening against her curves.

Ambria cleared her throat. "This isn't a peep show."

"Yes, I will help." Sonia walked around the table, tracing her fingernails across Baxter's scalp. He shivered, whether from fear or pleasure, I couldn't tell, and slumped in his seat after she'd gone.

Desmond smiled sheepishly. "I know she seems unpleasant, but my sister has been through a lot."

"So have we," Ambria said. "And yet we manage to act civil."

"When you're ready, message me on my phone," I told Desmond. "We can open a portal and bring you to us."

"Of course." Desmond ran a hand through his thick hair. "I'll be ready within the hour." He got up and left.

Lily sighed. "He's so charming and handsome."

"I suppose," Ambria said. "He's certainly nice compared to most vampires I've met."

"I'll go get those golems." Harris took out an arcphone. "Can I message you for a portal too?"

I bumped my phone against his to transfer my contact symbols. "Yes." I looked at the trio, still processing how we'd moved from enemies to uneasy allies. "This mission will be extremely dangerous. You do understand that we could end up fighting against battle mages, right?"

Baxter gulped. "Yeah, you made that clear earlier."

Harris didn't seem the least dissuaded. "I know it's dangerous, but we can't let the Overlord rise again."

"Agreed." Lily patted my arm. "I'm glad we can be on the same side again, Conrad."

Baxter pshawed. I ignored him and smiled. "Yeah, me too."

Ambria and I hopped on our brooms and flew into Queens Gate feeling much better about our chances. Our numbers had doubled, and two vampires would make a tremendous difference with the physical labor. I stopped by a magical hardware shop and purchased several self-sticking pulleys along with other items that might make our task easier.

"I can't stop thinking about Ansel's house," Ambria said as we left the store. "Why were Victus's men searching it?"

"I don't know, but we don't have time to go there now."

Ambria pursed her lips. "Probably not, but maybe Percival had some success healing Ansel. Maybe he could answer our questions."

I used the communication pendant to request a portal. Kanaan opened one in the alley behind the shop. We stepped through into the omniarch room where an anxious Max waited with Kanaan.

Max glared at us. "Where'd you guys go?"

Ambria smirked. "Oh, you're going to love this, Max."

He narrowed his eyes. "Love what?"

"Harris, Baxter, and Lily are going to help," I said.

"You've got to be kidding me!" Max's mouth dropped open. "That's awful!"

"Sonia and Desmond are coming too," Ambria added.

Max groaned. "I'd trust Sonia before letting Harris guard my back."

"Don't worry, Max." Ambria patted his back. "We'll keep an eye on you."

I handed the materials from the hardware store to Kanaan and hurried down to the gauntlet room, now Percival's makeshift healing ward.

The healer was bent over a beaker of purple liquid but straightened when he heard me come in. "You'll be happy to know that giving your cousin his allergy medicines has helped immensely. His soul is in dire straits, but now that his body is in nominal condition, it's starting to heal."

"Is there any way he can answer questions?" I asked.

"He's been in and out of consciousness, but not particularly lucid." Percival sorted through a small crate and removed a strip of red cloth. "This will wake him for a moment, but I don't know if he'll be in any condition to answer questions."

Ambria came up behind me. "What's the news?"

Percival ignored her and walked to the bed where Ansel lay. His skin was pale, but had a healthy color to it instead of sickly green. Percival laid the red strip on his patient's forehead. Ansel moaned. Jerked. His eyes flicked open and a scream tore from his throat.

Ambria and I jumped a foot. Percival snapped his fingers until Ansel stopped screaming. "What's your name?"

Ansel's head turned toward us. "Victus. Cumberbatch."

"No, your name," Percival said.

I leaned over my cousin. "We know about the foundry. What's in your house that Victus wants?"

"Golem spark spells," Ansel whispered. "Perfect copies. I said no. Wouldn't help."

"You have spells that would have helped him make perfect copies with his infernus?" Ambria asked.

"Yes. Before I knew you." He sucked in a breath. "Helped him and Delectra with original." Ansel's eyelids fluttered. "Demon creatures. Dark and so hot." Sweat broke out on his forehead. "So hot!" His body convulsed. Foam speckled his mouth.

Percival ripped away the strip. "He's going into shock!" He rushed to a shelf, frantically searching potions and came back with clear liquid. "Hold his mouth open, boy!"

I fought Ansel's bucking, glad he was restrained, and managed to get my fingers in his mouth. His teeth clamped down. I shouted in pain and jerked them out.

"Careful, boy!" Percival gripped Ansel's jaw and squeezed with thumb and fingers, forcing open the patient's mouth. He poured the liquid down Ansel's throat then pressed up on his chin to hold his mouth closed.

Ansel swallowed. Relaxed. His eyes closed and his breathing went back to normal.

"What happened?" Ambria asked.

"In case you hadn't noticed, the man isn't well," Percival said. "Now, I hope you got the answers you needed because I refuse to wake him again until I'm convinced he's much better."

"We're done here for now," I said.

"Once you bring in all those other coffins, I'll barely have time for anything," Percival said. "I hope they're easier to care for than Ansel. If only I knew more about healing demon-inflicted soul damage."

Ambria snapped her fingers. "What about Emily Glass's demonomicon?"

Percival quirked an eyebrow. "I thought that only contained information on demons."

"Well, it has all sorts of demon-related information." Ambria shrugged. "Perhaps it has something about countering demonic effects." She in the direction of the omniarch. "Conrad, can you open a portal inside the vault?"

"I think so." Anything that might help Percival heal Ansel and anyone we rescued was worth an extra trip. We walked down the corridor to the omniarch room. I envisioned the table my friends and I spent hours studying at and opened a portal directly to it, bypassing the need to enter the vault via the secret entrance in Moore Keep. Ambria flew her broom through the portal and vanished from view.

"How interesting." Percival peered through the gateway. "Is that a warehouse?"

"Something like that," I said.

Ambria returned moments later with several tomes in hand and gave them to Percival. "I grabbed all the books from her section."

Percival looked them over, excitement flaring in his eyes. "Fascinating. I'll let you know if I find anything useful."

My phone dinged. I flicked on the screen and found a message from Harris. *Waiting in front of your house for a portal.*

Max looked at my screen. "Are you sure it's a good idea to bring them along? What if Harris decides to stab you in the back?"

"I don't trust him with my life, but I also don't think he'll try to kill me." I deactivated the portal to the vault and imagined the front of the house so I could open a portal there.

"I'm not letting him out of my sight," Max said. "Not even for a second."

I couldn't blame him, but we needed all the help we could get. I just hoped it didn't cost me my life.

CHAPTER 26

A portal winked open. The house at the corner of Dowling and Bucket appeared through the gateway. Harris, Baxter, and Lily squirmed nervously next to a glaring Sonia. Two stone gorillas towered behind them—apparently the utility golems Harris brought with him.

The moment the portal appeared, the kids rushed through, eager to escape the vampire's chilly stare, the stone gorillas stomping after them. Desmond stepped through after his sister and nodded at me. "We're fueled up on blood and ready to go."

I closed the portal and led the group toward the gauntlet room.

The newcomers stopped to look at the mansion, eyes wide.

"This is the underground Slade mansion?" Harris said, awe in his voice. "It's huge."

"Whoa." Baxter took a tentative step forward. "I heard there was no way to get here through the Burrows anymore."

"Perhaps we should move here," Sonia told her brother. "We wouldn't have to sleep in the basement anymore."

I cleared my throat. "We can talk about this later. We don't have much time before we have to leave."

Desmond patted my back. "Yes, of course, Conrad. Lead on."

I took them into the gauntlet room where Kanaan waited with the holographic map of the plan on display. Asha, Stan, and Natalia were already there. Shushiel hung from a thread overhead, drawing a sharp gasp from Sonia.

"You didn't mention giant bloody spiders!" The vampire backed up a step. "Where did you find that thing?"

Shushiel's mandibles twitched. "You are rude."

Ambria scowled at Sonia. "She's our friend."

"She's a giant bug!" Sonia shot back.

"She's deathly afraid of spiders," Desmond said with a faint smile.

"A vampire afraid of spiders?" Baxter burst into laughter. "That's so lame!"

Sonia's pale face turned pink. "I'm not afraid of anything." She folded trembling arms across her chest. "Not even your monster."

Shushiel dropped to the floor and sagged on her legs. "I'm not a monster."

Ambria hugged the spider. "I know. Sonia is just mean."

"Told you Sonia is trouble," Max whispered to me.

Sonia bared her fangs. "I heard that, little boy."

Max bared his plain teeth. "Yeah, well maybe you should be nicer!"

"If I didn't hate people so much, maybe I would be."

Kanaan held up a hand. "Quiet yourselves or leave. Our plan has no margin for error."

Desmond gripped Sonia's arm and whispered something in her ear. Her lips pressed into a tight line but she kept quiet. Desmond looked to Kanaan and nodded. The magitsu master zoomed in the map to an area marked with a portal icon. "This is how we shall proceed." He walked the additions to our group through the plan he'd detailed earlier, assigning everyone specific roles.

"Sonia and Desmond form loading group one. The utility golems will form group two." Kanaan turned to Harris. "Will you need to be present to issue commands to them?"

Harris nodded. "Yes, they won't accept commands from anyone else."

"We have twelve transport carpets." Kanaan pointed to rolled bundles on the floor. "As each one is loaded, group three will tow the carpets with flying brooms back through the portal to Shushiel who will unload them with webs and pulleys with the help of Stan." Max opened his mouth, presumably to ask who was in group three, but Kanaan spoke first. "Conrad, Ambria, Max, and you two"—he pointed at Lily and Baxter—"will form group three."

"What about me?" Asha said.

Stan jabbed a thumb against himself. "You're making me stay here? I think Shushiel can handle unloading coffins without me."

"Asha will join me to guard the others while they work." Kanaan zoomed in on the sandstone butte hiding the foundry and marked the two entrances on the north and south sides. The south entrance was the one we'd use to steal the coffins. "Natalia will guard the southern side. Asha and I will watch the back in case any battle mages approach."

Natalia frowned. "Why am I guarding the front? All the enemies will approach from the rear."

"Enemies could approach from any side." Kanaan circled the top of the buttes with a finger. "You can easily climb to the top of the rocks and watch from above."

"I would like to be there too," Shushiel said. "I cannot protect my friends if I'm here."

"With a group so small, every role is vital. The cargo must be unloaded quickly, which is why we need you here." Kanaan handed out dull gray pendants. "These are for communication. If I give the abort command, everyone at the foundry will immediately stop what they are doing and gather at the front door." He turned to Shushiel. "Should that happen, you must rush through the portal and be prepared to come to our aid."

Shushiel bounced up and down on her legs. "I will not let you down."

Sonia grimaced. "Grunt work. I can hardly wait."

Harris clenched his wand in a hand. "Can we destroy the compound? Kill all the enemy battle mages?"

"You're a little fool if you think we can fight over twenty battle mages," Sonia said.

"No," Kanaan said. "The odds are too great." He held up a red vial. "I created a blood potion that will scar the demon pattern in the foundry and prevent it from working without extensive repair."

Harris reluctantly holstered his wand. "When do we leave?"

Kanaan checked a black armlet on his right wrist. "Victus, Zarin, and Garkin planned to leave thirty-nine minutes ago. I will scout ahead to make sure they have left."

"How long will that take?" Harris asked. "Can't we all go with you?"

"Patience, grasshopper." Kanaan looked around at the group. "I suggest you prepare while I am away." He left the room without another word.

Harris stared at the empty doorway for a moment before turning to the broom rack against the wall and choosing a broom for his part in our venture. Shushiel crawled over to us, her eight eyes large and full of concern. "I do not like you going without me."

Ambria touched her foreleg. "I don't either, but I think we'll be fine with Kanaan and Asha watching our backs."

"But I am much better at protecting you." Shushiel's mandibles trembled with agitation. "I can set webs and traps to warn of danger."

"I really would feel better with her around," Max said. "But since we need the vampires and the golems for loading, I guess there isn't anyone else strong enough to unload coffins by themselves."

"I know." I sighed and rubbed Shushiel's foreleg. "I think we'll be fine." I noticed the communications pendant affixed to her foreleg. "Just keep an ear out, okay?"

"I will be vigilant," she promised.

"Cute." Natalia strolled around Shushiel, her feline eyes narrow. "Your own guardian spider."

Shushiel rotated in place. "I am their friend."

Natalia nodded. "I think it's adorable how much you want to protect your friends." She looked at Stan. "Reminds me of him."

"Are there any other felycans back at his house who can help?" I asked.

She shook her head. "Two weeks ago, the answer would have been yes, but most of the older shifters found furever homes."

"Did you say 'fur'?" Ambria said.

"Yep." Natalia winked. "We call ourselves furkids."

"Interesting." Ambria quirked her lips with amusement. "I don't see how Stan keeps up with you all."

"He does his best." Natalia's lips stretched into a smile. "He's a good man with a big heart."

Max took a pouch from his backpack and emptied the contents on one of the healing beds. "I grabbed all my banana peel and brain fog potion bombs. I'm going to split them up so we each have a few, okay?"

"What a wonderful idea, Max." Ambria patted him on the back. "I'm glad to see you thought about something besides food."

Max narrowed his eyes. "I can't fight on an empty stomach."

"Hopefully we won't have to fight at all." I watched as Harris and crew prepared their brooms. I had no idea how they'd perform or if I could even trust them in a bad situation.

Natalia sidled up to me. "That boy carries around a lot of anger."

"Harris?" I said.

Max frowned. "How can you tell?"

"Body language." She nodded at him. "Whenever he looks at Conrad, his jaw clenches. His face turns pink. He has scars on his palms where his fingernails repeatedly cut into his skin." Natalia shrugged. "Small things like that."

Ambria's mouth dropped open. "Scars on his palms? Good lord, that's awful." She hooked her arm in mine. "Maybe he still wants to kill you."

Natalia looked back and forth between the two of us and smirked. "When you mentioned Victus, Harris nearly cut his hands again, but he forced himself to relax. I think Conrad is safe for now."

Lily walked over to us, Harris and Baxter trailing behind. "What are all these marbles, Max?"

"Potion bombs." He handed two yellow and two gray ones to her. "Throw the yellow ones on the floor if someone is chasing you. It'll make them slip." He held up a gray one. "This one will make them forget the last ten minutes."

"I'm glad to see you've turned lemons into lemonade, Max." Lily nudged him in the ribs. "Because you certainly aren't doing well in potions class."

Max rolled his eyes. "Ha, ha."

She rotated one of the marble-like potions bombs between thumb and forefinger. "Have you ever considered using these with a slingshot?"

Max's eyebrows rose. "Hey, that's a pretty good idea."

Harris held out a hand. "Have some for me?"

Max hesitated, then gave Harris and Baxter potion bombs. "Just be careful you don't throw them near allies."

"I'm not stupid, Max." Harris loaded the potions in the saddlebag on his hovering broom and looked toward the door impatiently. "How long 'til Kanaan is back?"

"I hope he takes as long as he needs," Ambria said. "This isn't a leisure trip, it's a mission. We can't afford for anything to go wrong."

"I've heard stories about you, Conrad." Harris sat on the edge of one of the empty patient beds in the makeshift healing ward. "About the strange silver girl you were seen with, and that you'd disappear for days at a time."

Ambria's arm tightened on mine. "We've been busy saving the world. If not for us, an evil queen would have taken over campus and destroyed us all."

"Talk about hyperbole," Natalia said. "What sort of nonsense are you going on about?"

"The truth." Shushiel's magically amplified voice rose in indignation. "The Glimmer Queen would have taken over this world."

"Exactly!" Max puffed out his chest. "We fought an evil queen and went to the ends of the world for an artifact that would restore the real ruler of the Glimmer. Now Cora is back in charge."

Baxter's face wrinkled with confusion. "What's the Glimmer?"

I held up a hand to stop Max from answering. "Maybe we should start from the beginning."

Harris's left eyelid twitched. "I'd like to hear everything." He worked his jaw back and forth, as if trying to loosen tight muscles.

"I would too." Lily perched on the bed next to Harris. "I heard about that woman who attacked people with vines, but everyone just assumed she was a powerful Arcane."

Max cleared away his potion bombs so I could sit on the bed. Ambria sat next to me and Natalia hopped on the other side before Max could, leaving my friend to stand. Asha and Stan approached, curious looks on their faces.

"What's this?" Stan asked. "It looks like someone is about to tell a story."

"How could you tell?" Ambria asked.

The old man winked. "Because I've seen that look on the faces of a hundred youngsters right before I tell them a story."

"Oh, it's story time for the children?" Sonia pulled Desmond behind her. "Who wants to hear about the little boy who lost all his blood?" She graced us with a wicked smile. "It's a wonderful tale with a happy ending."

Ambria snorted. "Oh, our stories are much more gruesome, Sonia."

Max dragged one of the other beds closer to ours despite Percival's protestations from the other side of the room.

"Put that back when you're finished!" the healer yelled.

Asha took a seat on the bed Max brought over. Stan and Sonia took seats, leaving my friend once again with no place to sit.

"What story are you telling, Conrad?" Asha asked.

I offered her a small smile. "Mine."

Her eyes flared. "I would very much like to hear it." She saw the sad look on Max's face and slid over to make room for him.

"It all started in a place called Little Angel Orphanage." I told them how my first few foster parents died in terrible accidents and how mean many were until I met the person who would shape me as a person: Cora. I told them how we'd lived with a man who abused her and how she'd killed him by pushing him down the stairs.

Lily grimaced. "What an awful childhood, Conrad."

I smiled wryly. "That was only the start." I continued with the story of how a man tried to kill me with a herd of animals, only to die by my hand when I hit him with a shovel. How that unintentional murder led me down a rabbit hole of adventure at Arcane University. My audience gasped when I told them how my parents came back to life and tried to kill me, but Ambria and Max rescued me.

Baxter looked at Max, impressed. "Didn't think you had it in you, Tiberius."

"He has his moments," Ambria said.

Sonia pshawed. "I'm surprised any of them survived at all."

I finished telling that chapter of my life and was about to tell them how I met Evadora and learned Cora's true origins, but Kanaan seemingly appeared from nowhere.

Kanaan started without preamble. "The principal enemies have left and the other combatants in the compound are far from the foundry. It is time to start our operation."

I gulped and shared nervous looks with the others. Even Asha looked uncertain. This feeling was nothing new to me, but it never seemed to get any easier.

Lily laughed nervously. "I'm shaking like a leaf."

Ambria patted her arm. "I always get nervous before we do something dangerous even though I should be used to it by now."

Natalia stretched and put on a show of unconcern. "Just do your job and we'll all be fine."

"I wish it was that easy." Max ran a hand through his white-blond hair and sighed. "Once more into the breach."

I got my broom, checked my equipment and the group moved into the omniarch room where an open portal hovered between the columns, the derelict cottage visible on the other side. We filtered through in clusters until everyone stood in Montana.

Max gripped his wand and gave Lily a grim look. "Welcome to the danger zone."

Ambria face-palmed. "Oh, god."

Sonia stalked toward the cottage. "My, what a charming house."

Shushiel's mandibles twitched. "I will come with you and return with the first load of coffins."

Kanaan didn't object.

Stan hugged Asha. "Be careful, Ashes." He ruffled my hair. "Watch your back, Conrad."

"I will," my sister and I replied at the same time.

My sister. It was still so strange thinking of her that way. I hoped we survived this mission so I could get to know her better.

CHAPTER 27

W e moved forward at the fastest walking pace the stone gorillas could muster while Kanaan and Asha scouted ahead. Shushiel took to the trees and shimmered into camouflage.

"I could crawl faster than this," Sonia complained. "Can't you put the golems on a carpet and tow them?"

Harris's face reddened. "Don't you ever stop complaining?"

Lily unfurled one of the wide carpets on the ground. Harris blew out a sigh and motioned the golems into the middle of it. The carpet rose a few feet off the ground and Lily hitched it to the back of her broom. She looked down at Sonia. "You're such a negative person. Have you ever thought about counselling?"

Sonia bared her fangs. "You ever thought about losing a pint of blood?"

Desmond put a hand on her shoulder. "No more bickering. We have work to do."

We reached edge of the forest ten minutes later and found Kanaan and Shushiel dragging bodies bound in webs into the bushes.

Harris's eyes widened. "Are they dead?"

Kanaan nodded. "Shushiel found two mages hunting a woman in the woods. She did not spare them."

Lily shivered. "Where's the woman?"

"I sent her back to the portal with Asha." Kanaan held up a hand and cocked an ear. "It is clear to proceed." He vanished into the sandstone canyon between the buttes.

Harris looked at the cocooned forms. "I'm glad you killed them Shushiel. Evil like that doesn't deserve to live."

Shushiel's eyes blinked. "In some cases, you may be right." She rotated toward me. "I will look through the forest and then return to the portal to unload the carpets. Be careful, my friends."

Ambria smiled. "Thank you for protecting us."

We proceeded down the trail through the pockmarked buttes until we reached the rounded black mound with the tunnel leading to the foundry. I hadn't noticed it before, but etched in the sandstone just above the tunnel entrance were the words, *Devil's Kitchen*.

The sides of the carpet holding the golems scraped against the tunnel sides as we followed it inside. Kanaan had measured the width perfectly.

When we reached the nine-sided room with the pattern in the center, Harris gaped. "How is it possible to design something so complicated?"

We steered wide of the pattern and went through the short corridor in the back to the coffin room. Lily, Baxter, and Harris paused to take it all in, but Desmond and Sonia grabbed a carpet and headed straight for the red coffins.

Max flew over to Ivy's coffin. "Get this one first."

Sonia looked through the glass on top and smirked. "Your new girlfriend?"

He blushed and looked as if he wanted to protest, then nodded. "I wish Ivy Slade was my girlfriend."

Sonia frowned, obviously disappointed she hadn't embarrassed the boy. Desmond nudged her and they easily hefted the coffin and slid it onto the flying carpet. It took them no time at all to fit two more into place and strap them down. Max hitched the carpet to his broom and set off across the room. Harris's loader golems started working on the black coffins, moving stiffly but efficiently. Even so, Sonia and Desmond packed two more full carpets by the time the golems finished their first.

Ambria took the next carpet and I followed behind. We gathered speed once we reached the trail in the forest, keeping a close eye on the coffins in case they rolled off around a curve. Thankfully, the straps I'd purchased from the hardware store kept them firmly in place.

We caught up with Max who watched as Shushiel lifted all three coffins with a single web bound to a pulley overhead. I parked my carpet beneath another pulley and Ambria did the same.

"Don't wait on the carpets, Max," Ambria said. "The person behind you will get the one you drop off."

Max snapped his fingers. "Yeah, totally forgot." He detached the tether and flew away. Ambria and I did the same, leaving Shushiel to continue her work.

I saw Stan rolling up Max's first carpet as we sped away and hoped the old man could keep up with the demand.

We passed Harris in the forest on his way to deliver his first load, and nearly ran into Lily on her way through the tunnel. There was no way around or over her, so we had to back up and wait for her to come out.

"Max just barely made it through before I entered," Lily said. "We might need traffic control."

I tapped the comm pendant on my chest. "When you're towing a load, announce when you enter and leave the tunnel so no one runs into you."

JOHN CORWIN

Baxter's voice piped through the pendant. "Okay."

"Got it," Harris responded.

Lily smiled. "Problem solved."

Once she cleared the tunnel, Ambria and I jetted through, passing Baxter in the room with the demon pattern.

"Why can't we just fly across it?" he asked.

"It might be warded or awaken a demon," Ambria said. "Best to avoid it."

Baxter gulped. "Good enough reason for me."

Back in the coffin room, Sonia and Desmond had loaded up the rest of the red coffins and moved over to the black ones.

"You children need to move faster," Sonia said. "We're nearly out of carpets."

"Trying," I muttered.

Baxter's voice emanated from my comm pendant and the ones around me. "Entering tunnel."

I tethered a carpet to my broom and set off once again. We worked feverishly, the only talking over the next twenty minutes that of radio chatter as those of us on brooms announced a tunnel approach and exit. The exercise improved our efficiency so much, we almost kept up with Sonia and Desmond.

Shushiel somehow managed to keep up with unloading, but poor Stan had a time rolling up the carpets quickly enough. Lily and Ambria hopped off their brooms and helped him catch up while the rest of us took the ready ones and headed back to the foundry.

I lost count of how many times I made the trip and was surprised when white coffins waited on the next carpet. *How many more?* I tried to count, but the haphazard pile of white defied me.

Soon, even the vampires' paces slowed, tired by the constant lifting. The golems and their precise clockwork motions began to outpace them, but not those of us ferrying the coffins through the portal. With over twenty of the white boxes left, a line formed. Max and I got off our brooms and tried to help, but the coffins were far too heavy for us to lift.

Kanaan rushed into the room from the back entrance, Asha right behind him. "We must go."

"Go?" I glanced at the remaining pile. "But we're not done."

"There is no time to argue." He waved a hand at the remaining boxes. "We must leave them."

"And allow Victus's people to murder over twenty people?" Ambria shook her head and drew her wand. "I don't think so."

I slid my wand from its holster. "Are the battle mages coming?"

"They started rushing around and grouping up." Asha shrugged. "It's almost as if something alerted them."

"Lovely," Sonia said. "I don't plan to wait around. I'm too tired to fight."

"Please," Ambria said, "we can't leave these people behind."

Desmond flexed his fingers. "I'll do what I can."

Sonia bared her teeth. "You're staying?"

"If you help me, we can finish faster," he said.

Sonia stomped a foot and looked as if she wanted to throw a fit. She took a deep breath, and went back to the remaining stacks of white coffins. "Fine, then. Let's die for strangers."

Kanaan shook his head, but instead of arguing, ran back through the rear exit. Asha gave us a concerned look and followed.

I tapped my comm pendant. "Where are they, Kanaan?"

He didn't answer. Seconds later, he and Asha burst back into the room. They turned, aimed their wands, and blasted the stone above the doorway, collapsing it. "It will take them five minutes to run around the outside," Kanaan said. "We cannot wait any longer."

"We can fight them." Harris brandished his wand. "I'm ready."

"I will lead them away from here," Kanaan said. "Get the rest of the coffins as quickly as you can." He dashed across the chamber and vanished.

Asha stood in place, seemingly uncertain what to do. "I'll go out front and guard the entrance." She tapped her pendant. "Shushiel, we need you here."

"Coming," said the spider.

Sonia and Desmond steeled themselves and picked up the pace, loading three more carpets. Lily, Max, and Baxter took off with them while Ambria waited next in line. Sweat broke out on my forehead. I felt as if an army of battle mages might burst through the door at any moment. Ambria took her load and left.

The rocks at the rear entrance shifted. I turned and heat washed over my body. A shockwave blasted rubble through the air. My broom tumbled through the air. I slammed into rock and everything went black.

When I came to my senses, I didn't know how long I'd been out. Something heavy pressed against my legs—a pile of rubble from the explosion. I dragged myself forward an inch, trying to get free. I saw a bloodied Sonia, Desmond draped over her shoulder, racing from the room.

I groaned with effort and managed to pull myself forward another inch. Footsteps tapped my way. I looked up and saw Harris. He stood over me for a long moment, wand clenched tight in his hand. His hair stuck out in all directions, and blood trickled from a cut in his temple. He said nothing as he looked down at me like a person considering whether to kill a roach.

I tried to speak through a throat that felt like a desert. I reached for my wand, but it wasn't in its holster. Harris's entire body shivered and tears formed in his eyes.

"I hate you and your entire family." Blood dripped from his clenched fists. "I don't want to hate you, Conrad. I don't want to blame you, but I can't help it."

Calm settled over me. I knew what happened next. I nodded and swallowed the dust in my mouth. "I understand."

Harris's lips trembled. "I want you all dead." With that, he thrust his wand back into its holster and gripped my hand with the other. He grunted and tugged me free then collapsed on his backside. "I want you dead, Conrad."

"I'm not your enemy," I said.

He nodded. "I know, but I still hate you."

"I wish I could bring back your parents, Harris." Tears burned my eyes. "I wish my father had never been born." I stood up and offered him a hand. Harris looked at it for a moment, then took it and let me pull him to his feet.

More rubble shifted in the back entrance. Shouts echoed from the other side. The way was almost clear for them.

"We'd better run for it." Harris wasted no time following his own advice.

A group of robed mages burst through the remaining barrier, wands and staffs at the ready.

My ankle hurt, but I ignored the pain and raced after Harris. I took out one of Max's yellow potion bombs and threw it toward the back doorway. It landed well short, but the battle mages ran right into the slick and fell all over themselves. I threw a memory fog bomb at the wallowing mages. It burst into a large cloud right in their midst.

Harris might have helped me escape the rubble, but he wasn't waiting around for me to catch up. He was already halfway across the room with the demon pattern. Great red scars ran across the surface of the diagram where Kanaan must have dumped his potion on the way out.

"Conrad!"

The familiar, dreaded voice stopped me in my tracks. I turned and saw Victus standing in the doorway. His thick hair was gone, head shaved bald. A scar ran across his eye where I'd hit him during our encounter in the Glimmer. Gone was the charming exterior, replaced with something more nefarious.

"Where did you come from?" I backed away. "I thought you'd gone to the Grand Nexus!"

"I did, but a hunting expedition returning from the mountains saw your activity and contacted me, so I came back." He held up empty hands. "Forget that for now. Let's talk, son."

"Son?" I could hardly breathe. "Talk? You killed Delectra! You sent Garkin to kill me!"

"Yet, you survived." Victus smiled. "You're powerful, boy. It would be a mistake to end you."

"A mistake?" I barked a laugh and took another step back. I didn't have time to chit-chat with my father, the murderer. "So you'll leave me alone?"

"I will leave your loved ones in peace if you agree to join me." Victus held out his hands imploringly. "Just think. No more running. All your friends will be well-taken care of."

"No." I raised my wand. "I'll never join you."

"Because I'll kill you!" Harris roared from behind me. He stepped in front of me, wand raised. "You murdered my parents, Overlord. Now I'll fulfill the prophecy."

Victus reared back his head and laughed. "Prophecy? Surely you don't mean Foreseeance Five-Thousand, do you?"

"Yes, I do." Energy gathered at the tip of Harris's wand. "Once again shall the evil rise. The son of the fallen is the only hope for victory!" The glowing ball of energy grew brighter with every word.

Victus wiped tears of mirth from his eyes. "Little Harris Ashmore, what do you even know of your parents' deaths?"

"I know that you killed them." Harris aimed the wand toward Victus, but with all the debris and distance between us, I doubted he'd hit the target. "You found out about the prophecy and tried to kill me."

"That would be foolish on my part, don't you think?" Victus tutted. "By killing your parents, I would only put the foreseeance into motion." He waved a hand through the air. "Besides, I didn't kill your parents. The Arcane Council did."

Harris shook his head. "Lying won't get you out of this."

"I'm not lying, boy." Victus folded his arms, completely unconcerned by the wand pointed in his direction. "No one ever told you the truth, did they? No one told you that your parents were killed in a fight with Blue Cloaks because they were working for me!"

CHAPTER 28

"That's a lie!" Harris screamed and unleashed a bolt of energy from his wand. It sizzled through the air, burning with the hatred of a thousand suns and the rage of an orphaned boy.

For a moment, I dared to hope it was enough.

Victus contemptuously flicked his wand and deflected the shot. It exploded against the wall, leaving a molten mass of lava. "Your father was on the Arcane Council. When they found out he supported me, they had him and your mother assassinated and blamed it on me." My father smiled cruelly at the boy. "Their deaths were used as propaganda. You're no pawn of prophecy, or a great hero waiting to rise. You're just another war orphan."

"No!" Harris flung volley after volley of energy at Victus, but my father deflected them as if batting away flies.

"Your parents were strong, Harris. If you were stronger, I might actually want you to join me." Victus whirled his wand and Harris's wand ripped from his grasp and shattered into splinters.

I conjured a shield, but another blast hurled me and Harris through the air. I landed on my back. Harris groaned and pushed to his knees. I saw Victus walking toward us, the cruel smile still on his lips. "Join me, Conrad, and I'll spare you and the boy."

I rose to my feet and looked him in the eye. "I don't think so." Fireblade sizzled from the tip of my wand. Victus tried to deflect, but it cut through his shield like paper. Eyes wide, he dove to the side. I traced the beam after him, carving rivulets of lava in the stone. "Die, you filthy murderer!" I slashed at him, burning the hem of his robe before he ducked behind a pile of rubble.

My arm trembled as my strength waned. I released the spell, slung Harris's arm over my shoulder and ran for the exit. Bodies of robed mages littered the trail outside. A dead man's torso hung over the side of one of the buttes. A webbed body swung from a rocky overhang. Blood spatters told the tale of a vicious fight.

"Conrad!" Shushiel shimmered into view. "I could not find you."

"We saw Victus." I continued to pull Harris with me. He looked frazzled, but otherwise uninjured. "Is the way clear to the portal?"

"Victus is here?" Shushiel's mandibles twitched. "Go faster, Conrad. I will watch the rear." She leapt onto the rock face and attached a web to it, then leapt across the gap to the other side, blocking the canyon with her silk.

I knew she could take care of herself, but Harris was dragging me down. "Can you run on your own?" I asked.

He blinked. Nodded. "I-I think so."

"Then do it!"

Harris broke into a run and I chased after him. We passed more bodies, some of them with their throats ripped out, others drained of blood— Sonia and Desmond's handiwork. When we reached the forest, Kanaan appeared from the trees.

"What happened?" he asked.

"One of Victus's people saw us moving the coffins," I explained. "Victus came back."

"Then Garkin is not far behind." Kanaan looked toward the foundry. "Are you the last?"

"Shushiel is behind us," I said.

He nodded. "Then go." He waved us on and paced behind us.

Harris soon slowed, holding his side. "I'm too tired."

Shushiel blurred into view twenty feet behind. "More come."

"I can't run anymore," Harris said.

The huge spider lowered her head and upended the boy onto her back. He shouted in fright and gripped the fur on her back. Shushiel's legs wrapped a strand of webbing across Harris's waist to hold him in place, and she took off at an eight-legged gallop.

Despite my magitsu training, I rapidly tired, but pushed myself forward no matter how heavy my feet felt. I wished I could make my body understand that dying was a lot worse than fatigue so it would cooperate.

At last the portal came into view.

A bolt of lightning obliterated a tree to my right. Splinters flew. Pain bit into my arm and face. I staggered, but a sure hand took me and threw me into the portal. I landed hard on the other side and spun to see Kanaan rolling away as another attack narrowly missed him.

Garkin appeared at the edge of the tree line, a wand and staff in his hands. "Face me, Kanaan. Let us duel for the fate of your apprentice."

Kanaan turned and ran toward the cottage.

"What's he doing?" I shouted. "Get to the portal!"

Garkin unleashed a blast at the cottage, destroying the front door. The next blast caught Kanaan in the side. He rolled to a stop in the dirt, lifeless eyes staring up.

"No!" I screamed. "Kanaan!"

Kanaan appeared from the other side of the portal and leapt in. He snapped his fingers and the portal winked away.

"W-what happened? I saw you die." I reached over and touched him to be sure I wasn't hallucinating.

"An illusion trick." Kanaan helped me to my feet. "As you said, the way of the monkey relies on trickery. I could not reach the portal without diverting him."

My body sagged with relief. "I thought you were dead."

"Not yet." Kanaan headed out of the omniarch room where the others waited.

Ambria and Max ran up and hugged me.

"I didn't know what happened to you!" Ambria said. She kissed my cheek. "Conrad, I thought you were dead."

"Lot of that going around today," I said.

Shushiel cut the web from her back and Harris rolled off onto all fours. He sat down and looked miserably at the floor.

"You okay?" Baxter asked him.

Harris nodded.

"What happened to you two?" Lily asked me.

"Victus," I said.

Gasps sounded all around me.

Asha came to my side. "You saw our"—she swallowed hard and grimaced—"father?"

"Yes." I looked at the dejected Harris and wondered if Victus had told the truth about his parents. "We escaped."

Ambria hugged me again. It felt so comforting that I wrapped both my arms around her and leaned my head on top of hers. For a moment, everything else went silent and all the demons in my head went away.

"How many coffins did we leave behind?" Asha asked.

"A dozen," Desmond replied.

I let go of Ambria and gathered my strength. "Let's find out who we have." Everyone drifted toward the makeshift healing ward in the gauntlet room.

Percival already had one person on a table that I instantly recognized. "Galfandor!" I ran over and touched the headmaster.

He groaned and blinked weary eyes. "It appears I'm back among the living."

"How did Victus get you?" I asked.

Galfandor tried to shake his head, but it barely moved. "I am as much in the dark as you, Conrad."

Max stood on the other side of the bed. "Zarin must have taken him from the healers and taken him to the foundry."

Ambria's eyes widened with worry. "Do you think they made a copy of him yet?"

"They have not used the foundry recently," Kanaan said. "I do not believe they did."

Max pushed through the crowd around Galfandor. "Where's Ivy? Why isn't she out of her box yet?"

"Will you give me some space?" Percival shooed everyone to the sides and administered a potion to the headmaster. He pressed a hand to Galfandor's forehead and grunted. "This is promising."

"What is?" Max asked.

"Liquid aether fortifies the torn soul and helps it heal faster." He swirled the blue concoction in the vial. "It's just very time consuming to make."

"How do you make liquid aether?" I walked around the bed and looked at the glowing liquid.

"It took me four days just to make this using the instructions I found inside the demonomicon." He put a cork in the vial. "Apparently it's much easier for someone who can channel aether than for casters."

Max peered inside the other ruby coffins lining the back of the room. "Ivy is Seraphim. If you heal her, she can channel all the aether you want."

"And Max can have a new girlfriend," Baxter said. "Right, Harris?"

Harris flinched and looked up from the floor. He looked at Galfandor and blinked a few times, then stormed toward the headmaster. Leaning in close, he said, "Who killed my parents, Galfandor?"

Galfandor's forehead wrinkled. "What do you mean, lad?"

"Victus said my parent worked with him. That the Arcane Council sent Blue Cloaks to kill them." Harris's fists clenched. "Is that true?"

Galfandor sighed weakly, his eyes toward me.

I didn't let him off the hook. Galfandor had kept things from me before, and I hadn't liked it. "Well, did he tell the truth?" I asked.

A long moment passed in which everyone seemed to hold their breath at the unfolding drama. "Yes, I'm afraid it is true, Harris."

Harris deflated like a balloon, folding in on himself and backing away. "Why wasn't I told? Why would my parents work for the Overlord?"

Lily and Baxter exchanged horrified looks. Max and Ambria gaped at the revelation.

"What's this about?" Max looked back and forth between me and Harris. "The Ashmores were evil like our parents?"

"James Ashmore was elected to the Arcane Council after his opponent mysteriously died," Galfandor said weakly. "He was the first Victus supporter elected and worked to get Victus elected as Arcanus Primus. When the opponent of another Victus supporter died, the remaining council members started a secret investigation and discovered James was killing them."

Harris shuddered. "No," he moaned.

Galfandor continued. "Victus overthrew the council not long after, but not before a secret order was given to a covert squad of Blue Cloaks to hunt down the Ashmores and kill them, making it look as if Victus had done it." He closed his eyes and seemed to rest for a moment, then drew a deep breath and spoke. "I know all of this because I gave the order."

Harris gasped. "You were on the council?"

"I am a member of a secret order of Arcanes, formed in the aftermath of the Seraphim War to prevent another such event." Galfandor squeezed his eyes shut for a moment. "Despite all our precautions, we were too late to stop the Overlord."

"This is awful!" Ambria gripped my hand. "Why did you keep this a secret from us, especially after all we've been through?"

"Because we thought Conrad might be the next big threat." Galfandor gave me an imploring look. "We decided to keep an eye on him until we decided for sure."

"That's why you've always been hesitant to help me?" It felt like someone punched me in the gut, but it should have come as no surprise. It made sense why Galfandor always listened to what we had to say even if he didn't directly help us most of the time. *He was spying on us.*

"I recommended we trust you, Conrad. I told the others we should nurture you more, but they wouldn't listen." Galfandor wheezed and tried to speak, but his eyelids fluttered and he sank back into the bed.

Percival set his hands on his hips. "You've overextended him." He motioned us away. "Give the old man some space, or you'll kill him!"

Harris stared at the headmaster, warring expressions twisting his features.

Lily patted him on the shoulder. "Harris, everything will be all right."

He jerked his arm away and shook his head. "No, it won't," he said in a rough voice. "All this time, I thought I was someone special. I thought I was born to be a hero." Tears poured down his cheeks. "I was just born to be a joke!" He stormed out of the room, never looking back.

Baxter looked around like a trapped animal, suddenly uncertain of his own place in the world. "I can't believe it. It can't be true!"

"Welcome to my world." Max looked adoringly through the glass on one of the coffins. "Thankfully, we have the answers to our prayers right here."

"Careful about placing people on pedestals, Max." Ambria looked toward Baxter. "It makes it so much easier for them to disappoint you."

Baxter's shoulders slumped.

I joined Max at Ivy's box. She looked so young, so pretty, even in this state, though her white-blond hair had been cropped down to almost nothing and her face was pale and gaunt.

"Victus must have really hated her to cut her hair like that," Max said. "I just don't understand how he captured her."

"Maybe she can tell us." I looked at the other ruby boxes, peering at the unfamiliar faces inside. "Who do you suppose these other people are?"

"No telling." Max ran a hand through his hair and looked at Percival. "Hey, Percy, when will you have a dose ready for Ivy?"

Percival spun on his heel and glared at him. "When it's ready!" He threw up his hands. "Now, will everyone kindly leave me alone to tend to my patients?"

Kanaan headed out. "Clear the room."

We reluctantly drifted out into the corridor.

Sonia stood near the door to the omniarch room, tapping her foot on the stone floor. "Now that we've single-handedly saved the day, will you kindly return us home?"

"Of course," Kanaan said.

I took Sonia by the wrist before she could leave. She bared her fangs, but didn't pull away. "What do you want?"

"I just want you to take a minute later and think about what you did here today." I felt uncomfortable holding onto her, but forced myself not to let go. "Sonia, you saved a lot of lives. You don't have to be a miserable person who can't let go of the past. You can be someone who helps us win back the future."

Her mouth dropped open, eyes blinking rapidly, but she quickly recovered. "I'll leave the heroics to the fools, Conrad." Despite her harsh words, her look softened. She gently pulled away from me and walked toward the portal Kanaan opened.

Desmond shook my hand and grinned. "I haven't seen an emotional reaction from her like that in ages, Conrad." He hugged Ambria. "Keep up the good fight, and let me know if you need my help again."

"We probably will," Max said. "Don't leave town."

Desmond chuckled and followed his sister through the portal.

Natalia prowled around the group. "This has certainly been an exciting day."

"I need a nap," Stan said. "Can I go inside the mansion?"

"I'm hungry." Natalia took the old man's hand. "I'll go with you."

Asha watched them leave then turned to us. "What happened with Victus?"

Max nodded eagerly. "Yeah, how did it go down?"

I gave them all the awful details.

"I don't like this one bit, Conrad." Ambria tapped her bottom lip with a finger. "Victus wanted you dead, but now he doesn't. After all you've been through against him, why would he suddenly change his mind?"

"There's no way Conrad would switch sides," Max said. "Victus has to know that."

"He's devious and twisted." Ambria's forehead pinched. "I'm sure he knew Conrad wouldn't switch sides, but he had a reason for trying."

"Perhaps he wished to plant seeds of doubt." Asha pressed her lips together. "Or maybe he thought it was worth a try. In any case, what we did today should cripple his plans."

"Oh, he's done for good." Max rubbed his hands together. "We've got all his valuable prisoners. I'm so excited I could burst."

Ambria groaned. "Ivy again?"

"Yes!" He pumped a fist. "We've brought back a hero of the Overworld. Once she's back in action, Victus can't stop us."

"Perhaps you should temper your enthusiasm until we've actually revived her," Asha said.

"Conrad!" Percival appeared in the corridor, his face tight. "I need you in here right now."

We looked uncertainly at each other and then went back into the room. Two more of the ruby chambers had their lids removed. One of them belonged to Ivy.

Max's eyes grew wide. "How is she, Percival?"

"I—I don't know how to tell you this." Percival's eyes flicked back and forth between us and the coffins. "I'm not even sure what's going on, or why Victus would do such a thing, but—"

Max's face twisted with fear. "Oh, god. Is she dead?"

Percival gripped Max's arm to keep him from running to the coffin. "The beings in those chambers are alive and well, but they are not real." He held up the orb Kanaan used to verify Asha was not an infernus. "Ivy and the woman in the other chamber are infernus."

CHAPTER 29

Max sagged and staggered, as if a great weight dropped onto his shoulders. "No." He shook his head. "It can't be. Why would Victus keep infernus in those preservation chambers?"

"What about Galfandor?" I asked.

"He's the real one." Percival held up his hands helplessly. "At this point, I have no idea who's real and who's not. I'll have to test everyone as I go along."

"Are the infernus awake?" I asked.

"I put them to sleep until we decide what to do with them." Percival ran a hand down his face. "My god, was all of this for nothing?"

"Can we spot test people from the black and white boxes?" I asked.

"Yes, but first I'll check the rest of the red ones." Percival shook a fist in the air. "Curse you, Victus Edison!"

It seemed a bit melodramatic, but I was so angry, I wanted to scream.

Max looked on the verge of tears, and Ambria stared blankly at the red coffins.

Asha's face hardened with anger. "Victus is more devious than we thought."

I couldn't process the enormity of Victus's treachery. *Why would he plant infernus in those coffins?*

Percival methodically removed the lid to each red coffin and held the infernus orb to the skin of the occupants. None of them were the originals. A spot-check of the black chambers found no infernus, as did an investigation of the white ones. Aside from Galfandor, none of the red coffin occupants were genuine.

Harris and his friends came into the room as we finished our work.

"What's going on?" Lily asked. "Why do you look so worried?"

"Where is Kanaan?" Percival said. "I need him here."

"The mansion," Harris said. "What's going on?"

Shushiel descended a thread from the ceiling. "I will get him."

"Yes, please." Percival dropped onto a chair and put his face in his hands. "This is a disaster."

Harris raised his voice. "What's going on?"

Percival held up a hand. "Please wait for Kanaan."

The magitsu master showed up a moment later, his calm face betraying no signs of worry.

"Aside from Galfandor, there isn't an original soul in any of the red coffins," Percival said without preamble. "The other chambers are authentic."

Kanaan turned to Shushiel. "Quickly, get Stan and Natalia from the mansion." He looked at Percival. "Can Galfandor and Ansel travel?"

"Yes, but—"

"Take them to the omniarch room at once." Kanaan glanced at the other preservation chambers and shook his head. "We must evacuate immediately."

Asha gasped. "You think Victus tracked the coffins."

"No, I think he can track the infernus within them."

Percival transferred Galfandor and Ansel to a flying carpet and ferried the unconscious patients out of the makeshift healing ward. The rest of us gathered our equipment and ran for the omniarch room.

"Why are we in such a hurry?" Max said. "There's no way Victus can get all the way from the States to here in a couple of hours, unless there's an Obsidian Arch in Montana."

A strange whispering noise cut off all conversation. We turned around, looking back down the corridor where it led into the Burrows. The susurrus grew louder. Kanaan closed the circuit around the omniarch and looked at it. Nothing happened.

"They're using a portal blocker," Kanaan said.

"How did they get here so fast?" Max said.

"The mansion," Kanaan said. "Hurry."

We piled out of the omniarch room and back toward the mansion, nearly colliding with Stan and Natalia as they ran to join us. Kanaan appeared a few seconds behind us. The wall at the end of the corridor exploded. Dust and rubble flew inward, quickly followed by a stream of Blue Cloaks on flying carpets.

"Get inside!" Kanaan shouted.

The rare display of emotion removed the paralysis gripping the group and everyone burst into full gallop. Natalia scooped up Stan and carried him bodily toward the house, her petite size belying felycan strength.

"The Blue Cloaks are coming!" Max shouted. "The Blue Cloaks are coming!"

We filed through the door, pushing Galfandor and Ansel through first. Kanaan shut and barred it after us.

"Why in the world are the Blue Cloaks coming?" Ambria said. "I thought they were the good guys."

Even before I looked through the window, I knew why Kanaan had been in such a hurry to get us inside. Agatha Grint and Esmerelda Quiff hovered before the small army of Arcanes robed in blue, their faces glowing with unholy delight as they moved toward the mansion.

"By decree of the Arcane Council, Conrad Edison and his co-conspirators are to surrender themselves to us," Grint cried out.

Kanaan traced a symbol on the back of the door and a low hum vibrated through the floor. A shield shimmered into place between the mansion and the Blue Cloaks. He opened the door and stepped outside, the magical barrier blocking the intruders a scant few yards away. "On what charges?"

Quiff reached a tentative finger toward the barrier and scowled when she found it solid. "We know the boy is working for Victus. We want him to answer some questions."

"The only people working for Victus are you," Kanaan said. "The only question is whether or not you are infernus."

Quiff and Grint recoiled at the word, surprise flashing across their faces. The twenty or so Blue Cloaks with them remained stony and silent. Either they didn't know what Kanaan meant by 'infernus', or they would follow orders no matter what.

"I have no idea what you're talking about," Grint said. "I demand you surrender yourselves this instant."

"How could they be infernus?" Percival said. "I didn't see them in any of the chambers."

"Because Victus has been a step ahead of us all this time and the originals are probably buried in that trench near the foundry." I stepped outside next to Kanaan. "There's only one way you could possibly know where we were, Grint. It's because Victus gave you our location." I looked imploringly at the Blue Cloaks. "These Arcanes are following the orders of the Overlord. You need to arrest them, not us!"

Quiff cackled with laughter. "I'm afraid you won't find a true Blue Cloak among them, boy." She raked her fingernails down the shimmering barrier holding them back from us, leaving scars of red light that vanished an instant later. "Each soldier was hand-picked by Garkin to form the new security forces for the Arcane Council." She held up a statue with a multi-pointed star on top of it. "Your portal access is blocked. You have nowhere to go. If you don't surrender now, these fine soldiers will camp here until you starve yourselves out."

Kanaan twirled a wand in his hand, seemingly unconcerned by the threat. "Now I understand how Xander Tiberius won the election for primus. You two are not the only infernus on the council."

"You are mistaken if you think we're infernus," Grint said. "We were loyal to the Overlord during his first reign, but remained unknown to the authorities. For years we worked our way onto the council, knowing that he would rise once again as he promised us the night before he died."

Quiff flashed a dimpled smile. "Many on the council were replaced. It is only a matter of time before the Overlord takes his rightful throne and makes Arcanes first in the Overworld."

A strange disjointed melody echoed from somewhere on Kanaan's person, drawing confused looks from Quiff and Grint. He shrugged. "The ringtone on my arcphone."

Grint waved away his explanation. "If you surrender now, we will only take Conrad and Kanaan. The rest of you may go."

"An appealing offer," Kanaan said. "I must have absolute assurances that you will spare the others."

Grint leaned forward eagerly on her broom. "Of course. I will see to it myself."

"I would like to have a cup of tea before I surrender," Kanaan said. "I will return in ten minutes."

"No, you can't surrender!" Ambria shouted. "They're lying!"

Right then I knew two things for certain: One, Ambria was right, and two, Kanaan would never surrender us to them. I grabbed Ambria's arm and gave her a sharp look. "It's the only way. We can't escape, I won't let you starve to death." I squeezed her arm twice, hoping she got the message.

Ambria's eyes narrowed, but she relented. "I hope you know what you're doing, Conrad."

Quiff displayed her dimples again. "One cup of tea and then you will lower this barrier and surrender. Any further delays and we will rescind our generous offer."

Kanaan nodded. "As you say." He turned and ushered everyone back inside, closing the door behind us.

Asha raised an eyebrow. "What are you up to, Kanaan? I know you don't mean to simply give up."

Kanaan tapped the pendant on his cloak. "Shushiel, you may try it now."

"The tea room," Shushiel replied.

"Are we going to climb out of here on webs?" Percival said. "In case you hadn't noticed, we're underground and trapped by solid rock."

Kanaan walked into the tea room. A portal flickered open in the middle of the room, shoving the table and chairs across the room. Shushiel stood on the other side of the gateway, bobbing up and down. "I did it!"

Max's mouth dropped open. "A ruby spider can activate an arch?"

Ambria frowned at Kanaan. "More importantly, how did you open an arch if they're using a portal blocker?"

"The portal blockers were used in the war." Kanaan tapped his arcphone. "I have the musical frequencies to turn them off, but required close proximity."

"That's what your phone was playing," I said. "Grint and Quiff didn't even know what you were doing."

Stan burst into laughter. "You realize they'll probably sit out there for hours without realizing we've gone."

Max snorted. "I hope they rot out there."

Once the group went through the portal to the omniarch room, Kanaan closed the gateway, and reopened it to somewhere dark and dim. Once more, we stepped through the gateway and into a cavernous room lined with arches of all sizes as far as the eye could see. Once everyone was through, Kanaan closed the gateway.

Max looked around in wonder. "We're in an arch control room, aren't we?"

"El Dorado." Kanaan leaned against a black arch that looked like the omniarch near the mansion. "We should be safe from Victus until we decide our next move."

Max groaned and sank to the black polished floor. "I don't understand how Victus outsmarted us. How'd he know that we were coming to rescue Ivy and the others?"

"Where did he put the originals?" Ambria said. "How are we supposed to find them?"

"This is the man who orchestrated the events that stranded Justin Slade and the Eden army in Seraphina," Stan said. "Hell, he planned his own death and resurrection when his back was against the wall. He probably planned for something like this too."

Asha turned to Kanaan. "Do you think Garkin knew you were spying on them?"

"I am certain no one knew I was there." Kanaan took out one of his wands and started polishing it. "I was careful to avoid all wards."

The discussion continued, but I tuned it out, too embroiled in my own thoughts. If Victus knew we were coming, why did he let us take so many preservation chambers? Why didn't he spring a trap on us? He could've surrounded and taken us long before we'd destroyed the pattern in the foundry. No matter how skilled Zarin might be, creating a pattern like that wasn't easy.

It only meant one thing. Victus hadn't known we were coming. The remote location kept the foundry secret from every except the people who worked there. He suspected that the soul fragments left inside me after his and Delectra's resurrections might have inadvertently given me information about the foundry, or maybe he thought Ansel betrayed his secret. Even then, he probably considered it unlikely I would launch a raid against his secret base. Sending Garkin to kill me had been insurance.

Victus didn't trust anyone, not even his associates. Ivy Slade and anyone else he kept in those ruby chambers were of immeasurable value. That meant Victus had put clones of them in the foundry and put the real people somewhere else because he wanted sole access to them. But where? For all I knew, he could have them hidden in a cave beneath the foundry, or stashed them in a warehouse anywhere in the world.

But he hadn't.

Ansel helped Victus with the first foundry. That's where the originals are.

There was only one other person Victus trusted nearly as much as himself. In fact, he trusted him so much, he'd staked his life on it. Rufus Cumberbatch had resurrected my parents and proven his absolute loyalty to Victus. If anyone knew where the original foundry was, it would be him.

"I think we're done." Stan's words broke through my mental dam. "You're all welcome to stay at my house. I think you'll be safe there even if Victus comes into power."

"No." I clapped my hands, drawing all eyes to me. "We're not running from this. We're going to confront Victus and win. If we don't, the Overlord returns and everyone loses."

"We've already lost." Max drooped. "We don't have Ivy to help us."

"Who needs Ivy Slade?" I said. "Every one of you just helped me raid Victus's foundry. We robbed him blind and nearly got away with it. As far as I'm concerned, you're all heroes."

Harris perked up at the word. "You really think so? Victus completely outsmarted us."

"No, he didn't outsmart us." I let that sink in a moment. "Victus hid the real Ivy and others because he doesn't trust his underlings enough to leave his most prized possessions lying around for them to steal."

"Whoa." Max scratched his head. "So he hid them because he's paranoid?"

I nodded. "Yes, and I think I know exactly where they are."

Ambria's eyes flashed wide. "The same place Victus and Delectra's bodies were kept."

"Exactly." I projected an image of a grand estate in St. Ives in southwest England. "In the wine cellar of Rufus Cumberbatch's estate, probably near the first infernus foundry."

"Victus probably thinks we were fooled by the infernus in the coffins," Lily said. "Quiff and Grint told him we're trapped in the mansion. I'll bet if we go to Cumberbatch's estate, we could take everything without him being any the wiser."

"If Victus is as paranoid as he seems to be, he will likely check with Cumberbatch to ensure the originals are safe," Asha said.

"It is possible," Kanaan agreed. He looked at the holographic image of the main gates guarding the entrance to the estate. "Do you have a picture inside the cellar?"

"No, this is all I have." I turned off the hologram. "Is it enough?"

"It means we will have to traverse whatever security he has to reach the cellar." Kanaan turned to Shushiel. "Unless one of us can sneak inside and take a picture."

The spider bobbed up and down. "Gladly."

"One problem," Asha said. "We don't have the vampires to help us anymore."

Natalia flexed a bicep. "Not to worry, darling. The spider and I are plenty strong to lift coffins."

"I don't think they'll be in coffins," I said. "More likely, they'll be hidden in large wine casks."

"I do hope the man has a good selection of reds," Percival said. "Because I need something to calm my nerves."

"Just because Shushiel can camouflage doesn't mean she can avoid wards," Max said.

"I could go," Natalia said. "I'm sure a small cat could slip through unnoticed."

Kanaan shook his head. "I suspect someone like Cumberbatch employs deadly wards scattered like land mines across the estate, but to prevent animals from triggering them, they are likely attuned to humans, wolves, and felines."

"Why wolves and felines?" Baxter asked.

Max looked at Natalia. "Because of felycans and lycans."

Natalia scowled. "Perhaps."

Shushiel's mandibles twitched. "But not giant spiders, I hope."

"Remain on the driveway," Kanaan said. "I doubt anything deadly is there. Otherwise, he would inadvertently kill someone."

"Yes, I will definitely stay on the road." Shushiel reached a mandible toward me and took the arcphone from my hand. "Wish me luck, my friends."

I leaned down and hugged her.

"Please do be careful," Ambria said. "I don't know what we'd do without you."

Kanaan opened a portal to the outside of Cumberbatch's estate. Shushiel rotated and bobbed goodbye before shimmering into camouflage and starting her dangerous mission.

CHAPTER 30

Kanaan closed the portal to avoid detection and we played the waiting game, praying for the photo that would give us access to the wine cellar. Nearly twenty minutes passed and still no word.

Harris huddled against the base of an arch, eyes squeezed shut while Lily and Baxter tried to talk to him. He shook them off. "I don't believe Victus. My parents didn't work for him."

Lily patted his arm. "But Galfandor said—"

"Galfandor doesn't know what he's talking about!" Harris pushed up to his feet and glared at the omniarch. "How much longer will this take?"

"Harris, it doesn't matter what your parents did or didn't do," Ambria said, "It's what you do that matters."

Harris's lips pressed into a thin line. "They were heroes. They died fighting the Overlord."

Max groaned. "Lying to yourself won't help. Do you think I like having a father who's nothing but a lapdog to Victus?"

Harris looked at the unconscious form of Galfandor on the flying carpet and shook his head. "My parents were good. I'm good."

Max rolled his eyes.

"We should go after Shushiel." Ambria approached the omniarch, but Kanaan shook his head.

"Ten minutes more." He checked the time on his arcphone.

Shushiel sent a picture of the entrance to the wine cellar several tense moments later and Kanaan opened a portal. Stan started toward it, but the magitsu master put a hand on his chest and shook his head. "Wait here."

Stan protested. "I'm not useless just because I'm old."

"Remain." Kanaan's voice was firm. "We must move quickly and your bad leg will hinder you."

Stan sighed but relented. "Be careful."

Asha kissed him on the cheek. "We'll be back soon."

Harris stepped through first, followed by Baxter. Lily remained close to me, Ambria, and Max, her eyes worried. Kanaan and Asha took out their wands and approached the door to the cellar. Shushiel shimmered into view.

"I could not get through the door," she said.

"We'll take it from here," Asha said.

Kanaan worked his wand around the brass lock for a moment. "This door is magically sealed. We may have to use brute force."

Stan poked his head through the portal. "I know you don't need the help of an old man, but it might help to know that you're looking at a Jenkins four-hundred series magical lock that's bonded with a diamond-fiber, hermetically sealed door. The lock is nearly impossible to pick, and forget trying to blow a diamond-fiber door off its hinges."

Asha raised an eyebrow. "You know this from your days as a Blue Cloak?"

"Sort of." Stan smiled sheepishly. "Damien Shelton and I became bounty hunters after we left the Blue Cloaks. Let's just say we acquired some necessary skills."

Kanaan stepped back from the lock. "Can you open it?"

"Gladly." Stan stepped through the portal and slid his compacted staff out of its holster. Instead of expanding it, he traced a rune along the edge and the end popped open. Inside was a leather pouch. Stan opened the pouch and removed a piece of chalk and two balls of beige clay. He pressed one piece of clay to the lock and the other to his ear.

"What the heck does that do?" Max asked.

Stan was too intent on his work to hear the question. He tapped his wand around the lock and used the chalk to draw symbols next to his feet on the stone walkway. As he worked, Asha and Kanaan took positions at opposite ends of the walkway, peering around the tall hedges that lined ornate gardens to the side of the mansion.

The old man grunted and crossed out a symbol, replaced it with one that looked similar. Stan put down the chalk and checked his wristwatch. "Seven minutes. Damn, I've lost my touch."

"Is it open?" Max asked.

"All but opened." Stan pressed his wand to the door and traced the symbols he'd drawn on the sidewalk. The lock clicked and rotated. What sounded like bars of metal slid somewhere on the other side and clinked to a halt. Stan pushed on the door and it swung open silently on well-oiled hinges.

"Cool," Baxter breathed. "Can you teach me how to do that?"

"He won't even teach me," Natalia said. "Probably thinks I'll turn to thieving."

"Well, they aren't called cat burglars for nothing," Max said.

Natalia shot him a dirty look. "Not all felycans are thieves."

"Maybe I should think about passing on these skills," Stan said. "I'm not getting any younger."

Kanaan stepped past us and went inside the door. I followed close behind, my chest growing tighter with every step. I'd been to Cumberbatch's residence several times as a child for testing meant to gauge my magical potential. The Goodleighs took all their orphan wards to Dr. Cumberbatch for such an evaluation because Arcane children were valuable on the black market.

Since I'd been under the living curse that kept my parents' souls bound to my own, I'd been dull-witted and a magical zero. Cumberbatch had known the truth about me, but kept it from the Goodleighs. Now they were dead by my hand, but I could still feel their presence in this foreboding place.

I swallowed the lump in my throat and led the way, a vaguely remembered path to a metal chair with straps. The breath hitched in my throat at the sight of it. Ambria gripped my arm and stared at the shining metal. Crusted blood still clung to the edges of the seat—my blood drawn by my own mother shortly after her resurrection.

Concentrate! I shook my head to free myself from the visions of that day and located the large wine barrels my parents had risen from, still lying open even after all this time. "Why did Cumberbatch leave them lying here?"

"They're kind of big." Ambria pointed to a series of hooks and pulleys that had probably been used to move the barrels into position. "Maybe we can use those to move the others."

I pointed down the aisle to a back wall filled with more of the large wine barrels. "Then I suggest we move back there."

Natalia walked around the barrel that had held my father. She heaved up on the hinged top quarter half and closed it. "These things are a lot bigger than the coffins. It'll take us ages to get them up on the pulleys, onto carpets and through the portal. I don't even know how to keep them from rolling off."

"We'll figure out something." I headed to the back with the others where the oak barrels sat atop thick concrete blocks. I turned the spigot on the first one I reached and red wine dribbled out of the end. Everyone else ran up and down the long line of barrels testing each one.

Percival took a long draw from the one he tested. "Hmm, very dry, but nice."

Harris dashed out from between two of the barrels. "I think I found them."

We followed him between two barrels and along a stone wall. A tall stack of crates blocked the view of a doorway. Beyond it was another large room. In this one, the wine barrels lined up to either side of us. None of them had spigots, but they also didn't have clasps like the ones my parents had been in. Stan used his tricks to locate levers hidden in the sides. When pulled open, slats in the barrel slid back to reveal the clasps.

Kanaan opened the first one to reveal a young woman lying inside on a small bed, her brilliant blond hair splayed like a sunburst. A shimmering preservation spell hung over her like webs of gossamer.

"That's not Ivy," Max said.

Ambria peered at the woman. "Who is it?"

"A test subject." Kanaan waved Percival closer. "We must remove these people from the barrels so we can move them quickly."

"Why don't we just open a portal inside here?" Lily said. "Then we don't have to carry them far."

Kanaan raised an eyebrow. "An excellent idea. Can you do it?"

"Yes, sir!" Lily saluted him and ran out of the room.

"I certainly hope removing this spell doesn't kill her," Percival said as he waved his wand over the woman. Numbers danced in the air around his wand as he scanned her. "Her soul seems mostly intact. Perhaps it's had plenty of time to heal."

"Let us hope," Kanaan said.

The portal flickered open a few feet from the doorway and Lily stepped through from the other side. "Mission accomplished, sir."

Kanaan's lips twitched. "Good work." He turned to Percival. "It is in your hands now, healer."

Percival cracked his knuckles. "No pressure, eh?" He worked the wand around the edges of the spell. Cracks formed along the preservation shield. The webs flickered and faded. The woman gasped a ragged breath and jerked upright. She shouted in a foreign tongue, eyes wide with panic.

Kanaan held up a hand and spoke slowly in the same language.

Her eyes narrowed. She raised a hand. A small globe of light flickered and vanished.

"What in heaven's name?" Percival said. "What sort of magic is that?"

"She's Seraphim," Kanaan said. "She doesn't remember her name or what happened to her. She only speaks Cyrinthian."

"Seraphim?" Percival rubbed is hands together. "Memory loss is common with long-term preservation spells. I'm sure she'll be right as rain eventually."

Kanaan spoke to the woman again. She shivered and held out a hand to me. I took it and helped her out of the barrel. She collapsed against me and I struggled to hold her up. Max took her other arm and we walked the woman through the portal and into the dim arch control room at El Dorado.

We couldn't offer her much in the way of accommodations, but she took the cushion we offered her on the floor.

"She's so beautiful." Max backed away, unable to take his eyes off her. "An angel, Conrad! Can you believe it?"

"I wonder who she is." The time to answer that question would come soon enough. We went back through the gateway and waited to see who was in the next barrel.

Max's breath hitched in his throat as they opened it to reveal Ivy Slade. She looked very young for someone who should be nearly twenty, a sign that she'd been under the preservation aegis for years. Max could barely stand still as Percival loosened the magical bindings and released the spell.

Ivy's eyes fluttered. She stretched, yawned and sat up. "Is it time for breakfast, Big Daddy?" She blinked a couple of times, forehead squinting as if she couldn't quite focus on the rest of us. Her eyes flared. "Who are you?" Teeth bared, she tried to rise, but collapsed against the velvet sheets inside.

"Friends," Kanaan said. "Do you not recognize me?"

Ivy tilted her head sideways. "You do look familiar, but where am I? Where is Big Daddy?"

"Jeremiah is not here, child." Kanaan held out a hand. "We are rescuing you, so we must act quickly."

"Oh, in that case, let's get the flock out of Dodge!" Ivy took his hand and let him pull her out.

Max bounded forward. "Oh, can I? Can I? I'd love to help her through the portal."

Ivy smiled. "Who is this cute boy?"

Max's face flushed pink. "Did you hear that? Ivy Slade thinks I'm cute!"

"Who is Ivy Slade?" Ivy asked. She scratched her head. "What's my name?"

"We've got a lot to talk about." Max took Ivy by the arm and headed for the portal. "You're kind of a big deal."

Kanaan turned to Asha. "We should patrol the perimeter while they work."

Asha tore her eyes from the rest of the barrels and nodded. "Yes, that's a good idea."

Once they left, the rest of us opened the other barrels to make Percival's job quicker. Out of eight, only four held occupants—three females and one dark-haired male.

Ambria counted each one with a finger. "Why were there so many more of the red coffins at the foundry? This only makes six people."

"Not counting Galfandor we're short two people?" I said.

She counted again. "I hope we haven't missed any occupied barrels."

"Unless there's another hidden room, I think this is it." I walked around the back of the barrels to make sure we hadn't missed anything. All I found were two white boxes mounted to the wall. Opening one revealed a thick glowing crystal held between two stone prongs. The other held a switch.

I flipped it and the wall grated open to reveal a room half the size of this one with six different demon patterns engraved into the stone floor.

"This must be the original foundry." Ambria put her cheek to the floor and peered at it sideways. "These aren't three-dimensional."

"Or very complex." I took a picture with my arcphone. "They must have experimented with the process here."

"These look like children's drawings compared to the masterpiece in the Montana foundry." Ambria stepped back out of the room. "Let's hope they can't use this one to make more infernus."

I went to the other white box and inspected the glowing crystal. "I think this is an aether power converter for the house."

"If you say so," Ambria replied.

"There's a room in the mansion with something similar." I walked back around the barrels to watch Percival when Max skipped back through the portal, looking like the cat who ate the canary.

"Ivy is so amazing." He wore a huge grin on his face. "I told her all about her past, but she couldn't remember a thing."

Ambria groaned. "Max, you realize that once she's back to normal, she won't be the same, right?"

Max nodded. "I know. I'm just a kid and she's the epic Ivy Slade, hero of the Overworld. But at least I can enjoy the moment."

I patted him on the back. "Yes, you can, Max. Enjoy it while it lasts."

"Don't encourage him, Conrad." Ambria walked over to Lily and the others as Percival dissolved the preservation spell holding the lone male.

Stan chuckled. "Someone needs a haircut."

The man leapt from the barrel the moment Percival disenchanted the spell, thick curls of black hair bouncing around his head. He promptly fell, legs too weak to support him. He looked angrily at us, shouting in Cyrinthian.

"Another Seraphim." Percival held up his hands and pleaded with the man in slowly pronounced Cyrinthian, finally calming him down enough so Stan could escort him through the portal. "How in the world did Victus capture so many Seraphim?"

"Good question." Ambria gazed down at the petite form of a woman with olive skin and dark hair. "I hope none of them think we kidnapped them."

Max shuddered. "They'd rip us apart."

"What if these people are as bad as Victus?" Lily said. "For all we know, they could be former business partners."

"Even if they are, maybe they'll be angry enough to help us fight him," Harris said.

Baxter stared down at the woman. "Angels are so pretty."

Lily shook her head disapprovingly. "Just because some are attractive doesn't mean they all are."

"Fine, but this one is really pretty," he insisted.

"Not as pretty as Ivy," Max said. "She's half Seraphim and half Daemos, so I'll bet she's even more powerful than all these other Seraphim."

Ambria and Lily face-palmed and rolled their eyes.

"Well, we certainly know who Ivy's number one fan is," Baxter said with a smirk.

Percival raised the petite woman from her spell. She blinked, looked around calmly, and sat up. Her green eyes locked onto me. "Hello?"

A warm flush crept through my face and a stupid grin spread. *Wow, she is pretty.* I waved back. "Hi." Max and the others snickered. I stiffened and shook off the effect of those green eyes. "Who are you?"

She frowned and touched a dainty finger to her chin. "Do not know."

I held out my hand. "You've been under a preservation spell for a long time. Let me take you somewhere to recover."

She smiled and it seemed the whole room lit up. "Thank you!" Her hand trembled when she took mine and she had trouble climbing out. Her legs failed her, but I was able to support her with my shoulder. Her hair looked as though it had been cut shorter on one side, probably by Victus, and she had faint but visible scars on the backs of her hands and left shoulder.

Damn that monster.

I took her through the portal.

"Ooh." She looked around at the arch control room. "Big."

I nodded. "Yes, it's big."

Ivy was carrying on an animated conversation with herself when I arrived with the newcomer. The male sat twenty yards away, looking with narrowed eyes at everyone around him.

"Yes, you will remember!" Ivy shouted. She seemed to suddenly realize we were there and stiffened. "I need to remember everything."

"Percival thinks you will," I assured her. I helped the other female sit down. "Can you keep an eye on her?"

Ivy pursed her lips and looked down at the woman. "Do you remember?"

The other looked up and shook her head. "No."

The blonde woman spoke in her native tongue, casting inquiring eyes our way, but I had no idea what she said.

"I'm sorry," I said. "I don't understand."

She sighed and looked down at the floor.

"Whoever did this to us will die horribly," Ivy hissed.

I backed away from the cold malice in her eyes. "You'll definitely get the chance."

Ivy seemed unbalanced and eager to kill. I hoped Victus hadn't poisoned her mind like he had Delectra. If he'd used demonic influence on them, freeing these powerful beings could prove a terrible mistake.

CHAPTER 31

"**I** need to go help the others," I said. "Just relax until we get back."

"Thank you," the petite Seraphim said, looking up at me with her jade green eyes.

I felt that stupid grin coming out again. "Y-you're welcome." My doubts faded. There was something about this woman that made me believe there was good in the world. What it was about her, I had no idea. I turned and hurried back through the portal before I gaped like an idiot at her.

Percival freed the last prisoner moments after I returned. The female sat up as calmly as the last and took in her surroundings. Her first query came in Cyrinthian. When she saw we couldn't understand, she switched to English. "What realm is this?"

"Eden," Max said.

She nodded. Tried to get up, but like the others was too weak.

"I'll help you," Baxter said.

"Thank you." She took his offered hand and we lifted her out.

She stood a head taller than the rest of us, and her silvery hair reached all the way down to the backs of her legs. Slightly pointed ears poked from beneath the hair, and her upturned nose gave her an elven appearance.

The woman leaned heavily on Baxter. He didn't seem to mind struggling with her weight, but Lily pitched in and helped, an amused smile on her face.

Percival wiped his hands. "Well, that's all of them. I certainly hope they can help."

"Me too." I tapped on my comm pendant. "Kanaan, we're done here." The pendant hissed with static and turned off. I tried again. "Kanaan?"

"This cellar is probably shielded or warded against communications," Percival said. "You'll need to go outside."

I wanted to believe his explanation, but something told me it was more than that. "Percival, go back through the portal. Be ready to close this one and reopen it to a new location if I send you a picture, okay?"

"Send me a picture on what?" Percival said. "I don't have an arcphone."

Max handed him one. "Use mine." He took out his wand. "Let's go."

"Keep the others in El Dorado," I told him. "They may need to come rescue us."

Harris gripped his wand tight. "Do you think something's happened?"

"I hope not." I ran around the portal and went through the doorway leading into the main wine cellar. All was quiet as a tomb. I held up a hand to slow the others. We crept up the stairs to the door leading outside, stopped and listened.

A faint scraping noise emanated from somewhere to the right, like leather dragged on concrete. Ambria cringed. Harris tip-toed to the corner and looked around it. I peered around him and barely held in a gasp. A monster the size of a small dog, but with black, leathery skin dragged itself by two dagger-sharp legs. Green ichor oozed from several stumps where other legs might have been.

"What is that thing?" Ambria whispered.

"I don't want to find out." I looked over the hedges bordering the walkway and saw other signs of fighting. Blackened grass and charred husks of creatures like the injured one lay only feet away. I stepped through a gap in the hedge and looked across the lawn. Flashes of light emanated from a glass-enclosed pool near the back of the house. I motioned the others to follow.

We gave wide berth to the injured monster and ran toward the pool. Broken glass and more monster bodies littered the ground. I soon saw the source. Rufus Cumberbatch stood in one corner of the room, a shield shimmering around him while a giant black scorpion thrashed in the pool. Instead of a stinger, its tail held a humanoid face with razor sharp teeth. Asha pressed her back to Kanaan, fighting off flanking hellhounds with her wand.

Harris rushed forward, but I grabbed his arm and pulled him behind a bush. "Wait."

"For what?" He jerked his arm free. "We have to kill Cumberbatch!"

"He's behind a shield and we don't know where the demon spawn are coming from." I looked around for any sign of Zarin, but there didn't seem to be anyone except Cumberbatch.

"Do you think Cumberbatch is skilled enough to summon demon spawn?" Ambria asked.

"He's a power demonologist, but from what I read in Emily's books, humans aren't strong enough to control them." I focused on Cumberbatch. He held a wand in a gloved hand, but didn't seem to be using it, which made me wonder how he maintained the shield. "He must be using aether generators like the ones at the mansion to keep that barrier up."

Ambria looked aghast. "There's no way to break through."

"We need to help Kanaan against the spawn," Harris said. "Then we can focus on Cumberbatch."

"No, then we leave," Ambria said. "No doubt Cumberbatch alerted Victus."

"What in the world is that?" Harris pointed to an inky black pool on the lawn near the house. Tentacles writhed from within. Alien bodies squirmed to break free.

Ambria gasped. "That's a spawn pool. I read about them in the demonomicon." She shivered. "That's how Cumberbatch is pulling through so many spawn."

"But how is he controlling them?" I asked.

She shook her head. "He's not. Spawn pools are made by opening a nether portal with a summoning pattern and leaving it open." Ambria's grip tightened on her wand. "Whatever comes through that thing is unleashed."

I scanned the area, looking for more spawn pools, but only saw the one. "Can we deactivate it?"

Ambria shrugged. "Maybe. I don't know."

I turned back to the main battle in the pool house. Something seemed off about the shield protecting Cumberbatch and I soon realized why Kanaan and Asha hadn't made a run for it. The shield dome didn't cover Cumberbatch—it surrounded our friends. "Look there and there." I pointed to the barriers hemming them in. "They can't escape unless we turn off the shield."

"But how?" Ambria threw up her hands. "There's no—" Her mouth dropped open. "The power box in the cellar might do it."

Harris's eyes flared. "Can you turn them off?"

"Maybe by knocking out the crystals," Ambria said.

"Don't touch them," I warned her. "They might shock you." I didn't know if aether generators worked like electrical ones, but it was better safe than dead.

"Don't do anything until I get back," Ambria said.

I watched helplessly as Kanaan and Asha kept the hellhounds and demon scorpion at bay. Cumberbatch did something with his wand, and the shield around the battle shrank, driving the demon spawn closer and backing my friends up to the edge of the large pool.

I had to do something, but what?

The barrier isn't protecting Cumberbatch.

The Arcane flicked his wand and the barrier shrank again. Another few steps and Kanaan and Asha would have no choice but to fight in the pool against the monstrous scorpion.

There was no time to waste. I darted left, skirting past shrubs to keep myself concealed the best I could and ran for the pool house, Harris right behind me. So focused was Cumberbatch on Kanaan and Asha, he didn't see us coming.

There was no door on this side of the pool house, so I blasted the glass with a concussive spell. Shards flew through the air. One stabbed Cumberbatch in the shoulder blade. He screamed and spun on his heels. The wand clattered to the pool deck.

Cumberbatch staggered back a step. Blood dripped on the concrete beneath him. He held up his hands defensively "Conrad, my boy. Have mercy on your old doctor."

"Mercy?" I shouted. "Turn off the shield and send the demon spawn away!" I took a picture of the area, hoping Percival could open a portal inside so my friends could escape.

"Conrad, just go!" Asha shouted, her voice muffled by the shield dome. "Victus is probably on his way now!"

"No!" I turned back to the doctor. "Let them go."

Cumberbatch moved his arm and winced. "I did not realize you were with these people, Conrad. I thought they were simple intruders."

"Turn off the shield now," I demanded again. I sent the picture to Percival and prayed.

"Yes, yes, of course." He backed up a step. "I need to go into the house to do that." A bead of sweat trickled down the side of his face and his eyes darted to the sides.

He's stalling for time. That meant only one thing—he had help on the way. But even if Victus and his minions travelled to Queens Gate with an Obsidian Arch, it would take him hours to fly here even on a broom.

The shield flickered. Cumberbatch looked up at it. "What?" With a loud pop, the barrier vanished. "The shield!" The doctor staggered away from the pool. "I have no control over these spawn! I released them from spawn traps."

The giant scorpion seemed to sense easier prey than Kanaan. It spun, sending waves of water crashing across the deck. The water upended Cumberbatch, carrying him straight into me and Harris. We tumbled across the concrete and smacked into unbroken glass, the doctor sprawled on top. Cumberbatch's panicked eyes met mine. He elbowed me in the face in his haste to escape as the great demonic creature skittered out of the pool and came toward us.

The doctor staggered to his feet and stumbled out of the broken window. Harris cried out and rolled to the side. My nose ached terribly, but I ignored the pain and scrambled to my feet. Harris and I dashed out of the broken window, running after Cumberbatch and away from the demon spawn.

I looked back and saw a portal open inside the pool area. Kanaan and Asha killed the hellhounds and ran after us, ignoring the portal. Despite the blade of glass jutting from his back, Cumberbatch didn't slow.

Having such a monstrous creature racing after us inspired my feet to greater speeds than I'd thought possible.

The doctor drew another wand from his cloak and fired bolts of energy at us, missing wide. I snarled and aimed my wand. Instead of returning fire, I cast a shield right in front of the man's head. Cumberbatch's head cracked against the translucent barrier. He cried out and went down hard.

Harris aimed his wand at the downed man, but I gripped his wrist and pulled him hard left. A screaming face pressed against the leather hide where the demon scorpion's head should have been, as if someone desperately sought escape from a black trash bag. The monster screamed in the chorus of a thousand tortured voices. Its pincers ripped into the doctor and its great maw chomped down.

Cumberbatch didn't even have time to scream before he died. His blood spilled across the nearby spawn pool, and the inky liquid turned gray and frozen.

A portal winked open thirty yards in front of us. *Bless you Percival!* But instead of seeing our friends waiting on the other side, Victus and Garkin stepped out. They seemed just as surprised to see me as I did to see them.

Harris and I skidded to a halt and backed up, the awful sounds of the demon spawn crunching Cumberbatch's bones not far behind us. I jerked Harris left again, and we ran back toward the pool house.

Bolts of energy blasted the turf around us. I cast a shield and pulled Harris down behind it. Searing heat blasted my barrier, and washed over us. Garkin readied his wand for another volley, but Victus stopped him.

"Last chance, Conrad." My father held out a hand. "You've proven your-self worthy. Join me, and we will make the Arcanes supreme in this world. We can rid it of the vampire and lycan menace."

"What about the Daemos?" I shouted back. "Do they have a place in your new order?"

"Of course they do," he said. "Who can better control demonic elements than them?"

I tried not to look at Kanaan and Asha as they circled the giant scorpion and flanked Victus and Garkin. "What does Zarin think of your plan?"

"He does not care who rules the Overworld, only that I return his Aerianas to him." Victus shrugged. "Once I am able to repair the Grand Nexus, entire new worlds will open to us."

It was of some small comfort to know he hadn't opened the gateway to an invading Seraphim army at least, but the scorpion was nearly finished with its meal, and Garkin looked ready to end us the moment Victus gave the word.

Victus looked toward the scorpion and frowned. "Is that Rufus?"

"Doctor Cumberbatch is dead," I confirmed. "And I guess I'm next, because I refuse to join you."

"Your lies won't save you, Overlord." Harris brandished his wand. "You can't convince me I'm not the son of prophecy. I don't believe a word you say."

Before I could say anything else, Victus sighed and nodded at Garkin. The Arcane flicked his wand and unleased a concussive bolt that shattered my shield and sent us tumbling backward. The scorpion rotated toward Victus and Garkin and shrieked, sensing its next meal.

Kanaan and Asha fired spells from Victus's flank, sending him and Garkin diving for cover. Zarin leapt from the other side of the portal and raised his hands at the rushing demon spawn. At first, I thought the creature would kill him, but the Daemos stood firm. The demon scorpion slowed, stopped.

It spun toward Kanaan and Asha and skittered in their direction.

The momentary diversion had given us just what we needed—time. I took out one of Max's banana peel potion bombs and threw it at Zarin. It exploded on impact, covering him and the ground in a thick yellow slick. The Daemos fell and skidded across the lawn, unable to stop.

With his concentration broken, the scorp stopped following his commands and charged Victus again. Garkin fired a withering blast at the creature, but the magic splashed off its hide.

With chaos reigning, Kanaan and Asha reversed course and headed back toward the pool house where the portal waited.

"Let's go!" I dashed away as shrieks of demonic rage filled the air. I hoped the demon scorpion got my father, but doubted it would prevail. I looked back at Harris and realized he wasn't there. I stopped, looked around. Harris had run the other way, creeping behind one of the ornate shrubs decorating the back yard and coming up behind Victus.

I wanted to shout, but doing so would let Victus know the boy was right behind him. Garkin uprooted a sapling with a spell and shot it like a giant arrow at the monster. The wood splintered on the chitin to no effect.

I stood rooted to the spot for an instant, then ran after Harris. There was no way he was strong enough to kill Victus by himself.

Harris sprang from concealment and blasted Victus in the back with a bolt of orange energy. My father stumbled forward. Two more blasts caught him square between the shoulders. He steadied himself, spun, and channeled a shield.

Harris fired again and again to no effect against the shield. "How did you survive that?"

Victus laughed and patted his robes. "Armor enchantment, boy."

"But I'm the son of prophecy!" Harris shouted. "You should be dead!"

Victus roared with laughter even as Garkin fought desperately to hold off the giant scorpion behind him. "Have you even read all the foreseeances, boy? If you had, you'd know that there is no *son* of prophecy." He aimed his wand and fired.

"No!" I cast a shield, but it was too far and too late. The blast caught Harris in the chest and exploded out of his back in a gout of boiling blood. He fell in slow motion, body rotating toward me, a look of disbelief on his face. For an instant, our eyes locked, and then Harris's eyes went dull and dead.

My mind flashed back. Cora dying of cancer, a victim of the curse that preserved the souls of Victus and Delectra. Delectra dying in my arms after she took the killing blow meant for me. This would happen over and over again. More people would die so long as Victus lived.

Rage surged through every fiber of my being.

I pulled upon the strength of my mothers, for they were the ones who gave me life and a will to live. A crimson bolt of fireblade from my wand seared the air. Victus channeled a shield. Fireblade sliced through it and smoked against his clothes. His magical armor burst into flames. Garkin spared an instant from fighting the scorpion, using a second wand to quench the fire. I sliced the burning ray toward the magitsu master, but Garkin wasn't foolish enough to fight on two fronts. He hauled Victus to his feet by the hem of his clothes and shoved him through the portal. Fireblade slashed the air, but Garkin vanished inside the portal an instant before it reached him.

The portal winked away. Deprived of its meal, the scorpion turned toward Harris's body. "No!" I waved my arms and the monster turned toward me. I waited until it was yards away before hitting it with a banana peel potion. The monster shrieked as it skidded helplessly across the lawn.

I raced to Harris's side. A blackened, cauterized hole gaped where his heart had been. Tears burned my eyes, but I couldn't afford to cry now. I hefted his body and tried to run back toward the pool room. Before I got even a few feet, the demon scorpion recovered and skittered toward me again. I dropped the body and took out my wand. I had no more potions and it was too far to run back to the portal.

The creature shrieked, the jaws on its stinger tail chomping as it closed in for the kill. Hands gripped me and jerked me to a hard stone floor. A portal winked off just as the scorpion lunged. I shouted and threw up my hands. I wasn't in England anymore, but back in the arch control room at El Dorado, my friends gathered around.

Harris's corpse lay next to me.

"No!" Baxter cried. "No!"

Lily screamed and burst into tears. I looked up at Ambria and Max. They wept like me, but with sorrow tempered by the knowledge of too much death and loss. I got up and hugged Ambria. She said nothing, because there were no words to make this right.

CHAPTER 32

Shushiel wrapped Harris's body in webs like a funeral shroud and put him behind one of the many arches so we wouldn't have the constant reminder every time we looked that way.

Meanwhile, Kanaan tested each of the freed prisoners and confirmed they were not infernus. Our mission was a success, but I felt as if we'd lost. Every time Harris's death flashed before my eyes, I saw Delectra dying in my arms, saw Cora rotting from cancer.

Damn you, Father!

I should have agreed to join him, won his trust, and betrayed him. What had Harris been thinking when he tried to kill Victus? Hadn't it occurred to him that someone as clever and paranoid as Victus would wear body armor?

Ambria squeezed my hand. "Don't let it eat you up inside. It's not your fault."

I caught an angry glare from the teary-eyed Baxter. "Not everyone here would agree."

She looked back at the ginger boy. "He's the only one who blames you."

"I blame myself for not realizing what Harris wanted to do." I blew out a breath. "He convinced himself what Victus said was a lie."

Ambria shook her head slowly. "What do you suppose Victus meant when he said there is no son of prophecy?"

"Maybe the foreseeances are lies?" I shrugged. "There's no telling."

Max sat down next to us. "Percival said it'll take a few days, maybe weeks, but Ivy and the others should start to recover their memories. He said if he had access to his lab he could make potions that would help."

"We're outlaws, Max." Ambria sniffed. "Going back to his lab isn't an option."

"We need food." Max rubbed his stomach and looked around the room. "And we need someplace more comfortable than this to sleep."

Asha walked over and knelt in front of me. "How you holding up, brother?"

My spirits lifted at the new and strange feeling of having a sibling. "I'm okay, but I don't know where we go from here."

"We can go anywhere." She looked back toward the omniarch. "For now, we need a place to rest and recover."

Kanaan walked into view from the far end of the room where a giant map spread out across the wall. He motioned for us to come, so we got up and walked over to him. Lily joined us, but Baxter scowled at me and remained behind.

I felt lost and adrift at sea and hoped this wise man could point the way. "What now?"

"Come." Kanaan turned and walked away.

I looked back where Percival tended to the rescued prisoners while a sulking Baxter stared at the floor. The woman with green eyes smiled at me and I couldn't help but smile back. When I turned around, my friends were already several paces away, so I hurried to catch up.

Kanaan led us through a door and into a great cavern lit by dim yellow light. Red and purple scales glittered on massive reptilian forms in the middle. We gasped and stopped in our tracks. Kanaan continued walking.

Max and I looked at each other, swallowed hard, and followed. The others regained their courage and caught up. The magitsu master stopped less than ten yards from the creatures. A massive eye opened, the slitted pupil of a reptile focusing on us.

"This is Altash and his mate Lulu," Kanaan said.

"Holy cow." Max reached out a tentative hand, but stopped short of touching the giant. "Earth dragons!" He squeed like a small child and clapped his hands. "Dragons!"

"Will they help us?" I asked.

"No." Kanaan sat in the shadow of the great red dragon and motioned the rest of us down. "Should they enter the fray, the great nemesis would end the truce and act against them."

"Who's the great nemesis?" Lily asked.

"They will not say," Kanaan said. "In fact, they do not say much."

I tried not to feel too uncomfortable with Altash's giant eye watching us. "Then why bring us here?"

Kanaan waved a hand at the cavern. "Once this place teemed with the undead husks of blighted angels. The destruction of the Grand Nexus drained them of light, turning them into monstrous creatures that craved the light of others. For thousands of years they roamed these caves, doomed to eternity as dark creatures.

"Then Justin Slade led an expedition here to confront Vaedaemos Slade. During a battle, many of the husks were devoured by earth dragons. It was after this battle that Altash realized the husks could be revived by nesting them in the intense aether radiation inside their maws."

Altash's long lean maw opened suddenly. Most of us screamed. I jumped up and ran several feet before realizing he didn't mean to eat me.

Shushiel bobbed up and down with laughter at our reactions. "People are so afraid of monsters."

"Bloody right," Natalia said with a growl.

Altash turned his head to reveal rows of jagged teeth. Brilliant light glowed in the depths of his maw. Heat washed out over me, but this time I held my ground. Apparently satisfied with the demonstration, the dragon closed his mouth and returned his head to its original orientation. A purple head, long and lean like Altash's, rose, and a great eye opened.

Lulu, I presume? Lulu's eye rolled the same way Ambria's did when she disapproved of something me or Max did. Maybe she thought Altash took himself far too seriously.

Kanaan continued his story as if there had been no interruption. "Justin discovered that the dragons were reviving the husked angels. Before long, nearly every husked Seraphim was returned to their original state, whole and renewed."

"In other words, what looks like a hopeless situation might not be," Lily said.

Kanaan raised an eyebrow. "Just so." He pointed around at all of us. "We must train in the ways of magitsu while the former prisoners recover. Once we know our capabilities, we can end the Overlord once and for all."

Max fist-pumped. "Yes!"

"Let's do it!" Ambria shouted.

A warm glow melted the icy despair around my heart. *We can do this.*

Justin Slade had overcome plenty of hopeless situations. With Ivy and the other Seraphim, maybe we could too.

"There is one other thing." Kanaan stood and brushed off his pants. "Even where there is death there is hope."

I grimaced. "What do you mean?"

"I recognize the green-eyed Seraphim. She did not die as we thought." Kanaan actually smiled. "Nightliss is alive and well."

"That's Nightliss?" Max said. "The Clarion of the Templars?"

Wonder filled Ambria's eyes. "That's amazing!"

I turned around and saw the green-eyed Seraphim looking out of the control room and toward us. Our eyes met and her smile filled me with hope. It was then I knew the truth.

We can win.

I HOPE *you enjoyed reading this book. Reviews are very important in helping other readers decide what to read next. Would you please take a few seconds to rate this book?*

WANT MORE? Touch here for more books by John Corwin!

FOR THE LATEST on new releases, free ebooks, and more, join John Corwin's Newsletter at www.johncorwin.net!

ACKNOWLEDGMENTS

To my wonderful support group:
Alana Rock
Karen Stansbury

My amazing editors:
Annetta Ribken
Jennifer Wingard

My awesome cover artist:
Regina Wamba

Thanks so much for all your help and input!

ABOUT THE AUTHOR

John Corwin is the bestselling author of the Overworld Chronicles. He enjoys long walks on the beach and is a firm believer in puppies and kittens.

After years of getting into trouble thanks to his overactive imagination, John abandoned his male modeling career to write books.

He resides in Atlanta.

Connect with John Corwin online:
Facebook: http://www.facebook.com/johnhcorwinauthor
Website: http://www.johncorwin.net
Twitter: http://twitter.com/#!/John_Corwin

BOOKS BY JOHN CORWIN

THE OVERWORLD CHRONICLES

Sweet Blood of Mine

Dark Light of Mine

Fallen Angel of Mine

Dread Nemesis of Mine

Twisted Sister of Mine

Dearest Mother of Mine

Infernal Father of Mine

Sinister Seraphim of Mine

Wicked War of Mine

Dire Destiny of Ours

Aetherial Annihilation

Baleful Betrayal

Ominous Odyssey

Insidious Insurrection

Assignment Zero (An Elyssa Short Story)

OVERWORLD UNDERGROUND

Possessed By You

Demonicus

OVERWORLD ARCANUM

Conrad Edison and the Living Curse

Conrad Edison and the Anchored World

Conrad Edison and the Broken Relic

Conrad Edison and the Infernal Design

STAND ALONE NOVELS

Mars Rising

No Darker Fate

The Next Thing I Knew

Outsourced

For the latest on new releases, free ebooks, and more, join John Corwin's Newsletter at www.johncorwin.net!